*Dee Willson is a born storyteller. Her worlds are freshly invented, meticulously considered, and richly told. With GOT she's created a remarkably original world that looks like ours but isn't ours at all; while A Keeper's Truth dazzles us with an entirely human protagonist and a love interest who is anything but. In all her work she manages to offer what we all want: surprise and delight and laughter, a remarkable achievement.*

**—Catherine Luttinger, Agent, Darhansoff & Verrill, New York**


*There are two standouts in the novel. Tess is a highly credible and original lead character and I felt bonded to her throughout the book. A great lead character alone, though, is not enough to make a book a stand out but when that combines with a surprising portrait of ancient lore that reaches far beyond recorded human history, the novel really comes alive.*

**—D. J. McIntosh, Author of *The Witch of Babylon***


*Dee Willson's characters cast shadows sharp enough to make even the most jaded reader uneasy. She juxtaposes comfort with peril and the beautiful with the grotesque until the simplest gestures are disquieting and the only way out is forward.*

**—Rob Brunet, Author of *Stinking Rich***


*I love finding books that don't go the obvious path... books that keep you guessing.*

**—Jennifer Foxcroft, Author of *Sanguine Mountain***

DEE WILLSON

A Keeper's Truth

Big hugs

Dee

Driven Press

A Keeper's Truth
Copyright © 2015 Dee Willson

First Edition March 2016
Published in Australia

Paperback ISBN: 978-1-925296-18-1

Also in Hardcover and eBook formats:
Hardcover ISBN: 978-1-925296-16-7
Digital ISBN: 978-1-925296-17-4

Driven Press
www.drivenpress.net

Cover Illustration by Vera Lluch © 2015
www.veralluch.com  mail@veralluch.com

Cover Layout by Mumson Designs © 2015
mumsondesigns@gmail.com

Cover content used for illustrative purposes only.

*For my mother,*
*who taught me a great many things,*
*like dream big.*

*It is now a recognised principle of philosophy, that no religious belief however crude, nor any historical tradition, however absurd, can be held by the majority of a people for any considerable time as true, without having in the beginning some foundation in fact. . . . We may be sure that there never was a myth without a meaning; that mythology is not a bundle of ridiculous fancies invented for vulgar amusement; that there is not one of those stories, no matter how silly or absurd, which was not founded in fact, which did not once hold a significance.*

—H. H. Bancroft
Late-Nineteenth-Century American Anthropologist

# TIME'S UP

It takes thirty seconds to die this way.

Two seconds to register the sound of exploding rubber. One second to grip the wheel with enough force to fracture bones. Skidding sideways across four lanes with nothing but the blur of passing cars and a transport truck consumes six seconds. The screech of metal on metal seems to go on forever but in reality lasts only five seconds. Five more for the metal to fold, glass to shatter, plastic to snap into bits.

Soaring through the air can be measured in six harrowing heartbeats. People don't fly.

For three seconds the physical pain is numbing, surreal. It takes the brain two seconds to make out the thick iridescent line only an inch away. But 124,000 pounds crushing bone and vital organs into asphalt is instantaneous.

Time's up.

Or is it?

Sure, everything that happens afterwards—the chaos, the heartbreak—is beyond the deceased. Only twelve know what really lies ahead, what happens to a soul, where it goes and why it returns. Twelve men know *everything*, have since the dawn of time, a place buried deep in our subconscious. Yet no one is listening.

As for the dead, they leave devastation in their wake: wives, husbands, mothers, fathers, sons, daughters—souls with a stake in this half-minute in time, scarred for eternity. What happens when loss attacks like beasts? How do you survive without the one you love?

You just do.

All things considered, there are worse ways to lose your life. You could be beaten, raped of your soul, left cold and alone to die. Slowly.

Old souls know this. Tess Morgan should know this.

Only she doesn't.

# Tess

# COPING

## Early September

**M**y name is Tess. I'm the daughter of a liar. And unhinged.

Tess is the name on the sticker stuck to my shirt above my right boob. I wonder why it says that, no one uses my name anymore. It should read: *Oh, I'm sorry*. Or the extended version: *Oh my God, I'm so sorry*. I'm greeted with pouty lips and sad eyes. Instant reminders . . . as if I need to be reminded my husband is dead. Meyer has been gone five months, two days, sixteen hours, and twenty-two minutes. The last two minutes only slightly better than the first.

I'm standing in my daughter's classroom, waiting for my turn to meet her kindergarten teacher, Ms. Bubbly. Actually, her name is Ms. Rainer, but since she wears no sticker herself, I've taken the liberty to provide her with an appropriate title, one with more verve. I hover in the back corner, pretending to be enthralled with drawings of horses stapled to the bulletin board. Well, I think they're horses, or ponies, or some sort of animal with four legs; they really aren't all that easy to decipher. I'm grateful for the distraction. I'm a shell, a remnant, a shadow of my former self.

I catch a glimpse of affection, a naturally intimate gesture between lovers. His hand on her waist, her leaning into his shoulder while whispering in his ear. I draw a mouthful of air, the word widow encasing me like a tomb, and scan the crowd again, hoping to see Thomas. He's the only other single parent I know of. He's not here.

It must be my turn to speak to Ms. Bubbly. She reaches out and with a strained voice says, "So sorry to learn about your loss."

Great, just what I wanted to hear. I look at my nametag and tighten my arms into their usual position, holding my insides, inside. I realize my lack of finesse a moment too late, and Ms. Bubbly drops her hand.

"So . . . Abby . . ." I can't think of anything more to say. My mind is mush.

Ms. Bubbly briefs me on her first weeks with my daughter, nothing I don't already know. Abby is quiet. Abby's working on her printing skills, her b's and d's are backwards. Abby likes to play with Thomas's daughter, Sofia, her best friend from junior kindergarten. Ms. Bubbly ends with, "Abby seems to be coping," and I stare at my shoes, the word coping caught in my throat. "Yes, under the circumstances, Abby is doing well," Mrs. Bubbly says, her animation dwindling.

I realize she's striving for sincerity, but I can't help but wonder which circumstance she's referring to: Abby being fatherless or my inability to raise her alone.

"Good," I say, because it's Tuesday, opposite day according to the blackboard.

Ms. Bubbly's attention wanders, and I consider revoking her title as I mumble goodbye, head for the door, and tear the name tag from my shirt. Head down, I smack my forehead into something solid, then recoil, instinct requiring an assessment of the battle wound.

It hurts already. Life just won't toss me a break.

"My apologies, Tess," says an unfamiliar voice. A rich, masculine voice.

My eyes follow the six feet four inches of triple-threat black—boots, jeans, leather jacket—to land on two-day stubble and a large hand rubbing the contours of a chiseled chin. Apparently life can get worse. I've collided with Adonis, the kind that stops your heart from beating just long enough to make you forget all the ones who came before, offering nothing but hollow promises and seasoned moves. Been there, done that, burned the shirt.

It dawns on me he said my name, no condolences.

"Do I know you?" I ask, my gaze rising from his chin to his eyes.

Wow. His gray eyes and dark lashes are . . . mesmerizing.

"I doubt we've met. Tess, it's the name on your sticker," he says, pointing to the name tag now on the floor. His hair, dark and cropped, is windblown and off kilter.

I grab the closest chair, attempting to overcome the strangest sensation, like I'm a feather, floating.

"You all right?" His European accent has an almost liquid quality, at odds with his rugged appearance. "Allow me."

Relocating his motorcycle helmet from one hip to the other and balancing it under his forearm, he bends to collect my sticker from the floor. Something shimmers, my vision suddenly malfunctioning, and for a split second he's draped in a luxurious white fur, a blanket of sorts, reaching for a bright colored scarf at his feet, big and bare. His movements are gentle and deliberate, but fast, as if I am watching in fast-forward. With the conclusion of one blink he's back to normal, leather clad arm outstretched toward me.

I stand stock-still, holding the chair for support, trying to bring my eyes into focus.

"You okay?" He thrusts the sticker at me a second time, I

think.

I survey body parts, grateful gravity has kept me intact.

"I've been better." I squeeze my eyes tight, trying to recall what I'd seen, but it's gone, as if wiped from memory, leaving just a weird sense of déjà vu. Man, I've fallen apart since Meyer's been gone.

"You have," he says, and my eyes pop open to stare. He's smiling, amused. "Too much caffeine maybe."

Have I met this guy before? He doesn't look like anyone I know, but there is something about him, something familiar. It's not a good feeling.

"Right, caffeine," I say, lying. I gave up caffeine when I was pregnant with Abby and never looked back.

He grins like a hyena. "Your eyes playing tricks?"

My mother, in one of her moods, would've wiped that smirk away with a kiss. And he'd have let her, stranger or not. She was intoxicating. But I'm not my mother, and my brief lapse in sanity doesn't require justification. I'm a twenty-six-year-old widow with no idea how to pull it together, so I ignore his question and settle for diversion.

"Are you a teacher here?"

"Not here," he says. "I promised my niece I'd stop by to meet hers." He takes my hand. "Bryce, Bryce Waters," he says, planting a soft kiss on the back of my fingers.

Stunned, I search his face for the slightest hint of perversion, a reason to club him, but I see nothing but a gentleman in wolf's clothing. Still, I pull my hand away.

"I'm not the teacher."

He tilts his head. "You're Tess." My name drips from his lips like melted butter and warning bells sound in my head, loud and clear. "You'll need ice for that bruise." He points to my head. "Take care of yourself."

A gritty moan vibrates my teeth when I touch my forehead and discover a bump the size of Mount St. Helens. It throbs, making me take note of the headache creeping in. Somewhere under the surface I'm mortified I plowed into this guy without an apology or concern for his chin. I can't bring myself to grasp the emotion, so I draw a deep breath and say, "Always do," as I shuffle past and without another word, walk straight out the door.

**Luckily, I live** close, and within minutes I'm home. Other than the entryway lamp, the lights are all out and the place is quiet. A glass of water sits on the bottom stair. Grams greets me at the door, sighing, her gaze aimed at my damaged forehead. Its days like today it hurts to look at her. Meyer's eyes. His lips. She's uncharacteristically mute as she pats the gift she'd given me earlier, along with a lecture, setting it beside the cup on the bottom stair. The lecture, I suppose, was necessary. Apparently there is no such thing as a woman's sexual prime, and it's important to recognize the body has needs at all ages, under any circumstance. Grams would know, she spent thirty-six years as a leading sex therapist and a decade specializing in women's sexual health. BOB is the gift tucked neatly in an unassuming tote bag, ready for travel, which is ironic considering he'll never leave my night table drawer. BOB stands for Battery Operated Boyfriend, and is, hands down, the most unusual gift anyone has ever received from their dead husband's grandmother.

But who am I to say: I never had a grandmother of my own.

Grams leans in and up onto her toes to kiss my forehead. "Good night." She takes hold of her loud flower-power purse and gently closes the door, leaving me alone with BOB and the weight of the world. There was a time the quiet soothed me like a hug. I was born Tess Reit, daughter of Celeste Reit, father unknown, and my mother suffered from severe depression and was bipolar, an endless roller coaster of maxed-out credit card highs and Titanic-worthy lows. When my mother would lock herself in her bedroom, lights out, begging for silence, I gave her what she needed. I'd have given her anything in those moments, those days, and the quiet did as much for me as it did for her. Maybe more.

Minutes wear on while I gather the energy to drag myself up the stairs.

As I approach Abby's room, I pause to listen to her incoherent chatter. I ease the door open and meander in to contemplate the sliver of light from between the curtains as it illuminates her face, an angel in slumber. I feel my way through the peppering of toys and books to tuck the blanket around her tiny form. While relishing her sweet smell, I catch a stray tear tickling my chin. I can't help but think of all the moments, all the momentous occasions this little girl will experience without a father.

Just like me.

This wasn't the plan. Other than being knocked-up and twenty, the reason I married Meyer was because he was stable, reliable, here. He was five years older than me and knew what he wanted, a family. He'd be the father I'd never known. Hell, he'd be the mother I never had. For five years he was all that and more to Abby.

"She takes my breath away," he used to whisper, watching her sleep. He'd rest his hand on her belly to feel her breathing, and she'd smile the content smile of a newborn while I watched in awe.

Tears gather as I try to collect myself from this all-consuming hallucination: my world before the car accident.

"Mama," slips from Abby's pink lips, and I panic to think she's caught me lingering, crying, again. It's a fleeting worry, stifled by her rousing grumble and diminished when she rolls over, kicking the covers, mumbling, "Push me higher, Mama."

I will, I swear I will.

Taking the cue, I blindly make my way through the onslaught of toys, shuffling out and into my bedroom to tug on baggy flannels. Hiding BOB in a drawer along with unwanted thoughts of Adonis, I pick another stray hair off my shoulder. I used to have beautiful hair, rich chocolate brown, long, thick, and bone straight. Shortly after the funeral the luster disappeared and my clothes and hairbrush were covered in hairs jumping ship. Doc said stress can do many things to our bodies, and my hair took a beating. I wash my face and lean over the sink to get a closer look at my head. The collision at the teacher open house has left a plum-size purple bruise above my right eye, and between the bruise and the hair, I look about as good as I feel.

*Get a grip*, says the woman in the mirror. She's someone unrecognizable.

An unruly laugh escapes me. I laugh again, intentionally this time, trying to mimic the noise, but it sounds fabricated, so I give up the charade. Popping a Tylenol, I turn off the light and shimmy into bed, determined to start afresh in the morning, no more tears.

I need to accept Meyer's gone, that I'm alone, again. I need to move on with my life. For my sanity. For Abby. I suck in a deep breath. I can do this. I've survived on my own my whole life, through some pretty bad shit. What's another twenty years of motherhood?

I drift into sleep, in search of thoughts vastly dislocated from my current life. *Who am I fooling* is my last conscious thought.

**"Meyer, slow down**." Buildings are flying by, colors blurring. "You're gonna hit something."

Meyer flashes me an as-if grin. His sandy-blond hair blows in the wind. His face, usually clean shaven, shows signs of his mad-dash to the office for some forgotten report that couldn't wait until Monday. He's in a rush, on an adrenaline high. Today is Abby's birthday party, her fifth, and he's late.

My stomach does somersaults. "Slow down, please . . ."

My voice fades into the distance, and the car seems to dissolve. Suddenly I'm cold and the view from the window has come to a complete halt.

"Lady, shut it and drive." The voice is rough, male, not Meyer's.

Heavy breathing pounds my right ear. My head is pinned against the headrest, and if I move, the knife against my throat will surely hurt me, so I look straight ahead, watching the rain hit pavement then pounce into the night air. My heart skips time with the idling of the engine. A lack of oxygen distorts the view.

"Drive," he says.

I open my mouth to scream but nothing comes out. I'm far from home, I think. My headlights are the only fragments of light, the only sign of life. I catch a glimpse of a rain-blackened sign through the half open window, and a fresh wave of panic overtakes me. Nothing good happens in a junkyard at this hour.

"You're a pretty one," he says.

Bitter air gnaws my skin. He's opened my blouse to run his fingers along my collarbone, his touch like shards of ice. I grip the wheel, knuckles white. I can feel the knife cutting thin slices into my neck as the car tires fill potholes. My head pounds, stomach churns. Warmth drips down my chest, the smell of blood and sweat flaring my nostrils.

"Drive round back." His eyes glow a turbulent shade of

indigo, inhuman and wild.

When I stop he's going to kill me. I know it to my core. Fear consumes me, and the car accelerates.

Claw-like fingers dig into my shoulder. "I'll make this hurt," he warns.

He will. This is how I die. This is how I always die.

Bile burns my throat, stomach muscles tense. Something tugs me from the inside, and I panic, the car picking up speed. "Please let me go." My voice is shaky and wrong. "Let me go," I yell, and the knife slices farther into my neck, the pain unreal. Blood oozes through my bra, spreading over my thighs, gathering on my lap.

His sneer glowers in the rearview mirror, a look I recognize with dread.

Fear consumes me, and I yank the wheel. The car veers to the right, stopping abruptly when I hammer the brake, and the front-end hits the guardrail with a vibrating crash that sounds of grating metal. A pop pierces my ears, the seatbelt rips into my chest, my eyes burn. I slump back into the seat and regard the white bag hanging from the steering wheel.

A wave of numbness blankets me, disconnecting senses, leaving my oblivious mind to tally injuries with little help. My arms and hands are grossly inflamed, several fingers out of shape. I no longer feel the knife on my neck, which is a relief until I see it in my chest. The white ivory handle is spotted with blood. It doesn't hurt, I don't feel anything. It points. I follow its aim, and there, outside the car, is Meyer, standing beside the twisted metal, watching me.

"Wake up." His voice is quiet and calm, as if he's sitting beside me and not standing in the rain.

Confused, I close my eyes. *You left me* is all I can think.

"Now!" his voice booms.

I spring upright, gasping for air. It takes a moment to digest my surroundings. The moon peeks through the blinds, the crumpled down comforter at my feet. I peer over the bed at the sheets and pillows abandoned on the floor. Tears have left sticky stains down my face and neck on their way to soak the collar of my pajamas. I lower my face into trembling hands.

What the hell is happening to me? I've had nightmares before, but lately they've been brutal. Meyer's car accident makes sense. I can't help but think I should've been there, stopped it from happening, held his hand while he died, but why can't I have nice dreams with happy endings? Why are my nightmares filled with strange, murderous men? Should it have been me to die that day?

If I believed in fate . . .

A shiver runs through me. I gather my stuff from the floor and climb back into bed.

There is no such thing as fate.

# MIND GAMES

## Late October

Time. It has no healing power. It just buries grief under a crapload of moments that dull the senses. Time forces you to eat, sleep, put one foot before the other, breathe. Everything that existed still exists, only altered: crumpled and ironed, crumpled and ironed, then laid out and pinned flat until it resembles something whole again.

Of course, I tend to be melodramatic. Without time I'd be a blubbering fool. Time and painting pulled me through the worst of it, the endless daze and the gaping emptiness of Meyer's absence. Time, art, and of course, Abby. Always Abby.

I slide on my rubber boots—covered in paint splatter in various tones—and head to the studio, burning my tongue on a piping hot tea as I slush through the fallen leaves of the Niagara Escarpment, otherwise known as home. More than 450 million years ago, an Ordovician-Silurian Age sea abandoned 728 thousand hectares, leaving a rigid shelf of shale and limestone stretching from Niagara Falls to Tobermory, a horseshoe outcropping in the heart of Ontario's Greenbelt. Nowadays, the Niagara Escarpment is recognized as one of the world's natural wonders and designated a World Biosphere Reserve by the United Nations. Hikers and bird-watchers flock to explore the caves and trails rich with wildlife, and vast tracts of farmland part to entice golf lovers and equestrians. Me, I came for an art festival and never left.

I met Meyer here, in the small town of Carlisle, on a similar Indian summer day in October. Luckiest day of my twenty years. I lived in Toronto at the time, about a forty-minute drive east, and a school friend was meeting up with a guy she'd met at a party the week before. So I tagged along to see J.D Picoult, a local sculptor I'd met my freshmen year at the University of Toronto.

Only two booths into the fair, my girlfriend ducked behind a tarp to make out with the guy she'd come to see, leaving me to wander the fair with the dude's buddy. He was a slightly older guy with soft blue eyes and an easy smile, introduced as Meyer Lemon, which I assumed had something to do with his yellow-blond locks. We'd barely uttered a dozen words that first hour. As usual, I was enthralled by the artistic talent hidden in tiny country towns and hardly noticed I had company until we both stood back to admire a canvas and tripped over a tethering cord, my entire cup of craft beer spilling down Meyer's shirt.

It was the first time I'd spent the day with a guy who didn't need to talk or touch. He made me laugh. And when Meyer confessed he'd lost his parents in a boating accident at fourteen, it was like some benevolent being pulled out a needle and thread to sew us together. My mother had stopped eating three years before, when I was seventeen. Which was, of course, when she really checked out, and not the date, some months later, listed on the death certificate.

I step inside the studio, my sanctuary, and the past slips away, splashes of burnt orange, yellow, and robust red surrounding me like a blanket. I stare at the glass ceiling, the morning sun heating my face. A brilliant hummingbird investigates a glass panel in the roof, his beak making tiny rat-a-tat-tat sounds. I'm in heaven.

My studio is actually a large glass greenhouse nestled in a grouping of ancient white cedars, exactly thirty-four steps from my kitchen and sixteen meters from the Bruce Trail at Rattlesnake Point. Meyer built the greenhouse from a kit as a gift for my twenty-fifth birthday, which was comical to watch since the man wore his corporate white collar like a badge. It's private, pin-drop quiet, and although the trees block the bluster of early winter and the harsh summer sun, they allow just the right amount of morning sunlight to pierce from above, May through November.

I take a deep breath, air expanding my ribcage like the gills of a fish, and wander about the studio in search of inspiration. Shelves of books call out to me. My fingertips glide over pages and pages of folklore and fantasy, realms that ignite imagination with fairies, goblins, witches, warlocks, and lessons of good versus evil. Wire strings attached to wooden dowels hang from the ceiling on delicate silver chains, and metal clips support canvases suspended in midair. Mythical creatures dance in my personal universe: angels surrounded by lush white wings, goddesses with crowns of gold and jewels, tempting fairies, and shimmering ghosts.

I spin in circles, allowing them to take me into their music.

Popping a few glass panels for ventilation, I set the fans to spin, just enough to circulate the air. Digging through my wicker basket of oils, the colors sing to me: tangerine orange, blood red, crisp white. I release them onto my pallet and prime my brush, feet planted, canvas ready. The brush pulsates. My heart pounds with anticipation. The colors join the dance and off we go, into a magical world, my solace, my escape.

Hours evaporate until thoughts of Abby float to the forefront.

She's at school, wearing her favorite dress. Lowering my brush, I soak up the sun and consider my canvas. I catch the movement of the clock, my mind foggy and distracted.

Ten to one.

Shit, I'm late.

**The spa is** fairly new, wedged between a Polish deli and organic café in what locals call "downtown," which is basically a strip plaza bookended by a steakhouse and post office. My guide makes a show of opening the set of double doors to an expansive room. Huge leather lounge chairs dominate various hubs throughout the spa, each decorated in a different theme. Romi, the aesthetician, inclines her head to the right and asks if I'm a bride-to-be. I shudder at the thought.

My wedding included a court justice and Grams's blue denim shirt and a skirt borrowed from Karen—the only things that fit over my whale-sized form. Abby was due to join us any day. Meyer was eager to marry, having asked me several times before I said yes, and I just needed the day to be over and done with. I wanted a family, yes. Badly. But a wedding? No. My little girl dreams never included iridescent pearls and white silk roses. All I ever wanted was a normal life and something to eat.

"Look who it is," says Karen, her fake southern drawl filling the room.

Karen is vivacious and loud and the best friend a girl could ask for. She's sitting in a pedi-chair, feet soaking in the tub. Her fingernails are already painted, a rather brilliant shade of lime green.

I smile, sheepish, and blow a kiss. "Sorry I'm late." Climbing into the black leather seat beside Karen, I shake my shoes to the floor. "Wow. The chairs rub you down." I feel like I should be strapped in for take-off.

Romi returns with a basket of pedicure tools, asking if I'd like some pineapple ice tea. I just stare at her, puzzled. I've never heard of pineapple ice tea. She tells me I'm in mini Maui and lights the pineapple scented candles surrounding my lounger before pointing to the headset. Apparently it plays Hawaiian music.

"She'll pass on the pineapple tea," Karen says to Romi before leaning back and miming throwing the headset over her shoulder, a heads-up to skip the cheesy music.

"Man," I mumble. "How much is this gonna cost me?" The chair has nubs that rotate in circles along my spine. It quickly becomes creepy, and I grope for the remote.

Karen dismisses me with a wave. "It's on Frank. He missed our anniversary. Again. Consider this his get-out-of-jail-free card."

Karen's husband is a doctor, a heart specialist. He's considerably older than Karen, who is thirty-five and a good ten years older than me. He's dull as a pebble and works a lot. Karen's his third and most patient wife.

"Speaking of jail," she says, "Katherine and I have been chatting, and we think it's time you bust out of that studio of yours. You spend too much time surrounded by imaginary friends, and it's time you joined the land of the living."

The land of the living. What an interesting choice of words. I'd sensed an ambush when Karen insisted I meet her at the spa today, only I hadn't realized it was a joint effort. Katherine is Meyer's grandmother, aka Grams. She's known Karen far longer than I have. I only met Karen five years ago, when Meyer introduced us at a charity art auction. I'd donated a painting and Karen was the organizer of the charity. She'd also been Meyer's babysitter growing up, which made for a fun night of jokes and jabs. Meyer's cheeks glowed pink whenever Karen described the various love notes and Valentines Meyer had given her over the years. Poor Meyer. I hadn't laughed that hard in ages.

"I'm living. I function. I take Abby to school, walk her home. I even bring Abby to Thomas's horse farm on McNiven Road to play with Sofia once in a while, which happens to have all sorts of living things wandering about."

Karen rolls her eyes. "I know where Thomas lives."

Of course she does. Karen is Carlisle's queen bee. She probably rang Thomas's doorbell a year ago, the minute he and Sofia set roots in town.

"So, what is it with you and Thomas then?"

I stare at her, dumbfounded. "He's a nice guy. Good with Abby. That's it."

Summer was rough with Meyer gone, and Thomas kept Abby busy with playdates, allowing me much-needed time to grieve without an audience.

I smile at Karen. "The guy bakes a killer apple pie."

I have a thing for apples.

Karen leans in, over the arm of her chair. "You don't think Thomas wants more from you?"

"No, I don't." Really, I don't. "His daughter is Abby's best friend."

"Sure, that's it."

Thomas is Carlisle's prime bachelor, or so I gather. Ladies shamelessly fawn over him at school functions, Karen included. I guess I see why. The guy has that summer fling look, like he just jumped from a jeep with a volleyball under his arm and sand on his feet, ready to play. Not my thing. Besides, I'm done with men. Meyer loved me, and lightning doesn't strike twice.

"Let it go, Karen, there is nothing between Thomas and me."

"Why not? You're beautiful, young. I see the way men look at you. It's shitty how it happened, but you are single, and Thomas is a nice specimen if you ask me."

"I didn't."

I glance at my feet. Romi's put her weight into rubbing my soles with some gritty concoction that stings. Like hearing I'm single. Before university, I had the usual string of crappy boyfriends and one-night stands. Usual, that is, for a girl who was willing to tolerate an awful lot of crap for some much needed attention. Shitheads, for the most part, their pockets full of DUIs and stolen goods. It wasn't pretty.

Karen rests a hand on mine. "Meyer loved you. I've never seen anyone so smitten. But he wouldn't want you crying forever, Chickpea. He'd hate to see you like this, with all the life drained away. He'd want you to be happy, to move on. We all want what's best for you." She squeezes my hand. "No one is saying you need to jump head first into the dating game, but consider getting out, opening your mind to a world of possibilities. You're too young to spend so much time alone."

Tears hover just below the surface, and I turn the other way, in need of a distraction. Karen keeps talking, of course, but I can't bear to hear what she has to say. I've grabbed a *Forgotten History Magazine* from the Formica shelving unit beside my lounger, under a shelf of strange looking bottles. The feature article asks, "How old are we?" and "Where's the proof?" It's quite fascinating really, "Archeological Finds that Baffle Scientists."

". . . I understand, but before you say—"

"Did you know they found spearheads and human remains beside extinct mastodon and mammoth bones in Mexico, proof man hunted large game as far back as the Pleistocene era?" I keep reading, pretending I don't hear Karen's dramatic sigh.

"Apparently the discovery, dated over 250,000 years ago, proves man walked the Earth long before originally thought."

"Look, Tess, I know getting out will be hard for you, but I've thought about it and I think a party is perfect."

I look up from the magazine. "A what?"

"I said we'd go to his Halloween party."

"Whose party?" I shake my head. "No, no way, I'm not going."

"Hear me out, just for a minute." Karen leans in farther. Her breasts roll onto the arm of the chair into a sitting position, and her spandex top stretches to translucency. "Everyone will be in costume, somewhat unrecognizable, so you can be whomever you wish, in disguise. A few locals will be there, so if you're not antisocial, you won't be stuck in a room full of—"

"It says here that water erosion on Egypt's Great Sphinx dates to 5000 BC, some 2,400 years earlier than archaeologists claimed, and twenty centuries before the dawn of Egypt itself."

I turn the page, the magazine slick in my hands, but Karen is relentless.

"There will be alcohol to ease your nerves, which I'm sensing you'll need, and food to keep your hands busy. Pig out if you want. You could use some meat on those bones."

"Karen, I don't—"

"His house is the old Vandemere estate. It's only a few blocks from the school, so you'll be close to home."

She's really thought this through and I almost hate to disappoint her, but it's too soon. A night of condolences would be nothing but hell.

"I'm not going, Karen, but 'he' who?"

"Have you not listened to a word I've said?" She huffs. "Bryce Waters."

Adonis. Oh my.

Karen grins at me, teeth showing, eyebrows lost in her

hairline. "He insisted I bring you to the party. Insisted."

"I have no idea who you're talking about."

"Liar," she says. She pauses, apparently waiting for a response from me. "You met Bryce Waters on meet-the-teacher night at the school, ages ago." She pretends to look hurt. "I heard all about it, just not from you."

Even with my eyes focused on the magazine, I can see her looking at me.

"We ran into each other. Literally. Actually, I walked into his chin. But that was it, so I'm not sure what you're—"

"He's hot, Chickpea. Like blow-your-mind hot. And single. You didn't think to mention you'd had a moment with the guy?"

A deep breath whistles past my lips. A moment? Ha! A mental breakdown is what it was, pure and simple.

"There was nothing to mention." Nothing I'm willing to spill.

She's trying to be serious, but there's a sneaky look to her eyes. "He asked if we're friends, you and I. He wanted to know about you and of course—"

"The guy looks like trouble, Karen."

"I was curious to know why he wanted to know. He said he found you intriguing. Oh, and *alluring*." She rolls the word like a red carpet. "He asked if you were *the* Tess Morgan, the artist."

Fish on a hook. I sit straight up, almost knocking the nail polish off the tub.

"He recognized my work?"

"Apparently he's a fan of your Wings series. He loved your showing, the one you had a few years ago at the Landmark Gallery in Oakville."

That show was amazing. I sold almost a dozen paintings including my personal favorite and the inspiration behind the Wings series, a massive, seven-by-seven-foot canvas titled *Crimson Spirit*.

"Bryce didn't meet you the night of the show," Karen says. "Apparently you were sick. He met Meyer though."

Abby was the one sick that night. An hour into the show, Grams called to tell us Abby had spiked a fever over a hundred and four, and I panicked. Meyer thought I was being silly, that Grams had it under control and Abby would be fine. But I couldn't stand it, not knowing, being so far away. What if Abby needed me? What if she felt alone or scared? I was home nearly twenty minutes before I realized I'd left Meyer at the gallery.

"Bryce didn't know about Meyer's car accident." Karen stares at the sponge-like substance sprouting around her ankles, and Romi, thinking it's her cue, lifts Karen's feet out and wraps them with a towel. "I'm sorry," Karen mumbles.

So am I.

"Come to the party with me." Karen pouts like a kid who's about to lose the battle after giving it all she's got. "Please. Frank won't go, and I need a wingman."

Romi taps my leg, drawing my attention. She's painted my toenails red.

"It's the color of exuberance, fun, and seduction," Karen purrs. "The perfect color to move you forward."

I let Karen bask in her theory. It's the least I can do since she'll be flying solo at the party. With any luck she'll get sidetracked before we head next door for tea and I can forget about this entire conversation. I grab my purse and slide my feet into sandals, trying not to ruin Romi's paint job.

I picked red because it reminds me of autumn, my favorite season.

And for some reason I don't care to think about, Bryce Waters.

**We fumble next** door: me walking awkwardly in flip-flops, Karen's three-inch heels getting stuck between stones. The pilfered magazine burns hot in my pocket. It's been years since I swiped something, but old habits don't die. And I couldn't leave it to rot with the likes of beauty tips and greasy oils. I need to read more.

The café is quite large, in the shape of a giant L. The smaller section up front has a set of glass showcases displaying pastries and baked goods. The smell of almond and custard sweetens the air. Massive chalkboards hang from the ceiling by chains. The bulk of the place is a stretch of street-facing windows featuring floating tables with backless stools. The sun is bright, setting patrons aglow. Wobbling to the end of the café line, I scan the signage for something good. There is an endless list of organic white teas and natural lattes. Not sure what makes a latte "natural," but what I really want is a drink, something strong or straight up.

Did I mention old habits?

Karen nudges me. "I actually saw Bryce with Sonia a few weeks ago, at the Olive Twist next door. My sister and I were having dinner with the kids, and Sonia was at the bar, hanging all over him."

I sigh. I can't help it. "I care because . . .?"

"It's a big deal. Well, sort of. It could be. The police don't think it's a big deal, but you never know. You gotta report this stuff, right?"

Karen picks a long silver hair off the jacket of the lady in front of us in line, and the woman turns and glares.

"You talked to the police? Why? And who the hell is Sonia?" I ask, peeking at my cell. I can't be late getting Abby from school. Karen's kids are older and don't need to be walked home. Two are in high school, Frank's from a previous marriage, and one is in her last year at Carlisle Elementary.

Karen glares at me. "You really need to get your head out of your ass," she says, shaking her head. "Do you not watch the news? There are posters at the school." She notices I'm not getting it. "Sonia, you know, the blonde bombshell with the two-inch waist. My neighbor's daughter."

I don't know anyone named Sonia. I step to the counter and order a decaf tea and bran muffin then turn back to Karen. "I thought your neighbor was the old guy with the blind parrot."

"The other neighbor," she hisses.

Karen orders a double latte with extra skim milk, heavy on the foam, three sugars, and two lids.

I shake my head. "Two lids? Really?"

"Burns my lips," she says, smacking her lips. She taps her fingernails on the glass showcase, directing the barista to the pastry she wants. He pulls out a chocolate donut oozing orange gel from various holes and places it on a plate, handing it to Karen.

I snicker with distaste.

"The neighbor farther down, to the right," she says. "The house around the bend. The ugly one with puce siding." Her eyes bug out: *puce siding*. "Sonia has been missing since Wednesday."

"Shit," I say, a sudden knot in my gut. "I hope she's okay."

"She works at the restaurant next door, the Olive Twist. Cops found her car out back, but she never came home from work."

We move down the line, waiting for Karen's latte.

"Her parents must be freaking."

That has to be every parent's worst nightmare, without question, no matter the age.

Karen hums. "That girl has always been trouble; heavy drugs, drinking, a revolving door of men. Her mother isn't much better. The woman spews profanities like a trucker. Sonia probably ran off with some badass biker. They're always gunning it up her driveway, shooting rocks."

I take a bite out of my muffin and look away.

That was me. When I was thirteen, we landed in Toronto and I fell in with the wrong crowd. I had good marks and went to school enough to fly under the radar, but nights were spent drinking, smoking anything I could roll, swiping necessities, and having sex. My mother never brought men home, but her suicide only made things worse, and by eighteen I was out of control. It took an unexpected pregnancy to set me straight. That and a school counselor who insisted I had talent and should enroll in art school. The baby didn't survive past the first trimester, but by then I'd gotten my head straight, straight enough to know what I wanted when I met Meyer two years later.

Maybe Sonia wasn't so lucky.

"If I was twenty-one and having the time of my life, I wouldn't call home either," says Karen. "She'll turn up. Someone must know where she's run off to, and they'll tell the police." A sly smile lights her face. "Secrets are hard to keep in a small town like this."

"Every day, Karen, every day I thank my lucky stars you and I get along."

Karen bursts into laughter. "We'd get along better if you'd come to the party with me." She waves a ten-dollar bill in my face. "Gotta pee. Grab Frank a caramel brownie to go." Her laugh tapers off as she heads to the bathroom.

The café is busy so I organize our stuff on a tray. I turn around to find a seat and instantly my body goes into shock, my mind fighting to rationalize what it's viewing. The entire room falls away, the hum of chatter gone. The sensation of nausea rises in my throat. Somewhere in the depths my gut instinct screams *run*, but I can't move.

It's a man. He sits, one cheek on a stool, leaning slightly forward, his weight supported by a foot firmly planted on the floor. His other foot casually rests on the bar around the stool base. Every muscle on his perfectly chiseled body stirs with flourishing, almost elegant movements. I can see every detail—he's naked. Not a no shirt, no shoes, no service kind of naked, but a run from the place screaming exhibitionist naked. In his arms is a woman. She's nude, wearing only a pair of high-heeled black leather boots and tiny black lace panties. She'd be beautiful if she didn't look so . . . stoned, drunk, drugged. He is fixated on her, his hands ravaging her ass and back. His face is buried deep in her neck, her head tilted back like a ragdoll's.

He moans and she shudders, her face turning toward me.

Holy shit! Sonia! My intuition screams this is Sonia, the missing girl. She looks familiar, I think, until she shimmers like her form is a hologram, and I squeeze my eyes shut and try to focus. My hands are shaking, the tray held tight in my grip.

He moves, slowly, running his fingertips over her stomach. She drops back, her body falling into a dramatic arch. Her long blonde hair sweeps the floor. She lifts her head, her chest rising and falling, grappling for air. Her nails hold tight to his sides. His skin is dark, tanned, and his jet-black hair hangs chin length in disheveled curls. Tattoos of intricate wave-like symbols cover large portions of his body, the sun providing a radiance that nearly gives life to the raised contours.

I can't believe this is happening. How is this happening? I scan the room, frantically searching the faces of people within view, but no one looks in their direction. No one cares at all.

My muscles lock in place, stunned motionless. I can't take in enough air and my chest heaves in protest. I try to scream. Only a gasp escapes my lungs.

He looks at me, his eyes an unnatural shade of blue. For a moment he seems to stare right through me, as if I don't exist. Then his lips part and he belts out a snarl, displaying two rows of thin, needlelike teeth.

Holy shit. What the hell is he?

My eyes grow wide and my heart quickens to a dangerous rate. A deafening ring vibrates the walls of my skull and the tray trembles in my hands. All this, yet I can't look away. He radiates evil, and I have the sense to know I should be afraid. I am afraid. But I'm scared for the woman in his arms. What the hell is he doing to her?

"What's up?"

My gaze flickers to my right, where Karen stands beside me with her arms crossed, a concerned expression on her face.

"Don't you see it?" I shriek. "Them?"

"Them who," Karen says, stepping back. "The guys in the suits? The tanned one is rather hot, although long hair doesn't do it for me." She shelters her eyes with her hand. "Cool stools."

This is insane! She doesn't see him? Them?

"Is it Sonia? The woman with him, is that your neighbor's daughter?" I search Karen's face for a sign, anything to show she sees what I see, that I'm not imagining it, but it's blank.

"Right there." I scream and point, but when I look back they're gone. "What the hell?" I turn in circles. They're nowhere. "They're gone! Gone!"

Karen pries the tray from my fists and sets it on a ledge then turns to cup my cheeks in her hands, forcing me to look at her. "Tess, you're scaring me."

"They were there," I say, my voice a whisper. "I swear."

Karen moves to inspect my face. "Who was there, honey? Customers?" She looks around. "There's a lady with a baby, an older couple eating bagels, some business men huddled for a meeting. You look like you've seen a ghost."

I squeeze my eyes, holding them tight. My fingernails gouge my ribcage, now throbbing from a lack of oxygen. This can't be real. He wasn't real. I must be seeing things.

I peer past Karen as the men in suits rise to leave. The guy with dark skin and the slightest hint of a tattoo showing around his collar looks in my direction before walking out the door. It's him. I think. It looks like him. Sort of. He doesn't seem to notice me.

"He's normal, and his eyes aren't blue. And where's the girl, the one in his arms?"

"Whose eyes, Chickpea? What the hell are you talking about?"

I move to stand by the door, watching them walk down the street through the glass, four men in business suits, not a woman around.

"Where is she?"

Holy shit, I'm having a serious mental breakdown. This is it, the moment I've dreaded my entire life, the moment I become my mother. Meyer's death pushed me over the edge. I need help. I need a doctor. I shake my hands out, panicking. Abby. Who will take care of Abby?

I search for Karen and spot her talking to someone behind the counter. She turns and walks toward me, a foam cup in each hand. "Here," she says, handing me a cup. "It's a double shot latte. Kill the caffeine ban."

I take the cup. "Air, I need air." I open the door and step outside.

Karen follows, sliding in beside me. "Did you see someone who reminded you of," she leans close, "Meyer?"

I focus on a piece of broken sidewalk, keeping the amount of air I intake equal to the amount I exhale, allowing no room for stale air to linger in my lungs. I need to think rationally. What did I really see? Nothing, it had to be nothing. I've never even met Sonia, so why would I think the woman was her? She wasn't real. He wasn't real. It was a daydream, a vivid daydream.

Karen guides me to a bench. "Talk to me," she says. "Did someone look like Meyer, sweetheart?"

What do I say? Should I tell her the truth? Like that would go over well. And Karen can't keep a secret. Grams will freak if she hears I'm hallucinating.

"Yeah, Karen, he looked just like Meyer."

"I didn't notice anyone who reminded me of Meyer." Karen speaks softly, every word pronounced as if consoling a child. "There is a phenomenon where someone recognizes a facial pattern or something like that, and I suppose hallucinations and flashbacks are a normal part of the grieving process, a stage."

That's it. A stage, a sleep deprived daydream and nothing more. I've been under a lot of stress and my body is reacting, like when I lost all that hair.

"You should speak with someone, you know. A doctor or grief counselor. Frank could recommend a good therapist, someone to help you through the rough spots."

"I'm fine. I'll be fine." I have to be. There is no way I'm telling a doctor this shit. He'll say I'm nuts and take Abby from me. It's the very reason my mother, with all her faults, didn't seek the help she needed. Death was a lesser fate.

Karen grins. "Maybe a shrink will tell you to get laid."

A chuckle escapes me. I take it Grams never mentioned BOB. I fiddle with my wedding ring. I've lost weight, and it slides on and off with ease. Physically anyway.

Maybe Karen is right. Maybe I've been cooped up too long. Maybe I need time outside my head, a little adult interaction. Maybe I should go to that Halloween party.

How bad could it be?

# TRICK OR TREAT

## October 31st, Halloween

*Some scientists believe Earth's first civilization, the Lemurians, were the Adam and Eve of mankind. Little is known about Lemurian culture, most tangled in ancient myth predating the written word. This theory, even when substantiated, is not popular. In fact, it borders on forbidden.*

*Forgotten History Magazine*: Archeological Finds Baffle Scientists

**A**bby is so full of pulsating energy she has difficulty sitting through dinner, and her eyes dart to the clock every few minutes, which is funny since she can't tell time. Peas lie scattered across the kitchen table, shot in all directions by anxious little hands having trouble holding a fork. The juice has been tipped over twice. I can't bear another minute, so I excuse her from the table, smiling as she makes a beeline for Gramps, Keds in full throttle.

Grams and Gramps wouldn't miss tonight for the world. Since Abby was a baby they've planned their annual Florida migration around Halloween. They usually spend winters there, *to warm old bones*, Grams says, but I suspect this year's escape has more to do with Meyer's death than their eighty-year-old bones. Gramps has always been a proud man, a quiet man. So much so, I used to think he didn't like me. But he had a hand in making Meyer the good man he was, having raised him when his parents died, and no man wishes to outlive two generations of sons. He's barely uttered a word since Meyer's funeral, and Grams is worried.

I stab peas, three and four at a time, popping them into my mouth. I've given up trying to collect them with the cloth as they keep rolling to the floor. I should get a dog, a self-propelled food vacuum. I track Grams, currently the big bad wolf, chasing Abby around the living room.

"Ahhhh," Abby screams, launching herself into the couch.

"I think I'll eat an angel for dinner tonight," Grams growls, hands over her head in a menacing pose. The threatening look is thrown off by laugh lines and tight silver curls. She looms for dramatic impact then drops her hands to Abby's belly, spurring massive strings of uncontrolled giggles. Arms and legs flail about haphazardly.

"All right, you two, that's enough." I playfully swat Abby in the rump. "Get ready to head out, baby. It's candy time!"

As much as Abby loves to be tickled, she loves trick-or-treating more, so she swiftly slides off the couch and runs upstairs for her wings.

Grams collapses, taking Abby's previous spot on the couch. "Her costume is adorable," she says. "Perfect choice."

"Abby picked it out. You should've seen how excited she was when we found it." I can't bear to repeat what she'd said at the time, *Now I'm an angel, Mama, I can visit Daddy.* It took everything in me to keep from bawling in the middle of Walmart.

Abby bounds into the room. "I'm ready!"

I look and my heart stops. She's slipped Meyer's hockey jersey over her costume.

"Abby, baby, what are you wearing?" I'm having trouble breathing.

"Daddy's pajamas."

Meyer was a die-hard Maple Leafs fan. Game days were pajama days. Always.

I fall to one knee beside Abby and pull her into my arms. I kiss her face. Grams has both hands over her mouth.

Abby weasels out of my grip and stands back, tapping her wings on the floor. "So Daddy can find me," she says. "He likes candy."

"He . . . does," I whisper, gently working out the creases in the jersey with trembling hands.

Grams rises from the couch and heads for the door. A bowl of candy waits beside the pumpkin we carved before dinner, and Grams picks it up, visibly relieved to find Gramps hasn't made it to the door yet. Her eyes are red.

I take Abby by the hand and open the door. "Let's go get some junk."


**The moon casts** an eerie glow onto the street sparsely dotted with kids fluttering about in their costumes. Most of the families out this early have young children in tow, making their way from house to house. I park Abby's wagon so no one trips over it, waiting at the end of a long driveway while she runs to the door. She skips, humming some muddled tune that sounds dubiously related to the theme song for The Addams Family. I find this amusing. Abby's never heard of The Addams Family and I've never watched it, not even as a kid. The show scared the bejesus out of me. And goodness knows my imagination didn't need any assistance on the horror front.

A muffled growl assaults me from the left and the cricket orchestra pauses in fear. I hold my breath, suddenly tense, cursing the city for placing the streetlights so far apart. Something snarls, and I search the trees where shadows come to life, spinning gruesome scenarios through my mind. A figure jumps to my right, roaring, and I tumble over the wagon.

"What the hell?" I scream as the man steadies me.

"Gotcha," he says. His laugh is a garbled mess under the rubber zombie mask.

Backing up, I twist the wagon between us. I can't see his eyes, but his smile can't hide behind the gaping mouth hole.

"Thomas?"

He raises gnarly rubber gloves. "How'd you know it was me?"

"You've got teeth straight out of a dental advertisement. And the hoodie and shorts kinda blow the look." Thomas removes the mask and runs a hand through his hair, throwing reckless curls into absolute mayhem. I run the wagon into his shins. "You scared the shit out of me!"

Thomas grins, shrugs. "Mission accomplished."

"You know it's October, right?" I point to the shorts then gather my sweater for warmth.

"Broken thermostat." He watches Sofia lock hands with Abby as they cut across the yard to the next house.

I study him, wondering, thanks to Karen, if he's holding out for something other than idle friendship.

"What's new with you?" he says.

Losing my mind, seeing things. "Nothing much."

Thomas pushes the sleeves of his hoodie up, mindlessly fingering a nasty scar that runs from elbow to thumb. I've seen the scar before but have never thought to ask about it. We never talk about anything personal.

"What's that from?" I ask before thinking.

Thomas tugs his sleeves down. "Boating accident."

He's lying. I have this way of knowing the truth about someone, a sixth sense you could say. He's hiding something, but I'm not about to pry. I glance at him sideways, curious. It's the first time I've noticed the color of his eyes, a bluish gray that matches the shade of his sweater.

We follow the road, the wagon looking like a miniature toy behind Thomas's towering stature. I hide my hands in my pockets. I've been brooding over my ring lately. Should I take it off? Are you no longer Mrs., no longer married, once you're a widow?

*Till death do you part.*

"How long did you wear your wedding ring after you and your wife . . .?" I immediately regret asking. Other than assuming Sofia had a mother at some point, I don't know a thing about Thomas's past. I think Karen once mentioned he's divorced, but I wasn't really paying attention to the conversation.

Thomas looks away, and for a moment I think he's not going to answer me, but he changes his mind. "I hadn't even thought of it until I ran into a friend a few months after . . . the divorce. He and his wife split the year before and he donated his ring to charity. Mine went by burial at sea."

"Boat or toilet?"

Thomas looks amused but doesn't answer.

"What happened to prompt a divorce?" The words are out before I think twice, and Thomas just stares at me from several feet away. I haven't known him long enough to read his face, but I'm not blind. Several emotions flutter through those glazed eyes.

"She left me."

I kick at a weed growing out the side of a clump of gravel and dirt. Abby comes running, almost tripping over the jersey, and shoves a handful of candy into the pillowcase stashed in the wagon. I wipe the chocolate off her chin, and she and Sofia head to the next house.

"I'll give you the pretty picture," Thomas says when the kids are out of earshot. "My wife wasn't sure she wanted children. We had Sofia, and I was the happiest man alive." He beams, watching Sofia twist from side to side to keep a chubby poodle from swiping the licorice hanging from her coat pocket. "We fought about having another—and other things, of course. There are always other things—I wanted a son."

A son. A sibling for Abby. That's what Meyer wanted. That's what we both wanted.

Thomas flinches as if slapped. "She got herself fixed."

Yikes. That's as drastic as a concrete wall. And that final. I opt to change the subject to something less bleak. That was his pretty picture.

"How's everything at the farm? Last time I saw you there was a situation with a foal."

Thomas houses some forty-odd horses and a couple of dozen goats. He's also got a donkey, a pig, and a flock of geese. Whenever I bring Abby by to play with Sofia, I have to wander about the farm to find them. Sofia is usually playing, Thomas close by working with the horses or tending to a repair. The guy wears the outdoors like a layer of skin, camouflaged by his surroundings.

"Filly's got her land legs now. She can even outrun her brother."

For the first time I notice Thomas has a slight American accent.

"Have you always worked with horses? Where did you live before moving to Carlisle?"

"Everywhere. Nowhere important. Chicago."

"The city?" I can't imagine Thomas living in a city.

"The one and only. I didn't work with horses then." He starts to look uncomfortable again. "I didn't work with animals much at all."

"So what did you do in Chicago?"

"Well," he squeezes the bridge of his nose, "I was a teacher."

Really. Now that I hadn't expected either.

"What did you teach?"

I pretend not to notice Thomas pulling himself together, picking at a hole in the seam of his shorts. He seems more tortured by this line of questioning than he did when talking about his wife. Maybe I should bite my tongue and avoid topics that don't revolve around the weather or our kids.

"I didn't mean to—"

"I'm a dad. Without a mother, Sofia needed me. And I needed her to know she was the most important thing in my life. I moved here, to Carlisle, to start fresh, to leave all that behind. Is it so hard to imagine needing a new life?"

Is it hard to imagine? Shit no. I'm the poster child. This spurs all kinds of questions, questions about Thomas, but I lay them to rest. He's his little girl's hero. I leave it at that.


**The air has** adopted a winter-like crispness, working its way under my sweater, and Abby's fervor has dwindled. Her pint-size feet take three steps for every one of ours, and the Keds, meant to give my angel a running start to fly, seem to drag behind. We plan one last stop before calling it a night. We can't miss Mrs. Maples on Halloween.

At the very end of our street, huddled behind towering cedars and white pines, is an ancient farmhouse. Although the house saw the raising of a half-dozen gangly boys into strapping men, it now enjoys the quiet bliss of one, Mrs. Maples. Mrs. Maples goes all out for Halloween. For weeks prior you can find her frail, eighty-pound body dragging decorations from the barn. Cocky kids and curious adults come from who-knows-where to brave the walk beneath ominous trees with frightening ghouls to pocket one of Mrs. Maples' renowned goodies. Even I'll endure this nightmare set-up for one of her candy apples.

We take slow, arduous steps toward the farmhouse porch, turning every so often in response to nail biting shrieks and piercing yellow eyes that assault us from the dark foreboding trees that line Mrs. Maples' driveway. Orange lights flicker, illuminating ghosts hung from branches, goblins sneering from under fake grass hills, and tombstones claiming the dead. Horrified screams and animalistic howls seem to pour from the wood siding as we approach the house, and less than two feet from the stairs, the girls stop cold. I stand on one side of Abby and Sofia, Thomas on the other, both of us watching their faces. Abby seems torn between ringing the bell and bolting as fast as her runners will take her.

The front door creaks open with an artificial screeching sound that must be from some sort of battery-operated device because no door really sounds like that, and there stands Mrs. Maples, all four and a half feet of the eighty-nine-year-old. A black wig matted into a once-chic sixties hairdo hangs to her knees in clumps. Ash colored net-like material clings to her body, chin to toes. A bodice covered with glimmering sequins flattens her chest, wrapping around her waist and over her legs, pooling into a black-feathered fish tail.

We all laugh.

"You're one nasty looking mermaid," I say.

Mrs. Maples snickers. "If Walt can take liberties, so can I."

She's referring to Walt Disney. We've talked about this

before, how ancient myths change over time, becoming twisted with every generation of storytellers.

Mrs. Maples swings her cane, motioning us to step inside while she holds the door. The smell of death permeates her skin, and gelatinous make-up blots her hands and face. Abby and Sofia leap into her arms, giggling, and Mrs. Maples plants a wet one on each cheek before stepping back to consider Abby's hockey jersey.

We exchange looks but neither of us comment.

"Vindictive oafs," Mrs. Maples huffs, waving a hand at the life-size mermaid statue that resides in an alcove off the foyer.

Mrs. Maples has a love-hate thing for mermaid folklore. Apparently mermaids were once people, legs and all, who deserved to be thrown from their land during the great deluge. Those who didn't drown adapted to life amid the waves. Many became bitter, angry. They'd lost everything that mattered to them: land, riches, power. They blamed others for their demise and in retribution lured innocents to their deaths for centuries. Misery loves company. Tonight the three-thousand-year-old bronze mermaid unearthed by archaeologists in the Middle East dons a dusty pirate hat.

"Fitting," Mrs. Maples says, eyeing the hat.

Mrs. Maples is eccentric. And slightly off her rocker.

She winks at me then disappears into the kitchen. Thomas stretches to investigate a wall of sepia photos and almost topples the table of tribal masks balancing precariously on metal stands. He steadies one then yanks his hand as if bitten.

"For my young ladies," Mrs. Maples says, tail swishing. She blows Thomas a kiss. "Candy apples, green ones, just how you like 'em." She pokes the end of her cane at a basket of apples. "One for each, your Grams and Gramps included." She points a bony forefinger at me. "One special, to bring sleep."

Man, how bad do I look if she can tell I'm not sleeping?

"Nightmares are getting worse," I say. We'd talked about them a bit the last time she stopped by the house for tea. I kept the café delusion to myself. Forgetting about it altogether would help me sleep. "How can an apple—"

"In times of stress, the mind opens. Some call it the third eye. It allows us to see things as they really are, keeping us mindful of our inner strength. Some are stronger than others. I say it's a gift."

"I say it's time to go," mumbles Thomas.

Mrs. Maples grabs a fist full of Thomas's sweater and pulls him down to her level, patting him on the side of the face. "'Tis our soul coming to the rescue." She shakes her head and a cloud of make-up dust billows from her wig.

"Sure it is." Thomas gently grabs Sofia by the shoulder.

"Do not fret," Mrs. Maples says, waving a hand in my direction, "the body will know."

"Know what?" asks Abby, taking my hand.

The doorbell shrieks.

"Thanks not necessary." Mrs. Maples opens the door, driving us out with her cane. I fumble onto the porch, trying to figure out what an apple has to do with an eye and why nightmares are gifts. A devil and his father step past us into the foyer.

"Enjoy that party!" Mrs. Maples calls out, slamming the door.

I wheel around, staring at solid wood, my breath swirling in the porch light. When I last had tea with Mrs. Maples I didn't mention Halloween. How does she know I'm going to a party?

"What party?" asks Thomas.

I step down the stairs, pausing for a second peek at the door. If Mrs. Maples heard there was a party tonight, I guess she'd assume I've been invited.

Thomas steps in front of me. "What party?"

"The Halloween party at the Vandemere estate."

Thomas runs a hand through his hair. "That's fishing the deep end of the pool, that guy is bad news."

"Aren't you going?"

"No. And neither should you."

Abby calls from halfway down the driveway. She's tired and wants to go home.

I allow doubt and confusion to slip from my mind and hurry to catch up, waving goodnight to Thomas and Sofia.

The night suddenly feels claustrophobic. The hairs on my arms stand on end. Fiendish cries echo through the trees and illusory claws paw at me from the dark. Fumbling, I try to shake the sensation of being watched, studied . . . stalked.

I scoop Abby up, placing her in the wagon, and hightail it home.

The Keds are just not fast enough.


**At home, Abby** sprints to the kitchen to sort candy with Grams, and I head upstairs to calm my nerves and dress for the party. Gramps is parked by the open door with a huge bowl of lollipops on his lap, waiting for the next round of kids. I'm at the door to my bedroom when he calls out to Abby, urging her to hurry to see what's coming up the driveway. The patter of Abby's feet rumbles through the floors as I wiggle out of my jeans and sweater, throwing them onto the bed.

I step closer to the mirror and glide my hands over my belly as I turn, the side view taunting me. If Meyer were alive, maybe I'd be pregnant. I'd thought I was—hoped I was. I'd missed a period after the funeral and dreamed, for a brief time, we'd created the family we so dearly wanted. But it wasn't meant to be.

I arch my back, filling my insides with air, pretending.

The air rushes out in a great whoosh, heat flushing my cheeks. Thanks to Meyer losing control of his car, that dream is lost. Now I'll never know the feel of another child moving inside me, the sound of a suckling newborn holding tight to my breast, the scent of creation. Abby will never be a big sister.

Damn you, Meyer, for leaving us, for leaving me. You promised I'd never be alone. Damn you for making me think we could be a family, for giving me hope. And while we're at it, damn that transport truck, and the drivers on the road that day. Damn you all!

I glance at the bed . . . at the Halloween costume. Adrenaline has me high.

I'm a widow. No longer half of two, but single?

To hell with that!

I scroll through songs on my cell looking for something to spur my mood then crank the volume, Pink drowning out sounds from downstairs.

"I got a brand new attitude and I'm gonna wear it tonight." I dance around the room, naked, singing at the top of my lungs. "I'm gonna get in trouble, I wanna start a fight!"

I spin in circles then fall to the bed. I haven't had this much energy in a long time. I almost feel like my old self, the girl who laughed, challenged all authority, and kicked up a fight just to get the blood pumping. The girl who took destiny by the balls.

"Tonight," I declare to the woman in the mirror, "I'm going to have a good time in spite of my status."

I'm gonna dress to kill and act the part.

# WHITE KNIGHT

**I** arrive just after nine, wondering if I'm early since there are only a half-dozen cars parked in the drive. Even in the dark of night the estate is magnificent. Its entire façade is clad in ivory limestone and massive windows line several stories. Three soaring arches announce sets of oversized mahogany doors and every ornate post is lit with a wrought iron lamp. Scaffolding and equipment sits to the left, the place obviously under renovation. No one has lived here in years. Before Bryce, that is.

What the hell am I doing here? I shouldn't be at a party. I should be home, grieving, tucking Abby into bed. The bravado I had getting ready has evaporated on the walk over, and my stomach is considering giving back the peas. Beaming faces come to mind. Grams, pleased to see me going out, Gramps holding me tight. They'd be disappointed if I returned home now, tail between my legs.

*Among the living.* Karen's words taunt me.

A few minutes later I'm in the same spot, second-guessing my outfit. A taxi pulls up and the back door swings open an inch from my hip. Curvaceous legs and navy heels swing from the back seat. "You came," squeals Karen. She comes to stand beside me, squinting to see my face in the glow of the lamps. "Oh no you don't," she says, hauling me up the stairs. She knocks on the middle set of doors, holding my arm in a death-grip.

A man opens the door in a butler costume and a nervous laugh escapes me. "Good one," I say, pointing at his outfit.

"Ma'am." He nods. "I am Clause, Dr. Waters' chef, and butler when the need arises. Please do come in and allow me to take your coats."

I make a face at Karen and she grins from ear to ear. Clause disappears with our coats, and Karen takes a good look at my outfit. "About time the old Tess showed up for something," she says.

I'm dressed in gold from head to toe. I glow.

"I found the gold tights and body suit at a thrift shop and I painted the shoes." I raise a leg. The once black stilettos reflect light with glitter. My hair is pulled back into a tight ponytail coated in gold sparkles from a can. My facial features are strikingly inhuman, painted on with shimmering makeup. Long eyelashes twinkle, my lips glisten with gold lipstick, and Abby's wings hang down my back, even though I know they don't belong with the outfit.

"Let me guess, you're a hot fairy," Karen remarks.

"That'll do. I'm actually a Tuatha Dé Danaan." Karen lifts an eyebrow. "The Tuatha Dé Danaan are ancient fae, mythical creatures thought to live in a parallel world among the Irish." She just stares. "No one will get it. I expect to be pegged a fairy all night."

Karen shrugs without further comment. She's just happy to have a wingman.

I take a step back, appreciating Karen's outfit. She's a police officer. Well, a scandalously clad police officer. The navy polyester uniform holds tight to her curves, top three buttons hanging free. Her long red hair is tied into a bun tucked beneath an authentic-looking officer's hat.

I laugh, delighted. "Who'd you buy this outfit for?" Her husband is a self-absorbed prude who'd never volunteer for this type of foreplay.

Karen looks herself over. "Hubby would poop his pants to see me like this. I figured since I felt like a teenager sneaking out of the house I might as well have some fun with it."

God, I love going out with Karen.

We're about to wander when Bryce blows into the foyer. "Thank you for coming," he says. He looks dashing, slightly menacing, but distracted. "The bartender will serve anything you wish to drink and waiters are wandering around with things I couldn't possibly name." The party is obviously catered. "Please, make yourselves comfortable." He ends with a hospitable bow, cape in hand, then turns to greet the next wave of arriving guests pushing us from the foyer.

"You need a drink," says Karen. So we head for the bar.

"This party is packed." We push through the crowd. "How did all these people get here? They couldn't possibly fit in six cars."

Karen scans the crowd. "This is nothing." She hates being outdone. Her parties are legendary, and she has no intension of being knocked from her throne.

The bar consumes an entire corner of the great room. It's illuminated with candles and small pot lights that showcase glass cabinets filled with an assortment of expensive-looking crystal glasses and stone sculptures. An attractive young man stands behind the counter, his suit starched stiff, making him look like a penguin. I lean over the bar, inquiring about martinis, my voice straining to be heard above the chatter. "Any kind you wish," he says, flashing a smile containing more teeth than should fit into one mouth.

"Candy apple martini," I say, Mrs. Maples coming to mind.

"But not the sour kind."

Bar boy nods. "And you, officer?" He ogles Karen's barely-contained boobs.

Karen leans forward, giving him a better appreciation of her finer points. "Corona with lime, please and thank you."

Man, her husband has no idea what he's missing.

With drinks in hand, we scan the room. People have put great effort into looking the part, most in elaborate costumes. I watch a tall fellow in a pirate outfit talking to a group of people with an animated hand and one hook flying every which way. The group consists of an extra-large Fred Flintstone, Obi-Wan from *Star Wars*, and a doctor and nurse, a couple. To our left a knight is involved in a heated conversation with a lanky woman dressed like Wonder Woman. The man holds his sword outward, demonstrating its advantages, and Wonder Woman, lasso coiled, stands with both sets of knuckles on her hips, impatiently waiting to get a word in.

Everywhere I look waiters filter through the room with trays of shots and fancy pastries. As one approaches, pausing to serve several shots to a boisterous woman in a witch costume, I gently place my almost full martini onto the tray.

"It's much too strong." I can feel myself becoming light-headed already.

"Let's flaunt our stuff," declares Karen. She leads the way through the crowd, chatting as we go. Most of the people look to be from out of town, but I recognize a few locals: Manny and his wife Loraine from down the road, the Fedwicks, dressed in matching ghost attire. Henry is here, the chef from the corner bistro. I don't know his wife's name, but she's beside him dressed as a baby, diaper and all. Mostly couples. A lot of frowns and soppy eyes. Just wonderful.

Karen talks while I survey the room, admiring the

architecture. The house was custom built in the sixties for some European nickel tycoon, or so I've heard. The attention to detail is impressive. One end of the room boasts the largest fireplace I've ever seen, surrounded by intricate woodwork and glossy black granite. An elegant antique mirror crowns the mantle framed by two ornate statues of dancing women. Along a never-ending wall are three sets of French doors. Beyond them the night is dark so I can't see out, but I'm inclined to think they lead to a beautiful patio oasis. Everything is layered in textured shades of creamy ivory, and the walls are Venetian plaster, heavily rubbed to shine like marble.

I expected Bryce's home to be littered with modern pieces and showy man-cave stuff, but it's not. Sure, there is a lot of open space not yet filled, but his possessions are obviously historical pieces gathered from around the world, both elegant and unique, and I'm surprised.

I take it all in, Belle in the Beast's castle.

Bryce sweeps into the room, smiling, aiming straight for us, I think. Guest's stop him every few steps to chat. I find myself fidgeting, which pisses me off. He's well dressed in a cultured black suit and crisp white shirt, opened to reveal a purple silk scarf stylishly folded and pinned with a diamond-encrusted emblem. Over the suit, draped on his back and clipped at the neckline, is a black satin cape with blood-red silk lining. His handsome features are highlighted by slicked hair and pale makeup, making him every bit the regal vampire he's meant to be. He's got a glass of bubbly in each hand.

"At last," he says, coming to stand beside Karen and me. "I'm so pleased you could make it." He leans in to kiss Karen on each cheek as she mumbles words of gratitude, and I wonder, for a split second, why she gets kisses and I don't.

Bryce turns to me. "For you," he says and grins, handing me

a glass.

Am I so pathetic he thinks I need alcohol? "Thanks," I say, slightly agitated. I wait for the words of sympathy, the condolences, but they don't come.

"If you're anything like me," he says, "empty hands make you nervous." His sly smile reveals two dangerous teeth.

I'm not entirely sure what to make of this guy. I've dated men with more money than class, good-looking guys with the confidence to approach a pretty, self-sufficient girl without fear of rejection. They usually had egos the size of mountains and rough hands. Not the manual labor kind.

"Thank you," I repeat, wondering for the umpteenth time why he insisted I come to this party . . . and why I came.

Karen mumbles something about a costume malfunction as she fumbles with the buttons on her jacket. Everything looks fine to me, but she says she needs to find the ladies' room and slinks away before Bryce can offer directions, leaving me alone with him beside the fire.

I make a mental note to thank Karen later. And kick her in the ass.

"Vampires have a long history," Bryce says, maneuvering his cape like a bat wing. His face glows, dancing with the flames of the fire. "They date back almost four thousand years. Ancient tribal traditions speak of living sorcerers, immortals capable of absorbing one's life-essence or chi. These magicians didn't rise from a grave or suck blood, but the end result was the same. Over time, the word vampire evolved to a catch-all phrase encompassing a variety of creatures, some based on tribal traditions, most on modern imagination."

I'm blown away. Some of this I've read before. A lot of my books cover vampire folklore. But I've never met anyone else who has read this stuff.

"No one told Stoker." I teeter on my toes, searching the mirror for his reflection.

Bryce clears his throat with a raspy chuckle. "Folkloric vampires have little in common with literary vampires. Vampire myths exist throughout all of Eastern and Central Europe and references abound in scripture as old as documented time. In fact, the word vampire is found in hundreds of languages, most deriving from the Turkic word, witch." He swigs the last of his champagne, oblivious to my shocked expression.

"Perfect choice," he says, staring at my costume.

I feel the need to explain. "I'm a fairy. An Irish fairy, to be precise."

"The Tuatha Dé Danaan," he says, matter-of-factly.

Bubbly drizzles down my chin.

"The Tuatha Dé Danaan," he says, "are remembered as myth, folklore, and are a perfect example of how ancient history predating the written word has been twisted and misinterpreted throughout the ages, making it impossible to distinguish fact from fiction."

I can't tell if he's serious. "Most of the books I've read paint the Tuatha Dé Danaan as mythical creatures who guard the passage to the underground, to the land of the fae." I peer at my gold tights and shoes. "And look like this."

"Today the Tuatha Dé are an important part of Irish mythology, their story always evolving. But what if, thousands of years ago, the Tuatha Dé were mere mortals, migrating people from an advanced civilization displaced by a great flood or catastrophe? What if they were people no different than you and I?" He leans in to whisper in my ear. "Who knows, maybe you're a direct descendant? The Tuatha Dé were tall women and men with fair red hair and pale skin, and your stunning green eyes are a dead giveaway."

I suddenly feel like a stranger in my own skin. My hair is dark but my mother was a red head.

"The wings are cute though." A devious smile plays on his lips. "You ought to be careful tonight. The vast majority believe the Tuatha Dé Danaan were sensual beings. You may get hit on something fierce."

I scan the room, feeling somewhat targeted. No one is looking in my direction. No one but Bryce.

"I'll be your white knight and protect you from the demons that lurk," he murmurs in my ear.

I laugh but my heart is not in it. Who will save me from Bryce Waters?

Nerves and alcohol wreak havoc with my insides, my pluck gone the way of the dodo bird. I take a sip of Champagne and gaze out into the room, people watching. Suddenly, the room seems even more crowded, the notion making me dizzy.

"You have a lovely home," I say, avoiding his eyes. If I didn't know better, I'd swear the fire is making the silver flecks in his eyes spark.

"Thank you. There is still a lot to do, much to update, but I'm settling in."

"What made you buy in Carlisle?"

"It's 1625 feet above sea level."

I stare, dumbfounded, and Bryce grins.

"I have family nearby," he says. "I fell in love with the town ages ago, when I was here to assist an archeologist studying the area. The Niagara Escarpment has more than one-hundred sites of geological significance, including some of the best exposures of prehistoric rock and fossils to be found anywhere in the world."

"Are you an archeologist? Do you travel a lot?"

"I'm a historian. I teach, but not here. My work takes me

around the globe, although I'm trying to cut back, to spend more time with family."

A historian. Hmm, my inner nerd is giddy.

"Aren't historians, like, book worms? You're not what I envision. You got a pocket organizer hidden somewhere?"

Bryce tut-tuts me, smiling. "How cliché. I specialize in anthropology, the study of human origins, societies, and cultures. Most of my time is spent teaching ancient history: Mayan, Inca, Roman, Egyptian, civilizations that thrived for hundreds or thousands of years." He frowns, seemingly bored.

Not me, I studied art history in university, even spent an entire semester addicted to Egyptian pottery.

"Have you published any articles or books I might've read?"

He shrugs. "I mostly speak at conferences, schools."

He looks too young to have such experience.

"Do you get to go on archaeological digs?" Bryce doesn't strike me as someone who likes to get dirty . . . in the dirt.

The right side of his mouth twitches. "Every once in a while one of the archaeologists or geologists I work with calls me to a site." He reaches behind me, his scent, soap mixed with vanilla and apples, engulfs me as he pulls something from a shelf. "Gotta love the dig," he says. Cradled in his hand is a tiny porcelain dish encased in plexiglass. The dish is covered in symbols of various shapes and sizes, all encircling a naked woman standing waist high in water, holding a tree branch above her head. My breath blooms over the plastic box as I investigate the etching too intricate for tools of this century, let alone one past.

I take a stab at dating the piece. "The Minoan civilization, sixteen-hundred BC?"

"Add a thousand years. Early eighteenth century. A rare find." He points to the center of the plate. "The woman is Xi

Wang Mu, known as the goddess of immortality. Here, she's following the other gods of life across the sea, away from her former Palace of Immortality, which has been swallowed by angry waves. Her chief duty is to tend to this peach tree, the tree that bestows eternal life to anyone who eats the fruit." He returns the priceless plate to its haven on the shelf and turns to me, now brimming with excitement. He's young, my age I'd guess, and articulate, speaking with a maturity beyond his years. His knowledge is mesmerizing.

"Truth be told, my specialty is prehistory, cultures that existed prior to written language. I'm especially close to Lemurian culture."

This sounds familiar, the concept floating close to acknowledgement, but still out of reach.

"Lemurians . . . I've read about them before. They're more myth than fact, right?"

"Depends who you ask," he says, not bothered by my skepticism. "Unlike the Atlanteans, who were obliterated before sunrise, Lemurians struggled to survive the catastrophic remains of comet bombardment for thousands of years, until they were eventually overtaken by tsunamis."

"Atlantean, as in Atlantis?"

"Atlantis was a fantastical place, brimming with scores of people. The sun shone for all but a few hours of the day, bringing life to boundless acres of garden. The land, laced with volcanic soil and fed by an immense irrigation system of fresh mountain water, offered feasts of fruit, flowers, vegetables, and herbs. The markets were busy day and night with trade beyond wonder, and the evenings filled with song, laughter, and dance. Oh, the dancing," he says, sighing. "The imperial palace was a magnificent mega of early Etruscan architecture, and clad with silver and copper, it radiated warmth that could be felt for miles.

One could spend countless days exploring the city's streets, the gardens, the temples, the shrines, and the royal residences that encircled the heart of the city. From atop a bridge you could look upon a canal bustling with import or take in the glory of one of four grandiose harbors. And that," he says with an awe-inspiring smile, "was just the place. The people, ah, the people were something to behold."

His account, so vivid, takes my breath away. I tingle from the inside out and feel like I've magically returned from a stroll down the stone-lined streets of the majestic city only seconds ago.

"You are a fabulous storyteller," I say, truly impressed.

"I get carried away sometimes." He smiles. "Enough about me. Tell me about your work. I know you're an artist."

Art—my favorite subject. Before I get a word out, someone calls Bryce from across the room. A waiter waves frantically from the doorway.

"Hold that thought," Bryce says, frowning. And away he goes, my white knight in black.

Nothing like I'd imagined.

# THAT BAD

The party gets louder as more guests squeeze in. I sip the last of my Champagne, keeping an eye out for Karen or someone familiar. The fire has my right side toasty.

A man stumbles toward me, polishing off a bottle of Heineken. "Yummy," he says, his beady eyes grazing my body.

"Excuse me?" He'd better be referring to the beer.

"Power wrapped in foil," he slurs, leaning in close, his weight supported by the mantel.

Mental note—avoid the drunks.

"What are you supposed to be?" I say, looking for a way to get past him. His skin is pasty white, almost translucent, and gives me the creeps. Gauzy material clings to his limbs, a couple of rounds in the dryer too many. His head twitches on his shoulders and his lips move, but I don't think he's speaking English. I'm busy trying to stay out of his reach. With every step he takes toward me, I take two steps back.

"Dude, you're bugging me out."

I'm planning an escape via body slamming when a hand takes mine, pulling me away from the wall and more than an arm's length from the freak. Bryce has materialized out of nowhere. The freak looks startled, then embarrassed. He turns and disappears into the horde of costumes.

"I appreciate—"

"You need to eat," says Bryce, leading me from the room.

I'm about to protest but he's right: I'm hungry. I didn't have much dinner and the wine is dousing my defenses, which apparently I need to keep sharp. We zigzag through the crowd, and I glance at our interlocked hands, tempted to pull free. Bryce holds tight, as if he has the right, and I wonder what kind of playboy this guy really is. I've seen them all, but he's an enigma.

In the dining room, Bryce hands me a plate and I make my way around the table, collecting goodies. I dole out compliments—the spread is amazing. It's just the two of us in the dining room, and the chatter filtering through is quiet. While I munch, we talk. Bryce adores art and seems truly interested in my work. Of course, when I talk about painting, I have the tendency to ramble. At one point I scrutinize his eyes, curious to note if I'm boring him, but he stares right back, a corny grin on his face until I look away.

"I'm a starving artist lately," I joke. I'm lucky Meyer was well insured and the house is paid off. "It's been a while since I completed a painting and even longer since I've sold one."

"You have gorgeous curves for someone starving," he says.

And the tiger returns, a man on the prowl.

I lower my plate to the table, no longer hungry. "Yes," I say, suddenly the hairless body-pierced Goth teen I once was, "but you're chasing the wrong tail."

An uncomfortable silence fills the room. I turn to leave, and Bryce appears before me like a ghost.

"Please don't," he says, mock punching the wall. "I can be a gentleman."

I open my mouth to comment and he places a finger on my

lips. My mother, when I was twelve, broke a guy's finger for silencing her. It was the first time I considered her illness, her lack of control, dangerous.

"Promise," he says, his expression extinguishing my fire.

I remove his finger, gently, and collect my plate.

A few minutes pass before either of us speak, but soon enough the charismatic Bryce makes an appearance. For twenty minutes he revels in stories about his family and how they've thrown Halloween parties for generations, "As a way of keeping friends in check," he says. "It's my favorite holiday, and like Lemuria, predates all known religion. The Romans first recorded Lemuria as the name of their oldest ceremony, conducted every year on the ninth, eleventh, and thirteenth of May. Like modern-day Halloween celebrations, Lemuria was staged to win the favor of restless souls or spirits."

I take another look at his costume, my imagination running wild.

We talk about Carlisle, the people in it, where I live, and how long I've lived here. We laugh.

Not once does Bryce mention Meyer. He offers no condolences. There is no awkward shuffling of his feet, no pouty lips, no sad eyes. I chew on this while duty calls him to help with a red wine disaster. Bryce makes me feel free of my widow status, as if time has rewound and I am a single, independent, well-educated woman. It's been ages since I've felt this way.

For some reason this frame of thought leads me to contemplate Thomas. He is handsome and kind and we've become friends. So why don't I feel this way around him? Is it because our relationship revolves around the loss of my husband and our daughters being close? Maybe. It's obvious that Thomas cares for Abby, and I'm grateful for all he's done for me, but . . . he makes me think of Meyer. Sometimes I appreciate that about him. Sometimes I hate him for it.

**With Bryce gone**, the dining room feels drained of life, so I decide to wander, to see what Karen is up to. Only I can't remember which door leads to the living room, so I end up in the kitchen. It's a beautiful kitchen. One wall runs the entire length of the room, spotted with gorgeous creamy-white cabinetry built flush with the soaring ceiling. The cabinets are faced with leaded glass doors and the walls are covered in elaborately detailed wainscoting. The center of the kitchen features a long island topped with a thick slab of granite that glitters in the light of a wrought iron chandelier.

I amble over to the floor-to-ceiling window in the middle of the far right wall, between what looks like two walk-in pantries. The window is draped with a sheer curtain that puddles elegantly on the floor. I'm about to pull back the curtain, with the intention of peeking into the yard, when it swings open, revealing a set of French doors. Two men stumble toward me from the night and before I have the chance to move they're standing at my toes.

"Fucking A it is," one says.

"Just the thing I needed," says the other.

I glance from one to the other, aware of two things: they are brothers and both are drunk. They are physically boisterous, elbowing each other in the ribs. Deep, mischievous laughs rise from their chests. They are not dressed in costumes but in suits finely cut to showcase buff bodies. One brother closes the doors behind him and the stench hits me—cannabis. The other one stops short and stares at me.

"Well, now, what do we have here?" he says.

They both sway, raking me with their eyes, alcohol and pot

seeping from every pore. An array of suggestive expressions cross their faces, most racy and sexual, all promising mayhem.

I hold my breath and my body tenses, knowing something is off.

They look at each other then back to me. "I think we have ourselves an Irish fae out of her realm," one says. He laughs. "What do you think, Brother?"

I wonder how all these people know my costume when Grams struggled until I put the wings on. Even then she came to the same conclusion as Karen. I'd taken the wings off in the dining room and they hang from my hand. Both brothers follow my line of vision.

"The Tuatha Dé don't have wings, never have. Fuckers could've used them at one point though." He elbows his brother in the side. "Suppose you know the stories, so you can flutter over here and sit with me a while." He flutters his fingers, suggesting I follow to the antique bench in the corner. "I bet I've enough experience to keep a sex fae pleased."

The other brother practically falls over laughing, and I stand frozen in silence. I'm not scared but I'm shocked. I can't believe these men are being so blunt, so obnoxious. And there is something strange about their movements.

Bryce walks in, head down, carrying a cloth soaked with red wine. He looks up and drops the rag, leaping to my side, wrapping his arm around my waist, our bodies touching from shoulder to thigh. My body is slightly tipped into his, one foot hovering, the other rooted to the marble floor. I can feel his muscles through our clothes, solid and strong. It's a possessive stance and I should be mad, or at least embarrassed, but I'm so relieved I just gaze like a fool.

"I see you two have met the lovely Tess," Bryce says.

The brother on the right is suddenly anxious. "We've met.

Tess is it?"

Bryce looks down at me, grinning. "You might want to stay away from these two. They are notorious seducers. They may prove to be a bit more than you can handle tonight."

The more serious of the brothers, the anxious one, waves at Bryce. "You know she can see," he says.

"What the hell is that supposed to mean?" I say. I look to Bryce for an explanation, but his attention is on the brother to the right, his expression amused.

"I do," Bryce replies. He flashes the brothers an ominous smirk followed by a subtle nod.

The three men glare at one another, ignoring me completely.

Suddenly two sets of hands fly up in surrender. "Okay, okay," the brothers mumble. They saunter off, falling over each other laughing.

I push away from Bryce.

"What was that all about?"

"You have a knack for attracting the life of the party," he teases.

"And you keep strange company." I'm absolutely baffled.

His face reads, *you have no idea,* but he says, "Those two fancy themselves the Taungbyone brothers from Myanmar mythology. They are reasonably harmless, if not troublemakers, and their history fascinating," he pauses, smiling, "of legendary proportion. I hope to tell you all about them sometime but for now just avoid them. I've known them for many years, and I've seen what they can do when they pick a lady to admire."

I shake my fists out. I'm pretty sure I can protect myself, but this sounds like a better plan.

"I was trying to find my way back to the main room," I say, aiming to justify how I came to be in this situation for the second time this evening. I smile, blushing. I know it's a weak explanation, but a valid one isn't coming to mind. These types of things just happen to me.

More so lately.


**Taking my hand**, Bryce walks through a maze of hallways until we come to stand at the entrance to the great hall. It is loud, voices competing with the music. It's even more packed than it was before, and I wonder how I'm going to find Karen in this never-ending crowd of costumes.

Bryce raises my hand, pulling it to his shoulder, forcing my body to follow until it collides with his, and before I even recognize what's happening, we're dancing.

The man can dance.

The crowd disperses like a ripple of water, gathering around the perimeter of the room. Bryce holds me tight, leading gallantly, and for the first time in a long time, I feel like I'm part of something special, like I'm one of two, adored. Our bodies move in time with the beat of Sting. *When we dance, angels will run and hide their wings . . .*

My feet follow, led in graceful circles. I hear only music and my blood pumping fast and heavy within my skull. I look into the awed faces flying by, some clear, some blurry, and at one point catch a glimpse of Karen, jaw agape. I float—the princess swept away by her Beast.

Until I catch the word widow as I flow past the throng.

One word is all it takes. My legs abandon me and Bryce floats away without a partner. My stare wanders the room, listless, until steady hands direct my hips toward Karen.

"For now," Bryce whispers into my ear in parting.

I watch him fade into the chaos that has resumed its place on the dance floor then turn to Karen with disappointment, relief, and a myriad of emotions clouding my judgment.

Karen, on the other hand, is annoyingly giddy.

**An hour of** mingling passes without incident, allowing me to nurse another glass of wine, enjoying the sensation of it dissolving the slight edge I have to my demeanor. Bryce has taken his self-appointed role as my protector seriously. As he socializes around the room, he keeps an eye on me. I'm not sure how I feel about this. I am conflicted. I'm loitering beside the bar with Karen, half listening to her drone on about something someone said about something someone did.

". . . what do you think?" Karen says, hands on her hips, awaiting an answer to the question I only caught the tail end of.

I don't bother lying. "Sorry. I wasn't listening."

Her eyes follow mine to Bryce. "Someone is awfully enamored with you."

"Who? What do you mean, 'enamored'?"

My view of Karen about to speak is blurred as a burly lady who has clearly had too much to drink falls into me spilling her entire cocktail down my arm.

Great. Another drunk.

It takes all my strength to help the woman up, but when I try to peel her hat from the floor, I can't. Her entire overweight frame is located on the rim of her witch hat. I surrender the hat while the bartender tosses me a stack of napkins to soak up the sticky liquid running down the left side of my body.

"Thank you," I say to bar boy.

I clean myself, pacing backwards. The woman reeks of alcohol in massive doses. She stumbles forward, taking in my outfit, matching my steps until my back is pressed against the bar with no escape.

"Seriously," I say, "this is too much."

"O'boy. Sorry, luv, sorry. I've had some too many, I'm thinkin'," she says, loud and slurred. She dabs at my arm, managing only to spill the last of her drink before dropping her glass. Shards tumble across my feet. "O'boy. I'll make it up. I'll fix it, I will. I'll tell your future—everyone loves a fortune!"

The people surrounding us sacrifice their conversations to stare.

"No. Thanks, but no thanks," I mumble, hoping she'll take my lead and lower her voice. I'm embarrassed and slightly nauseated. I've no energy for this.

Karen bounces on her toes, excited at the prospect of hearing my future. "Do it!"

"I'm wet, tired, and I don't want to know my future." Especially from some obnoxious half-baked witch.

"Oh, come on, how bad can it be?"

I look at Karen, deadpan. "I'm going home."

I try to push past the witch but she grabs my arm, digs her nails into me, and screams, "Your life is filled with death! Lots and lots of death!"

Everything within my vision freezes. My mind flashes images of my mother's suicide, Meyer's funeral, haunting nightmares. This can't be happening. I search for the door and spot Bryce, a drink in each hand. Beside him a lady is yanking stockings gathered around her ankles. His eyes lock with mine, frantic.

"Love finds—death chases! Past is future. Grave danger follows. A son, a Keeper's heir!"

The crowd releases a collective gasp, and stunned, I stare at the witch still clutching my arm. Her eyes are wide and bloodshot. Glass shatters on the floor from Bryce's direction. Tears threaten to spill, my neck and face hot.

I need to get out. Now.

I pull free and run for the exit, a clear line to the front door. Hands try to stop me but I shake loose, tears blurring my vision, needing only to escape.

It was that bad.

# CHESHIRE GRIN

## November 1st

*Deep core samples prove our planet has experienced several cataclysms of epic proportion. One of these close encounters with "the end" wiped the dinosaur from the map. We know this now. We have proof. But had you told the story of dinosaurs prior to 1907 you'd have been dubbed imaginative or mad.*

*Forgotten History Magazine*: Archeological Finds Baffle Scientists

Since Meyer's death, Sunday has become family day, a day to bring what's left of our pint-sized brood together. Death will do that, make the living closer. Abby and I putter around the house in our pajamas all morning. Just after lunch, Grams saunters in pushing Gramps's wheelchair, sliding him into his spot by the back window where he claims he can see everything, from the raindrops gathering on leaves to his lovely ladies bustling round the house. Like me, Gramps has a special place in his heart for the woods around us. Grams and Gramps live in a quaint bungalow the next town over. They settled there long before Meyer was born, when Meyer's father Marty was just a boy, his sister Sarah a beating heart in the womb, and only planned a temporary stay. But this place has a way of sinking its teeth into your bones, in a good way, a comfortable way, and the woods took the Morgan's as their own, embracing them like family.

Today marks the last of our family days for a while. Tomorrow Grams and Gramps leave for Florida.

"I don't know what I'll do without you," I say to Grams, looking away so she doesn't see the tears welling in my eyes.

"You'll do exactly what you've been doing," she says, "exactly what you must. For you and Abby."

I know if I asked her to stay, told her I couldn't do it alone, they wouldn't go to Florida. Selfish as it is, the thought has crossed my mind, but I can't bring myself to say the words, to make them stay when I know its best they take care of themselves. They were in their late sixties when Meyer moved to Toronto for university. When most are facing retirement and slowing down, they were busy raising a little man. My man.

"I'm not the best mother. I panic when Abby is hurt and suffocate her when she wants independence. Meyer always knew what to do. He always had the right answer. What if I raise her wrong? What if I screw up and she ends up like . . . like . . .?"

*Like me*, I want to say but don't.

We're digging through my closet, looking for clothing with resurrection potential. The people of Saint Ann's Cathedral embraced me, designating me chief costume designer of their Christmas performance. Apparently being an artist qualifies me to make costumes. Abby begged me to be involved, to do the pageant with her, and after such a commendation from the committee, as well as Karen's praise, how could I refuse? I didn't mention I'd never touched a sewing machine.

"You know," Grams says, sitting on my bed, "I've never told you this, but you scared the daylights out of me when Meyer first brought you around."

"I can believe it. And I had the bulk of my shit together by then." I can only imagine what Grams would have thought of me a few years before I met Meyer, before art school and my hair grew back. "I actually thought it was Gramps who hated me."

Grams guffaws. "Ted was over the moon. His grandson had snagged a looker and it was all he could do to keep his mouth shut in your presence. He teased that boy something awful when you weren't around, slapping Meyer on the back and hoot'an and hollerin' like some silly frat boy. All that fuss over a girl, over you." She smiles at the memory.

"It was me who worried you were all wrong for my grandson. It was my job to worry, and you were this firecracker who had my baby boy in a trance. You were too beautiful to stay loyal. You had no family to speak of and lived in a bar. Sure, you were well spoken and polite, but under the tight jeans and belly shirts you were this wounded bird determined to fly, and I was convinced Meyer would get hurt wanting to fix you."

I recall the fight Meyer and I had the second time he dropped to one knee and I said no. We'd only been dating a few months, and I thought he was nuts to want to marry me. I was five years younger than him, in school, working nights, and didn't have a clue how to be a family. Hell, I didn't even have an address. He had a good job in Toronto and shared a townhouse with some buddies. Why on earth would he want to marry me?

"Meyer never wanted to fix me, or change me, or make me into something I wasn't, something I'm not. He didn't want to—"

"Exactly," she says, shifting closer to where I've joined her on the bed. "Meyer had no doubt you were the one, that you'd be a loving wife and good mother. He saw a spark in you, different than the one I saw, and refused to listen to a single point I made. That boy had faith in you from minute one." She rests a hand on mine. "Now you need to believe the same."

Grams holds up a pair of baggy jeans that read *hip to be* across the butt. "How old is this stuff?" she says. "Christ, child, set foot in a mall once in a while."

I snatch the jeans, laughing, grateful for the distraction. "I shop . . . sometimes."

That's a lie. I'd rather walk on fire than go to a mall. My mother always had nice clothes when I was little, when we lived in Ottawa, in the attic apartment of a three story brownstone she dubbed "the Ritz." By the time I was six, I resented the silk pantsuit with gold belt, the red dress with the plunging neckline, the rhinestone stilettos. Friend's gave her these things, of course, we didn't have the money to buy shit with logos, but I never understood why they couldn't just buy us something we really needed. Like heat.

Grams laughs then shakes her head, sighing. She stands and pulls me into a hug.

"I know you think you have to go it alone," she says. "And there was a time I thought the same, when I thought I'd lost Tom. I felt nothing but despair and had no doubt I'd live out the remainder of my life alone."

When Meyer was nine, Gramps fell from a ninth-story balcony rescuing a woman from a burning apartment building. His fire chief gave the family his condolences. The doctors didn't think Gramps would make it past sunrise.

"I know better now. Tom survived—thank our lucky stars—but had he died in that hospital, I'd have gone on. I'd have found love, or a companion to share my life with. Because that's what people do, that's how we survive. We give love and thrive when it's returned. This is what life is all about, my love."

I hold Grams tight. She's warm, soft, and smells like grapes.

"Grams, I married an amazing man."

She stands back, holding me at arm's length. "Yep, you did. And yes, he was a good boy, a wonderful husband and father. Now what? Meyer is no longer here and you are."

I fiddle with my wedding ring.

"You are young. You have needs, to be held and loved and touched."

"Grams, Katherine."

"Well, it's natural to—"

"Seriously, Grams—"

"Fine, but answer one question. Have you had a date with BOB?"

"Grams!" I'm mortified.

Grams shrugs, waiting for an answer. I throw the jeans at her and we double over laughing, tears streaming from our eyes.

The doorbell rings, saving me from hell.


**"Who could it** be on this dreary afternoon?" says Grams, following me down the stairs toward the front door. "Maybe it's a gentleman caller." She dances behind me with a Cheshire grin.

I roll my eyes. The woman is relentless.

The front door opens to reveal a huge umbrella sheltering black jeans, a thick dark-gray wool coat, and the finest scarf I've ever seen on a man. The scarf is all my favorite shades of fall: burnt orange, red, gold, and deep mustard yellow entwined in three-dimensional thick cotton. My fingers tingle, wanting to touch.

"Bryce," I say, tearing my eyes from the scarf.

Grams looks like she was expecting someone else. Thomas maybe?

Bryce's smile is somewhat strained. "I came to apologize," he says.

"What did you do that you need to apologize for?" Grams says, giving Bryce the evil eye.

I move past Grams and open the door wider, welcoming Bryce inside. "Come in out of the rain." I say, only slightly embarrassed by my pit bull.

Grams lets it go. For now.

"I don't want to intrude on your family—"

"Intrude away," I say, laughing. "You have good timing."

Bryce looks confused but steps in anyway, shaking his umbrella free of rain then leaning it into the hall corner before shrugging off his heavy coat.

"Ma'am," he says, taking Grams's hand. He nods then bows. "My name is Bryce Waters."

Grams looks at me, not quite sure what to make of Bryce Waters. I shrug. Her guess is as good as mine.

"This is Katherine, my Grams-in-law." I say, taking Bryce's coat and hanging it on a hook. "My daughter Abby is playing in her room and the old guy in the kitchen . . ." I motion for Bryce to follow us down the hall, and Grams's feeble attempt at hiding her appreciation for Bryce's rear-end doesn't go unnoticed. She clicks her tongue at me. I point to the back window, "He's Gramps."

Gramps waves, secures the Game Boy in his lap, and wheels away. He's been trying to top Abby's Tetris score all afternoon. Meyer found the hand-held relic at a garage sale last year and gave it to Abby for her fifth birthday, claiming she should learn to respect the classics.

"You two have a seat," Grams says. "I'll put the kettle on for tea."

Bryce pulls a chair at the kitchen table, studying my face. His cashmere sweater attempts to hide his physique without success, and my dream scarf sits casually around his neck, pulling my gaze into its awe-inspiring colors. I sit across from him as Grams putters around the kitchen, clanging plates and mugs.

"I'm sorry to come unannounced and on a Sunday," says Bryce. "I wanted to make sure you were all right." He eyes me with a serious expression. "And apologize for my party guest."

Grams knows nothing about the Halloween party, but having heard Bryce isn't guilty of harming me directly, she saunters off, mumbling something about checking on Abby, and I slide my hand under the table, hiding the Band-Aid. Somewhere between Bryce's living room and home I broke a heel and sliced a finger. It wasn't the only scar of the evening. Events of the Halloween party sway through my internal vision, ending with the drunken lady and crying in my driveway.

"I've survived worse," I say, trying to make light of it.

I touch the raised contours of the tiny scar on the peak of my left cheek. When I was fifteen, my mother caught me sneaking out with cigarettes and tequila. She'd crashed the week before, when depression's darkness swallowed her whole, and hadn't left her room until she heard me in the liquor cabinet at two a.m. She set the pack of cigarettes on fire and smashed the tequila on the kitchen counter, the broken bottle slicing my face.

"You have," Bryce says, glancing at my wedding ring. "I am sorry Angitia upset you. She tries to keep herself contained, but I'm afraid alcohol got the better of her."

"Angitia was the—"

"Witch." He attempts a smile. "She hasn't been the same since the witch hunt."

I stifle a chuckle. Then notice he's not kidding.

"Weren't witch hunts in the sixteen-hundreds, in Salem?"

Bryce shakes his head, deadpan. "Salem is known for their witch trials, not witch hunts," he says. "The hunting of witches, or those suspected of having magical powers, goes back thousands of years. Ancient texts from Egypt and Babylonia speak of sorcerers capable of influencing the mind and prophesying. The Japanese fox witch, for example, could change shape and create powerful illusions. Most were slaughtered across central and southern Europe in the fourteen and fifteenth century. Hundreds of thousands of people, the majority women, were imprisoned, tortured, and executed."

A shiver runs through me.

"Sadly, witch hunts still take place. Saudi Arabia continues to use the death penalty for sorcery, even executing a man in 2007. In 2008, more than fifty people accused of practicing witchcraft were killed in New Guinea. Every year, hundreds of people in the Central African Republic are convicted of sorcery. Angitia hasn't been back to India since 2003, when her sisters were lynched in a witch hunt that killed over seven-hundred and fifty people."

I had no idea. "So the inebriated woman with the shrill voice is seriously a witch? In real life?"

"Witch is an ugly word, riddled with fear. Angitia is a registered Reiki master and a shaman."

"A shaman." I try to process this.

"Um hmm," he replies. "She is open to her inborn ability to connect with the natural world in ancient ways. And she has a knack for communing with the dead." He smiles. "She's been on Oprah."

The kettle whistles, and I leap from my chair, almost knocking it over. Bryce doesn't comment. His eyes follow me as I move to the counter where Grams has laid out all the necessities on a tray. She's taken my candy apple and sliced it for dessert.

Mrs. Maples comes to mind. I'm not sure if it's the conversation or the candy apple that makes me think of her.

Chair legs rumble across the floor. "I've upset you more by coming," says Bryce.

"I'm fine. Sit down, please." I should be the one apologizing. I'm not upset by anything Bryce has or hasn't done. It wasn't his job to save me from every intoxicated jerk at the party, no matter their vocation, and I've encountered enough drunks in my life to know to walk away. "Please, sit" I repeat, and ask him how he drinks his tea.

Bryce sits but the air between us is thick and consuming.

Upstairs, Barbie and Ken's Volkswagen Beetle hums across the hardwood floor followed by the muffled sounds of laughter.

"Abby loves her dolls," I say, sighing. "To be five again."

"Yes. I should've enjoyed my childhood longer than I did."

"If only we had that choice."

"Oh, yes, if only." A half-hearted grin inches the right side of his face. "You shouldn't be so bitter, so young."

I shrug. He isn't insulting me, just stating a fact. "I suppose I'm a little lost lately."

"There is no need to feel lost," he says, radiating sincerity. "I have found you."

I fidget in the chair, no clue how to respond. I appreciate his efforts, I think, but I'm not ready for this. Not in my kitchen, our kitchen, mine and Meyer's.

Bryce leans forward resting an elbow on the arm of the chair. "Is this Abby?" he says, pointing at a framed black and white of a woman and toddler plastered in ice cream and gummy worms. I was three and we'd just returned from the Royal Ontario Museum, one of the few places my mother was truly happy.

I put down the half eaten slice of apple. "My mother was a photographer."

My mother, Celeste Reit, had her fifteen minutes of fame. She was known for her photos of swingers: the subtle touch of a woman's hand accepting an offer to get closer, a sexual expression, clubs for the wealthy and open-minded, classy depictions of an alternative lifestyle. For a time, her art was sold in private circles for good money and garnered the attention of celebrities worldwide.

"It's the only photo she ever took of the two of us together."

"She was stunning," he says, studying the picture.

"She was, always, even when sick."

*Heartache,* she used to tell me, *I have a heartache that will one day swallow me whole.*

"Another artist."

"You know what they say about apples . . . I held a crayon before a spoon. As a toddler I had a compulsive fascination with colors and textures. After a day at the museum my fingers were blistered from running my hands over every object I was allowed to touch. I loved nature and could spend entire days at the park. I'd follow the geese, the water in the stream, the bugs as they climbed the trees."

I tell Bryce about my childhood, skipping the shitty stuff. My youth wasn't all bad. My mother did the best she could with what she had. She never abandoned me or gave me away like she did my brother Stephen, and she never physically hurt me, not on purpose anyway.

"I got a scholarship to the University of Toronto and spent five years earning an Art and Art History degree," I say. Bryce nods toward my book collection: history, art, parenting books by the dozens. They line an entire wall of the living room. "I was obsessed with art, especially renaissance and late twentieth century post-impressionism. I fell in love with sculpture, photography, drawing, and painting. I love painting." I swipe the last slice of candy apple.

"Where have you been all my life?" Bryce mumbles.

I close my eyes, hoping Grams hasn't heard his quiet comment. She's wandered into the kitchen to make herself a tea.

"Your grandson was very lucky," he says, raising his voice so Grams doesn't need to eavesdrop. "You must've been proud."

"Uh huh," she says, grabbing her mug and pacing out of the kitchen.

Bryce and I burst into laughter. It feels good to laugh with him.

"Where do you work now?" he asks, glancing over his shoulder, probably in search of art paraphernalia.

"I paint in my greenhouse." I rise from the table, instructing Bryce to follow my line of sight out the window. Spread before us are acres of old evergreens.

He comes to stand beside me, one hand encompassing the entire mug. "Peaceful," he says.

I point to the cobblestone path. "My studio is hidden in that mass of trees." A hint of glass peeks through branches of blue spruce. "It's beautiful, my sanctuary. There is no place I prefer to be. When I'm not with Abby, that's where I am."

We stand in silence, taking in the vista. With some people silence is awkward. With Bryce it feels calming, like I'm weightless, floating.

"You hum when you think about your art," he says, and I chuckle.

"I know. I've been called out before."

"You glow as well. Your aura shimmers. You've found your calling." He smiles.

"My aura? Ah, okay. Calling is the right word though. I've never considered any other career. I was born an artist."

"A creator," he corrects, still smiling. I don't understand but he doesn't seem to be mocking me. "Every soul has a purpose. Yours is to create," he says matter-of-factly. "In another life you created peace, justice, love."

"You're being an ass if you're teasing me."

"I'm not. Most souls spend entire lifetimes searching for their purpose. To have found yours is true evidence of your strength. I'm impressed and honored to be a witness."

I purse my lips. I've always considered myself an atheist. As such, I avoid topics that smell even slightly spiritual, and this smells iffy.

Bryce doesn't push for commentary. Instead, we spend the better part of an hour talking about school, art, and showings coming to a local gallery. Bryce's knowledge of Shang dynasty jade carvings makes me giggle like a silly schoolgirl, and I bombard him with question after question. He answers them each in turn, but eventually raises his hands in surrender.

"I'll elaborate another time," he says, avoiding my last question. "I better head home." He chuckles. "It's a school night."

He's right. I got carried away.

I lead Bryce to the front door, and he puts his coat on then steps toward me, shoving his hands in his pockets. We mumble goodbyes. I can smell him, a mix of man and rain. My heart skips a beat.

He turns for the door, pausing mid-step. "Almost forgot," he says, "Karen brought your coat home from the party."

I nod. "She called this morning."

"Good." Bryce steps out onto the porch and opens the umbrella before turning back to me, a frown stealing the spark from his eyes. "Are you concerned about anything Angitia said to you? Anything at all?"

*Death, lots of death.*

"My mother died when I was seventeen, and my husband passed away in April. I guess I'm just a little sensitive regarding the whole death thing."

Bryce doesn't look to be breathing. "And . . .?"

"And what?" Isn't that enough?

"Well then," he says. "I'm sorry the party ended the way it did and that your night was ruined. I hope you let me make it up to you someday."

"You have nothing to make up for."

Grams peers around the corner, demanding an explanation with her eyes. I haven't told her about last night. There is nothing to say. I didn't even register everything the witch said. The general theme of death was enough for me.

"Goodnight, Tess. Ma'am." Bryce waves and Grams steps out from behind the wall.

"Goodnight," I reply.

Bryce turns to leave and I close the door, spinning to find Grams in my path, arms crossed.

"Spill it," she says.

I smile. Times like these I'm happy I'm a liar.

# DO TELL

## Mid-November

The clock ticks, but I have no idea what time means as I float in my fantasy world with my colors, brush, and canvas. The sun's light has just started to seep life into the woods around me. I stare into the wilderness watching a black squirrel run from tree to tree gathering debris and food for the cold winter ahead. Blue jays, cardinals, and a medley of bright winged finch fly in and out of view. Most of the foliage has fallen from the trees.

I spent most of the night mixing paints, trying to match the vivid colors of nature. Anything to keep from sleeping. Or not sleeping, as it were. My nightmares have a new flare for the dramatics, killing me in places I could scarcely imagine in daylight, in centuries I've never known. I've watched the sun come up for days.

Today is the fall fair. I'm thankful the day has finally arrived. For weeks I've been inundated with the details: so-and-so's mother is running the rubber duck game, and so-and-so's father is cooking hot dogs. I've heard all about who's bringing the cotton candy machine and which family donated hay bales for the maze. Originally, I'd told Abby we weren't going, but I've watched her enthusiasm grow with the little things that entertain a five year old, the fair currently topping her list, and in the end, I couldn't refuse.

Now I'm anxious for her to wake.


**It's mid-November** and brisk enough to require a winter coat—that is what I told Abby. I layered her for forty below, just in case.

We surrender our shortbread cookies to the lady in charge of the bake sale then set off in search of friends. Abby spots Sofia and runs ahead, her scarf hanging from her coat pocket. I trail behind, attempting to keep the morning sun from my eyes.

Thomas sees me coming and smiles. "Perfect day or what?" he says. He's not wearing a coat at all, just jeans and a long sleeve shirt.

"Lots of fun things to do this year." I scan the area. The playground is divided into sections and scattered among the games are adults gathered in conversation, their kids running amuck. Although the fair is a fundraiser run by the school's parent council, for most the fall fair is a chance to socialize with local families while the kids burn steam.

"Let's get the games in first," says Thomas. "The prizes are candy. Sugar can do its thing while the girls run the maze."

Smart man. Meyer would've made the same suggestion.

We each buy a roll of tickets and make our way to the dart game, where the lady manning the booth is dressed like Anne of Green Gables, pigtails and all. Before I have the audacity to suggest Halloween is over, we move to the next game, where the girls *oh* and *ah* over the ring-pop prize. They aim and throw but neither come anywhere close to the hoop, so Thomas forks over another round of tickets and grabs a ball. I watch him align the basketball, his expression that of a young boy, and I'm struck by how normal this feels, how easy it is to be with Thomas and his daughter. Even Abby seems at peace when we're together.

Like a pro, Thomas sinks three balls in a row, then claiming his prizes, turns to me with a candy ring.

"I do," I say on impulse, and Thomas's ears turn red.

**It's been an** amazing day. The kid's feed their tickets to the gargoyle guarding the haunted maze and take off, running through the cobwebs and plastic spiders that surround the entrance. Thomas, looking to cause trouble, follows close on their heels while I make my way to the exit, elbow deep in cotton candy. I can hear Abby's laugh, the sound muffled by mountains of hay, and Sofia's cries to Thomas, who thumps his feet heavily on the ground, growling. Shrill screams bellow from somewhere in the maze, and a few minutes later Sofia darts from the exit followed by Abby, yelling "again, again!"

Thomas comes out panting but smiling. "That was fun," he says.

I suck cotton candy from my thumb. "They've gone back in."

"Awesome." Thomas's mischievous laugh follows him through the exit.

A strange sound catches my attention, alerting my stomach. It sounds like an animal's whimper or moan. I pace the perimeter of the maze, slowly. The noise stops and I pause, trying to ground myself to its location, but I can't place it. Part of me dreads the thought of finding a dying animal, and part of me worries for Abby's safety. What if she were to stumble across something in pain or afraid?

I scan the grounds. There is nothing but hay bales and acres of open field dotted with people. For some reason the man/thing from the café comes to mind. The woman in his arms made similar sounds. A nervous chill inches up my spine but I ignore it, walking until I come full circle. Screams hit me from the left, and I jump, cotton candy laced spit running down my chin.

"Ha, ha," Thomas cries, flying from the maze, his entire body shaking with laughter. He picks me up with one arm, swinging me in circles. My hand is still buried in cotton candy, so I have trouble balancing when my feet touch the ground.

"Do that again and I'll puke blue," I say, laughing.

This feels better. The lack of sleep has my imagination on overdrive, on edge, and I'm not sure what scares me more: seeing something freaky again, something that proves I'm going mad, or Abby witnessing my insanity. I shake the thought, determined to put bad images to rest and enjoy the day. Thomas is amazing with kids. He gets Abby laughing, giving her the male attention she needs. This makes me think of Meyer and our days out as a family. I'd give anything to give that life back to Abby. Anything.

The girls run from the maze, pleading, wanting to go through again.

"Later, monsters, there is still lots to do here," I say, ruffling Sofia's dark curls. "While I man the craft table, your dad will take the two of you to the book sale and to play more games." I glance at my watch, figuring I've got an extra five minutes to find a bathroom before heading for the gym. I gather the remaining tickets and hand them to Thomas, watching him shake his head.

"I'll use mine for now." He snatches the tickets from my hand, tucking them into my coat pocket. "When we switch, you take them to the games we miss."

Thomas volunteered for the bouncy castle and his one-hour shift starts right after mine.

"Deal." I kiss Abby goodbye and stick my bright-blue tongue out at Thomas.

"Best five bucks I ever spent," he says to my back as I walk away.

There are two women at the craft booth, and as I approach one grabs her purse from under the tablecloth skirting, preparing to leave. She picks at paint splatters on her shirtsleeves, obviously displeased. She mumbles goodbye to the other woman, the mother of a boy in Abby's class. I don't know her name.

"So," the lady says, "we're painting white T-shirts for five bucks a pop." At one end of the table, a stack of folded white cotton shirts sits, and scattered about the other end are tubes of fabric paint in various colors. String is duct-taped to the wall behind the table, displaying newly painted masterpieces. "Make sure you write a name on each shirt to ensure the correct one is collected. Parents get testy when their kid's art goes missing. Oh, and the money box is on the chair behind the table." She turns to leave. "Good luck."

I'm confident I can manage without requiring luck's involvement. Art is my thing.

I'm on one knee shoving my coat under the table when black leather boots appear an inch from my face. My eyes follow snug jeans to a leather motorcycle jacket, James Dean minus the cigarette. I grip the table, pulling myself to standing, staring at the scarf that throws my head into tiny spirals.

"What's the deal, boss?" says Bryce, shrugging off his coat.

"The deal?"

"I volunteered to help with the craft table. You're the artist by trade, so I've appointed you governor."

I haven't seen Bryce since the day he stopped by to apologize, and something about his one-sided grin and windblown hair makes my stomach do flip-flops.

"Oh. Okay." It hadn't dawned on me that my shift partner

hadn't appeared yet. Or that she'd be a he in the form of Adonis. "Well, hello then."

"Hello." He's obviously pleased he caught me by surprise.

Within minutes I've gone over the instructions, and due to a lack of clientele we have nothing to do but chat.

"Is your niece enjoying the fair?" I ask.

"She's home sick, actually. I was looking forward to bringing her today, but she woke this morning complaining of a stomachache. Her father thought it best she stay home and rest."

"That's too bad. At least you won't catch what she's got." I smile then quickly purse my lips, hoping I don't have blue teeth.

"No worries, I don't get sick," he says.

"Never?"

"Never."

He must be joking. Who never gets sick?

Customers wander over to our booth, twin sisters. They each hand Bryce five dollars while I dig for shirts their size. They're debating what to paint on their shirts when Bryce suggests they get help. "She's a professional artist," he says, pointing a thumb in my direction.

The girls seem pleased with the recommendation, probing me for advice. Bryce steps to the side, tucking his hands behind his back, allowing me center stage. This is right up my alley. I ask a few questions about their likes and dislikes then suggest they close their eyes, which they do. I tell them to listen to the sounds around them, to take a deep breath, and to think of things that make them happy. Then I instruct them to say the first thing that comes to mind.

"Candy," says one.

"Friends," says the other.

"That's what you paint on your shirt," I say, pleased with the results.

Bryce beams, vastly entertained, and the girls get to work.

"I have a confession to make," says Bryce. He's being playful, leaning in close, pretending to gaze in the opposite direction. It's all for show.

"Uh, oh. That's never a good opener."

He crosses his arms and turns, a mischievous grin igniting his eyes. "What's wrong with confessions?"

"If you have something to confess, then you were doing something crooked to start with."

"You never do anything wrong, anything you need to own up to later?"

"No," I say. Liar.

"Never?"

"Never."

"Ever?"

"Nope."

"Hmm," he hums through puckered lips.

I laugh. "Maybe you shouldn't taint me with your criminal intent." I'm joking, of course. I'm no saint, and I stole the magazine from the spa not too long ago. Still, I enjoy our easy banter.

"You might be right," he says. He seems to stare right through me. "You're as pure as they come. I promise not to rub off on you." He rubs his forearm against my shoulder, releasing a throaty chuckle.

I play along. "Confess, my son."

"When I signed up for the fair, I put my name down for the sucker pull game." He hesitates for a moment. "Then I noticed you'd volunteered for the craft table, so I switched to be with you."

I'm not really sure what to say. I suppose I'm flattered, but it's been years since a man's been so forward, and I find myself a fish out of water. Should I be freaking out? Should I fall at his feet?

"All right," I say, my voice barely audible.

Bryce stands tall, relaxed and unfazed. "I'm not stalking you. I just wanted to get you alone, to ask you out."

I feel winded, sucker punched. A dozen thoughts collide in my head, none making it to my lips.

"You know, a date. Like dinner and a show," he says.

A date. Goodness. He's had a lot of practice at this. There is absolutely no fear of rejection apparent in his features.

"I don't know, Bryce, I'm not—"

"Look, I fly out tomorrow, and I'm away a few weeks. Just think about it, and we'll talk when I get back. Okay?"

A group of kids only a year or so older than Abby run to our booth, money in hand. We have work to do, and I'm rather relieved. Bryce is not so easily distracted. At one point he leans over and whispers, "No pressure, I swear, just consider it," his lips lightly brushing my ear, the tingling sensation numbing the butterflies swooping in my stomach.

"I will," I say, not so sure I should. Reasons jump to both sides of the debate.

Pretty soon the conversation is buried under layers of paint. With the lunch lull over, there's a constant flow of customers at our table and laughter surrounds us. A mound of soiled paper towels threatens to topple the garbage can. We've run dry on three colors. Bryce smirks, taking in the paint splatter covering my arms and shirt. I'm not even slightly embarrassed. Paint is my friend. We belong together. Bryce seems to know this somehow.

"Why do I feel like I know you from somewhere other than here?" I say.

Bryce laughs. "You do know me. You are an old soul."

This isn't an unfamiliar term. "I've been told that before. Several times in fact."

He's pleased with this answer. "Do tell," he says.

"The first time I was just a baby, so of course my mother used to tell this tale best . . . Anyway, I was a few months old and my mother was strolling through the market, cradling me against her chest so I could see the world passing by over her shoulder. She'd nicknamed me 'the observer' because I would sit and watch people for hours. I wasn't shy, and seldom scared, I just liked the hustle-bustle of others. Anyway, my mom was pushing the stroller with one hand and holding me with the other when a lady, a complete stranger, rushed up and blocked the stroller, stopping my mother in her tracks. The woman was older, around Grams's age now, and she seemed normal at first, asking my name, my age, so my mother answered her questions, turning me so the woman could see my face. That's when the lady went nuts. She looked into my eyes and started yelling in some foreign language, trying to take me from my mother's arms, and my mom freaked, backing away, hoping the lady would get the hint and leave us alone. But the woman followed, screaming, telling my mother I was an old soul, that I knew things. She said she could see me, see that I had been here before, several times. She kept repeating 'old soul' over and over until my mother was on the verge of tears and security came to cart the woman away."

I expect Bryce to laugh but he only stares at me, obviously lost in thought.

"Crazy, huh?" I mumble.

"And the other times? You mentioned several," he says.

"The other times weren't nearly as entertaining." I chuckle. "That's my only good story. The rest were strangers claiming they knew me from another life. A few called me an old soul." Childhood scenes flash before me. "I've met a few freaks. You know, people teasing a kid, trying to scare me. Once, when I was at a party, this girl a grade or two higher than me grabbed my hands, following invisible lines up my arms. I'd had a bit too much to drink and couldn't pull away. She kept saying I was an 'ancient one,' and that I knew things. It was disturbing but avoiding her turned out to be easy. She left the party a few minutes later."

"And you think these people were crazy?"

The line between sanity and insanity can be thin, but I know what crazy looks like.

"I think they believed what they were saying, which made them slightly off. Come on, what's that supposed to mean . . . an ancient one?"

"The concept is a lot to swallow," says Bryce, his tone strange.

A recurrent nightmare from my youth comes to mind, the shimmering man, stalking me, always whispering, *it's a lot to swallow.*

"My husband used to say I attract the loonies. They flock to me like I'm some sort of nut magnet." I look away. I hated when Meyer said that. I could say it, sure, but not him, not someone who had no idea what it's like to watch someone you love struggle with mental illness.

Bryce still appears adrift in his thoughts.

Another four kids come to our table, swallowing me in the chaos, and as I help a little girl hold a paintbrush with her tiny fingers, my hair falls into the paint.

Bryce chuckles. "You have almost as much paint in your hair as you do on your hands."

I pull my sleeve back with my teeth, revealing the purple

hair-band beside my watch. "Would you mind?"

Bryce slides the elastic over my hand, avoiding contact with the paint, then moves to stand behind me. I can feel his breath on my neck. He gathers my hair in his hands, gently catching strands with his fingers, easing through dried clumps. His weight shifts forward. My scalp tingles, and his body heat radiates through his shirt, warming my skin. My heart accelerates, and for a moment I feel like I'm floating, like my limbs have lost all substance.

Oh my.

Bryce takes his time, his supple fingers caressing my neck, lingering on the sensitive spot behind my ears. With delicate movements he twists the elastic, dispersing the scent of raspberry shampoo into the air around us. The heat of his breath causes my eyelids to sink, my lips to part, and a gush of air to escape my lungs.

This feels . . . this feels . . .

I slowly open my eyes, and for a split second I'm rushed by guilt.

It's Thomas. He's standing barely twenty feet away. He isn't looking at me but over my shoulder, at Bryce.

And if looks could kill . . .

# BATTER UP

## November 21st

*Accounts of a great people, an entire civilization obliterated by epic catastrophe, have been passed through generations for over 8000 years, in almost every language, in every culture. In comparison, Christianity is approximately 1000-1500 years old, and is practiced by 33% of the world's population.*

*Forgotten History Magazine*: Archeological Finds Baffle Scientists

**T**oday, Saturday November 21st, is officially marked on my calendar. So, after lunch, Abby and I head over to Saint Ann's Cathedral for the Christmas pageant meeting.

Abby is thrilled to be here, doing a church play, and I can't believe I agreed to this. My mother would spit on her own grave to see me in a church. Her mother died giving birth to her, and her father was a minister, or priest, or some sort of religious big shot, a man who apparently took every opportunity to tell his daughter he wished it had been her the Good Lord took. My mother didn't mention her father much, only to say he was a son-of-a-bitch with a fucking foul mouth and a fucking short temper and didn't deserve to meet his granddaughter, ever. I've never thought to look for him. My mother was many things, including a liar, but the only time I ever heard her swear was when she spoke of that man.

We slip into a timeworn pew, Thomas relocating so Abby and Sofia can sit together.

"I thought you might not show," he says, "and I'd have to kill you."

Thomas wants to be here as much as I do, for reasons he wouldn't relinquish, and I admit I twisted his arm. The things we do for our kids.

A stout woman shaped like a pear stands before the group wielding a tea cart weighted with stacks of papers and books. I highly doubt these books contain what I've been looking for. When I couldn't find Atlantis or Lemuria references in my literary arsenal, I spent hours scouring the library. Although Atlantean myths abound, there was very little regarding Lemurian culture. This only has me more intrigued. I'd like to say I'm searching only to satisfy a curiosity, but the honest woman in me knows it has a bit to do with Bryce.

Something about him has me agitated, yet fascinated, and explicit thoughts, definitely unwidow-like, have forced me to consider my feelings for him. Date, he wants to date. Me. Am I ready for that, for dinner out with a man? I suppose it's just dinner, no big deal. Or is it? Am I ever going to be ready to move on from Meyer? And what about Thomas? I'd never considered us anything more than friends, but what do I make of that look at the fair? That was pure jealousy.

Apparently I'm the only one worried though. Thomas has slid back into place, just as before. Not a word of the fair.

The minister raises his arms and claps his hands three times, yanking me back to reality. This is immediately followed by the congregation's claps, three times, as if there is an echo. I bite my tongue, keeping amusement at bay. I've only seen this type of attention-getting ritual done with toddlers and the hall is filled mostly with adults. Of course, this could be normal, I've only been in a church once before. I was sixteen, stoned, and there with a guy who had a foot fetish and pyro problem. When he set fire to the church, I ran. He later claimed he preferred my feet un-charred, but I dumped him anyway. I'd seen him with a match.

Pear-lady pulls small stacks of paper from the cart, handing them to the end person in every pew, belting instructions for the play, the *Three Wise Men*. While she does this, my mind replays my favorite jokes about wise men and I giggle to myself, stopping when I notice pear-lady staring at me, silently chastising. Thomas does a pathetic job of stifling a chuckle and I elbow him in the side. She tells us to flip our booklets to the second page. Listed are the characters and children chosen for each role. Abby is singing three songs in the choir and playing a shepherd.

"How vogue," I whisper to Thomas, "a female shepherd." I chuckle and Thomas follows suit.

I didn't think I'd feel comfortable here, in a church, but I do. The people are welcoming and I didn't go up in flames when I walked in. To be fair, I love the idea of organized religion. I love that an entire community can come together on a common thread and share in each other's special moments, special occasions. Like Christmas. Karen talks fondly of her "family" at Saint Ann's, and I even felt sort of envious when Meyer died and I lacked that kind of support. Maybe this place can be someplace special for Abby.

Thomas draws my attention to the script, which makes up the next twelve pages. I turn to page sixteen and see my name beside several jobs, the final being: *Make sure all costumes and accessories are in the appropriate hands by the final dress rehearsal on Saturday December 12th.*

No problem. My only worry is the church's mammoth forty-year-old sewing machine, aptly named Old Reliable. I doubt she comes with instructions.

Pear-lady approaches with a stack of books slung in her arms, eyeing me suspiciously. She hands me a *Three Wise Men* storybook and a thick folder. The folder is filled with paper scraps that possibly, at one point, resembled costume patterns. She leans over me, her boob nudging the side of my face, and passes Thomas a thick book covered in weathered red leather. Her stare darts between Thomas and me as she explains the set design on pages forty-four through forty-eight and where to find reusable wood from last year's play. Her voice is like nails on a chalkboard, and I'm dying to tell her to blink once in a while. When her dictation dwindles to a close, she looks at Thomas, smiles, and says, "A strong, splendid man like you oughta have no trouble pulling all that heavy stuff from the storage room." She's suddenly all soft and sweet.

"Sure," Thomas mutters.

She reluctantly drags her stare from Thomas's biceps to my face. "And you, do you have any questions?"

A few come to mind. Why are we given instructions for set design? Thomas's name is clearly noted beside that job, not mine. Where is Karen, isn't she the director? How do I work a sewing machine? Why did I volunteer for this? And the more nagging question, are you allowed to flirt with your congregation?

I settle for a quick, "Nope, see you Tuesday."

'Tis the season to be merry.

**The next two** weeks pass by in a blur. At any given hour I'm in one of three places: my studio, the church, or my bed. The only productive spot is the church. Poor BOB.

Every Tuesday, Thursday, and Saturday, Abby and Sofia rehearse with the other kids while Thomas and I work like slaves. Thomas helped me decipher the inner workings of Old Reliable, and he's been helping with the sewing, so I've painted the set. He's been a good sidekick. I have to admit, it's been great spending time with Thomas. He's got this cute way of finishing my sentences and he makes me laugh like Meyer used to.

Only seven days until the big event and we still have lots to do. The sequined belts and head-wraps must be hand sewn and the paper-mache star needs a final layer, along with a coat of glitter glue. Thomas built the nativity set, but we ran out of yellow paint so it requires some creative tweaking, and Old Reliable deserves a good cleaning before being put to rest another year. Still, Thomas insists we call it an early night. He has dinner to prepare.

**Abby and I** make the short drive to Thomas's in silence. We've been here before, for Abby's play dates with Sofia, but we've never been invited to dinner.

"Very casual," Thomas said, "just a dinner date to reward ourselves for a job well done."

Dinner sounds delightful. It's the date part that's making me itch.

I pull into the long winding driveway and press on the brake, pausing to watch dense puffs of snow drift to the ground. The trees surrounding us are draped in shimmering powder, their beauty only slightly tarnished by the claustrophobic feel. Nerves kick-up a fuss in my belly. It might be the date. Or it could be the snow, a reminder of the nightmare I'd had last night.

I was cold, so unbelievably cold. That in itself wasn't unusual, I've had nightmares of dying in the snow before, but this one was different. I was the audience, the casual observer crippled by someone else's pain. I could hear her cry out, sob, beg for the end. I could feel her under my skin. I wanted her dead. I wanted her gone so she didn't have to suffer. So I didn't have to suffer. But when I woke with a thin veil of sweat covering my body, all I wanted was to forget.

I roll down my window, suddenly in need of air. The smell of rotting leaves and wet nips my nose. Winter has arrived. I hope the police find that missing girl soon.

I release the brake, inching forward in small intervals. Thomas's house comes into view. The ranch-style bungalow is nestled in the woods. A plume of smoke rises from the chimney. The sage green door is adorned with a seasonal wreath, the only embellishment on the otherwise simple facade. It oozes family, which doesn't explain why I can't get my foot off the brake. The man inside the house is much the same: comfortable, warm, family oriented, every woman's dream. So why am I itching to turn around? How can this place feel comfortable yet wrong? I've been here several times over the last few months, but this time feels different. Not good different, not bad different, just different. Maybe I'm reading too much into this. Maybe I'm not giving Thomas a chance. I suppose he's is a great catch. Why shouldn't I consider him a great catch for me? Perhaps I'm not ready to move on from Meyer. Maybe I am but not with Thomas.

"Mom, you gonna park or what?"

Abby is working on her adolescent sarcasm. It's coming along just peachy.

**An hour later**, I realize I was worried for nothing. Between mouthfuls, Abby and Sofia chatter about school friends and the church pageant, and Thomas and I talk about the kids, the weather—safe, easy topics.

"You don't look thirty-two," I say, bubbles dripping from the glass in my hand. I insisted on helping with the dishes. It's the least I can do after Thomas cooked such a scrumptious dinner. The man can cook. Hmm, sweet potato and honey ham, plus apple pie for dessert. All my favorite things.

Thomas grabs a cloth to dry. "Older? Do I look older?"

Abby places her plate on the counter then sprints to catch Sofia running down the hall. Thomas has put a movie on for the kids.

"No, younger." I wouldn't peg Thomas for a day over thirty.

"Maybe I am younger. I don't keep track. My family doesn't celebrate birthdays."

I peek at Thomas. He never mentions his family as anything other than him and Sofia. "You mean as adults your family doesn't keep up with birthday celebrations?"

"I mean never," he says. "I don't recall ever doing the birthday thing, even as a child. It's never been important, I guess."

"Did you grow up somewhere birthdays aren't customary?"

Thomas focuses on a glass bowl, gently turning it within the folds of the towel. "Um, no. I lived in several countries, wherever my father's work took us. We were in Europe for most of my childhood, and when I was older, I spent time at a boarding school in the United States."

This is more than Thomas has ever told me about his childhood.

"Europe, huh? Do you speak other languages?"

"Oui, a few." He shrugs.

"I'd love to learn another language. I think I'd choose French." Everything said in French sounds romantic. "Was it hard to have a normal childhood while moving around?"

"I guess moving didn't help," he says, "but normal wasn't really an option."

Thomas looks uncomfortable so I scrounge for a change of topic. Nothing comes to mind. I kinda like this topic. "You must have had interests. You know, hobbies and stuff?"

Thomas grins. "I was great at sports. Not just one or two, but any sport. I was captain of the rugby team for three seasons. I played football and baseball and could swim from our boat to the beach and back, which was pretty good considering the boat wasn't usually visible from shore."

"Your parents must have beamed with pride."

"You'd think, but my brother is the one who walked on water." For some reason this makes him laugh. It's not a nice, lighthearted laugh, but a bitter stroll down a not-so-good memory lane kind of laugh. "My parents are scholars. They don't have much interest in sports."

I grope the sink, empty-handed, and pull the plug. Thomas returns dishes to the dining room credenza, obviously on edge. He's not comfortable talking about himself and I don't want to pry.

It's time for Abby and me to head home.

"The girls didn't even make it to the best part of the movie," says Thomas, walking back into the kitchen. "They've crashed." He raises a wine bottle and two glasses. "Time for a toast. Come, let's take advantage of the quiet."

Oh no.

My mind races, conflicting emotions crashing into one another. Something feels off, like the vast territory ahead is best left untraveled. I'm not sure being alone with Thomas is a good idea, even though Abby and Sofia are technically here. Thomas ignores my dubious demeanor and wanders into the living room, waving me to follow.

Oh hell, one glass of wine shouldn't hurt.

My princess is asleep on the floor, in a pink tent, wrapped in a Dora the Explorer sleeping bag. Beside her, Sofia dozes upright, huddled between a dozen pillows from various pieces of furniture. I'm jealous. It's been a while since I've slept with such peace.

Thomas turns the movie off and toys with the stereo. "Sit," he says when he sees me hovering.

I perch on the end of the couch, a pillow held tight to my stomach. The couch is chocolate-brown chenille, and so soft, so uniquely textured, I run my hand over the surface, almost sated.

An expansive window floods the room with moonlight. The fire pops. Thomas sits a suitable distance from me but not at the other end of the couch. I smile halfheartedly, digging my big toe into the area rug. It's supple, lush, a deep woodsy shade that reminds me of moss. And Meyer's car. I push thoughts of Meyer from my head and concentrate on the distinctive voice emitting from the sound system.

"When I was younger, this was my most played CD," I say. "My mother loved The Cranberries, and it's been years since I've heard this song." I take a deep breath. "Years."

I'm nervous. I'm trying to act casual, to go with the flow. It's not going well. I don't want to say or do something I might regret. Thomas is a good friend and I'd like to keep it that way.

"A good choice then," says Thomas. He pours the wine, balancing the glasses on the leather ottoman, then hands me one. He taps our glasses in cheer and the crystal sings.

"Dinner was awesome, Thomas. You're an amazing cook. Did your parents teach you?"

Thomas chuckles. "Not a chance. My mom and dad aren't much in the kitchen. Louis, our cook, taught me." A memory distracts him. "Louis was constantly chastising me for playing in the pantry or swiping food. As punishment he'd put my sticky fingers to work. By the time I was ten, I'd hang out in the kitchen just to watch him cook. He'd listen to classical music, whipping together culinary masterpieces, rarely uttering a word, and as long as I was learning, and quiet, I was allowed to stay in the kitchen."

"Sounds inspirational. My cooking skills—or lack thereof—contribute greatly to my physique." I laugh. "We eat a lot of fresh fruit and vegetables."

Growing up, my mother didn't use appliances of any kind. If food had to be baked, roasted, or fried, Celeste wasn't buying it. My mother would sell a few of her photos, and we'd eat fresh fruit and veggies till we puked. Then a dry spell would hit and we'd spend months living on chips and soda, or whatever came out of my mother's magic purse. I drank a lot of tap water.

"My father says I learned to cook by osmosis. Good thing too. I ate twice as much as anyone else in the house." Thomas looks away. "And I liked having a place my brother wasn't bound to be."

"You and your brother didn't get along?"

"I guess we did when we were kids. I have very few childhood memories that don't include him. Once we were older, though, things changed."

"Changed how?"

Thomas thinks about this for a minute, gulping his wine. "Have you ever known someone who is good at everything? Not just good but the best: top grades, awards, all the praise, all the girls." His eyes pierce mine. "That's my brother, Mr. Perfect."

"He's a jerk?"

"Yeah, a real piece of work . . ." He snickers. "Well, I don't know, I guess he's a jerk sometimes. My brother is the one who was born to be. I was the surprise, the mistake. My parents adored him." He swigs his wine. "Still do."

I wasn't planned, and my mother never told me in so many words, but I think she loved me from day one, even facing odds.

"Your parents didn't want a second child?" I ask.

Thomas slams his empty glass to the ottoman. "They wanted a girl."

"Seriously? They told you that?"

"They didn't need to say it. It's complicated." His mouth says *complicated* but his face says *not to be discussed further.*

I don't push.

"Where does your family live now? You never mention them."

"My parents retired in the south of France. We don't speak much."

"And your brother, does he live in France as well?"

Thomas leans forward, nodding, spinning the empty glass between his hands. "Like I said, we don't talk much," he says. He pours himself another wine.

I sip from my glass, wondering why Thomas doesn't communicate with his family. My half-brother, Stephen, lives in Paris, and although we weren't raised together, we email each other weekly. Stephen was conceived on one of my mother's bipolar highs when I was six. She'd yanked me out of school to catch a flight to Spain, determined to see the running of the bulls. We never made it to Pamplona. Our overnight stay in Barcelona was extended when she met Gregory Tindell, a corporate lawyer for some investment firm, in Barcelona on business. The whirlwind affair lasted four days and ended when he returned to Paris, to his wife and kids. I got a black eye from the hotel's on-staff babysitter, and Mom got knocked-up. Fun had by all.

"My family didn't approve of my choices," says Thomas.

"Choices . . . they didn't like your wife?"

"They didn't want me to marry her. They said I wasn't ready, the timing was wrong, she wasn't the woman they'd choose for me, etc, etc. They refused to acknowledge what I wanted, how I felt. And they were against us having children." He looks tortured, staring into his wine glass. "All I wanted was a family."

Now that's an emotion I can relate to. Stephen moved to Paris six weeks before my seventh birthday. By then my mother had renounced medicine, allowing her illness to bloom, and as hard as I tried, I couldn't raise a baby on my own. Stephen got a new start with Gregory Tindell and his family. I was never the same.

Thomas plops his glass on the ottoman then falls back into the couch, hands tucked behind his head, long legs stretched out. He stares at the ceiling, eyes glossed over. "I wanted a son," he says. "I wanted Sofia to have a brother and maybe a sister. I wanted a wife that loved me and only me. I wanted to be happy."

He wanted it all. Just like I did—like all of us do. We want the pretty picture, the perfect life, the happy days, the endless nights, the kids, the good health, and the money to enjoy it all. Nobody wants an ex-wife. Nowhere in this pretty picture does the husband die.

Shit. Now I need more wine. I fill both glasses to the brim.

Thomas releases a gust of air, pulling his hands from under his head. In one fluid motion, he grabs the glass and swallows the entire contents. He stretches, this time turning onto his side, eyes fixed on mine. We're close. Too close.

"I want a family, a whole family. I want a wife that loves me as much as I love her. I want . . ."

No, no, no, please don't say it.

The space between us is paper-thin, and I can smell wine mingled with sweet ham on his breath. Thomas reaches out and tucks strands that have fallen over my face behind my ear, and I freeze. Part of me wants this: to be touched, to be wanted. His fingers are gentle, lightly caressing my ear, my cheek, my chin. I'm caught between desire and dread. I hold the pillow tighter to my chest, fingers anxiously moving through the chenille trim. I can hear my heart pounding.

"Your eyes are the most beautiful I've ever seen."

Blood races to my head, making me dizzy. "Thomas, I—"

"We want the same thing, Tess. I know you want a family, siblings for Abby. I've seen it on your face, a longing I recognize."

Thomas stares at my hand, where my wedding ring sits heavy, suddenly hot.

"This isn't right, Thomas, I don't think—"

"We could be great together, you and I, we could—"

"Abby and I should head home." I jump from the couch, clutching the pillow to my chest. "I'm tired and Abby should be sleeping in her bed."

Thomas rises, stepping close. He opens and closes his mouth like a fish gasping for air then sighs.

"I'll carry Abby to the car," he finally says, tenderly loosening my grip on the pillow tassel and turning me toward the door.

I'm stone cold sober as I walk to the car in a daze, wondering what the hell just happened. When I look up, the sight of Thomas cradling my baby girl steals my breath, the emotion too strong to explore, and I have to look away.

Thomas is everything Abby needs and exactly what I want.

Yet only one thing is for certain: sleep won't be coming any easier tonight.

# JUST MAYBE

## December 12th

Last night I was burned alive on a pyre of sticks and tar. Fitting, I suppose, considering the nature of my thoughts regarding Bryce and my date with Thomas. I'm supposed to be a grieving widow.

I was paraded around town, naked, men, women, and children sneering. The bishop's sermon, spoken with utter disdain, reeked of blasphemous retribution, and through a small opening in the swollen and bloody folds of one eye, I could see him flail about. The town folk clung to his every word while hurling potatoes and stones at my body locked in the pillory. The stench of urine wafted from below. Cuts and bruises were nothing compared to the overwhelming ache of emptiness, of starvation.

Three men and a boy no more than ten dragged me to the pyre. A woman stepped close and spit. I raised my chin. The sheriff lit the fire and I didn't even flinch. But when the mass of tar and sticks erupted into a black inferno, cooking me from the outside in, I screamed bloody murder.

It wasn't the kind of nightmare you shake. It was the kind that has you sitting at your computer at two a.m., desperate to find something, anything, to erase the horrific images from your mind. It was the reason I spent three hours scouring websites about Atlantis's demise. Even then, the hissing of burning skin kept haunting me, forcing me to reiterate my findings out loud as a distraction from the torturous cries that erupted from my imaginary charred body.

"It is estimated that Earth has been brought to the brink of extinction at least five times in the past five-hundred million years. One of these close calls was Comet Encke, a killer comet that passed by Earth unleashing a bombardment of meteoric material that set off a cosmic chain of events that culminated in major global catastrophe."

It was a burn beyond anything comprehensible, heat devouring the tar smeared on my feet, arms, and legs.

"Every living creature scrambled to avoid sudden death at the hand of massive volcanic explosions, a firestorm of collapsing sky, and tsunamis that swallowed entire continents whole. Those who survived the onslaught were caught between Earth's fractures, stranded by the sudden and dramatic shift in tectonic plates."

Begging for the pain to end, willing my body to surrender, to die.

"What was left of obliterated Atlantis dropped beneath the sea in a day and a night."

And I thought I had a morning from hell.

The day gets better over brunch, thank goodness. Though I'm exhausted, my plan to chat with Abby about the impending holidays and how she feels about celebrating fatherless goes better than predicted, proving Grams right, yet again. Grams thinks Meyer's death was awful but well timed for Abby. She's old enough to have made some great memories of her father, yet young enough to rebound from devastation quickly.

I wish I could say the same for myself. Between my frazzled

nerves and analyzing Abby's reactions to my questions, I don't get much food down. Still, I'm pleased with the choice of locale. The bistro is at full capacity, not an empty chair in sight, and the surrounding bustle keeps me strangely focused. While I talk, Abby fills her belly with child-sized portions of pancakes, fruit, bacon, eggs, toast, and a bottomless glass of orange juice. She allows me to poke and probe, showing a maturity beyond her years. She doesn't shed a single tear. Her bravery, along with an audience and my will to stay strong for my daughter, keep my tears at bay as well.

Abby and I shake on our deal to make our first Christmas without Meyer a happy holiday. It's not going to be easy. But I have a plan.

On the way through the bistro door, we pass the kitchen and the incessant sizzling of the chef's frying pan combined with the restless chatter of people standing in line brings visions of last night's nightmare back to the forefront of my consciousness.

Flames snapping from my tar-tattered hands, the putrid smell of burning flesh. The horde, hatred and fear in their eyes.

I forcefully ignore the nightmare in my head and commit to focusing on the day with my daughter. We're getting our Christmas tree today, a tradition I think is important to keep, but is bound to carry memories of Meyer. I need to stay focused. I need to give Abby my full attention. And tonight is the final pageant rehearsal, so I have to make this day special, uphold the pact with my angel.

Death and Christmas cannot coincide.

**We ease into** the parking lot of the tree farm then grab a shopping basket at the entrance. Abby, familiar with this shop, makes a run for the large wicker baskets surrounding the bases of heavily decorated Christmas trees. The overwhelming quantity of twinkling lights gleaming off reflective surfaces is breathtaking, almost dizzying, and I realize I am looking forward to the holiday despite knowing this season will be difficult with Meyer gone. I love Christmas. I love the wreaths, the trees, the lights, and the endless streams of decorations. I love how Santa brings a smile to every kid's face. I love fresh-baked shortbread cookies, oven roasted turkey, and large glasses of eggnog. I love how families gather from across the globe, putting aside busy careers and differences to be together, and that our world becomes a happier place. People smile brighter, greet with more cheer, and give. It reminds me that there is more to this life than the tiny world I've built.

I follow Abby from tree to tree, absorbing the grand sparkle. My foot taps to the festive music coming from the store's sound system, and I catch myself singing out loud. What a great holiday, one that allows you to sing something as ridiculously jubilant as "Rudolph the Red-Nosed Reindeer" in public and not look like a total wacko.

Abby squeals from the other side of the Disney themed tree.

"What've you found?" I say, picking through Mickey Mouse ornaments.

"She found us."

I look up and it's Thomas, his forearms smothering the handle of a shopping cart. He smiles big.

"What are you doing here?" I'm equally pleased to see him, a reaction I find surprising after my tense exit from our dinner date last week.

"Sofia has never had a Christmas tree. I've never celebrated Christmas. We thought this would be a good year to start a new tradition."

"Tree virgins." I laugh and Thomas chuckles. "How is it

coming along?" I look down. "Your cart is empty."

"We haven't been here long, but I have to admit I have no clue where to start. I don't even know what we need exactly. I was about to ask for the store manager when Sofia spied Abby."

The girls are on the other side of the tree, giggling.

"Well, I'm no expert, but I'm confident I can help with the basics. First things first, you need a base to hold the tree." I call attention to the Christmas tree beside us, demonstrating its upright pose.

Thomas smirks. "I don't just lean it into a corner?"

"Call for the manager," I say, pretending to walk away.

Thomas grabs me. "Kidding. Help. Please."

How can I refuse that face? "I saw tree bases over there," I say, pointing to the entrance. "Pick one that holds water, then meet us at the Harry Potter display. Today is your lucky day. I'm giving free lessons in tree decorating 101."

Thomas snaps to attention before following instructions, and I round the tree, curious to know what warrants such giggles. I'm relieved Abby has Sofia to distract her from the memories this place evokes. We've come here every year since Abby was born.

Me, I choose to ignore the knot in my gut and concentrate on my pet project.

My guided tour has the four of us ambling through the store, fiddling with every shiny object that catches our attention. The possibilities are endless and narrowing down select ornaments proves to be a daunting task. At one point Abby stops dead, enthralled with miniature white lights that flicker to the beat of "Jingle Bells." As the music accelerates, so do the flashing lights.

"I gotta get me some of those!" bellows Thomas, knocking an entire shelf of boxed lights into his cart. We all laugh and Thomas declares the spree a success, requesting my assistance with a verbal checklist.

"Tree base," I say, an invisible check sheet and pen in hand.

"Yep," says Thomas.

"Lights."

"Oh yeah," he laughs. He's got enough lights to blow the area's power grid.

"Tree topper?"

Thomas holds up a funky metal star. "Check."

"Garland?"

"Ah, these things?" He's got several strings of bright-red beads. I think they're painted cork. I give Thomas a high-five. My protégé's done me proud. Reaching into his cart, I examine ornaments, making sure there is a good assortment. Thomas eyes me digging. "What are you looking for?" he says.

"Did you choose ones with meaning or are they just random?"

"I picked ones I like," he says, eyebrows high, challenging me.

"You are supposed to choose ones that speak to you."

"You do things your way, and I do things my way. Besides, I picked some that speak to me." He shoves an arm into the loaded cart, seemingly in search of something specific. "See," he says, handing me a box. "It reminds me of you." It's a ceramic Minnie Mouse. She's wearing a painting smock, a paintbrush dripping red paint in one hand. Little red dots cover the Christmas tree on her canvas. It's adorable and I'm speechless. Thomas thrusts another box at me. "And this one speaks to me."

I turn the box as it repeats, "This one speaks to me, this one speaks to me, this one speaks to me . . ." over and over in Thomas's voice, only monotone.

Thomas covers his mouth to contain a gut-wrenching laugh. "See, I can be taught," he says.

The box repeats, "I can be taught, I can be taught, I can be taught . . ." and the two of us double over laughing.

A curious stranger stops to ogle us. "What's the fuss?" he says, and the ornament belts a repeat of his inquiry, but in monotone it sounds like "What the fuck?" so Thomas and I crack-up even more, until we're swiping tears.

Laughter, what a drug.

I tighten Abby's coat belt and steer my students toward the back door.

"Come, tree virgins. Nothing says Christmas like the smell of fresh pine."

Thick ringlets fly every which way while Sofia attempts to persuade Thomas to give our tree-cutting tradition a try. It's not an easy sell.

Thomas groans, holding tight to the door handle. "A real tree? I was thinking a plastic one would work, maybe one with fake snow on the branches."

I roll my eyes.

"Seriously, Mr. Outdoors? No way, I can't let you do it." I pry Thomas's fingers from the door.

Every year Meyer stood in this exact spot, cataloging the downsides to cutting our own tree, listing the virtues of a fake. It's a good memory, one that makes me smile. Of course, Meyer never won the tree debate. And Thomas doesn't stand a chance either.

"A cut tree smells great, looks natural, and is biodegradable. Don't contribute to landfill problems." You gotta love the power of environmental guilt. "Grab a saw!" I slip on a customary Santa hat and toss Thomas the mouthy ornament.

The ornament says, "Grab a saw, grab a saw, grab a saw . . ."

Thomas searches for the off switch, laughing. Then he slides

---

on a Santa hat and follows me outside, grabbing a saw from the bin.

My, my, he can be taught.

**By evening I'm** pooped. Both Thomas and I receive calls to say the girls aren't required at tonight's rehearsal, but I still spend an hour dispensing costumes at the church while Mrs. Maples supervises Abby and Sofia's sleepover at my place, giving Thomas a kid-free night to himself. It's the least I could do, since the guy has not only been there for me, but he delivered and set up our ten-foot Douglas fir, getting sap and pine needles all over his truck.

I'm about head home, to grab my coat and purse from their usual hidey-hole behind the stage curtain, when I run into Karen scanning the auditorium.

"Looks good, doesn't it?" she says.

"The set looks awesome, the props are in place, and the star decorations Lou Ann hung from the rafters look really cool. I see the old piano is being tuned, so that should pretty well cover it. You've done a great job, Karen. If only everything ran so smoothly." I chuckle. "Wanna use your magic to finish my holiday shopping?"

Karen snorts. "Only the crazy enter a mall this close to Christmas. And you hate shopping."

"I'm desperate. I don't know what to get for Stephen. And if I don't courier his gift by tomorrow, it won't arrive in time for Christmas. Got any ideas?"

"You're on your own. It takes everything in my power to find a gift my husband won't forget by New Year's Eve." A memory makes her scowl.

"I'll find something, I hope."

"Take Thomas shopping. He'll help you find something good for your brother, something manly and masculine." Mischief pulls tiny wrinkles at the sides of her mouth.

For some reason Bryce comes to mind. When Mrs. Maples arrived to babysit tonight, eyebrows drawn on lopsided, she told me to call Bryce Waters. No reason, no explanation, I was just to call him. Tonight, I was to call him tonight. I studied her, confused. I wasn't even aware she knew Bryce. And what would I call him for? Like many of my chats with Mrs. Maples, it was an odd conversation without segue. And as usual, she waved away my questions, smiling, swatting me out the door with her cane.

I shake my head clear. "See you tomorrow, Karen." I grab my stuff and leave.

What is it with friends and their need to hook me up with men?

The car is cold, slow, and by the time I stand on his doorstep about to knock, my confidence has waned. What the hell am I doing? This is a bad idea. I can't drag some guy from his house to go to the mall with me. I should just go by myself. Pulling my coat tight, I turn around and walk back to my car.

"Tess? Is everything okay? What's wrong?"

I turn around to see Thomas standing in his doorway, obviously concerned. He's naked, but for shorts and a tiny towel slung around his neck. I quickly divert my stare. Now I know what all the fuss was about. The man looks quite nice all sweaty and ripped.

"Nothing has happened, Thomas, don't worry. Sofia is fine. I phoned Mrs. Maples and the kids are sound asleep."

When I asked Mrs. Maples if she minded staying another hour or two, she said she'd raised a brood the size of a wolf pack and two itty-bitty girls wouldn't pose a break in her stride.

"You okay?" Thomas says, his voice coming closer.

"You must be freezing, go back inside. I'm sorry I bothered you."

"No bother, what's up?"

"I'm thinking about heading to the mall," I say to my car.

"Okay," he says, drawing the word out slowly.

"I need a Christmas gift for my brother and could use a guy's opinion."

Thomas chuckles. "I'm a guy."

I think of him holding Abby in his arms. "Um hmm." Somewhere in my subconscious a proper invitation prances, just slightly out of reach.

"Give me twenty minutes to—"

"I don't want to interrupt. Tonight is your free night."

"Right," he says, "my night, my choice, and I'd like to be with you. I was working out, but I'm done. It'll only take a few minutes to shower and get dressed."

I'm wondering if this is such a good idea when Thomas grunts. I hear him head back to the house and when I spin to see if he's ditched me, he throws me a set of keys from the doorway.

"Either come inside or wait in my truck," he says then chuckles. "I won't fit in that miniature shit-box of yours."

I pretend to be shocked. "Don't dis the Magic Carpet," I yell, making my way to Thomas's truck. "Ignore him," I mumble to my car in passing. Magic Carpet is the beat-up Volkswagen Bug I inherited from my mother. She's sunflower yellow and qualified for the seniors discount at Jiffy Lube fourteen years ago when my mother and I drove her to the Grand Canyon. I love her, but she is a shit-box.

Unlocking the doors to Thomas's truck, I shimmy into the passenger seat and make myself comfortable. It's a nice truck, new and fully loaded from the looks of it. The smell of pine is overwhelming. I shake my coat off. Fatigue hits me, the dark insisting it's bedtime, but I can't get the damn seat to recline so I toss my jacket over the console and climb onto the back bench, spreading out. I've got twenty minutes to catch a quick catnap.

*Tap, tap, tap* . . .

I hear a faint tapping but my body doesn't respond as I float in a blissful state of sleep.

*Tap, tap, tap* . . .

I move in slow motion, the dim dashboard light confusing my retinas. My skin is toasty warm, muscles placid. I tilt my head, a slight shift toward the tapping sound.

*Tap, tap, tap* . . .

A dark shadow appears in the window and for an instant fear raises the hair on my scalp.

"Thomas!" I reach to unlock the door.

Thomas climbs in the back, all teeth, rumbling laugh vibrating his throat. "You sleep like the dead," he says, grabbing the headrest to turn around. "It's all right, don't get up." He lifts my feet and sits, placing my feet in his lap.

I plop into my original spot and attempt to pull my feet in, but Thomas holds tight. He smells like soap and cologne. It dawns on me how intimate this is. We're in tight quarters, alone. Being surrounded by tall, thick trees doesn't help either. I steal a glance at Thomas; the words *now what* hang in the air like the smoke from a sparkler.

"Well, this is weird," I whisper.

"Are you still tired? You were out of it when I knocked on the window."

"I'm awake now." And my heart's pumping at full throttle, like the Titanic plowing through mountains of ice.

Thomas looks at me, gathering the sleeves of his snug sweater. "You're still half asleep."

I close my eyes. "No. I'm here." But I shouldn't be. We should go.

"Can I kiss you?"

I look at Thomas. He's puffed up, holding his breath. My head feels thick and I can't think clearly. Do I want him to kiss me? Will there be sparks?

"I . . . guess."

Thomas looks as stunned as I feel. He expels a full chest of air with a long whoosh and then goes rigid, his eyes piercing mine. I wait, thinking he's changed his mind.

"Maybe we should go," I murmur, questioning my use of the word maybe.

The man decides quickly. His arm slides over my chest and he threads his fingers through my hair, cradling my head. Our body's touch, blood heating my face and neck. I wet my lips, mimicking him. His lips touch mine, warm, and we both freeze.

It isn't happening.

"Let's try this again," mumbles Thomas.

He kisses me, slow, careful, lips cautious. My eyes close and I'm able to melt into the kiss.

The pace quickens, his grasp tightening in my hair. I match his vigor, my fingers plunging into his thick curls. Thomas groans a deep growl trapped in his throat. The sound releases heat that spreads throughout my limbs, burning extremities. His torso presses into me, pinning my arm under its weight. The sound of wet lips and heavy breathing fills the air and my head swims in heat.

Is this wrong?

His lips rush over my jaw and down my throat. His fingers slide under my shirt and I shiver. My back arches in response to his touch. The echoes of hungry moans ricochet off the windows. My previously pinned hand shimmies beneath his sweater, groping strong muscles in his side. Man, he feels good. But what the hell am I doing? His muscles contract as he pulls me closer, tighter, our clothes inconvenient. His thigh slips between my legs, and heat surges into aching parts, wanting parts, parts barren too long. Soft fingertips slip under my bra, and I gasp. Thomas moans. This feels good. Really good.

Holy shit, this feels like Meyer.

Thomas stops, his entire body falling motionless. His mouth hovers on my neck, over the spot where my beating heart confesses to his swollen lips. Nothing but the sound of labored breathing pierces the silence.

"You don't bite, do you?"

"I might." His lips form a smile on my neck. "We should save this for somewhere other than the back of my truck."

Panic provokes the butterflies in my stomach. Save this? As in do it again? I can't do this again. I shouldn't have let this happen this time. What is wrong with me?

Thomas places soft kisses on my ear. "Do you want to go inside?"

A part of me screams *yes*. Not the most rational part, but the part supposed to be dating BOB. I ignore it. I stare at the window. Moisture plummets in suicidal streaks. How appropriate.

Thomas wants love. He wants a wife. And I'm not volunteering.

Thomas feels my resolve without me having to say a word, which I'm grateful for, since I'm currently not capable of articulating a thing. He carefully untangles his hand from my hair and gathers my arm from under his sweater. We maneuver into sitting, sets of arms and legs finding ways to fit.

"To the mall," he says, gripping my hand.

It's a simple statement. With so much meaning.

# SHOW TIME

**I** navigate the church parking lot, slowly, begging Abby to keep the door closed until I park. Her tiny fingers are jammed into the door handle, and I've got her dress held in a vice-grip while I beep and buzz, pretending to be a car alarm, a computerized voice suggesting she *keep all limbs inside until the vehicle has come to a complete stop.*

What I really need is a battery-operated advisor who counsels regarding life. One that says, *do not kiss men who should remain friends.* Or, *stay away from men who have you questioning your sanity.*

For a while, after fooling around with Thomas, I felt like a teenager, like a touch could set me on fire. But these feelings of lust came with other not-so-nice feelings. Like guilt. And by the time we arrived at the mall, the spark, if I hadn't imagined it, was gone. Thomas fell back into our routine of comfy friendship, walls thin, but up, we didn't hold hands, didn't kiss. Intimacy didn't change our relationship into something more. Why not? It should have, shouldn't it?

And then there is Bryce. I haven't even figured out why he enters into the equation, but he does. Reality is, I barely know the man. Yet there is something about him I can't shake. Do I let these lingering feelings lead to something? Or do I stay away and pretend they don't exist?

Being with Meyer taught me a lot about myself, my wants and needs, but I am no longer the reckless teen I once was, and I'm no longer alone. I have Abby to think about.

As I ponder this, a more rational thought enters my mind. I really miss Grams. Florida is too far.

"All right, kiddo, now you can open the door."

We leave our coats in the car and shuffle between parked cars. I escort Abby through the stage door and tuck my purse into its usual spot behind the velvet curtain while Sofia dances toward us in her camel costume.

"Okay, my little birds," I say, drawing Abby and Sofia in for a mommy-sandwich hug. "You two go out there, be the best shepherd and camel you can be, smile, and have fun." My attempt to plant a kiss on Abby's head is thwarted as she runs off with Sofia, giggling.

Time to find my seat for the show.

Standing on the bottom stair, I attempt a head count. Bodies bop every which way, the air thick with perfume and cologne. It looks as though our entire town's population has packed into the main hall of the church. This is an enlightening phenomenon, seeing Carlisle is dusted with a potpourri of faiths. I lose count when I see Thomas and Bryce making their way toward me from opposite directions.

"Great turn out, huh?" says Karen, embracing me with a hug. She's come out of nowhere.

"Full house."

I look over Karen's shoulder. Thomas has stopped dead in his tracks.

"Good evening, ladies."

Bryce's voice slides up my spine like silk. I turn around.

Ah, those eyes. It's been weeks since I've seen him, the flesh and blood him that is, and my daydreams don't do him justice. He's traversed somewhere tropical, bronzing his skin, making him even more beautiful than I remember.

"Glad you made it," says Karen, pulling his gaze from mine.

Bryce plants a kiss on Karen's cheek, first the right and then the left. "Wouldn't miss it for the world," he says.

Karen hugs Bryce, lingering in his arms, and I'm shocked by my instinctual urge to pull them apart.

"How was your trip?" My mouth delivers the words but my head wants to know where my hello kisses are?

Bryce sways toward me, stopping mid step.

"Productive," he says, thrusting his hands into his pockets. He looks great in a suit and tie, debonair. "I was at a conference in Athens, presenting bone flutes from a site in Jiahu, China."

Karen taps her watch. "Almost show time." She blows kisses and disappears into the crowd.

"Bone flutes, huh, made of animal bone?"

"Some animal, some human. Most musical instruments of the time were crafted from degradable materials like leather or wood," he says, "but flutes made of bone have survived years of elemental abuse, and these examples, while dated slightly later than 8000 BC, were still playable."

"Fascinating," I say, truly intrigued. "I've been reading about Atlantis. I can see why you're—"

"Drivel," says Thomas, surprising me from behind. "Atlantis is nothing but myth, a legend touted by decaying minds."

"Thomas, this is Bryce. Bryce, this is Thomas."

Neither man moves to shake or exchange greetings. No one even cracks a smile.

"Troy was myth until 1871, when a German archaeologist discovered it under layers of mountain in Turkey, proving the legendary Trojan War to be historical fact," says Bryce.

"Fact is subjective," says Thomas.

"Results are subjective. Fact is theory proven. The Ice Age theory was born when geology was in its infancy and technology primitive. Today, facts show the obvious flaws in the theory, disproving it."

"Sure . . . and we didn't evolve from apes," Thomas says, sardonic.

"Evolution. Also a theory."

The two of them argue without emotion, the effect disturbing, yet I sense I've been here before, like the three of us have had this same discussion.

"Freaky," I mumble.

"I agree," says Thomas, glaring at Bryce.

"I mean the déjà vu. I just felt like I'd heard this before."

"Déjà vu is your soul recalling a snippet from a past incarnation," says Bryce. "It's your—"

"It's time we had a seat," says Thomas, attempting to take my hand.

I pull away and step back to view the two of them standing a few feet apart, glowering at each other.

Bryce sighs, turning to me. "I saved you a seat if you wish to join me."

"Tess is sitting with me."

Bryce stares past me at Thomas. "Tess can sit wherever—"

"She sits with me."

"Enough!" I regard them both. "What is it with you two?" Thomas's possessiveness has me pissed, and Bryce . . . I point to the right of the stage. "I'll be sitting over there. Alone. I'm responsible for the light switches during the performance. Lucky me."

I inhale deeply, about to give Thomas a piece of my mind,

but he stomps off, swiftly vanishing into the throng.

"I guess I'll see you later," says Bryce, shifting uncomfortably. He endeavors to pull together a smile but falls short.

I wave and walk away, already devising a plan to avoid them both after the show.

The music starts and my brooding fades as I rush to my seat and focus on the curtains that have opened to reveal three boys walking through a desert setting. The boy in the blue velvet robe I painstakingly sewed steps forward to speak his lines. "I am Melchior, and I am wealthy. My entire life I've watched the stars and I know them all by sight. Tonight, there is a new star that dazzles my eyes as it outshines, by far, all the others in the sky."

The second boy jumps forward to stand next to Melchior. He says, "My name is Caspar, and I believe I know the story this star tells. Soon there will be a birth; the birth of a prince, a king, our ruler!"

The third child raises his hands, displaying a large perfume bottle. Stepping to stand beside the other two, he belts, "I, Balthazar, will bring myrrh to the new babe. We shall follow the star that will lead us to our savior." His exuberance prompts a rumble of laughter from the audience.

Another boy steps out from behind the curtain dressed in the outfit that took me over four hours to make. It has gold buttons and gold-sequin trim, giving him the royal air due to his character. He searches for his spot on the floor marked with masking tape and a red dot and when he locates it he pounces like a lion, coming to stand tall and proud. Again the crowd erupts. "I am Herod, the king," he says, pointing a finger. "You three men, you shall go forth and find this babe!"

The boys flee the stage, ducking their heads to run under a raised section of curtain. Herod is the only one left on stage and this is my cue. I flick all three sets of switches, bringing the house into complete darkness. One spotlight highlights Herod, casting a villainous shadow as he announces, "There shall be no other ruler but me. I will find this babe, and he will cease to be." He laughs a menacing laugh, the kind you hear in horror movies, but it sounds so strange coming from a child with a high-pitched voice that the crowd laughs again.

The curtain closes and people take the opportunity to chat. Comments are hurled across aisles to friends and family, mingling with the noise of skidding shoes, and the squeal of the piano as its pushed center stage.

When the curtains open I immediately search for Abby. She's at the far end of the front row, holding tight to Sofia. Her patent leather Mary Janes tap in anxious spurts. I'm so proud I could scream, and it takes a conscious effort to keep my ass in the chair. I reach to adjust the lighting, and Mrs. Johnson pounds the piano keys, cueing the kids. The kids sing off key and slow but they try really hard. I fumble for my cell. Abby looks adorable in her holiday dress, and my view through the lens is so distorted I have to swipe tears to take the picture.

What I would give to have Meyer here right now . . .

The choir sings their last song, the curtain closes, and the noise resumes. I sense someone staring. I pivot and locate Thomas two rows in, sporting the forced grin of the guilty.

"Sorry," he mouths.

I keep my response to myself, determined to keep my attention on the show, which has resumed, to Abby as a shepherd standing center stage with the three wise men.

Melchior says, "The route is clear, the light is strong, I hardly think we can go wrong." He points to the paper-mache star hanging above the stable by a skinny wire. It glows from within, utterly magical, and I steal a glance at the audience, delighted to witness their rapture in my handmade miracle. I should ask Karen if I can keep the star. I hate the thought of it collecting dust in the church storage room, and it would make a cool light fixture in Abby's room.

The three boys pass the camel reins (one attached to Sofia) to Abby. She says her first line, "Inside the stable a wonderful . . . oops, I mean wondrous . . . a wondrous sight that filled their hearts with great delight. A baby lay in a wooden manger yet smiled upon these three rich strangers." Abby beams, sticking the end of her tongue out from between her teeth, and I clap with extraordinary enthusiasm, trying to keep my hovering rear in the seat.

A distant part of my brain registers laughter so I scan the audience for the source only to find all eyes on me. Heat flushes my face and I drop to my chair.

The wise men present their gifts to baby Jesus. Mary lifts the baby from the manger, pulling a cord, and he cries over the audience's collective *ah*. The camels spit, the donkey heehaws, and my daughter speaks her last line with perfect clarity. An angel appears on the roof of the manger, having climbed a ladder unseen, and when the last word is spoken the audience rises, hooting and hollering their endorsement.

The show was a resounding success.

A moment later my baby girl is tightly wound around my legs.

"You were wonderful!" I say, swinging her around.

"Did you see me, Mom? Did you see me?"

"Are you kidding? I watched your every move. Totally cool." I plant a mushy kiss on her cheek then chuckle as she wipes my saliva off her face, annoyed. "I'm so proud of you!"

"The lights were bright. I couldn't see you, Mama."

"I was here the whole time." I show her the yellow chair that had difficulty containing me for the performance.

Bryce walks over and tickles Abby. "Good job, young lady," he says as Abby squeals, almost falling from my arms. He looks at me. "What a wonderful show. I heard you made the beautiful costumes."

"Yes, a comical sight. You should've seen me work the old sewing machine."

"Lots of laughs," says Thomas, having snuck up beside me. "We were a great team."

I take a deep breath. I'm pleased the two of them are behaving, but I'm too tired to maintain a pretense. "Fun had by all. Now if you'll both excuse me, I should congratulate Karen before I go."

"You're not going to the bistro?" Thomas says.

The families involved in the pageant made plans to celebrate at the bistro after the show. I hadn't decided if Abby and I were going. "I think we'll pass, Thomas." I peek at my tiny shepherd, noting her slight wobble. "I'm beat and Abby's had a busy weekend."

Thomas shifts his weight from one foot to the other, at a loss for words.

"Well, goodnight guys." I take Abby's hand. "Hope you have a wonderful Christmas."

I shuffle past the chairs now scattered about the room in an unruly manner.

How appropriate.

**Twenty minutes later**, I'm still looking for Karen. There is a caravan of cars waiting to escape the parking lot, and Abby and I shiver on the church steps scanning the crowd for a mass of red hair. Friends pass and I enquire about Karen's whereabouts, but nobody has seen her.

"Perhaps she's already left," I say to Abby. "We should head home and thank Karen later, baby girl."

Abby can barely summon the energy to agree.

We maneuver through the obstacle course of vehicles until we find our Magic Carpet. The doors are unlocked as always. I'm helping Abby with her car seat buckles when I hear a distinctive voice.

"Was that great or what?" Karen says.

We hug. "Flawless," I say. "You must be stoked."

Karen eyes Abby almost asleep in the back seat. "You're not going home, are you? No! Come to the bistro with us."

I assume Karen's church buddy, Marjorie, is the other half of us since Karen's husband is AWOL.

"I'm too tired to be good company, Karen. Besides," I point my chin toward Abby, huddled for warmth, "Abby is officially out."

"That sucks." She embraces me, pouting. "We'll talk soon," she says, and smacks me on the ass in parting.

I spread Abby's OshKosh blanket across her lap then grope my pockets for keys. Shit, I've left my purse in the church. I catch Karen chatting two cars over, her hair glowing under a parking lamp. She agrees to watch Abby while I run back for my purse, rolling her eyes dramatically when I remind her—more than once—not to leave Abby alone.

Two feet from the stage door I wonder why I hadn't grabbed my coat. I'm freezing.

The lights are out and the stage is deserted. I'm fumbling through the shadows, feeling for my purse, when a deep voice rings through the darkness, halting me. Thomas? Is that Thomas? It can't be.

Now there's a second voice, deeper still. I root to the floor, not wanting to disturb what is obviously a private conversation. The sound of shoes scuffing hardwood only a few feet away has instinct dropping me into a crouch. Pine floor cleaner burns my nose. I rummage through thick velvet. Where is my purse?

The voices move closer, becoming clear.

"We shouldn't have this conversation here. Come to my place. We'll talk."

Shit. That's Bryce.

"There isn't anything to say. Just go away," says Thomas.

My eyes pierce the blackness, confused. I've never heard Thomas so angry. What the hell are they fighting about? They barely know each other.

"Thomas—"

"Go away. Leave. Go back to France or London or wherever you were last."

I cover my ears, not wanting to hear this Thomas.

"You haven't told her anything," says Bryce, his voice lucid.

"Christ, she just lost her husband."

Husband? My hands drop to my knees.

"You're supposed to teach her, help her. You're a—"

"The one that wasn't meant to be." Sarcasm drips from Thomas's every word.

"That's not true. How can you say that?" They pace the floor, moving farther away. I can barely hear. "You have to help her before someone finds her, before it's too late."

"She should be left alone."

"Thomas—"

"I'll protect her."

Bryce sighs. "She needs to learn how to protect herself."

"You're the one throwing parties and introducing her to your freak show."

"I didn't know at the time. I had a hunch, but I wasn't sure.

And I would never put her in danger."

"No?"

"If you were so worried about her, why didn't you come?"

"I want a normal life," says Thomas, pausing. "That would exclude you and your friends. Go away. Leave her with me."

"She doesn't love you."

"Think she loves you?" Thomas sounds venomous.

"We've been together before. She's the one. I can feel it."

"Bullshit! You've never believed in that love at first—"

"It's not like that," says Bryce.

"She's mine."

Excuse me? Who does Thomas think he is? My mind spins in confusion.

Bryce sucks in a mouthful of air, whistling. "Thomas, you know you can't control an old soul, you can only guide and—"

"You arrogant fuck. Don't you dare throw her in my face. I wanted a son."

Her? Her who? Is Thomas talking about his ex-wife?

"I know, we all do, but it doesn't work that way and you know—"

"But only one of us can, and it's going to be me. I want it more than you. I don't know what happened but I'm telling you she loved me."

Bryce sighs. "I'm sure she did. Still, you shouldn't have pursued her. And you should've told her the truth before you got her pregnant."

"If it wasn't for him, she would've come around."

"She had her ovaries butchered, Thomas. Not everyone can handle being taught in this century, and you were aware of the ramifications. Even when she left you to go back to him, you couldn't leave her alone."

"She loved me," Thomas repeats.

"Love isn't enough."

"Fuck. Sometimes I hate you." Clothing ruffles. "You're taking Tess from me as punishment?"

Taking me?

"I would never take anything from you, Thomas. She's not yours to take. She makes her own choices."

Damn right I do.

Thomas steps forward, his features highlighted by a faint ray of light. His eyes look chafed, both literally and figuratively. His body stands rigid, his shoulders back and defiant, his visible hand locked into a fist of contempt. "We'll make it work," he says. "She'll love me and I'll have my family."

"You already have a family," says Bryce.

"I don't want you here. Go."

Huh?

Bryce starts to speak then stops. "I'm not leaving you. And I won't leave her now that I've found her, Thomas."

Thomas lowers his voice to a lethal whisper, "She is not yours."

"I don't want to hurt you—"

"You don't give a rat's ass—"

"Of course I do, how can you say that? You're my brother."

Brother? They're brothers? No fucking way!

"Don't call me—"

"Brothers!" I sputter, launching into the dim light.

Thomas's body tenses, his startled eyes locked on my face, and Bryce, now vaguely discernable, has one hand wrapped around the back of his neck. My eyes drill them, moving from one to the other. "You're brothers?" I gape at Thomas. "You . . . you lied to me. You told me your brother lives in France."

"He did," Thomas says, inching toward me, reaching.

I step back. "You lied to me."

Bryce paces forward. "Tess, I'm—"

"And you!" I verbally lash out. I don't know what to say so I throw daggers with my eyes, pursing my lips in frustration. I can't believe this, brothers fighting about . . . what exactly? The room starts to spin and every ounce of my being needs to get the hell out. I cradle my head, shock and fury pounding my skull. I need my keys.

I turn abruptly, intent on one thing and one thing only. Now that I'm out of the shadows I can see the plush navy curtains gathered in the corner, the prize sitting right where I left it. With two long strides, I seize my purse and open the stage door, slamming it behind me without another word.

My mind is thick and dazed. I want to be home, to be swallowed by the comforts of familiar walls. I stomp my way through the church parking lot and mumble a curt thanks to Karen as I slither behind the steering wheel.

Rage slams the door and I take off, escaping on my Magic Carpet.

# MEN

## Mid-December

*In Earth's history, entire continents and countless islands have been swallowed by the sea, the earth, and covered with volcanic sediment. Our planet is in constant flux, an ever-changing cycle of water level, temperature, and the resulting natural disasters. The sudden extinction of mammals and plants worldwide is proof that Earth's surface changes rapidly, violently. Add the vast array of pyramids and stone monuments built beyond current knowledge and you've set the stage for a lost advanced civilization, a possible Atlantis.*

*Forgotten History Magazine*: Archeological Finds Baffle Scientists

"Tess, I need to talk to you. I know you're pissed, and you have every right to be, but please talk to me. Call me back. Please."

*Beep.*

"It's me again, Thomas. You're obviously still mad. I messed up and I'm sorry. Please call me. I need you to forgive me."

*Beep.*

"Tess, I'm going crazy not talking to you. Please call me back so we can work this out."

*Beep.*

"Hello, honey. This heat wave is making Ted irritable, so we're coming home a little earlier than planned. I'll call when we get in. See you soon. Give Abby hugs for us."

*Ping.*

Text message: Tess, if you don't return my calls, I'm coming over there. Call me, please. Please.

*Ping.*

Text message: Karen here. I've got something for you and we need to talk. Anyway, call me as soon as you get this message.

I've been avoiding the phone for days. It's childish and obnoxiously rude, but I haven't been in the mood to speak to anyone, so I've let it ring. I've been busy with Abby. Well, Abby's been the perfect distraction. We've plastered the house with Christmas decor, played in the yard, baked banana bread, poured over our favorite books, and bumped our way through the grocery store, twice. No time to brood.

Abby's been asleep for hours, so at peace I can't bring myself to carry her from the couch. I'm stretched across the floor, comfortably propped, a tower of assorted pillows bearing my weight. The fire has my feet toasty. It's late and all the house lights are off. Every once in a while lightning flashes, throwing the steady flicker of the tree lights out of sync.

I'm two hundred pages into the book I ordered, a book about lost civilizations. It arrived this afternoon along with the storm, and I've been reading by candlelight—bad for the eyes but great for the soul. I think Edgar Cayce would agree. He's the famous prophet who, in the late 1800s and early 1900s, proffered medical cures while in a trance-like state. An entire chapter is dedicated to his fascinating romps into the psyches of thousands; most tracing back to previous lives in Atlantis. He believed the sins of Atlanteans lead to bad behavior that carried over into subsequent reincarnations, affecting their soul's development through many lifetimes. In other words, Cayce's patients were paying in this life for their soul's previous misdeeds.

I flip back a couple of pages, trying to find the last sentence that actually stuck. Fatigue has my concentration by the balls. Or maybe it's the lights on the Christmas tree, blinking snippets of my life. Like the battery-operated ballerina ornament. As her lavender tutu spins, a distant memory whirls.

I'm standing outside the Princess of Wales Theater, downtown Toronto. It's a remarkable evening. Snow drifts from the night sky on slow-moving waves. Trees, cars, buildings, everything is coated in a thick blanket of ice. Meyer slides his fingers under my thick parka, skimming my taut belly, the sensation provoking internal feet and hands to flutter. I smile and a smug grin illuminates Meyer's face. I take one last look at his gift, a precious ballerina ornament holding show tickets. It's Christmas Eve and the *Nutcracker* is a delightful surprise.

Wind blows down the chimney, a plume of smoke as witness. I turn to Abby asleep on the couch and gently pluck stray strands from her flushed cheeks. Not a trace of Meyer lies within her features. Other than reckless curls of red, she's a mini me, my mother incarnate.

I look back at the Christmas tree, memories flooding my senses. The tiny hockey jersey was bought to commemorate the day we brought Abby home from the hospital wrapped in Meyer's jersey, and he introduced Abby to Gramps as "the enforcer" because her nose was slightly off center, her face bruised. The pink teddy bear makes me think of Abby's first birthday, and how we found Meyer asleep on the floor beside a big girl bed with pink teddy bear sheets and quilts, none present the night before. I remember Taxi, Meyer's old golden retriever, and the Christmas we spent in Paris with Stephen. I recall the first time Meyer and I made love under a Christmas tree, our tree, decorated just like this one.

Now, enthralled with ornaments commemorating our life, I see Meyer more clearly than I have in months. My handsome, loving Meyer . . .

I close my eyes, resting my head on a cushion. I search my mind for a vision, one that will allow me to feel his caress, the strength of his embrace, warmth of his lips. I'm granted the view but the sense of touch hovers beyond my reach, and frustrated by the bombardment of emotions, tears drip from my chin.

*Ring, ring, ring.*

I hear the telephone but ignore it.

*Ring, ring, ring.*

I rub tiny circles over my temples, striving to divert my attention back to the lights.

*Ring, ring, ring.*

I grab the damn phone.

"What?"

"Tess? Did I wake you? It's Karen."

I try very hard to remove the edge from my voice. "I was . . . just thinking."

"Sorry to phone so late but you didn't call me back, and when I drove past your house, I could see your tree lights on." Karen's house is just past mine on the main road into town. Three-quarters of the year our small house can't be seen from the road, but winter spurs leafless trees, allowing for a better view of my home and, apparently, my living room. "Are you all right?" she asks. Her voice sounds hollow and I wonder if she's still in her car.

I take short steps in time with the intermittent lights, aiming for the living room blinds. A chill creeps through my spine, my sixth sense suddenly on edge. I feel watched, on display. I almost drop the phone.

"You don't need to worry about me," I say, peeking out the window.

The sky is dark, almost black, the clouds so low they cut the tops off trees. The rain is not just falling it's jetting a path of destruction, pelting the few leaves that managed to hold onto trees and bushes, leaving everything bare, wet, and gloomy. The sight is depressing. Christmas is meant to be bright white.

I shut the blinds.

"Bryce thinks there's reason to worry. He called yesterday, suggesting I check on you. He wouldn't tell me why, just that you might be upset and need a friend. You sure you're okay?"

I swallow a massive amount of air. My need for a confidant swims against a current of self-preservation.

Ah, hell, Karen will find out anyway.

"They're brothers, Karen."

"What? Who?"

"Thomas and Bryce, they're brothers. And Thomas lied to me about it."

"No way," she gasps. "Shit. That's complicated."

The line falls silent.

For days, I haven't sacrificed more than a scattered minute or two to reflect upon Thomas or Bryce. But now, presented with a suitable sounding board, I have no control over the path my mind opts to wander. I'm furious with Thomas. Not only did he lie to me about where his brother lived, but he had several opportunities to mention Bryce was his brother and didn't. For heaven's sake, Bryce is Sofia's uncle! Where did all this loathing come from? And where does Thomas get off claiming me like he has the right? One brief encounter and a developing friendship does not mean I am his. This is a side of Thomas I've never seen before. A side I never want to see again.

Karen snorts, startling me. "That explains a lot," she says.

"Explains what, exactly?"

"It sheds light on the tension between those two. Siblings can be pretty competitive. It also explains why Bryce stormed from the church looking like he'd been hurt."

I recall Bryce's expression when I caught them arguing, how sad and torn he looked. His words roll in my mind, twisted, blurred, not making any sense.

"That night, when I ran back for my purse, Thomas and Bryce were backstage, arguing. I tried to get the hell out of there, but I didn't move fast enough, and I overheard them talking. The fight was heated, Thomas especially. I've never seen him so irate. I didn't catch all that was said, and what I did hear I don't quite understand, but I'm sure of one thing, the two are brothers."

At odds with her trigger-happy personality, Karen remains silent. When she finally decides to broadcast her notions, her voice is riddled with concern. "Thomas left the church with his daughter Sofia in tow. The kid was crying. When they passed me in the parking lot I asked Thomas if he was joining us at the bistro. He said he wasn't going, that he had to get Sofia home. Minutes later, Bryce exited the church and while heading for his car I saw his face under a light. He looked like someone had clocked him."

"Literally?" My chin collides with the phone. "Hurt, as in beaten?"

I can't believe it. Thomas wouldn't actually deck Bryce, would he?

"He had a shiner and a bloody nose. I only caught a glimpse, but he didn't look great. At the time I'd figured he'd fallen or banged into something."

"And Thomas, did he look battered? I hope Bryce gave as much as he got."

"Not at all. That's why it never occurred to me that the two of them might have been fighting. That and the fact that I didn't think they knew each other. Thomas looked slightly concerned, stressed maybe, but that's it."

"Why didn't you stop Bryce? Maybe he needed help."

"The man shot out of there like a bullet." Karen pauses for a moment, catching her breath. Thunder rumbles in the background. She sounds distracted, like she's trying to talk and drive at the same time. "Now I understand why Thomas left with Sofia and Bryce followed after. Who wants a kid to know they've been clocked by their own brother, the kid's father to boot. It also explains why Bryce took off."

"What do you mean by 'took off'?"

"Bryce called yesterday—like I said, he was concerned about you. He called from France. He'd grabbed a flight to spend a few days with his parents. Apparently he does this often. His family is really tight."

Not his entire family.

I can't help but think of Thomas, about the conversation we had the night of our dinner date, of all the things he said about his brother, the jerk.

Karen huffs. "It was a short conversation, and I didn't get the chance to ask questions. He probably doesn't want his niece to know what happened and a black eye is hard to hide. Especially in Carlisle, where people talk."

"Karen, seriously, you can't—"

"Relax, Chickpea, I'll keep everyone's privacy on this one." A car door slams. "What are you going to do?"

"Nothing. Everything. I don't know. I've been avoiding

Thomas."

Thomas lied to me, big time. I thought he'd opened up, let me within his walls, given me a glimpse of the man inside, but there was no truth to it. What else has been a lie?

"I have nothing nice to say to Thomas, especially now."

"And Bryce?"

"I've had it with men. I'm barring the whole lot."

All but one. BOB and I are going to get to know each other really well.

The line is quiet for a moment. I'd guess Karen is grappling over her promise to sweep this under the proverbial carpet. Finally, she says, "This really sucks."

"Yes, yes it does."

The doorbell chimes and I jolt, almost knocking the curtain rod from the wall. It takes a moment to shake the nerves from my hands. I've lost the phone.

"Who is it?" I say, clutching the deadbolt.

"Karen, you dolt, and I'm getting soaked."

Tension subsides and I open the door, *what the hell* written on my face. Karen flashes her cell phone then thrusts her coat at me, rainwater soaking the floor. In Karen's world, visiting hours don't follow any clock. I lay her coat on the mat and follow her into the kitchen, flicking light switches on the way.

"Do you want tea? I only have—"

"Decaf, I know. When are you gonna give that up?"

"I came close this morning. I'd have given a small fortune to have Abby back in school so I could take a nap. I've always been prone to nightmares, but since Meyer's accident they've been brutal." And real, too real. "I was butchered twice last night."

Karen hovers in my personal space, analyzing my face. "I can see that," she says.

Nice.

"If you came to make me feel better, it's not working." I turn to fill the kettle.

"I came to give you this." She plops a large black garbage bag on the kitchen table.

"What the hell is that?" I hadn't even noticed she was carrying anything. "How did I miss a garbage bag the size of a toddler?"

The bag is dripping rainwater all over the table, and now that the lights are on, I spot puddles down the hall.

"Bitch about the mess," Karen says, smiling. She's a force of nature and knows it, no apologies necessary. I grab a tea towel to collect the water while Karen grapples with the knot at the top of the bag. "Am I great or what?" she says, lowering the plastic.

It's my paper-mache star from the pageant.

"Oh, Karen." I help her shimmy the star from the bag. "Thank you. Abby will be thrilled. I'm going to hang it in her room." I oust the final remnants of irritation from my voice, grateful to have Karen as a friend. "You know me so well, huh?"

"Ah, I shouldn't tell you this, considering your man ban and all, but it was actually Bryce who told me you wanted the star." She grins, sheepish. "But I made sure Irving took it down gently, and I recommended he put it in a bag so it wouldn't get wet."

Irving is the superintendent at Saint Ann's.

"Such talent," I tease, handing Karen a mug.

I stare at the star, confused. How did Bryce know I wanted the star? I don't remember saying anything to anyone about it.

"Have you ever noticed anything weird about Bryce?" I say. "Anything at all?"

"Other than the fact that he's insanely gorgeous, obviously wealthy, and highly intelligent, which is too much scrumptiousness to squeeze into one man? Not really, why?"

I peek over my mug at Karen. She's got that look, the look a person gets when thinking about an attractive version of the opposite sex. A *hmm, yum,* kind of look.

I fidget, slightly rattled by a pang of envy.

"I never mentioned wanting the star," I say. "I don't see how Bryce would know to tell you."

Karen emits a low humming sound from her throat, clearly mulling over my statement. "Maybe you mentioned it to Thomas and he told Bryce. Or maybe Bryce assumed you'd want it, considering the work you put into making it. It is a cool star. Did you see it glow at the pageant?"

"I don't recall saying anything to Thomas . . ."

Strange. I should just come out and say, *What is so unusual about you, Bryce Waters? How is it you know things you shouldn't, as if you are one step ahead of me when we chat? Why do my eyes do funny things when you are around? What is it about you that puts me on edge and at ease at the same time?* Maybe he'll confess to something really wild. Maybe he's Batman or an alien from another planet. Maybe he was born with supernatural powers and can shoot laser beams from those silver eyes of his. I snicker. And maybe stress has me over the edge, short-circuiting my faculties.

"What's so funny?" Karen eyes me suspiciously.

It is bad enough Karen witnessed my slip on reality at the café. I'm not about to fill her in on my deranged thoughts regarding Bryce.

"I'm just being superstitious and foolish," I say, opting for a quick change in topic. I suppose I'm hoping there is something wrong with Bryce so I don't have to face what's wrong with me. "Other than delivery of my star, why are you out in this crappy weather so late?"

Karen answers with her hands. "I had to grab Eric from work. Alicia forgot her allergy pills, so I had to drop them off at her girlfriend's where she's staying the night. I ran out of bread for lunches, so I had to make a pit stop at the grocery store. And of course I had to stop at the . . ." Karen gives me a look. "Just you wait. You'll blink and Abby will be a teenager. You'll see— you become taxi driver and errand boy!"

We laugh. The woman speaks the truth and we both know it.

Suddenly Karen is serious. "Regarding your moratorium on men. I should warn you, I ran into Thomas this morning. He said you're not returning his calls. I assumed you'd had a lover's quarrel." I roll my eyes. "He's considering a siege on your barracks." She chuckles. "Had it been anyone other than you, I'd have supported the lunatic. I could use a juicy scandal. Unfortunately, I'm loyal to the bone. I advised him to keep his distance or I'd make his life a living hell."

Karen smiles and I ooze gratitude.

"You're diabolical, Karen."

Karen shrugs. "Christmas will be hard enough this year. The last thing you need is men fighting over you." She is quiet for a moment, waiting for a reaction. I stare into my empty mug. "They could fight over me if they want to," she says, grinning.

Laughter erupts from my belly. Not because the idea of two men fighting over Karen is absurd. On the contrary, she's smart and funny with a profusion of style. I just can't imagine why anyone would want grown men brawling and slugging it out around them, never mind over them.

Karen grasps my meaning. "I guess it's not all it's cracked up to be, huh?"

"Not even slightly entertaining."

"You should throw all these troubles to the curbside and focus on Christmas with Abby," says Karen, placing a hand on mine.

"That's my game plan."

That and a dog.

# RELEVANCE

*There is a bias that supports accepted dogma while rejecting evidence that does not support convention. As a result, archeological evidence proving man is far more ancient than originally theorized has gathered dust, suppressed because it conflicts with an entrenched belief system that refuses to consider it might be wrong.*

*Forgotten History Magazine*: Archeological Finds Baffle Scientists

**T**he sun is shining, but debris and scattered foliage divulge proof in the wake of yesterday's storm. In spite of the desolation, I feel pretty upbeat. Grams and Gramps are home, their return providing something I'm desperate for. Hugs.

"What's happening with you and this Bryce fellow?" asks Grams.

We're folding laundry, and the overwhelming scent of lavender dryer sheets crams the limited space in my laundry room.

"Happening? Nothing is happening."

Sharing with Karen is bad enough. Grams will worry

incessantly. And I can't stand the thought of giving her more to fret about. She's got Gramps to take care of.

"You can't fool an old pro, Tess. I see it in your eyes. They sparkle at the mere mention of his name."

"You don't know what you're talking about," I say, settling for evasion.

"Guess it was all in this old head of mine," she says, twirling a L'Oreal Golden Brown #36 curl around her index finger.

I can't get used to the color change.

"You lit up like a lighthouse when he dropped by after Halloween."

I toss underwear at her head. "You're delusional."

"I might be, but I haven't heard you laugh like that in a long time."

She's right. Bryce has a way of making me feel alive.

"It's irrelevant," I say. Right now, I'm too confused and cross to feel anything for him.

"Really."

Eventually she'll pull the story from me, if only one aggravating detail at a time, so I submit to a partial confession. "Bryce asked me out on a date and I said I'd think about it."

"Hmm," she mumbles.

This is it. This is all she gives me.

"He's intriguing and intelligent and I like his taste in clothing," I say, picturing Bryce in nothing but his scarf. "Like me, he's fascinated with art and history, so we have lots to talk about but . . ." I don't really know how to complete this train of thought. Why won't I go out with him?

Oh wait, he's trouble. And Thomas's brother!

"I see."

She's killing me with these one-liners.

"You see what? Enlighten me, please, because I don't see

what you see."

Really, I don't. So what she says next throws me for a loop.

"I think you have feelings for Thomas."

"Thomas? What makes you think I feel anything for Thomas?"

She eyes me suspiciously. "You've talked about him quite a bit lately, and spent a lot of time together at the church and such. I thought you might have found something more than friendship."

Her words flicker a bulb in my head. This is why I'm so angry with Thomas. We were friends, good friends on the verge of discovering something more. I'd finally opened my mind to the possibility of a relationship after Meyer, and that I could someday, maybe, create a family for Abby. Thomas made me think I had a chance at happiness again. But now . . . now that's gone. I can't trust him. He threw our relationship, our closeness, in Bryce's face . . . and over brotherly competition. I was a game, a calculation, a prize to be won, and Thomas thought he could bully Bryce out of the equation.

"That time has passed," I say, bitterness rolling from my tongue. "Thomas and I are friends, if that, but nothing more."

Grams leans close, inspecting, evaluating. "If he hurt you, I'll—"

"Relax, Grams. Thomas would never hurt me."

Even knowing Thomas struck Bryce, I don't believe he'd ever physically hurt me.

"Then why are you so upset?"

I take a deep breath. So much for a partial confession.

"Thomas told me his family live in Europe and he seldom speaks with them. He failed to mention his brother lives down the street. And that his brother, Sofia's uncle, is Bryce Waters."

The silence is deafening.

"Bryce," Grams finally murmurs.

"Before Bryce came into the picture, Thomas hadn't shown the slightest bit of interest in me. He never let me peek at who he really was, and he never suggested a physical connection. Not until Bryce did. Then he put his game face on, giving just enough to lure me into thinking he could be trusted. He wanted to win something over Bryce. But that's all I am, a trophy."

"Brothers," Grams repeats, evidently as disturbed with the concept as I am. "Where is Bryce's responsibility in all this?"

Good question. Bryce didn't tell me Thomas was his brother either. He mentioned he had a niece he was close to, and that he'd moved to Carlisle to be close to family, but not that his family included Thomas and Sofia. Was that intentional?

"I don't think Bryce knew that Thomas and I were close. Not before the fall fair, anyway. And Thomas, Thomas wanted me because Bryce did." I take shallow breaths, lost in my own statement. "I'm not ready for all this Grams."

Grams steps close, inviting me to fall into her embrace, which is exactly what I do. There is nothing I need more at this moment than a hug.

"I was looking forward to watching you find love again," she says. "Unfortunately, love doesn't always come wrapped in pretty paper. Sometimes it's wrapped in garbage."

"I'm done thinking about it," I say, resting my forehead on her shoulder. Her sweater smells like mothballs. "I need to focus on getting Abby through Christmas."

She rubs my back with both hands. "Yes, Abby needs you to be strong."

"Speaking of Abby," I say, deciding to spill the details of my plan. "I could use your help with something . . ."

**Hours later, Abby** is curled on her great grandpa's lap watching an episode of Franklin, and pots and pans are banging in the kitchen—Grams preparing dinner. I take the opportunity to creep out the back door and slide my sneaky rear behind the wheel, tossing my purse onto the passenger seat where it normally lands with a thump but today smacks into place, knocking a small red box to the floor. I fetch the box. It's wrapped in crimson foil paper, a thick satin ribbon of the same color tied in a dainty bow. Where did this come from? I turn the box and notice a miniature card that simply reads, *Tess.*

Am I supposed to open it now or save it for Christmas morning? Curiosity consumes me and I claw the paper with vigor.

Inside, wrapped in tissue, rests a glass bauble on an elegant gold ribbon. I gently lift it from the box and hold it to the light, illuminating the vibrant bubbles in various shades of red. It's beautiful. On the bottom is a tiny black button, begging to be pressed.

"Merry Christmas! We miss you! Merry Christmas! We miss you! Merry Christmas! We miss you!" repeats the mechanical voice of Thomas and Sofia. It's not the same ornament as the one Thomas bought at the tree farm, but I can't help but smile at the memory. In the bottom of the box, there is folded paper, a letter.

Dearest Tess,

Sofia and I were hoping to spend Christmas with you and Abby, but it's been suggested you need space over the holidays so we're spending Christmas in Belize.

Please let me talk to you when I get back. I'm very sorry I didn't tell you about Bryce earlier and that you had to find out the way you did. I screwed up.

Bryce wants to be an uncle to Sofia, and I can't deny her family, but there are parts of my past I don't like to talk about, and I wasn't lying when I said my family and I aren't close.

Don't be upset with me. I apologize for being an ass.

I miss you,
Thomas

Loneliness wanders into my psyche, and fury jumps ship. We hadn't made plans, Thomas and I, but I assumed we'd spend time together over the holidays, while the girls were out of school. I guess this isn't happening now that they're in Belize. Now I feel bad. They've abandoned their first Christmas tree and new holiday traditions because I wouldn't answer the phone. I hadn't paused to listen to Thomas's perspective and maybe I should have. Maybe the bile spewing from Thomas that night, the hatred toward Bryce, is the result of a lifelong chasm between the two. Jealousy is a nasty emotion and when marinated for years . . .

Yes, Thomas blatantly lied to me, but why? What could keep a man from communicating with his own brother in a town the size of a baseball league? And what does that say about Bryce? What has Bryce and his family done to warrant Thomas and his daughter moving to another country for a fresh start?

Either way, I can't dismiss the scene that played out that night at the church. Knowing Thomas let his anger lead to physical abuse . . . After years of witnessing my mother lose control, the thought sickens me. And yet, how many times have I seen sibling's battle over a toy and the parents plead indifference: *Boys will be boys.*

I guess the question is, can I forgive and forget?

I chuckle at a thought, Pocahontas and her pet raccoon in the wooden canoe, stopped at a fork in the river. Which path to take? The steady, calm route leading to . . . or the rapids that promise excitement? Even with a risk of drowning my body steers toward the rapids.

"Enough of the Disney movies," I mumble, shoving the keys in the ignition.

The fluorescent green of the clock makes a point of warning me ten minutes has passed, limiting my time at the animal shelter. I've got to get moving. I'm determined to put a smile on my baby girl's face Christmas morning, and crowning Abby's wish list is a dog.

Top of my wish list? I wish, more than anything in this world, that the last eight months were an awful dream from which I only need to roll over and wake to see Meyer lying next to me asleep.

Good luck with that one, Santa.

# GRIM REMINDER

## December End

I'm in bed, it's four in the morning, and my eyes are locked in an unnatural stare that wouldn't be focused on anything in particular, even if there were a shred of light. I'm thinking about Christmas.

In the past, Christmas in the Morgan household was a time of joy and jubilation. Christmas morning was a six a.m. wakening spawned by Abby, brimming with excitement. It included an adrenalin-fueled rush that undoubtedly rendered at least one of us injured as we skipped steps to make it down the stairway at breakneck speed. Nothing was more important than finding out what old Saint Nick snuck into our stockings while we slept. Abby would squeal over the half-eaten cookies and empty glass with milk-stained smudges then investigate every dollar store gift that Santa had stuffed into her oversized red velvet stocking. It would take her all of fifteen minutes to rip open the gifts that took me three hours to wrap and countless hours to source, and Meyer and I would watch, riveted, cell phone's documenting a show worthy of an Oscar.

When the sun was actually awake, Meyer's grandparents would wander over for a feast. While Grams and I whipped together a royal breakfast, Meyer and Gramps poured themselves over Abby and her gifts, hacking into packaging capable of housing a nuclear warhead, skimming instructions, and inserting umpteen batteries. Festive music would blare from the radio and each and every one of us would float about the kitchen with a dance in our step. We'd stuff ourselves silly, leave the mess for house elves, and huddle on the couch to watch Meyer's favorite Christmas classic, *It's a Wonderful Life*.

This Christmas wasn't remotely similar.

After a second glance at the clock, I sprang from the bed in a panic. I bounded down the hall, haphazardly tugging my housecoat, only to find Abby sound asleep, head where her feet should be, and toes on the pillow. Her sheets were strewn about as if a brawl had taken place in the night, leaving her quilt abandoned on the floor. I stepped closer, relocating sweaty strands to peer into her face. It was blotched and puffy. My baby girl's Christmas Eve hadn't been spent in blissful anything.

I rescued the quilt from the floor and tucked Abby's headless bunny under her arm. Abby slept another forty minutes, well past daybreak, while I cried.

As hard as we all tried, this was pretty much the theme for the entire day. Abby's unenthusiastic attempts at joy were almost more than I could handle, and it took every ounce of willpower I had not to drop to my knees and bawl.

After opening the gifts we made our rounds, lingering in each other's arms, letting love defrost our extremities. We cooked breakfast but lacked the appetite to eat, so it sat, barely picked at, until Grams surrendered with a huff and threw it into Tupperware. Abby showed no interest in her toys. No one turned the music on. No one suggested we watch Meyer's movie, the movie he'd watched every Christmas since his parents passed.

By noon I'd read Abby every Dr. Seuss book ever published and my ass was numb. So was my brain. If it wasn't for Grams and her not-so-subtle reminder, I'd have forgotten to implement my plan.

The plan was to allow Abby her usual Christmas morning routine before presenting the gift capable of resurrection. This wasn't only for Abby's sake, but for the dog's as well. Her name is Magpie and her previous family called her Magsie. During her short stay with Grams and Gramps, everyone kept calling her Maxi by mistake. She reminded us of Meyer's dog, Taxi, and our mouths would start the *m* in Magsie then naturally switch to Taxi. Magsie / Maxi, both seemed to spur the usual responses, so Maxi it was. She was everything I was hoping for and much more needed than I'd originally imagined. The dog was the savior of Christmas in our house.

Grams made a commotion at the front door, announcing Maxi's presence in a grand voice. The dog trotted, dodging furniture as though she'd lived here her entire life, directly into Abby's waving arms. Maxi's tail swung in full force, knocking a cup from the coffee table. Abby laughed. Not an artificial rehearsed laugh, but a true deep from the belly laugh. Tears soaked her cheeks until they dripped from her chin, leaving dark circles on her fleece pajamas.

Overwhelmed with emotion, I covered my face, body quaking, relief flooding my senses. I looked at Grams and Gramps crouched in the doorway. Gramps was in his chair, arms stretched around Grams's shoulders, her face buried in his neck.

This is how the death of one man can turn a holiday meant for merriment into a sad testament of his absence.

Tears sting as they follow the contours of my face and neck, down to a shallow puddle nestled within my left collarbone. I wipe my cheeks in the dark. Dawn peeks around the blind's edges. I'm tired but I think I'll get up, maybe head to the studio.

My skin feels itchy in this bed.

Needless to say, other than the addition of our dear Maxi, this Christmas will be tossed with the tree.

And not enshrined in any photo album.


**We're rolling shortbread** at the kitchen table when, for the third time in two days, Abby demands to be entertained.

"The shelter had the perfect dog just waiting for us," my story begins. I'm animated, the rolling pin cutting air as I speak. "The first dog to join me in the petting room was a one-year-old Weimaraner named Peppy. Sleek and powerful, if looks were enough he'd have been our winner. Unfortunately, his exuberance had me doing tailspins of my own. Even the shelter staff couldn't get Peppy to calm, which was frustrating because I needed to see his eyes." I lean across the table and stare into Abby's eyes, nose to nose. Abby giggles.

"It was a crazy theory," I say. "I thought if I could peer into a dog's eyes, search their depths, a connection would spark, and I'd know that this dog, the one whose essence could be seen, was the one." I laugh. "Peppy was a bust."

I stick my fingers in flour and splatter Abby with white dust. Her laugh ignites her face, making my heart dance. "More," she pleads.

"The next dog sauntered in, not a care in the world. Her name was Magpie. At first glance she looked like any golden Lab, but as I watched her sit for the shelter attendant, I could see the resemblance to Taxi."

Abby slides from the chair, running her flour laced fingers through Maxi's fur. "This dog lost her family," she says, stealing my thunder.

I smile, agree. "She'd been loved." I place a dough ball onto the mat and ready the rolling pin, coating it with flour.

Apparently my tale is in need of more gusto. A blind man could detect Abby's *keep going* expression. I laugh, picking up the pace.

"I patted my knees and Magpie sauntered to where I was sitting on the bench. Her tail swayed, giving flight to the mix of dog hair in its path. The six-by-six room held the aroma of animal pee and bleach. She nudged my hands with her wet nose, her tongue lazily hanging over yellow-white teeth. I obliged, rubbing the soft spot behind her ear."

"This is the part! The part I like the mostest!" Abby says, climbing back onto her chair.

"The most, baby, there is no such word as mostest."

Abby sticks her tongue out at me.

"It was time to put my theory to the test," I say with a wink. "I placed my fingertips under Magpie's furry chin and gazed straight into those big brown eyes." I pause for effect. Even Maxi looks up in anticipation. "Love rolled in waves from her body, the universe floating within her milky stare. Her eyes said it all. She was the one."

"Ha, ha!" Abby claps and a plume of fairy dust coats everything in sight.

The doorbell rings.

"In short," I mutter, concluding today's two o'clock performance, "Magpie unfurled her long, gooey tongue, licking me from chin to hairline, sealing the deal."

Abby skips down the hall. "Love that story."

Maxi follows, torn between seeing who has come to visit and staying close to the sweet smelling cookies. I peek in the oven, two steps behind my mini clan.

"Good evening, ma'am," says a voice as I step around the corner.

I stop short.

Abby is holding the door for a man in uniform. He is tall, slim. A faded rim of purple surrounds his eyes. My heart plummets to the balls of my feet.

"Officers Smith and Becale here," he says. The second officer, a woman, steps out from behind him. They flash their badges. "Could we speak with you for a moment?"

"Alone," she adds, her stare shifting to Abby.

Lunch has lodged somewhere between my stomach and tonsils, thickening my throat. The last time the police came to my door it was to tell me Meyer had been in a car accident and hadn't survived.

I'm about to vomit. Please no, no more.

The officers step inside and I turn to Abby, my movements coming in slow motion. "Roll more cookies in the kitchen." I tuck Abby's fingers under Maxi's collar. "Take Maxi with you. Do not touch the oven."

I try to focus on Abby and Maxi waddling down the hallway. In my head I skim a list of loved ones I haven't seen or spoken to today. Panic sets in when I realize I haven't heard from my brother Stephen since Christmas day.

Officer Smith inches forward. "We're sorry to interrupt, but this is rather important," he says. "The body of a local woman has been found close by."

Oh no, Sonia, Karen's neighbor. It must be. A wave of relief crashes through me. My family is safe. The euphoria dissipates instantly, replaced by remorse. My heart aches for the parents and family who must be beside themselves with grief. It's an emotion I'm all too familiar with, and I don't wish it on anyone.

"Who? Close by where?" The thought of a body being found close to home makes me tremble.

"We cannot discuss the crime scene, ma'am. I'm sure you

can appreciate the sensitivity—"

"Of course."

A chill makes me think of a recurring vision, of lying naked in the snow, alone.

"Ma'am, did you know Sonia MacKinnen?"

So it is her.

"Oh, my, no, I never met her. I didn't even know her last name. I assume you mean the Sonia that went missing a few months ago?"

"Sonia MacKinnen was reported missing October 18th. Could you tell us how you came to hear about Miss MacKinnen?"

"A friend of mine lives on the property around the bend to Sonia and her mother. She mentioned that Sonia had disappeared and her mother was worried."

"And since then?"

"I heard Sonia was still missing, but authorities thought she'd run off with a man."

"When and where did you hear that Sonia was still missing?"

"I don't really recall. Just before Christmas maybe. Probably at the church. I was involved in the Christmas pageant at Saint Ann's and I overheard tidbits. Most thought she'd fallen for some guy, someone her mother wouldn't approve of."

Officer Smith nods, his face expressionless. "Have you seen anything or anyone unusual around town lately?"

I stifle a nervous chuckle. Have I seen unusual? I'm an unusual magnet. But fast, telepathic men, naked lovers, and loopy old neighbors aren't what this cop is searching for, I'm sure.

"Nothing I can think of." Or speak of, I muse.

"We appreciate your assistance, Mrs. . . . ."

Why hadn't I inquired about Sonia? Was it because I didn't want to be nosy or because I was so utterly wrapped in my own problems that I'd forgotten all about her? I should have called her mother, offered to help in some way. I look up to see Officer Smith watching me, eyebrows raised.

"Morgan. Tess Morgan," I finally mutter.

Officer Becale jots something on a pad of paper, my name I presume. Apparently Smith is the designated interrogator and Becale is the note taker.

"Is your husband home?" says Officer Smith. "We'd like to ask him a few questions as well."

"My husband passed away in April." Saying that never gets easier. "Only my daughter and I live here." The officers glance at each other. "Should I be worried?"

Smith smiles. It's not a friendly smile. "We see no reason to think this isn't an isolated case but suggest you keep your doors and windows locked and stay in contact with friends and family until we find the perpetrator. It's always best to err on the side of caution."

I fiddle with the deadbolt on the door.

Officer Smith steps onto the porch. "Enjoy the rest of your evening," he says, pausing so his sidekick can pass me a business card. "And call if you see or hear anything that might be of assistance."

The police make their way down the steps.

"Extend my condolences to the MacKinnen family," I yell after them.

I shut the door and lean against it, eyes closed, praying to some unknown god that Sonia was killed quickly and without pain. Somehow, deep inside, I know this is not the case. Nightmares have given me more than enough experience in the brutal death department to know what Sonia might have gone through. I shudder at the thought.

The sound of muffled voices catches my attention and I open

the door.

Officer Smith stands a few feet from Bryce on my walkway, nodding as Bryce speaks. Officer Becale scribbles in her notebook then reaches out, a card between two fingers. "Much appreciated, Mr. Waters, we'll see you soon," she says, grinning.

Not having heard her speak much, I'm caught off guard by her mouse-like voice. Bryce takes the card. No smile, no charm, all business. Officer Becale scurries down the walkway on the heels of Officer Smith, back to the cruiser parked in the driveway. Halfway there she hesitates to sneak a peek at the man in black, suddenly crowding my doorway with his presence.

"This is bad timing," Bryce says. He's standing in a strange position, hands behind his back. He has an uncomfortable, almost tortured expression on his face. This is the first I've seen him since his fight with Thomas. I scrutinize his eyes and cheekbones, searching for telltale signs of bruising.

"I'm fine," he mumbles. He is. I see nothing. "I wanted to . . . I thought . . ." His breath billows, cloudlike, hovering mid air. He looks like he'd prefer to be anywhere other than my porch.

This Bryce baffles me. I'm accustomed to seeing him ooze confidence.

"I can't really deal with this right now, Bryce." I'm not sure where this is headed, but it's irrelevant since I'm not in a place to go there with him. My Christmas wounds are too fresh. "Is something wrong, something more important than a young woman found dead?"

"Like I said, this is really bad timing," he says. "I should go." He fidgets but doesn't move to leave.

"Look, Bryce—"

"These are for you." The movement is instantaneous. One second his hands are tightly tucked, the next they're before me, displaying a bouquet of white daisies. I stare at my favorite flowers. "This feels wrong but I can't leave without you seeing them," he says, extending farther, suggesting I take the flowers.

"These are stunning, Bryce." I take the bouquet into my arms. "But I don't—"

He raises a hand. "Please," he says. "I only wanted to say merry Christmas." He has a way about him, a talent for melting me. I form a natural, easy smile, and struggle to recall why I'm upset.

"Thank you for the flowers," I say, fingertips dancing over velvet petals. "They'll look perfect in the vase Grams gave me."

Bryce nods. "I should let you get back to your baking."

"How do you know I was baking?"

"Look, I—I was hoping we could talk soon, possibly over dinner."

I'm willing to listen to what Bryce has to say, just not at this moment. "I'm not sure a date is in my near future, but I will talk to you. You and Thomas. I just need—"

"I should've given you more time," he mumbles, shoving his hands in his pockets.

"Seriously, I'm all right. We'll talk another time. Christmas was rough and this local girl has been found dead and I—"

"Say no more." A forced smile clouds his features. "Another day." He turns to leave.

"Yes," I say. I have questions that need answers. "Another day."

# BREATHLESS

## December 31st

*Darwinism, which is rooted in the assumption that all existence is matter-based, cannot account for the most human characteristic of all, consciousness. The human mind is capable of far more than necessary for mere survival. Why?*

*Forgotten History Magazine*: Archeological Finds Baffle Scientists

**A**bby sucks on the curved end of a candy cane patiently waiting for a chance to snatch another hot chocolate from one of the perky elves in bright red stockings. I lean on the red and white striped metal pole that claims this very spot as The North Pole. Kids squeal, on sugar highs. Our boots make sloshing sounds in the slush while we stand in line, the bus six line. There are a lot of us here and it's quite chaotic.

The teachers of Carlisle Elementary, Ms. Rainer included, were nice enough to plan this field trip to Elves Village over the holidays, providing good reason to implement one of my New Year's resolutions a few hours early. Resolution: refrain from all mental jabs pertaining Ms. Rainer. I've devised this pledge for two reasons, the first being that the lady really doesn't deserve my attitude. She's chosen a career that requires her to be in the company of twenty children, seven hours a day, five days a week, and I suppose one would either need a whole lot of drugs or an upbeat personality to handle that kind of environment. The second reason is quite simple: Abby adores her.

Somewhere in this mass of students and parents are Sofia and Bryce, although we haven't seen them since this morning when we were placed in separate groups for the day, sorted by surnames in alphabetical order. We're shoulder to shoulder, M through P, exhausted and clammy, awaiting our yellow submarine rides back to the school. Hot liquid burns my insides and I flap my coat in the cool air. Abby's scarf hangs from my coat pocket, rescued from a botched expedition. The day has been chilly, but beautiful, the sun setting the snow to glimmer. Today we built snowmen, decorated cookies, doused popsicle-stick ornaments with sparkle glue, pet the fake reindeer, and climbed the Winter Wonderland jungle gym. Before calling it a day we visited Mr. and Mrs. Claus, who did a great job feigning interest in Abby's dismal recount of Christmas. I was most grateful.

We file onto the buses, Abby plopping beside a plump boy with white-blond curls and ice-blue eyes. Abby stares at him, enthralled. The boy blushes, adding another dimension of color to his face. We're bundled in snowsuits, boots, scarves, hats, and mittens—great for a cold day, but not for an overpopulated bus. I loosen my scarf and scan the crowd for familiar faces. I notice Bryce is on the bus to the left of us, nestled beside a heavy-set woman in a bright-orange parka. Sofia is sitting on Bryce's lap. For the first time I notice how alike Bryce and Sofia look. Same dark hair, same shaped eyes and lips. They are more alike than Thomas and Sofia. How did I not realize they were related before?

Thomas called this morning. He and Sofia had just returned from Belize and he wanted to talk, but I was running out the door and hadn't figured out what I wanted to say to him, so I said we'd talk later. He got snippy when I said we were on our way to the school for the field trip. He was mad that I'd changed my mind and decided to go. Once I got to the school and saw Bryce with Sofia, the pieces fit and I knew why Thomas had given me attitude. He must have agreed to let Bryce bring Sofia because he thought I wouldn't be here.

In fact, several pieces fell into place. The day of the fall fair, when Thomas saw Bryce standing behind me, maybe that look wasn't just jealousy. I think Thomas was shocked to see Bryce at the fair at all. I mean, why would he be there without his niece, who was supposedly home sick? I bet Thomas didn't know Bryce had volunteered and would come without Sofia. Did Thomas pull the plug on Bryce's day with Sofia when he heard I'd decided to take Abby to the fair? Was Thomas playing the game long before I imagined?

The lies just keep piling up, burying Thomas deep. Who the hell does he think he is?

A second wave of people crowds the bus, forcing me to make room. I shuffle down the aisle, trying desperately to protect the paper bag containing Abby's masterpieces. The bus moves, heading to the main road, and I rise to my toes, hoping to catch a glimpse of Abby honing her flirting skills. All I can see is the fluorescent puff crowning her ear warmers as it bounces with the potholes.

Close to the school a toddler tugs my scarf. "Whath doth a new year mean?" he says between missing teeth.

I explain until the bus stops. We're back in the school parking lot.

"Abby, wait outside the bus for me," I yell around bodies.

People are gathering loose pieces of clothing, peering out windows to locate their cars in the parking lot, chatting with their kids. It takes forever to get off the damn bus, and when I do I search for Abby's lime green parka and a head of red curls.

I don't see either.

I stroll around the buses, calling, "Come out, come out, wherever you are."

After the second lap I freak.

"Abigail Morgan, this isn't funny. Where are you?"

I turn in circles, searching, inspecting anyone wearing green. I sprint across the parking lot, dodging cars blocking my path to Magic Carpet. When I get there, I don't see Abby. A line of vehicles exits the parking lot. I run from child to child and car to car, bordering on hysteria, pushing people out of my way, no regard for pleasantries.

"Abby!" I run another lap around all three buses, pausing periodically to inspect the underbelly for hide-and-seek participants. There is no sign of her.

Climbing back onto bus six, I search under the seats, calling Abby's name. She's nowhere. "Abby!" My scream reverberates through the empty bus. Horrific thoughts bombard my head, visions too gruesome to absorb. I cover my mouth, my stomach threatening to explode.

I leap from the bus to run to the next one but stumble forward, falling into Ms. Bubbly. She flies sideways into a garbage can, shocked, and maybe hurt. I should care but I don't.

Fuck resolutions.

"Abby!"

"Mrs. Morgan." Ms. Bubbly says, righting herself. "What's got you all worked up?"

I lower my head between my knees and suck a mouthful of

air. The oxygen slows the spinning, enough for coherent thought. "I can't find Abby. I'm an awful mother. I've lost her. I've lost her!"

"Your daughter was on bus six, Mrs. Morgan, she wasn't left behind."

"Abby was at the front of the bus and I was stuck at the back. She got off without me, and disappeared."

"Well, she must be around here somewhere."

"I've searched everywhere," I say, breathing heavy. I might pass out.

Mrs. Bubbly peeks around the bus, tapping a headlight with her knuckles. "Maybe she's hiding." She climbs the stairs of bus six, calling out to Abby.

"I've already looked there. She's not on the bus."

My heart is beating a mile a minute. I'm trying to think straight but can't. I've lost my scarf and gloves in the heat of the hunt. Where is my phone? I gotta call the police! I dig through coat pockets for my cell but only find car keys. The car. I left my cell charging on the passenger seat of Magic Carpet.

I run for the car like it's a lighthouse in a storm, throw the door open, and lunge for my cell.

I'm begging my phone to hurry, to turn on faster, when Mrs. Bubbly rushes to my car out of breath. "Maybe Abby went home," she says. "You live walking distance, don't you?"

For a second I think that's it, Abby's walked home. How many times did I wander away from my mother when I was a kid? I need to get home. She's there, safe and sound. Then I shake my head clear.

"Abby's never walked home by herself."

Ms. Rainer takes a hold of the car door. "You'd be surprised what a five-year-old can do," she says. "They get a taste for independence and make decisions adults find rash."

I study her, desperation clawing my gut. But for the teachers and parents searching the buses for Abby, the parking lot is almost empty.

"I'm calling the police."

My phone finally comes to life. It beeps. There is a message, left a minute ago, titled *Abby*. Someone's found Abby! Please tell me she's somewhere safe. Please! The phone trembles in my hand as I listen to the message.

"Tess. Bryce here. I got your number from Karen. Look, ah . . . I'm hoping you know this . . . Abby's at my place playing with Sofia. Abby said she asked for permission, but now I'm not so sure." His voice wavers. "Anyway, she's here. And if by chance you didn't know that she . . . I'm sorry. I'll call you again in a few minutes if I don't hear from you first. Or come by whenever you wish."

I grip the steering wheel for support. Bryce took Abby. He took her. He took her!

But Abby is safe. She lied about asking permission. She's safe.

I turn and stumble from the car, landing on all fours beside Ms. Bubbly's boots, where I puke, candy sprinkles and all.


**The drive to** the estate is a blur. I only know that I'm here and relief floods every vein. Abby is somewhere on the other side of this door. Before I even knock the door swings open.

"You!" I thrust a fisted hand at Bryce's chest.

Bryce braces the doorframe. "I'm so sorry," he says.

I storm past him into the foyer. "Abby, where are you?"

"She's upstairs with Sofia," says Bryce. "Nanna, my housekeeper, is watching them play. Look, you're obviously upset and—"

"Upset? Upset? You have no idea how fucking upset I am!"

I prod his shoulder, pushing him backwards. He doesn't say a word. I cup my face. It's hot, flushed. My coat has disappeared. I should be cold but adrenaline has me heated to a sweat.

Bryce inhales deeply then releases it in a dramatic whoosh.

"Abby and Sofia told me they asked you for permission to come play here," he says. "Abby claimed you said yes. I looked for you, but when I didn't see you I figured you'd already gone home." I just stare at him, trying to envision this scenario while making a willful effort to calm my nerves. "I didn't think anything of it until we got here. I bought Sofia a dollhouse and the kid's ran upstairs to play. I went to check on them and overheard them talking. Sofia was teaching Abby to say the word permission in French. Only then did it dawn on me that you might not have understood what she said if she asked you in French. Or that she might not have asked you at all." He stops for a moment, catching his breath. "I called you immediately and left a message."

He reaches out to me and I back up, banging into the wall. He flinches, his hand dropping to his side. "You have no idea how sorry I am."

"Abby . . ."

"Abby is fine. Come in and relax a moment." He motions for me to lead the way inside. "I don't think you should drive in this state."

I don't move. I hear the faint sounds of children laughing but fury has a hold of my muscles.

"I know it's no excuse," says Bryce, "but I am new at this play-date thing. Sofia said her father lets her play with Abby all the time, so I thought it was okay. She begged to have Abby over to see her new dollhouse. You should see it. It's cute. It's got windows and these little wooden shutters that open and close, and a doorbell that chimes."

I stare at him.

"She was beside herself with excitement, and I got caught in the moment, totally losing my wits."

He attempts to take my hand but I pull away.

"I'm sorry," he says. "I never meant to scare you."

"I should have you arrested."

Bryce just looks away, obviously crushed.

I'm wrapped like a mental patient in a straitjacket, arms clinging to my chest, hands in fists so tight my knuckles are white. How appropriate. I draw a gust of air then hesitate for a moment, counting to ten.

Okay, I have control, I think. I lead the way into the kitchen, bypassing Bryce's hand still floating midair.

"I need to speak to Abby," I say. The oven's heat reaches out to touch me as I pass. The smell of roasting poultry fills the room, but short of a dirty pot soaking in the sink, the kitchen is spotless.

"Of course." Bryce attempts to draw my eyes. "May I suggest you take a moment first? You could blow any minute."

I glare at him, rage bubbling to the surface.

"See," he says, my instant indignation proving his point.

"You took my daughter."

He frowns. "Let me get you a glass of wine. It'll help calm your nerves."

He escapes through the double doors.

My ears prick at a muffled voice. I raise my chin to the ceiling, my mind's eye spying Abby through layers of plaster and flooring. That little lady is in big trouble.

Bryce enters the room with two glasses of white wine.

"My nerves are shot as well," he says, raising a glass. His jaw muscles twitch. "I've never had a woman storm my house, guns blazing."

He presents me with a glass. I don't move so he places it on the granite beside me. He takes a swig and sighs, allowing me my silence.

The quiet grants me the chance to conduct a physical assessment. Stress has knotted my muscles into thick clumps that ache with the slightest of movements and a raging headache assaults my sinuses. My temper has subsided leaving an empty cavern that quickly fills with humiliation over my display of aggression. I lean forward, resting my forearms on the cool countertop. I close my eyes. Bryce allows me a moment, but his presence does strange things to my insides. My body pulls him in, an invisible array of connecting wires that feed off each other's energy. Even in the utter quiet, I sense him inching closer.

"Hey now, relax," he says, his voice a whisper.

The heat of his breath on my skin is euphoric. Gentle hands slide over my fists, their warmth alleviating tension. His fingers move in slow circles kneading taut skin and muscles, his chest rests against my back. A distant thought comes to me, foggy, something about another man, but serenity overwhelms my senses, forcing the images to dissolve into nothingness. Tranquility seeps from his body to mine, his existence coddling frayed nerve endings. I sink into him, resting the back of my head against his chin.

"Feel better now?" he asks.

I float within Bryce's personal space, the stone countertop absorbing anxiety through my flattened palms. "You have no idea what I was thinking."

"I might," he mumbles.

"I couldn't help but picture the worst. I thought I'd lost her. I thought someone had taken her. That I might never . . ."

"This is my fault. I'm so sorry. Please forgive me."

"Abby and I are going to have a serious talk about strangers."

I have no clue what I'm going to say. My mother's lectures usually had something to do with finding strangers to help me when she couldn't, not avoiding them.

Bryce's body deflates around me. "I'm not a stranger, Tess."

He's right, he's not. But what is he exactly?

"I would never intentionally hurt you or Abby," he says, pain entwined in every word. "Please tell me you know this."

I don't know how or why but I know this to be true. It's a feeling from deep within my belly, a quiet, content feeling. I didn't realize I was still holding tension, but it releases and I ease back the last bit into Bryce's embrace. He lowers his head to my collarbone and rests his lips on my skin. It should feel intimate, too intimate, but it just feels natural, his breath warm and welcome. His hands gently grip my waist and in one fluid motion I'm turned and lifted, effortlessly, into a sitting position on the counter. My body tucks into his like a puzzle piece. We're silent for a while, both of us taking quiet, controlled breaths.

Now, face-to-face, I can see silver sparks dance in his eyes. They're beautiful, intoxicating, but not real. I'm about to say something but the subtle texture of his hand cradling my face brings thought to an abrupt halt. A stray tear slides down my cheek only to be caught by his caressing thumb. Exhaustion takes over my body, and my limbs feel too heavy to hold up. More tears follow the contours of my face, gathering at the base of my chin. Bryce wipes the collection with the back of his hand. His eyes lock on my wet lips. He leans in, softly gliding his lips over mine. The sensation draws my breath and he pulls back slightly, just enough for me to witness his mesmerizing silver-gray eyes.

I think he expects me to pull away but my body is paralyzed

and I have no desire to move. This is all so new, yet familiar, like I've kissed these lips for a lifetime. I close my eyes, allowing other senses to govern my emotions. I take in the smell of wine on his breath, the feel of his hands on my lower back. I swear I can hear his heart pound through his shirt.

Bryce's lips touch mine again, not really kissing, just sliding, tasting. His hand inches up my spine before becoming tangled in the hair at the nape of my neck. I'm torn between leaning into his mouth and surrendering to his hand. His breath catches and his lips follow the line of my jaw, dusting my ear. My head falls back, yielding of its own free will. The heat from his mouth makes me dizzy.

I can hear . . . what is that . . .?

Footsteps and laughter resonate off the walls, coming down the stairwell toward us.

Bryce's body stiffens, hand dropping to the counter with a thud.

Abby bounds into view having passed over the bottom step entirely, and Sofia tumbles to fall in line beside her, both girls taking in our intimate stance, tension filling the air like a sentient being.

The cloak of serenity is suddenly gone, and I recall why we're here.

"Time to go," I say, pushing Bryce away and sliding from the counter.

"Mom—"

"Not a word." I grab Abby, steering her toward the exit.

Bryce paces forward, not blocking my way but positioning himself to get my attention. "Please stay," he says. "Join us for dinner."

Anger is returning with a vengeance, so I need to leave before I do or say something I'll regret. Bryce is no good for me, or

Abby, and this fiasco only proves it. I escort Abby down the hall to the foyer where a quick scan shows no sign of her coat or boots. I lift her into my arms, throw open the door, and barge down the steps.

The crisp air bites but I barely feel a thing. I'm numb, confused.

Not another word is spoken . . . to Bryce or Sofia.

# TALK TO ME

## New Year's Eve

**I** tuck Abby into bed, give Grams and Gramps a kiss goodnight, and hop into the taxi. Covering my bases, I hand the driver a ten before confessing our destination. Cabbies don't like coming so far out of the city for such a small fare and ten dollars is generous considering the fare won't be much more than two. Still, the driver gets pissy when I tell him the address of the party and that it's technically eight houses down the street.

"The houses are far apart and nothing but acres of snow, dirt, and tree debris lies between them. To walk in the dark would be downright dangerous," I explain.

He thinks I can trek the distance and is still idling in my driveway when I show him my Jimmy Choo red satin heels.

"Lady—"

"Cops found a dead woman around the corner less than a week ago. Unless you plan to drag my ass from your cab, I suggest you drive because I am not walking."

This shuts him up.

Every New Year's Eve Karen and her husband throw a memorable bash. Well, Karen does. Her husband sulks in the corner nursing a gin and tonic while the hostess directs the festivities herself. I had wondered if Karen would cancel this year's celebration due to Sonia's murder investigation, but apparently the show really does go on and life resumes for the living. Even so, my attendance was in question until Karen called pleading. "You absolutely must come," she said. "This is what friends do, they show up." I wasn't really in the mood for a party, but as far as friends go, Karen has been a good one, so I agreed to be there for her. "Besides," she said, "if your best friends don't show for your party, what does that say about you?"

Karen's house is more of an estate. Not quite the size and grandeur of Bryce's or several others in Carlisle, but large enough to deserve the title. A winding driveway lined with cedars ends at two stories of sand-gray brick and over six thousand square feet of designer style. Everything inside, outside, and around Karen's house is the best. She has a world famous interior designer on retainer and a budget that allows her to purchase almost anything she wants. And she does just that.

I leave the driver with little fanfare and make my way to the front door, unlocked and labeled with a sign that reads, *Party's here, come on inside!* The glass dining room table is covered with coats and more hang on chairs. The credenza holds a smorgasbord of party favors, the gold and silver tiara's glittering in the candlelight. I add my coat to the pile and knowing my way around Karen's house, head for the living room.

The place is packed.

"Nice turnout," I say, sliding in beside the hostess.

Karen shrieks, throwing her arms around me for a hug. Her gown is emerald stones, to die for, the color making her dyed auburn locks pop.

"Chickpea," she says, "you sure you're going to be okay with the men here?"

"The men" would be Bryce and Thomas. Karen invited them

weeks ago, long before the games. I don't foresee a problem. I've had a reconciliation of sorts with Bryce, the kid thief, and Thomas the liar, well, if he shows I'll avoid heavy conversation, saving it for a more appropriate time and place.

"I'll be fine." I pump my biceps.

Karen laughs. My arms are quite puny. And apparently useless, considering I was putty in Bryce's hands only hours ago.

"You show'em, girl." She points to the kitchen. "I gotta check on the servers. Mingle and let me know if anyone looks bored."

I make my way over to Karen's husband. Frank is perched on a stool in the far corner of the room, four feet of empty space around him.

"Hey, Frank. Thought I'd come say hello."

Frank raises his glass and flashes a smirk that leaves his face faster than a mouse sprints from a snake. I don't take it personally. "Sorry to hear about Meyer," he mumbles. His glass turns in his hand, ice cubes spinning round and round, jingling as they go.

"Me too," I say, opting for diplomacy.

Time ticks in slow motion. I stand in silence, picking invisible dust bunnies off my dress. The only thing Frank and I have in common is Karen, and history has proven Karen isn't a topic Frank participates in. I scan the crowd and recognize Frank's ex-wife, Felisha. I smile to myself. Karen likes Felisha, sometimes more than she likes Frank, and invites her to every social function just to piss him off.

"Why don't I refill that drink?" I finally say to Frank, itching to abort.

Frank gives me his glass and what might be a genuine smile.

The bar is a wall-to-wall make-your-own, fully stocked, with most bottles sporting pewter pour spouts. Like a mad scientist, I measure and mix the ingredients for my infamous Chocolate Monkey Martini. I'm in need of a buzz sweet enough to gulp. I'm pouring gin into Frank's glass when I sense someone hovering behind me, radiating tension.

"It's a big house, Thomas. We'll talk another time."

"Thomas isn't here. He doesn't like—"

"Parties," I say, spinning to face Bryce. "What's wrong, why do you seem so . . . intense?"

"Do I?" He throws his shoulders back, lifts his chest.

"Puff up all you want, I can still read you like a book. Something is bothering you. It surrounds you like a black cloud. Are you worried about Thomas coming?"

"Thomas is a big boy. He can do as he pleases. I'm just a tad disturbed tonight. I don't want to talk about it now though." He grips the back of his neck. "You can really see that?" It's more of a statement than a question, and it causes him to put great effort into changing his demeanor. His facial features soften and a smile makes an appearance. He leans into me and my heart skips a beat at the thought of his touch.

Bad idea, bad idea, bad idea.

He halts mid-motion, thrusting his hands into his pockets.

"You look beautiful tonight," he says. "You remind me of Hekate, the queen of the night and goddess of witchcraft. Ancient myths tell of Hekate patrolling the frontier between life and death, her thigh-length hair flowing down an ebony gown made of coral."

I never know what to say when he talks like this, so I curtsy, holding the hem of my fire engine-red dress.

"I wasn't sure if sleepless nights and lack of iron go with retro chic." The low, scooped front gathers around my neck with braided straps. Very sixties. The dress makes me look classy yet sexy, but the holiday from hell has done a number on my hair and skin, so the dress is working on its own tonight.

"I love you in red, and gold, and black." His composure evaporates and his eyes drop to stare at my Jimmy Choos.

When has Bryce seen me in black? The red is this dress, and the gold was my costume for Halloween. I seldom wear black anymore, the widow thing and all.

"When have you seen me in black?"

"About the playdate earlier—"

"Abduction is more like it. 'Playdate' would suggest it was preapproved. And I'm still pissed at you."

"I should've done things differently, and I regret causing you to worry about your daughter's safety. Really."

My anger has long since lost its fizzle. Blushing, I recall the intimacy of his apology and my response to it. Forgiveness was granted, I suppose.

"You and Abby gave me the scare of a lifetime, but I'm over it. Abby and I had a long talk, and she won't be leaving my side anytime soon."

Until she's forty.

"I've learned my lesson as well. Felines come for their kittens nails out and teeth bared."

"Ya, well, take my kid and you'll feel the wrath of the hunter." I squint in an attempt to appear menacing. "That isn't why you're agitated, is it?"

"No." He moves closer, a rogue smile toys with his lips, his bravado having found its way home. "Hmm, I like it when you fret over me." The sparkle, the dashing silver I've come to appreciate, slowly ignites his pupils.

"Why so stressed then?" I ignore the way my body responds to his mischief.

He waves, whisking the question away. "I've decided to focus on you this evening. To let trouble fade into the darkness for one night."

Well, that's good, because I've got questions.

"You'll need a drink," I say, showcasing the array of bottles. "What's your vice? A Chocolate Monkey Martini might do the trick."

"Four shots of liquor is three too many. I'm not much of a drinker."

"How could you possibly know how many shots go into a—"

"Maybe I was watching you create your concoction." He points to my martini glass and peeks over my shoulder. "Any red wine here?"

I eye him suspiciously, uncorking a bottle of wine. "Maybe, Mr. Waters, you can tell me how you know what you know while I pour your wine." I expertly navigate the bottle from his grasp.

He smirks. "An artist who knows her way around a bar."

"An education isn't cheap. I worked nights at a club."

I also lived there for a time. The club owner let me stash my stuff and study during the day while the club was closed and quiet.

"Ah. I was trying to find an artist. Had I known to look for a barmaid, I would have found you sooner."

Although I'm sure Bryce's lines are well rehearsed, I have to admit I like this side of him. I can see how a woman could fall for his charms. I, on the other hand, am privy to the wily ways of a man on the prowl.

"You'll have to excuse me," I say, raising the glass of gin and tonic. "An interrogation is forthcoming. First this barmaid needs to make a delivery."

Bryce nods and smiles as I breeze past him in search Dr. Social.

A minute later there is a light tug on my elbow as I pass a group of people talking in a circle.

"Have you seen anyone not having a good time?" Karen asks.

"Does your husband count?" I tease.

"Is he still sulking?"

"Not for long." I raise the G&T and Karen frowns.

"After you've sated Frank, make rounds, will you, Chickpea? I need help steering conversations toward topics less gruesome. Police have been scouring the area for days, and the residents have their knickers in knots." She sips her martini. "Dreadful this girl was killed, but ruining a perfectly good New Year's party isn't going to bring her back."

"You are obnoxious," I say with a smile. Karen is as distressed by Sonia's death as everyone else in this town. I know because we've talked about it. "Just give me a minute with Frank, then I'll do my best."

Karen blows me a kiss, waving me away.

When my second attempt at a conversation with Frank fails miserably, I down my martini and follow Karen's instructions, socializing with the townspeople present. Bryce has disappeared and Karen is right, the mood is tense, most talking about Sonia's murder.

My first steps into the kitchen reveal a tight-knit group of local landscapers, headed by Manny and Loraine Capore. Apparently Sonia's body was found on their land and someone suggested a monument be raised on the site. I hover on the verge of the circle listening to varying arguments. Most think the idea has merit but aren't willing to fork over the funds to create such a memorial.

The woman standing beside Mr. Jenkins is the cousin to the owner of Smith's Funeral Home in the city. It's suggested she solicit her cousin for a freebie. The woman fidgets, obviously uneasy with the suggestion, until the Capore's lodge their complaint. They are sorry Sonia was killed but they don't really want a monument on their land. Loraine steps into the circle, her face and neck several shades of flustered. She doesn't want to be reminded of the dead body every time she steps out her front door. Who would? The entire group falls quiet, obviously ruffled.

This is my cue. I slide between Mr. Simpson and Mr. Capore, displaying a red satin stiletto in a way that hikes my hemline and calls attention to my long legs. It's an attention-grabbing trick I've learned serving drinks to the intoxicated, and works every time.

"Hey, guys, gals, hope everyone is having a good time," I say, smiling. "I'm thinking of taking my daughter to Disney World this week. It'll be our first time there. Any recommendations?"

I'm grateful that this is all it takes. Instantly the group, obviously relieved to be presented with a topic change, begins reminiscing about family trips to Florida, comparing notes and making suggestions. The discussion quickly takes on a life of its own, venturing from Disney to fantastical holiday destinations, and before making a clean escape, I take one last look at my handiwork. The group is no longer gloomy but roused and enthusiastic. I smile and duck from the circle, in need of a bathroom break.

Only a few steps down the hall, I'm forced to stop in my tracks. The obstruction is solid man.

"Talk to me," Thomas says.

I try to squeeze past him.

"I thought you hated parties."

He blocks my way.

"I came to see you. To get you to talk to me."

"This isn't the time, Thomas."

"When is? And why not now?" His voice is sad and pleading, but his stance is arrogant. "Were you gonna leave for Florida without talking to me?"

How the hell does he know I'm thinking about going to Florida?

"Were you listening in on my conversation? I can go anywhere I want without your approval, Thomas. Besides, I don't recall participating in Belize plans, so who are you to talk?"

"I didn't mean you need my permission, and I left to allow you time to grieve. I left for you, because I thought it was what you needed, not because I didn't want to be here." He folds his arms across his chest and leans against the wall, blocking my path. "Please talk to me. I'm going crazy without you."

I feel sorry for him. For a moment. Until my hibernating anger bubbles to the surface.

"What do you want me to say, Thomas? Why don't you talk to your brother? You know, the guy who lives a few blocks over? Sofia's uncle?"

He rubs his eyes. "I want you to say you understand. I want you forgive me. I want you to say you miss me too."

I search aimlessly for the words to describe how I feel. Do I understand? Sort of, I guess. Thomas's reaction the night of the pageant, though possessive and aggressive and not a response I condone, was obviously a character flaw that Thomas has difficulty controlling. This doesn't mean I like those qualities, just that I can see how they can exist. He is a liar, yes, but has part of me already forgiven him? I know I'm not willing to ruin Abby's friendship with Sofia over this. But I can't deny that the side of Thomas I saw that night changed my feelings toward him. Did I miss him? Hmm, I don't think so. But I've been deep in holiday grief and shock over Sonia's death to feel much else.

"I would do anything to bring us back to the way we were before that night," he says, studying me. "Abby and Sofia are close, and we could have something . . ." His voice fades, resolving not to go there.

He's still after his happily-ever-after.

I juggle conflicting responses. As much as I hate to admit it, my entire being yearns for a man to hold, a father for Abby, and more children. I want a baby kicking inside me, a child shared with someone I love. But is that someone Thomas? I look into his eyes, which are dark gray at the moment, trying to find my place in them.

The words tumble without a conscious decision to speak.

"I wouldn't live walking distance from my own flesh and blood and not be on speaking terms. I wouldn't deny my daughter a relationship with her uncle when it doesn't suit my purpose. And I sure as hell wouldn't use fists to vent my frustrations." I don't let his tortured demeanor stop me. "We make choices, Thomas. This life offers us one chance to make a difference and experience love and you're throwing it away. Take it from me, someone who would give anything for a family, there isn't a reason big enough."

I step closer. "Still, I treasure you and want you in my life." Thomas looks hopeful, and I cringe at the thought of my next words hitting him hard. "As a friend. I forgive the person you are because I care for you. And I acknowledge that, as a friend, your choices might not be the same as mine. But that's where it ends."

Surrender hits his eyes and his shoulders slump.

"Tess, I know we can—"

"I hope you find your happily-ever-after, Thomas. I really do. But I doubt you'll find it in me."

Thomas bolts upright, the movement so fast I barely see it. One minute he's leaning on the wall and the next he's looming over me.

"You can't want him," he says, seething.

"I can want anyone I choose, Thomas."

"He'll hurt you."

"How is that, Thomas? Will he spew mythical rhetoric until I pass out? Flatter me to pieces?"

"Open your eyes, Tess. And close your legs."

I gasp.

Son of a bitch!

Not about to be bullied, I scramble for a retort to hurl but don't get the chance. One second Thomas is standing in front of me, the next he's gone.

Lucky for him.

# INSANITY

The clock ticks while I make my way around the room, chatting with friends. Bryce is nowhere within sight and Thomas, I assume, has left. To dilute outrage over my confrontation with Thomas, I've downed another three martinis and am on the verge of making a beeline to the bar for another when a set of large hands casually rest on my hips.

"Hey you," Bryce whispers.

His breath warms my ear.

"Hey you back."

I lean into him, feeling his muscles through my dress. He smells amazing.

All my thoughts, all my worries, even the curiosities I'd been pondering evaporate to nothing of consequence. The air between us thins until all that is left is an energy snapping from his body to mine, releasing gravity's hold.

Something has changed; something about Bryce is different. He always stays an appropriate, almost careful distance from me in public and his hands are usually behind his back or in his pockets. And what would have been a simple touch with little meaning had it come and gone in a fleeting moment, instead lingers until it feels like much more.

Still, I don't move and neither does he. Lost in this connection I forget about time, place, about the circle of people around us.

A familiar voice pierces our bubble and we both jump.

"Most murders are committed by someone the victim knows, someone close," says Thomas, glaring over my shoulder at Bryce. "I heard you were close with Sonia MacKinnen."

Bryce clears his throat, removing his hands from my hips. "You are not helping your case, Thomas."

"You attract trouble. Had you stayed away—from Sonia that is—trouble wouldn't have come to this small town."

The crowd's gaze darts from Bryce to Thomas, surprised by the sudden friction. Some realize this isn't heading anywhere good and slink away in search of a less hostile environment. Curiosity gets the better of the few remaining and they hover to watch the show.

"I met Sonia once," says Bryce. "I was at the restaurant where she worked. I was—"

"Picking her up. Typical Bryce style, of course. You have a way with the ladies. She went home with you, right? And then what?"

What the hell?

"Suggesting Bryce was involved in Sonia's murder is pretty dark, Thomas," I say.

"You have no idea what my brother is capable of."

Bryce turns me, gently, drawing my attention. "Tess, Thomas knows I had nothing to do with Sonia's death. I was at the restaurant waiting for him. I asked him to meet so we could talk, work out our differences, but he never showed. Sonia was drunk and—"

"All over you, no doubt."

"Thomas, you shouldn't—"

"No, Tess, you shouldn't. You need to know what you're getting yourself into."

"Yes, she does," says Bryce, calm and controlled. "I've been telling you that for—"

"That is not what I mean, Bryce. I don't want that shit here." He moves closer. "Keep your mouth shut."

"Thomas—"

"She needs to be warned," Thomas grumbles, a finger in Bryce's face. "She needs to know you haven't had a relationship outlast a season. And that you'll crawl under another skirt the minute you're bored."

Bryce steps forward, guarded. "You are way over the line and you know it."

"I'll cross countless boundaries to keep her away from you."

"You need to stop."

Thomas sneers. "Worried she'll realize you're a player? That you wine, dine, and—"

"If you care about her at all you'll stop right now," says Bryce, suddenly cross.

"Man, you two really know how to clear a room," says Karen from the doorway. She's clearly displeased.

I sweep the perimeter. A few spectators loiter in corners, eagerly waiting fists to fly.

"I'm sorry, Karen."

"I don't blame you," Karen says, placing a pity pat on my arm. "But you two . . ." Her irate eyes drill *the men*. "Get control over yourselves. You fight like toddlers but with much higher stakes. Now, I don't know what this argument was about," she pauses, looking at me, "but I'm sure it could've been conducted with more respect to the guests in this house."

"You're right, Karen. I apologize," says Bryce. "We should go."

Bryce reaches for my hand and Thomas, moving like

lightning, swipes him away.

"Thomas! What has gotten into you?" I say, astonished.

Bryce stands tall. "That is enough."

"I should say so," says Karen.

My head starts to pound. "No more," I mumble. "I'm heading home."

Karen wraps an arm around my waist. "You don't have to leave."

"I do," I say, glancing at Bryce. "And I'll call a cab."

I leave all three of them in the almost empty living room and slam the front door behind me.

**Minutes later, I'm** pacing on Karen's porch, vigorously rubbing my arms, cursing my impulse to flee.

"I cannot believe that man," I grumble.

My breath billows in the night air. I left without my coat and didn't bring my cell to call a ride, but I refuse to go back in there. I'll wait out here all night if I have to. I stare into the darkness, contemplating the atrocities my satin shoes would endure if I were to attempt the hike on foot. "Eventually someone has to leave this party," I say, looking at my Jimmy Choos, "and when they do, we'll catch a ride."

"Are you talking to your shoes?"

I look up and see Bryce. He's three feet away with my coat folded over one arm.

"Don't judge me." I attempt to grab my coat but he swings it out of reach and points his chin at my hands. Surrender comes quickly. I'm freezing. I sigh and slide into warm sleeves. "How did you know which coat was mine?"

"Karen. She would have come out here herself, but she didn't want to leave Thomas and me alone." He brushes the hair from my face and places a silver tiara on my head. "She asked Thomas to wait inside while I check on you. Actually, asked is a nice way to put it. That woman has claws. She told Thomas if he took one step out this door she would tell the entire population of Carlisle he has a temper problem and cannot be trusted."

The night air nips my skin so I retreat into my coat, bundling tight. I study Bryce's face. His chiseled features are accentuated by the glow of the porch lamp, and I'd be rapt if not for the absence of silver in his eyes. The sizzle is gone. He's worried about his brother.

"She wouldn't do that you know. Karen. She's all talk."

"I know. I doubt Thomas will take any chances though. Besides, he knows he needs to chill."

Bryce reaches out, the tips of his fingers touching the wool collar of my coat. His gaze follows his fingers down my front. I swallow and a ball of air idles in my throat. He slips a finger into a buttonhole and pulls me to him. I ricochet softly off his chest, coming to a standstill against him, staring into his eyes. So close.

"You are always running out on me," he murmurs, finger still holding tight to my coat. Tiny silver flecks shimmer in his eyes, fading in from a distance.

Chemicals churn in my head and blood pumps to my mouth, making my lips tingle.

Bryce grins, smug. He tugs my arms free and my coat falls open. With concentrated motions he pulls the top button through the hole then slowly works his way down my coat, the quintessential gentleman.

"I'm sorry you had to see that. Thomas and me at odds, again." His stare hasn't wandered from his fingers holding me captive. "It wasn't always like this, Thomas and I. No matter what he says or does, I will not leave him to fight his demons alone. Not this time." He sighs, gently leaning his forehead to mine. "Are you all right?"

I am now. Perfect, I'd say, other than my cold hands with nowhere to hide. This coat has no pockets.

Bryce takes my hands in his, squeezing them flat between his palms. Heat soaks deep, warming my bones.

"I wish you and your brother would get along. I'd like to be friends with you both, but with fights breaking out at every turn you guys make it very difficult."

"I understand and I'm sorry."

"I am as well," says Thomas, standing coatless in the snow. Footprints behind him lead to the back gate.

The cold penetrates my hands floating in midair, suddenly unattended. I don't know if it's the crisp night or the quiet hum of hydro wires but something has made the atmosphere stable and serene. I look back and forth, between the two men, taking in their altered states. They seem to converse with their eyes, a sibling talent no doubt, but a discussion I'm not privy to. I dread the same argument, the same accusations being rehashed, so I say the first thing to come to mind.

"I can't stand out here and not think of Sonia lying in drifts, freezing to death, only a couple of houses down. I hope he killed her before he left her in the snow. I can imagine the hell she went through."

Both Thomas and Bryce abandon their stance to gape at me, their expressions making further explanation a must. "I have vivid nightmares. Have my whole life. I've been brutally beaten and left for dead more times than I can count. I know what it felt like for her."

I search Bryce's face hoping to find reassurance that my confession hasn't pegged me a psychotic freak, but he just stares. I try to backpedal, to lighten the mood. "Hopefully it was painless and she didn't know what was coming. Maybe it was a vampire," I say in jest.

Thomas and Bryce flinch in unison but neither utter a word.

"Will you two lighten up? I'm sorry. I know this is no laughing matter. I really do hope they find who did this to her." The solemn vibe has taken on a life of its own, thick and heavy, pulling me down like quicksand.

Bryce steps back to better view my face in the light. "Vampire? What makes you think Sonia was killed by a vampire?"

Shit. Why did a vampire come to mind? The guy in the café came to mind, the thing with the girl in his arms, but I hadn't thought of him as a vampire before.

"I don't know. I haven't been myself lately." I think up a lie real quick. "I'm reading a vampire book and it's got me seeing vampires in my dreams," I pause, wondering if I should let go of the precipice I'm hanging from. "And at the cafe." I chuckle then stifle it with a cough.

Bryce lowers his head to gaze directly into my eyes, but I'm so embarrassed I look away. I peer out into the yard in time to see Thomas turn around, hands entwined in his hair.

"Please look at me," Bryce begs. Even though his voice is delicate and soothing, I can't bring myself to move. He draws close, his breath warming my scalp. "Have you seen something, someone who reminds you of a vampire, here in town?"

"Seriously, guys, this is stupid. Go back to fighting. Stop freaking me out."

The men glare at each other. Minutes pass as I watch them locked in an unspoken argument, their body language disclosing some of the tension but none of the facts.

"Leave her out of this," Thomas huffs.

"If she saw him, maybe he saw her," Bryce snaps back.

Again, two sets of eyes penetrate my shield of self-preservation. Breath comes in spurts and my chest aches, experiencing some sort of panic attack. I showcase a pathetic smile, striving to look like I get the joke.

"Tess, it's very important you tell me what you've seen," says Bryce.

I know he's referring to my vision in the café, but I'm not willing to play their game or pretend any of this is real. I look to Thomas for help.

"None of it is real," he says. "You've lost your husband. You are under a lot of stress."

Bryce glowers at Thomas, a rare show of ire that catches me by surprise. When his attention returns his countenance is new, resolved, as if he's decided to ignore Thomas altogether.

"Please tell me what you saw in the coffee shop," he says, resting his fingertips on my cheeks.

"Don't touch her," growls Thomas.

Bryce groans, dropping his hands to his sides. "Trust me," he whispers, his breath swirling in a ray of porch light.

Trust him . . . with my secrets . . . The truth collides with lies in my head as I struggle to find solid ground in a landscape where I'm released from gravity. Do I entrust Bryce with my private delusions, my lapse from reality?

"I, ah . . . I was waiting in line to get a caramel brownie for Karen . . ."

"Where? Where were you?"

"At a café downtown, the new one next door to that fancy spa." Reluctance overthrows my attempt at disclosure and I stop, picking at a button on my coat. Do I really want to publicize my insanity? I take a deep breath. "He was leaning on a stool by the front window."

"What did he look like? Had you seen him before?"

"No. I've seen many things but nothing quite like him."

Bryce's eyes push for more.

"Well, he was a big guy. Muscular I mean. Dark skinned, strange tattoos covering most of his body." I hesitate, waiting for them to notice I've mentioned physical details without alluding to clothing. "His hair was black, shoulder length, and curly. I didn't see much of his face at first. He was making out with—"

"There was a woman with him!" Bryce roars, losing all composure.

Thomas's hands fly to his head again, his feet pacing in nervous circles that throw snow into mini drifts.

"I don't understand why you guys are freaking out. It was a figment of my imagination. A daydream. A vision. I was the only one to see them, and Karen was standing right beside me!"

Thomas speaks through clenched teeth. "Did he see you?"

"No . . . yes . . . maybe. I don't know!" My head is spinning. "He just looked at me and snarled."

Thomas: "Fuck."

Bryce: "What did you do?"

"When I looked back he was gone, my daydream was over. There was a guy who looked like him, sort of, but he walked out and down the street. So I left the café with Karen."

"And the woman? The one with him," Bryce urges.

"They were both gone."

"What makes you think he was a vampire?"

"I don't. Or didn't. I don't know. He didn't have two pointy teeth like you see in movies. His set was needle thin and sharp. He didn't have red eyes or white skin and there wasn't any blood. I'm not sure why a vampire came to mind. You can't possibly think that what I saw that day was real, can you?"

"Don't you dare, Bryce," warns Thomas.

Bryce looks at me, his expression professional, calculated.

"Remember what I told you on Halloween? Vampires are not the creatures embellished by generations of storytellers. In fact, most vampire stories are birthed from mermaid mythology. Current day vampire and mermaid tales stem from ancient folklore describing demons that siphoned souls, robbing the living of their energy, aura, or chi. Over the years, blood was dubbed one's lifeline, one's essence, spurring the notion that these demons sucked blood. Nothing could be further from the truth. They are people, humans, souls of a different time, an ancient era. They are old souls who have forgotten their purpose, lost their grip on humanity."

I'm lost and this charade is getting more ludicrous by the minute.

"You think he was a mermaid?"

"A lost soul. His tattoos, did they depict water?"

"Yeah. But he had legs."

"Myths, Tess. Fairies, vampires, witches, mermaids, they are all but tidbits of facts from a time long before the written word. Witches are just people capable of tapping into natural psychic abilities. Mermaids were human beings who adapted to aquatic life when the alternative was death. And vampires are nothing but manifestations of ancient folklore retold in a gothic age. All are human beings with old souls. Lost souls."

"Fuck, Bryce, no more," Thomas yells from across the yard. "You're gonna scare the shit out of her!"

"She needs to learn, Thomas, you know that. You of all people know that."

My whole body starts to tremble.

"He was real?" I gag on the word, "Alive?"

"Nothing dead walks," says Bryce. "But real isn't the right way to put it. Lost souls are just people, alive and real as you and me. Only their souls are tainted, marred, angry. And you can see the soul within."

"No more!" barks Thomas. His long legs make quick strides across the lawn.

A wave of nausea crashes over me and I shake my head, trying to dislodge images from the café. That man, that thing, was someone's soul? How is that possible? What does that mean? And why is my body reacting this way? Why am I not laughing like this is all a big joke? Why do I feel, deep in my marrow, that this is a truth I've known all along? My forehead rolls against the rough stone of the house while voices argue around me. I've had too much to drink, that's it. Stress combined with alcohol has pushed my imagination into overdrive. I need to go home. When I wake this will have been a weird dream, an evening of comical admissions said on an alcoholic high and quickly forgotten.

"I think I'm gonna hurl."

"You'll be all right," whispers Bryce.

Thomas reaches for me. "She will if you leave her alone!"

The door flies open, almost hitting me, and a large man in a navy suit steps out. "The party is inside, people!" he bellows, spitting a cloud of stale booze and cigarettes. More people file out and Bryce adopts a protective front as the group links arms for the icy trip down the walkway. They're drunk, stumbling, and obviously couples, the last stopping every few steps to kiss.

"It's midnight folks," the man in the overcoat sings. "Another year has arrived!"

About time. I really need a new year. The last one sucked. And frankly, this is a crappy start to a new one.

I watch the couples stumble toward the taxi and realize a moment too late that I just missed a ride.

"We can't talk about this here," Bryce mumbles in my ear.

"I've had too much to drink." I swear my words are slurred.

They must be slurred.

"How many martinis did I have? I think I had three or four. Maybe five. Over the course of hours. That's enough to feel tipsy but not so loaded that I . . . I'm drugged! Oh my God, that's it! Someone slipped something in my drink!"

Bryce shakes his head. "The martinis aren't helping, but you are not drugged."

"Maybe you are," says Thomas, "and you'll wake recalling nothing but a foggy hallucination."

"Thomas," grumbles Bryce.

"Don't Thomas me. She can ignore all this shit."

"How's that working for you?"

Thomas leers. "She can go back to the way things were."

"She can't and you know it."

"Bullshit."

Bryce taps his thigh with his knuckles. "You are not helping."

"Didn't say I would, Brother. I don't want you teaching her anything. Leave her alone."

"She is stronger than you—"

"Enough," I cry out. "If I have to spend one more second in this cold, I'm going to pass out. I'm going home."

I wobble down the stairs, my equilibrium and heels working against me.

Bryce takes my arm. "I'll drive you," he says. "Get some sleep and we'll talk tomorrow."

"I don't want you telling her *anything*," yells Thomas, following us down the walkway.

"Too bad. He's seen her."

"He got what he wanted and left. There is no reason for him to stick around."

Bryce pauses, supporting my weight while he turns to

Thomas. "Call a cab, walk, drive, but go home. There is nothing we can do or say in the middle of the night that will make a difference. We'll deal with this later."

At least a foot of crisp night air separates our bodies as we amble down the path.

Thomas swears under his breath and stomps up the steps, slamming the front door.

I shudder.

Bryce sighs.

# INNATE NEED

## January 4th

*Think of the devastation caused by the bombing of Hiroshima, 2004's Indian Ocean tsunami, and Cyclone Nargis. Now imagine bombs the size of Texas, tsunamis bigger than Mount Everest, and volcanic ash that has the entire planet in darkness, all happening at the same time, on every continent. Total annihilation. If this really happened at any point in Earth's history it would be clear why mankind's past is shrouded in mystery. And yet it has. We know it has.*

*Forgotten History Magazine*: Archeological Finds Baffle Scientists

These are really quite comical.

The plane hits a turbulence pocket, almost knocking my cell from my grasp. "Look at this one," I say, "you have spit coming out the side of your mouth." I laugh and Abby giggles.

"I didn't like that ride. The spinning made my tummy hurt."

"Well, those ones can do that to you," I say. "The loud music didn't help. The pizza, candy apple, and ice-cream probably didn't help either." Abby squirms as I yank a pigtail. "Check out

Gramps's chair, it looks like it should tip with all those bags hanging off the back."

Abby huddles close, inspecting the photo on my cell. "That one is funny. Grams has her hat on backwards." She leaves tiny fingerprints on the screen.

Abby adjusts her blanket, long limbs dangling awkwardly in the cramped space. Her eyes grow heavy, reflecting the sunset and cotton candy clouds. Someone close has a serious case of body odor. I adjust the air knob above Abby's head and breathe through my mouth.

I skim through countless pictures of our day at Animal Kingdom, Magic Kingdom, and Grams and Gramps's place, pulling the camera closer to examine Gramps. I'm shocked to spot the differences between my mind's perception of him and the real-life man everyone else sees, the man the camera reveals. Where is the pride in his posture? Why are those piercing blue eyes sunken, surrounded by wrinkles I haven't seen before?

Tears well, blurring the view.

Our time here, our very existence, is so limited. A lifetime is nothing but the tiniest of blips in mankind's storyline. For all our endeavors, all our accomplishments, what will be remembered? What do we know about Mesopotamian lovers, Sumerian geniuses, or Minoan trailblazers? History is a fickle beast, mutating with changes in culture, politics, and religion. What's it all for? Why do we exist? What is our purpose, and do we even have one?

A steward hovers to my left, smiling. Her twisted skirt and stained blouse confess to hours of doting on the impatient and nauseated. "Miss, you and your daughter will need to raise your seats. We'll be landing soon."

Life, this is why we don't know and don't care about our history, our purpose. We are swallowed by the mere effort it takes to get through everyday tasks, to survive. We breathe, eat, work, sleep, who has time to contemplate why?

I unfurl Abby's blanket and dab her chin with my shirtsleeve. "Abby, baby, we're home."

Abby approaches consciousness gradually, reassembling body parts from disjointed positions.

The landing is uneventful, and before long we're stretching in front of a circular baggage belt. My simple black case marked by a bright orange ribbon tumbles down the chute followed by Abby's Barbie suitcase. We extend the handles, steady the wheels, and take off in search of a cab heading west. We're following taxi icons through a maze of hallways, bodies, and luggage, when I navigate to the left and behold a different kind of sign.

I stop short.

"Thought you might need a lift," says Bryce, thrusting his fists into jean pockets. His coat is on the floor, propped against the wall, and his hair is slightly disheveled. Something foreign lingers in his eyes, something that worries me immensely.

"We were about to catch a cab."

"Well, now you don't have to." His gaze pans to Abby.

Something is wrong and whatever it is, it's not for Abby's ears.

"All right," I say, my reluctance visible. "Thanks."

Bryce takes our suitcases and leads the way to the underground parking garage. He is a catalog of tense body parts, so I follow a few steps behind holding tight to Abby's hand. In my head I rekindle thoughts that have plagued me for days.

New Year's Eve, after crawling into bed exhausted, I lay staring at the ceiling. I should have felt anxious, confused, maybe even afraid, but I didn't feel any of those things. In fact, every inch of me was overwhelmed with a sense of relief.

Everything was clear, as if I'd discovered a reclusive part of myself, a knowledge I'd always known existed but didn't accept or understand. My whole life I've seen unusual things. More so since Meyer's death. I've always pushed these things from rational thought. To do that, to ignore reality, was a lot of work. Discovering that my visions might have substance, that I'm not delusional, that I am not my mother, took a huge weight from my shoulders, and I slept like the dead.

The following morning was a whole different story. The full night of rest gave my common sense a chance to recoup. I recalled Bryce's words: myths, ancient souls, lost souls. But what are these things exactly? And this man, or soul, or whatever I saw—was he dangerous? And if he was, what was he doing to that woman? Was that woman Sonia? Why could I see them when others, obviously, could not? And why wasn't I scared? Or was I?

By breakfast, pandemonium overwhelmed logic, igniting an innate need to bolt. Abby and I were in Florida by noon.

"Are you getting in?" Bryce says, pulling me from my head.

I stand, lost in a stare of total appreciation while Bryce holds the door to a Porsche Panamera, a stunning four-door turbo with glowing aluminum rims and sleek headlights that scream, *get the hell out of my way.* If this is the car Bryce drove on New Year's Eve, I was either too drunk or too shocked to notice. I climb in.

This car doesn't drive; it soars.

The velvety texture of the leather seat and console distracts me while we ease onto the highway, but the allure dies when I'm hit with Bryce's tension, suffocating me like an avalanche.

"Are you okay?"

New Year's Day it was liberating to have someone know the inner rumblings of my psyche and not think I need medical care, but I fret about Bryce's sanity. How does he know these things? What more could he possibly tell me, and should I believe him? All the unusual things I've noticed about Bryce have filtered through my brain, fostering more questions. If those weren't optical illusions and mental lapses generated by my overstressed wits, what does that make him? Not normal, that's for sure. And should I trust him? My heart tugs from the inside out, insisting I should, but my head says run like hell.

"I didn't know you were leaving for Florida," says Bryce.

"Yet you managed to meet us at the airport, just as our flight landed."

I lower the window in spite of the brisk January bite, and the remainder of the thirty-minute drive is conducted in a charged silence.

At a fork in the road, just before the Carlisle Corner Store, Bryce turns left instead of right. Before I get the chance to protest he addresses Abby in the back seat. "Hey, kiddo, what do you say about a sleepover at my place with Sofia?"

Abby tosses the books aside, thrilled with the idea.

I'm livid.

"Excuse me, but I don't think you—"

"Please trust me," Bryce says softly. "Abby will have fun with Sofia and Nanna, and I've asked Clause to stay so they're not alone. You can collect Abby whenever you wish, but you need to believe me when I say she is better off at my house tonight."

Something about his expression scares me.

"Where is Thomas?"

"Out."

I look at my daughter, a restless ball of anticipation bouncing around the back seat.

"Okay," I say, and Abby squeals.

I trust Bryce. For some deeply embedded reason I can't peg,

my entire being believes he has Abby's best interest in mind.

Bryce pulls Abby's suitcase from the trunk while I walk her to the front door. Nanna introduces herself, obviously expecting our arrival, and Sofia locks arms with Abby, brimming with excitement. Nanna is older than I expected, almost Grams's age. She speaks with a heavy accent layered in obscure adjectives but her smile is infectious and she hugs me smelling of apple pie and cinnamon. I love her in an instant.

I plant a wet kiss on Abby's cheek. "I'll be back to get you first thing in the morning."

Abby tugs Sofia into the house before I can change my mind, and Nanna assures me my daughter is in good hands. Of this I have no doubt.

"I waited at the airport over six hours yesterday and five hours today." These are the first words out of Bryce's mouth when I sink back into the leather seat of his Porsche.

"Why?" My heart drums so loud it echoes in my ears.

"I didn't know when your flight came in. I didn't know this because I had no clue you'd left. I only found out when I dropped by your house to talk and discovered you were gone." His grip tightens around the steering wheel. "Karen said you took Abby to visit Meyer's grandparents, so I stalked every flight returning from Florida."

"Why would you do that? And why are you acting so strange?"

The car stops in my driveway and Bryce kills the engine before turning to speak to me, his stare aimed everywhere but my face. "I called you the morning after the party. I hoped you were able to get a reasonable night's sleep and would want to speak with me. You didn't return my calls."

"I didn't get the travel package on my cell."

He ignores me. "I stopped by your house to make sure you

were okay. You weren't home. I knew this because the front door was ajar, and worried about your safety, I went inside."

"Why would the door be open? I locked it and Karen—"

"Someone has broken into your house, Tess. It's quite a mess. And there's something else . . . ."

It takes four heartbeats to process his words. I leap from the car taking the walkway at a full run and skid to a halt at the front steps. Bryce is already there.

"How the hell did you—"

"I'm sorry," he mumbles, opening the door.

I gasp, dizzy, and step inside.

My living room couch is flipped onto its side and the coffee table is broken into several pieces, some strewn about the stairs. The Christmas tree Abby and I painstakingly decorated with precious ornaments lies flush with the floor, most of the decorations broken and scattered around the perimeter.

I'm numb from head to toe. The scene before me is incomprehensible, surreal. My body gravitates to the tree and I drop, groping for pieces of my life. The top half of my purple ballerina is crushed.

"Who would do this?" I mutter.

I stand in the center of my living room, turning in circles. Decorative pillows have been torn open. White feathers float on every surface, making the entire setting a demented outdoor wonderland. Plants are tipped over, dark soil offering a drastic contrast to the pristine down, and chips of pottery jut at odd angles. Pictures have been thrown about the room leaving broken glass in their wake and every wall naked. A cold breeze whips past. The window to my left is broken, a small puddle of melted snow curdling a semicircle of hardwood flooring and window trim.

I peer into the adjacent room. Food, dishes, and appliances

have been pulled out of every cupboard, smashed, and abandoned across the floor. Chairs are toppled over and several have streaks of what looks like mustard and salsa across them. There is no odor. It's too cold.

Bryce stands a few feet away, hunched. His every feature screams sorrow and concern as he watches me take in the destruction.

It is difficult to find the words to say or a train of thought to hold on to. I'm angry. I feel violated. I feel as if someone has ripped open my insides leaving me exposed and raw.

"What the hell happened here? It doesn't even look like anything was stolen. Who would do this? And where's Maxi?" I inhale sharply. The door to the mudroom hangs by a top hinge.

The mudroom. Where Maxi sleeps.

"Tess." Bryce stops me mid-lunge.

After a moment's hesitation, I rest a quivering hand in his, and he leads me through the chaos, toward the stairs. A glimpse of gold fur peeks out from behind the loveseat. My knees buckle and I sidestep until I hit the stairway and fall, clutching the railing with both hands.

"Is she . . .?"

"I'm so sorry."

The tears flow, fast and hot. I can't believe this.

"Poor Maxi. My baby girl, Abby," I whisper. I taste salt on my lips.

"I knew you wouldn't want her to see this."

"No. Absolutely not." Bryce backs away, giving me room to breathe. "What kind of person would do this?" I mutter, moving toward Maxi, to hold her.

Bryce stops me again, running a nervous hand through his hair like Thomas does.

"It could've been kids, restless teenagers out to cause

trouble."

His eyes say something altogether different.

"But you don't think so."

"Might have been random, but no, I don't think it was kids."

I study his face, my confusion escalating. "I don't understand."

Bryce sucks in a mouthful of air, his cheeks bulging like a chipmunk stuffed with nuts. The air finally escapes in a forced whistle.

"You keep running out on me," he says.

My stomach gathers into a tight ball and breathing becomes laborious. My body is preparing for an aftershock.

"I don't—"

"You are not ready for this, but you keep walking out on me and danger is close, so I have no choice." He rubs day-old stubble. "I can't help you, can't explain what you need to know, when you don't trust me."

"Danger? What danger? Should I be worried about the person or people who broke into my house? Will they come back?" I'm panicking now. "Is Abby safe?"

"Abby is fine." Bryce nods but looks away.

"Then what, what is it?"

"I think this break in has something to do with the lost soul you saw at the coffee shop. The man who made you think vampire."

I shiver. "I don't even believe what I saw was—"

"Yes, you do. I know you do. I know you feel it."

"What makes you think this," I scan the room, "was done by that same man, lost soul, whatever? And why? What would he want with me?"

"I think you piqued his interest at the café. I think he noticed your reaction and sought you out. I bet he's anxious to know what you really saw in him."

"Why would he care what I—"

"I think the woman you saw, the old soul with him, was Sonia MacKinnen."

I freeze, every muscle in my body trying to summon the energy to deny truth to his statement. But I can't. Bile inches up my chest and the room spins, throwing equilibrium to the wind. I drop to the floor with a thud.

"Oh my God."

"New Year's Eve I was troubled," says Bryce, stepping close. "I was stressed because the police came to speak with me. Again. They had questions about Sonia's death they thought I could answer. They showed me photos of her injuries: severe malnutrition and dehydration, broken bones, burns, and bite marks. I couldn't identify Sonia but I recognized the cause of death."

I know exactly how Sonia died, without the graphics. I know it like I was there, beside her, feeling her pain.

"Lost souls have various issues, scars from multiple pasts that manifest in many ways. But the lost soul you described, the man with aquatic-like tattoos, they thrive by seducing, controlling, and slowly stealing a person's free will. It starts innocently, the victim blinded by lust. Soon they lose themselves in pleasure, no longer eating, sleeping. The stronger the victim's will, the longer the game lasts, until the victim becomes catatonic and the lost soul becomes bored, restless, and loses control."

"He. Killed. Her." I say between sobs.

Bryce looks at me, anguished.

I spring upright. "I could have saved her. At the café. Maybe I could've—"

"No. Listen to me. You saw his soul, a memory, obviously

recent, but in the past. Tess, there is nothing you could have done."

I should be relieved but I'm not. He killed her!

"I know you're scared. And I know this is a lot for you. But there are things I must tell you, things you need to understand."

"He was here, in my home." I scramble to standing. "He touched our things. He killed Maxi!"

Bryce reaches out for me but I back away.

"Tess, try to stay calm. I swear we'll figure this out, we'll find him. Thomas is looking—"

"I don't want Thomas to find this man. He killed Sonia. He could hurt Thomas. Oh my God, what if we'd been home when he came here? Abby could've been killed!"

Bryce steps close to embrace me but I push him away.

"What if he comes back?"

"Listen, Tess, I can better explain what we're dealing with. But you need to know what you are, what you see. I can tell you but you won't believe me, so I have to show you. Tess," he says, waving a hand past my eyes, "please, pay attention."

"Pay attention? To what? How?" I feel dazed, drugged, like something foreign floats within my brain, something that won't allow me to think logically.

Bryce moves closer to the couch. "Watch me." With one hand he picks up the entire three-seat sofa as if weightless. He flips it like a penny then sets it down, upright, without so much as a sound.

"What the hell was that?" I shout. Every strange thing I've seen, all my suspicions about Bryce, jump to the forefront. "How did you do that? Are you a magician? Was that real or an illusion? What else can you do?"

Bryce shifts his weight and looks to the ceiling. The lights flicker before going out.

"I did that," he says, matter-of-factly. "I need you to focus on me and only me. Now look. Really look at me."

Only moonlight pours over the mess and it takes a moment for my eyes to adjust to the dark. I try to focus but it's hard when the guy before me just lifted my sofa with one hand. Questions claw the backs of my teeth, dying to get out, and for a fleeting moment I wonder if I've missed something. But I blink and my vision shifts, Bryce blurring.

Something squawks where Bryce stood and I jump. My heart pounds as my brain registers what it's seeing.

Standing in front of me is a bird, a large bird. A falcon, or some sort of eagle. Its feathers are dense, glossy, layered in various shades of black and gray. Massive feet rise and fall, nails tapping the floor in an anxious dance. I shiver and it squawks again. Instinct has me freaking, but I calm when I catch a glimpse of silver spark in the bird's eyes, an inhuman but tranquil illumination that looks strange yet familiar.

"It can't possibly be . . ." I lean forward to get a better look at those silver eyes, the thumping in my skull unbearably loud. The bird spreads its wings, the span covering a massive distance, and finding the breeze it flaps its wings and takes off, disappearing into the dark.

"Bryce, did you see that?"

When I look back, Bryce is standing stock still. He's in the very spot he was before, where the bird stood. He looks worried, maybe frightened. Frightened of me.

"What did you see?" he says.

I'm in shock. "A bird. An eagle, I think."

"An eagle? Really?"

"Was it real? Shit, Bryce, the thing had your eyes!"

Bryce starts to pace, hands gripping the back of his neck. The slow, nervous gait looks alien on him. He doesn't try to convince me that what I saw is a figment of my imagination. He doesn't deny the fact that he stood before me as something other than a man.

"Tess, you saw my soul."

"No! Are you kidding me? How is that even possible? You're a bird?"

Lucidity jumps ship and the room sways at an unnatural angle, forcing me to grab hold of a chair.

"Relax, please, try to stay calm," whispers Bryce, crouching before me. "I am not a bird. What you saw was a very important experience from a distant time, another life, when my soul could absorb energy to change into another living form, any animal, any living creature." His eyes flicker. "It is an ancient talent seldom necessary in this century. There was a time we needed to work in what you'd call the wild, and the ability to shape shift served a purpose. But what is really important, is that you can see it."

"We? We who? A purpose? What purpose? Why the hell would you need to change into an animal? How? If you can do this stuff, why do you hide from—"

"I do not hide," Bryce says, all signs of stress vanishing in an instant. He stands tall. "I am not ashamed of who I am." He shakes his head. "You're missing the point. Only the oldest of souls—specifically seers, creators—can see into someone's soul, to the good and evil there, to the experiences that have left permanent marks."

"A seer, what the hell is that? Are you a seer? Are you saying I chose to see you as a bird—your soul as a bird? That makes no sense!"

He laughs and it sounds unusual given the weight of our conversation. I stare at him dumbfounded.

"I am not a seer, you are, and you don't make a conscious

choice to see. This is who you are. This is who you've always been. Only now your soul is stronger. In times of great duress your soul awakens, becomes aware. Some describe this as the opening of one's psychic eye. It is the connection between your body and soul, a timeless fusion meant to help you through extraordinary circumstances, if you are willing to listen."

An abundance of information, too large for me to process, aches like a cancerous lump in my head. Confusion becomes tangible, pounding me internally. Stray tears cascade down my cheek as the absurdity of it all hits me like a brick.

"Shit. I've become my mother. I really am crazy." I hit the step quick and hard.

Bryce closes the distance between us, pulling me into his arms.

"You are not crazy." I fall limp in his embrace, a deflated shell. "You only see what is already there, what is real. It is a gift to see one's soul," he says, unleashing a brief chuckle. "You are not crazy."

He swipes at my tears.

Eye to eye I lose myself in his brilliance. He is beautiful, calming, almost entrancing, but not normal. I'd seen it from the start. I refused to accept what I was seeing. But it is real. Very real.

"I'm not crazy," I say, as if it becomes true when said out loud.

"No. You are amazing, strong, and I—" he pauses, changing course. "But you're not crazy."

I'm immersed in his eyes like they are fathomless pools of water and I am floating, watching the light show from within. I touch his face and his breath catches, his chin relaxing into my hand.

"What are you?"

"First and foremost, I am a man."

"Are you the same as that man in the cafe?"

"No. I am an old soul with unique talents, but I am not lost."

"What does that mean, to be lost?"

Bryce peers into my eyes.

"I will never lie or keep secrets from you. Ever. But I need you to trust that what I tell you is the truth."

"I trust you."

"Then know in time, when you are ready, I will teach you everything you need to know."

"Teach me. Teach me what? To do what you do? Why? How much time?"

"Our truth, history, purpose," he pauses, glancing at the front door. "Everything."

The doorbell chimes, making me jump. Someone bangs on the door.

"Police here!"

"How do they—"

"I called them when you were seeing Abby off."

"These things you can do. What if people find out, will you be in danger or trouble?"

A smirk inches the right side of his lip. "There is no governing body to control us, we make choices and deal with the consequences."

"So there are no rules?"

"I said there is no law, no governing body to control us. We are guided by our conscience. That doesn't mean existing rules don't have merit. Once the police have completed their investigation, I will help you put everything in place, so you and Abby will feel comfortable."

I scan the room, the mess bringing me back to the here and now.

"Mrs. Morgan, are you okay? We need to come inside."

"I'll be right there," I call out to the officers.

Bryce takes my hands, encasing them. He kisses my fingertips one at a time.

"I promise to tell you everything."

Everything. Now there is a loaded word.

# EVERYTHING

The police spend most of the evening inspecting the crime scene and asking questions I can't answer. I can't mention the man in the café. I have no idea who he is and no valid reason to explain why he'd do me harm. What could I possibly say? I saw some guy's soul molesting Sonia? I'm not about to tell the cops anything that would result in a straitjacket and Abby motherless, and although I'm sure Bryce can fend for himself, I don't want him in any more trouble than he already is. Clearly Bryce's involvement is of concern to the officers since two are assigned his interrogators and even after a thorough line of questioning remain his shadow most of the night.

It's after midnight before I get Bryce in a room alone, and when I do, I find it hard to speak. I'm stressed, somewhat nauseous, and my nerves jump like cats on hot coals. I want to know more about the lost soul who broke into my house, if Bryce thinks he'll return, and how I protect Abby if he does? I want to know how Bryce even knows this stuff. Only these aren't questions I can ask in a house crawling with police officers, and it's driving me batty. Well, battier. I can see people's souls, a murderer has ransacked my house because I witnessed something I shouldn't, and the man I've come to admire is . . .

something extraordinary. I suppose I've hit rock bottom.

"You keep referring to souls, old souls, lost souls," I whisper to Bryce. "Explain."

We're so close I can smell the lemon laundry detergent on his clothes. We're collecting cookbooks from the kitchen floor, skimming pages to steal a moment without an audience.

"Every living thing has a soul, or spirit, or conscience," says Bryce. "The name is insignificant. It's an enigma of energy that gives life to a body, like a battery. Our soul is part of our being, part of what makes us human. Our soul resides in our brain, guiding us through each lifetime, learning, and contributing. It's our connection to nature, to the elements, our plug to the network of life."

I attempt to absorb such a fantastical concept, but it's a bit out of my realm of belief. I try really hard and for a moment think I sense my soul, feel it inside me, but the moment passes. I twitch with that creepy-crawly feeling you get when talking about lice or spiders.

"What makes a soul an old soul?"

"Each time a soul's physical self—body, you could say—reaches expiry, it moves to a new one. You might liken it to reincarnation, I guess. Old souls are exactly that, old. They've experienced many, many lifetimes. Every one of these lives has a purpose, a goal, something to learn, to contribute. Some old souls are responsible for creation. Some focus on protection or the acquisition of knowledge. And a few," he stops to grin, "are here to teach."

I think back on all the times I've been called an old soul, an ancient one. Those people weren't nuts after all.

"If I'm an old soul, how many lives have I lived? What is my purpose? You say I'm a seer, what does that—"

Bryce shushes me, turning to look over his shoulder. An

investigator steps into the room and drops his coat on the kitchen counter. He loosens the collar of his shirt and unbuttons his sleeves. The window has been boarded, and I've blasted the heat so he's hot.

I inch closer to Bryce so I can whisper. "How does a soul get lost?"

"They aren't lost in the literal sense. Lost souls are old souls who have lost their purpose. They have trouble learning from past experience and therefore live immorally. It's a vicious cycle resulting in millennia of heartache, loss, and death, in one form or another. They've lost their way on the path to spiritual enlightenment."

I frown. "And we're back to religion."

The investigator fiddles with the door handle to my back patio then squats to pick through a mound of pottery and soil. The fern I've nurtured for years is barely distinguishable, mashed into the floor tile.

"Spiritual enlightenment and religion are not the same," whispers Bryce. "Developing one's soul and purpose is done from within, a power summoned internally in the quest to experience life and be a better person."

"How does a person learn from a past they can't remember?"

"They feel it. Like a computer, a soul stores past experiences, and lessons learned in previous lives make a person who they are. Memories are erased when the body dies and the soul starts a new life, but some things are permanently engrained in a soul's hard drive. Imagine a child born afraid of dogs or water. Not because he's been hurt or traumatized in this lifetime, but because his soul has learned something in a previous life to make him afraid. Your genetic make-up decides if your eyes will be green or blue and how tall you'll grow to be. Your soul contributes to the person you become."

"So the child is predestined to live in fear of the dog next door?"

Bryce shrugs. "Until he chooses to conquer his fear."

"Now we're back to choice."

"Always."

Bryce touches my arm, glancing at his shadows. They've come into the kitchen lugging kits with strange looking supplies. One starts taking photos while the other fidgets in the corner, organizing paperwork on a clipboard. I don't have time to contemplate what Bryce's touch does to me. His cell rings and he stands, turning away to talk while another officer passes through the kitchen carrying a roll of plastic bags, stopping to recruit brawn for bagging Maxi. The cops debate what a broken neck implies and my heart sinks.

I know what a broken neck means to me. It explains why Bryce wouldn't let me hold Maxi. It says Maxi died quick, thank God. And it reminds me I'm about to have one devastated little girl to console, with no clue how to explain Maxi's absence.

"Don't worry, we'll think of something," says Bryce, covering the mic on his cell to speak to me.

I push Bryce into a corner of the living room. He's still on the phone, listening to someone rant by the sounds of it. I think its Thomas.

"You read my mind," I hiss.

He shrugs. "Sort of, I'll explain later." He places a hand over his heart and grins at me.

And that's what it takes to push me over the edge. That and three men rolling poor Maxi in plastic. The air becomes thin, making it difficult to breath. I lean against the wall before sliding to the floor, dropping my head between my knees while I cry uncontrollably.

"Hey, hey now," says Bryce, lowering to sit beside me. He

pulls me into his arms and holds me tight. "Don't worry, you'll get through this. You're stronger than you realize. You and Abby will be fine. I'll make sure of it."

The officers leave the room with Maxi in tow, and I bury my face in Bryce's shirt. When I finally come up for air his shirt is wet and I'm a mess. Bryce wipes the tears from my chin.

"Was that Thomas on the phone? Is he okay?"

Bryce nods, grimacing. "He wants to be here, with you, but I convinced him to stay away. Since I'm under the microscope with the authorities and Thomas isn't on their radar, he has a better chance of learning more about this lost soul. We don't even know why he was here, in Carlisle. His kind usually stay close to well populated coastal regions."

"His kind? I thought you said lost souls are just people?"

"Ah, so you have been listening."

I shoot daggers with my eyes, but Bryce just smiles.

"Some of the most powerful old souls, ones most connected to ancient ways, became lost after the destruction of their homeland, Atlantis."

If I wasn't already on the floor . . .

"Atlantis? Are you serious?"

"Yes, Atlantis was an ancient civilization—"

"I know what it was. You're saying it was a real place? Not just a legend? This is insane!"

Bryce sighs. I think he regrets bringing it up.

"Tess, myths are passed through generations, stories originating from real life circumstances and lessons elders wish to impress upon their young. Atlanteans, for example, had been thriving for millennia when disaster struck, killing every man, woman, and child, and destroying everything they felt connected to. Those who were not crushed or burned were swept away by waves the size of entire cities, leaving survivors to scramble for higher ground, to find refuge wherever they could. This is a story of devastation at its worst. One that will never be forgotten."

"How . . . how do you know this? Were you there? No. That would've been . . . Was my soul there? Oh my God, there were survivors?"

"A few," says Bryce, obviously upset. "A limited number of people were able to hold on to small pieces of land that didn't sink. They refused to surrender their riches to nature's cruelty, and defiant, continued to dwell on Atlantis, adapting to a largely aquatic life. But nature has its way and Atlantis was slowly devoured by the sea, piece by piece, until all that was left was a fading relic of the once glorious city." He sighs. "The souls remaining lived on boats and man-made islands. They became bitter and indignant, determined to take the life of every sailor who dared enter their domain. If they couldn't control the sea, no one would."

"Hence the—"

"Mermaid legends. These lost souls have spent thousands of years struggling to shake the morally corrupt decisions their souls made after the destruction of their homeland. Very few still live in the depths. Some have found their way to a life of serenity, learning from their mistakes. Most have resurfaced to wreak havoc on land, taking from others what they believe was taken from them, free will."

I connect the dots. "Vampires."

"Um hmm, the origin of vampire folklore."

The sheer thought of Atlantis being a real place that was swallowed by the sea makes me quiver. What those people must have gone through, how terrified they must have been. To witness the entire world go up in flames, to watch everything and everyone you love incinerated, torn apart, or drowned. No modern-day movie could ever accurately depict this kind of horror and devastation. No amount of time would ever be enough for your soul to recover.

"Some people think it was for the best, that the fall of Atlantis was inevitable. Over the years Atlanteans turned away from the spiritual principles that guided their ancestors, and instead applied their skills to creating wealth. Ambition turned into greed. An obsession with material riches created a fear of loss resulting in the need for security, so they raised fleets and armies. Atlanteans ruled for eighteen centuries, but had their land remained above water they would have, eventually, self-destructed. Some think their end was nature's way of correcting a genetic flaw. Like karmic payback."

"But you don't," I say.

"Nothing living ever deserves to be torn from their soul, robbed of a lifetime."

Yes, what a price to pay, to lose everything.

"Is there anything left of Atlantis now?"

Bryce stares out the window, to the stars. "Seventy-one percent of Earth's surface is covered in ocean. More than half is over three thousand meters deep. Under four percent of our underwater world has been explored by modern man. We know more about Mars. Even if there is a part of Atlantis remaining, if there's proof of man's history, the technology to reach it doesn't exist."

**Bryce stays within** a few feet of me the entire night, coddling my nerves with his controlled demeanor and the odd gentle touch. Eventually his shadows leave, making the atmosphere slightly more tolerable, and as the remaining officers complete their investigation, Bryce and I are given approval to clean. We right smaller pieces of unbroken furniture, sweep glass and pottery, and discard food, even stuff untouched in the fridge. The vast majority is put into garbage bags or boxes labeled for the insurance company, and the broken Christmas ornaments I can't bear to part with are packed for future consideration. The place looks pretty bare and for a split second I think Meyer will freak when he sees our home like this. Then I remember he's gone and won't see a thing. Only Abby and I have to start over.

By daybreak the last of the men in uniform have left and Bryce and I have the house somewhat organized. I'm so tired I can hardly stand upright and anxiety has gone to bed. I've been awake almost twenty-four hours, the longest, most shocking twenty-four hours of my life. I've got questions and concerns by the dozen, only they're loosely formed concepts I can't grasp at the moment.

I turn a corner in time to see Bryce lift my credenza three feet off the floor and pull the curtain out from under it. Somewhere, buried deep, I know I should be blown away. But I'm not. It's like I've been electrocuted to the point of numbness.

"How do you do that, exactly?" I grip the doorframe for support. "It took four delivery guys to get that thing in here."

Bryce takes my hand and leads me to the credenza.

"Close your eyes," he says. I do and he places my hands on the credenza. "Everything has a magnetic currency that pulsates against the magnetic pull of gravity. If you concentrate, you can feel it."

I try, but all I feel is wood grain begging to be touched. And, to be honest, a tad dizzy.

"It's quite simple, actually. Every particle radiates at a specific frequency. The object as a whole need only resonate at the frequency of gravity, 1012 hertz, or the frequency between short radio waves and infrared radiation, to lose its weight. So, if you use electromagnetic force to suspend gravity, you can render anything, even stone, weightless."

I stare in awe. "Sure, that sounds simple."

"It is," he says. "Even Einstein's Unified Field theorized that gravity is really a frequency. How do you think all those heavy basalt monoliths got to Easter Island? Nan Madol? Stonehenge?"

I'm too exhausted to comment. My head is no longer working. I wander to the living room and plop onto the couch.

"I should call Grams and Gramps, they'll want to know what happened here."

I dig through my purse for my cell. I should've called them earlier, but by the time I had the chance it was almost midnight, and I didn't want to worry them. There wasn't anything they could do from Florida and Gramps has the flu. When I get their answering machine I leave a message, trying to sound light and breezy, but it comes off fake. I mumble something about Abby being okay then suggest they call me when they have a minute. I dread the thought of hitting them with more bad news.

I'm putting my phone away when the doorbell rings.

"Who the hell is that?" I leap from the couch in a sudden panic.

Bryce closes the space between us in an instant. "Hey, now, relax," he says, pulling me close. "I ordered breakfast. You mentioned you haven't eaten since brunch yesterday."

I deflate like a balloon. He's right, Abby and I had a late breakfast with Grams and Gramps in Florida and caught a midday flight home. The plan was to grab something to eat on the way from the airport.

Bryce lowers me to the couch to answer the door, returning with a wicker picnic basket.

"I didn't know the bakery had delivery," I mumble as Bryce arranges the food on a blanket.

"They don't." He smiles, all teeth, the confession of a rogue. He seems totally at ease now, as if there's nothing left he can't handle.

I wish I felt the same.

"You will, don't worry," he says.

"Stop that." I cringe. Now that I'm wise to this particular talent, I find it obtrusive.

"Sorry. I'll try to respect your privacy." He smiles, cocky. "Now eat."

Breakfast looks yummy and smells even better. I gulp the tea, burning my tongue in the process, and devour slices of apple and cheese without any recollection as to how they taste. The only sign I'm content is the rumble in my belly when I reach for another croissant.

"When will the caffeine kick in?" I mumble. "I need to get Abby." I'm holding my face up, elbows planted to support the weight of my head.

"It won't. I ordered decaf. You don't drink caffeine." He flashes another naughty grin. "And Abby is spending the day at Lil' Monster's Play House with Sofia and Nanna. You are going to sleep."

With that, Bryce scoops me from the couch without so much as a catch in his breath and carries me to bed. I don't have the energy to argue. He carefully lowers me onto my side, sliding me under my oversized duvet, clothes and all. The quilt adopts me in a womb of warmth. My eyelids flutter and my breath slows to a hush, preparing for hibernation. Tender fingertips brush the hair from my face, pausing to caress my cheek.

"I won't leave the house, so only sweet dreams."

I follow Bryce's fading silhouette to the door.

"Hey, you," I whisper, my vision descending into nothingness.

Like a distant dream Bryce rests his body beside mine, tucking me into his form and wrapping his arm around me.

Serenity rules my every cell.

There is nothing to fear with my white knight by my side.

# REVELATIONS

When I wake I have no idea what time it is. The clock reads 2:15, but I doubt it's correct. I roll over and bump another body in the dark.

"Hey," says Bryce.

"Hey," I breathe. "Is it really two o'clock in the afternoon?"

"Actually, it's two in the morning. You slept the entire day and half the night. I think you were hit with more than you could handle, and your body needed to reboot."

I can scarcely see his profile. He's stretched out beside me, his hands folded across his chest like a mummy. The blinds cover the windows and only a tiny bit of moonlight affects the room.

"Are you still tired? Do you want to sleep more?" He's speaking ever so softly.

I shake my head. I don't want to get up though. I feel strangely at ease considering what I've learned and experienced. It's Bryce that has me feeling this way, calm. It's in the way he watches over me, giving me just enough room to think. How he stayed with me, knowing the police would point fingers. The way he's trusted me with his secrets, his truths. I not only find myself believing his testimony, I'm attracted to him like never before.

And now, now I only want to listen to his voice, the smooth cadence of his European accent.

"Your Grams and Gramps called. I told them about the break in and they insisted on coming home. Their flight got in this evening and they came straight here but you were sound asleep and they didn't want to wake you. I promised I wouldn't leave you alone and convinced them to take Abby home to get some rest. They'll be back this morning. I called a maid service. They finished cleaning so the house is safe for Abby's eyes. And your insurance adjuster called, he'll drop in this afternoon."

Bryce attempts to smooth the wrinkles out of his shirt, to no avail. He sighs and continues with his summary.

"I apologize for taking the liberty, but I ordered groceries online. They were delivered last night, so the fridge and cupboards are stocked enough to offer a few days' respite. Nanna baked you an apple pie, which is in the fridge. Thomas came to see you. He wasn't pleased with me being here and things got a little out of hand until Grams suggested Thomas leave and call you later. Your cell has been ringing. A lot. Oh, and I talked to Karen. She's not happy with me either. I didn't want her coming to the house to check Maxi before the police arrived, so I lied, convincing her you'd agreed to have Maxi come stay at my place with me." He groans. "She expects you to call her when you wake."

"Wow, thank you. Like, seriously." Words can't describe my gratitude. "I can't believe I slept through all that."

I feel Bryce shrug in the dark. "No problem."

"Bryce." I pause, worried I'm about to ruin the relaxed atmosphere. "How do you know . . . everything you know? I get that you're an old soul, an ancient soul, but I am too, and I can't do the things you can."

He rolls closer and I see the strong lines of his face in the glow of his eyes. The sight takes my breath away when I realize this is something only I see, the silver sparks in his eyes. It makes me feel unique, special, connected to Bryce in a way I can't explain.

Bryce hesitates, but only for a second. "I was born and raised, just like you." He reaches for my hand then freezes when I entwine my fingers with his.

"You thought I'd flinch at your touch, didn't you?"

"Freak, actually." He falls quiet for a moment, taking in the sensation of my caress. "I figured when exhaustion wore off you would . . . I was pretty sure you'd be . . ." Firecrackers explode in his eyes. "You're not afraid of me."

"Should I be?"

"No. I'd give my life for yours."

I chuckle at the scope of his declaration then stop when I notice he's serious.

"Will he, the lost soul . . . will he return?"

Bryce stares into the dark, troubled, then shakes his head as if dislodging an image.

"It won't help you to worry. I'm here. And few lost souls will disrespect a Keeper."

"A what?"

He leans in close. "I am a Keeper."

I'm lost already.

"A Keeper. As in, 'that one's a keeper!'" I pretend to hold an imaginary fishing rod taut with a sizable fish.

"I can see this is going to be difficult," he says, deadpan.

I'll bite.

"What's a Keeper?"

"Keepers are the guardians of sacred mythology and the oldest of souls. The soul of a Keeper carries memories as far back as time itself, and can recall the knowledge with the dawn of each new life. We are born knowing our ancestral history, the powers of the ancients, and we use this information to do amazing things. We are the scholars and teachers of every lifetime, guarding the history and knowledge of the human race for eternity."

Holy crap.

"That's . . . epic. I was expecting . . ." What was I expecting? I think I was leaning toward superhero status, like Superman, or mythical like Hercules. "You're an old soul who remembers past lives."

"Yes. I am a Keeper, a Librarian of Lemuria."

"Librarian of Lemuria," I repeat, letting the words sink in. "Lemuria, the ancient civilization. What's all the hocus pocus for if you're a teacher and librarian?"

Bryce shakes his head and closes his eyes. "I don't mean librarian in the literal sense. I'm talking about my mind. I was born carrying knowledge of the entire human race in my head. Every catastrophe this planet has experienced since the dawn of man, every civilization to inhabit the Earth. All these experiences are filed in my mind. I hold the answers to questions that baffle man like, *where do we come from?* This information is within us, guarded by the Keepers."

Okay. That's big.

"Us, there are more of you?"

"Twelve."

"A dozen Keepers," I mutter in shock.

"Yes."

I pegged him for a one-off, a stranded breed from some alien planet, or a genetic quirk. I've tossed around the idea of an entire race of extraterrestrials that live among us or some sort of covert government project gone awry. Not one of my speculations were even close to the mark.

"Let me get this straight. There are twelve people wandering around who know everything."

"Twelve men."

"Seriously, all men?" There has got to be a joke in there.

Bryce rolls his eyes. "Our purpose is to enlighten, to teach. We help souls, new souls, old souls, lost souls, people of every race, every culture, from every geographical region on this planet. Keepers speak in private conferences, we teach at special schools, and we contribute to writings of historical relevance. We help scientists, scholars, archaeologists, and historians discover the truth in digestible doses. We wander, as you say, helping old souls understand our world, or as usually is the case with lost souls, find the way to inner peace."

"All twelve of you."

"You seem to have difficulty with this number. It's not really relevant at the moment."

"How do you know the exact number? What happens when one of you dies or reproduces? Can you make babies? And if you guys are all over the world, how do you keep track of each other? Do you mean that there are twelve of you right now?" I'm animated, hands flying this way and that.

Bryce chuckles, adjusting his position. He smells like soap and apples. It's distracting.

"I'm trying to tell you what we do, and you're hung up on quantity. There are twelve Keepers. There have been twelve of us since the dawn of man, and there will be twelve of us tomorrow, the day after, and a million years from now. We stay in touch like everyone else does. We don't just die, and yes," he stops to catch his breath, "we reproduce."

"You can make babies." I have no clue why I grab hold of this tidbit of info.

Bryce flashes two rows of brilliant white teeth. "We quite enjoy it, actually."

My throat runs dry. For the first time since waking I register the close proximity of our bodies and that we are in my bed. In the dark. Alone. The ceiling fan softly swishes, giving rise to stray hairs but offering nothing to buffer the heat radiating from his skin, warming me like a fire. I kick off the covers, piling the duvet between us. He spies my wall of down, my defense, a rue smile on his lips. I swallow the lump in my throat and change the subject.

"You said you're immortal—"

"No, I said 'we don't just die.' Our soul returns to experience another lifetime in another form."

Something awful occurs to me. "So, this lost soul, he could hurt you, kill you, the physical you?"

"I suppose."

"You suppose? What does that mean? You either die or you don't."

Bryce rights the blanket wall I've flattened. "If you held a gun to my chest and I let you pull the trigger, the bullet would pierce my heart, leaving me to bleed faster than I could heal."

"So, you can die."

"If I choose," he says, shrugging.

I growl, frustrated with talking in circles. "What do you mean, 'if you choose'?"

"I'm strong, fast, and smart. If you stood before me with a gun, I'd have many options. I could run, actually disappear from your line of vision. I could remove you from my presence, physically. Or I could convince you to turn the gun on yourself, with or without the use of my voice."

"Shit. What the hell happened to free will?" I mutter.

"Lost souls aren't the only ones who can manipulate a

person's right of choice. It's an option we use out of desperation, one we don't take lightly, and it comes with consequences."

I think about this for a moment. "How do you die then?"

"Old age. Most of us wish to grow old and die when our current bodies have lived enough. Occasionally we die by accident."

"All those super powers and you can be killed in an accident?"

"We're not perfect. We can be caught off guard and not react quickly enough. It doesn't happen often, but history has examples. A few Keepers have voluntarily ended a lifetime due to an overwhelming loss. Again, it's rare, but it happens."

Before Meyer died, I never considered ending my life, even when times were tough. I suppose I didn't think about it after either. I could never leave Abby. But there were moments I wondered what it would be like to put less effort into breathing.

"You elect to die of old age," I say. "Does this mean you can choose not to?"

"We can delay the process of cell breakdown, of age, but we can't stall it indefinitely. There was a time when every old soul could do this, could live for years beyond today's standard, but the power has been lost to all but the Keepers. A Keeper is born knowing who he is, where he's from, and what he must do. We are guided by our parents, our fathers, generation after generation, and taught how to use the knowledge and power we are born with. At times this can be an overwhelming burden." He accidently topples my barricade to sweep the hair from my face. "To help, we are able to slow the learning process, extend time. Coupled with a skewed grasp on maturity and responsibility, we sometimes linger, living off a natural high and relishing in life's perks."

This explains Bryce's promiscuous tendencies. It also

reminds me of Thomas's warnings. I look at Bryce's hand only an inch from my chest and wonder how it would feel on my bare skin, how I would feel if he were to touch me.

Bryce coughs and rights the covers.

I smile. *That's what you get for intruding on my thoughts.*

He ignores me. "Some think it's for the best. Just because we are capable of suspending time, doesn't mean we should. In fact, very few Keepers opt for more than one lifetime. I don't know any willing to experience the loss of more than one generation of loved ones. That and society changes too much to adapt. Most of us do, however, choose to halt the aging process at some point."

I think of all the folklore surrounding gifts of eternal life: sacred peaches, the fountain of youth, the Holy Grail. I study Bryce's hands. They are flawless and strong.

"How old are you?"

"I was born to Lina and Renault Waters thirty-four years ago." He pauses to investigate my expression. "I had a great time in my twenties. How many people can say they celebrated their twenty-first birthday eight times?" He flashes a devilish grin. "Based on appearance, you might think Thomas is my older brother, but he's actually my little brother by two years. Thomas looks older because he settled sooner, only staying three extra years in his late teens."

Even though I comprehend what he's saying, I'm shocked to hear a personal example. I think of Bryce and what I know of Thomas, and as inconceivable as this is, it actually fits.

"Now I know why your family doesn't do birthdays."

Bryce chuckles before an earnest grimace erases his laugh lines. "It's also why Thomas and I grew apart. As kids we were close, very close, but as we matured we became preoccupied with women and . . . other impulses. It was unheard of for a Keeper to have two sons. This is why Thomas calls himself 'the one that wasn't meant to be.' He thinks he was a mistake, an unwanted anomaly. But my family thinks Thomas is a gift, and I'm the luckiest Keeper of all time. I get a little brother. Thomas became competitive, always vying for the attention of our parents, girls, and eventually women. He's convinced only one of us can carry the male gene and have a son, so he's always rushing to beat me to some invisible finish line. It's foolish. And I've always been too busy to be bothered with his antics. But now that I'm older, I realize my mistake. If I hadn't been lost in selfish desires, maybe I would've seen what was happening with my brother. If I'd paid better attention, maybe I could've stopped him from making the decisions that plague him now. Maybe I would've been there to help him when he . . ." A cloud of guilt shrouds his face. "I moved here to make amends, to make up for lost time, to be the brother I should've been all along."

This blows me away more than his supernatural feats. Bryce moved halfway around the world to be with his niece and brother, in spite of Thomas's efforts to push him away. I've never had a family member give me the time of day. I'm about to ask what Thomas needed help with when I bite my tongue. Thomas is divorced, angry, and obviously experiencing some sort of identity crisis.

"Oh my God. If a Keeper's son carries a Keeper's soul, does that make Thomas a Keeper too?" I look to Bryce, in shock. "Can Thomas do what you can?"

"Thomas is my brother, Tess. A Keeper can only have one son, which is why Thomas is so special, but he is an old soul, one of twelve who remembers his past."

I can't believe this. Heat flourishes across my neck and cheeks as my temper kicks in. Thomas is everything Bryce is, a Keeper, and he never told me, never even hinted that he was anything but a regular guy. Everything I've ever thought him to be was a show, a mask, a lie. And I didn't see it. I didn't suspect a thing. Thomas and I were close. We were—whatever it was we were. He kissed me. His hands touched my body.

Bryce clears his throat. "Thomas makes his own choices. We all do."

"He should have told me. Why didn't he tell me?"

"That's something you'll have to ask him. But I'm sure he had his reasons."

All this information sits heavy in my mind, and I close my eyes to rest. Minutes pass. Even though I no longer see Bryce, I feel his energy crowding my space. Air whistles past his lips, the rhythm of his breath slightly euphoric. He moves closer and my mouth moistens, awaiting his kiss. It doesn't come. Instead he takes my hand and gently pulls me across his chest, heart pounding at high volume. I gasp for air as his mouth explores the tenderness behind my ear. His tongue, hot and wet, participates in delicate kisses down my neck. I hold tight, barely breathing as his hands glide over my—

"Tess!"

I wake to reality. The duvet is still propped between us. Bryce is a foot away, on his back, both hands over his face.

"We need to get up. Now." he says, literally leaping from the bed. His voice is nothing but a garbled mumble as he disappears downstairs.

Oops.


**I'm up and** the easy breezy feeling is gone. Without Bryce I have a hole, a void that quickly fills with doubt and fear, with the harsh reality of my situation, and it only escalates as I shower, unable to wash myself clean of a burden too heavy to bear. I make the bed because I need order. I get dressed and brush my teeth to set things right when everything feels so wrong.

I hear the kettle whistle and the tinkle of flatware. Bryce is prepping something in the kitchen. Pausing at the door, I consider climbing back into bed and drowning myself in layers of bedding, but the thought passes. I'd probably have a nightmare.

And I need to get myself in check for Abby.

My first step into the living room is met with a crunch. I step back and pick the dried play dough from my sock, emotion flooding me. It's a miniature dog leg from Abby's masterpiece of Maxi. There are three tiny slits in the foot where Abby used scissors to separate the toes and Maxi's hair sticks out at odd angles. Maxi. Maxi is dead. The enormity of what's happened wallops me, stealing my breath. A killer was here, in my house. I look at my feet, wanting to raise them from the floor so as not to touch what he's touched. I look around the room, suddenly struck by the enormity of it all. It's clean, too clean, like it's been stripped of personality, of life. There are no family photos, no heirlooms. It could be anyone's house, a builder's empty showroom, and the boarded window and smell of cleaner are nothing but camouflage.

My heart rate rises another notch.

I hear Bryce in the kitchen and force myself to take a few steps in his direction, but movement is limited. That man, that lost soul with the piercing eyes and ripped body etched with tattoos was in my home, touching my things, destroying memories I hold dear. How dare he. I look around the room, seeing him in everything. I can smell him over the scent of cleaning solution. His snarl tears through the room.

I've got to get out of here. It's all too much to take in, too much to handle. I can't do this. After Meyer passed, I panicked over how I'd survive on my own, how I'd raise Abby alone. Now I need to protect her from a man who killed a woman, destroyed our home, and snapped the neck of a dog!

I stumble through the kitchen, practically knocking Bryce over in my mad dash to the patio door. I need air. I need to think.

The lost soul killed Maxi!

I burst through the doors and out into the light, panting.

He murdered Sonia!

What if Karen had been at the house to feed Maxi when he came? What if Thomas finds him? What if he doesn't and this guy comes back? What if he hurts Abby? Grams and Gramps, they're not safe!

I trip and fall face first in the snow. I look to the greenhouse just as Bryce lifts me from the ground. Everything is a blur. Bryce is speaking but I can't concentrate, can't hear his words. He's worried. He says something about returning to the kitchen but I push him away. This is too much, too much for anyone.

"The studio," I sputter, voice not mine. I need to be there, the only spot he hasn't been, the one place the lost soul didn't leave his mark.

Bryce lets me go and I run.

I throw the door open and stumble inside, taking deep breaths. The scent of oil paint and pine instantly calms my nerves and the sight of my paints and brushes gives me focus. Still, I barely move. My pants are pasted with snow, my socks heavy with clumps of ice. The cold stings my skin.

"You'll be okay," whispers Bryce from behind me.

"Will I?" I snap. "How? If he comes back, if he chooses to inflict more on me, what can I do? Can I fight? Call the cops? Can I beat him off? Can I run?"

Bryce covers his mouth with his hand, and I realize I'm yelling.

"He's going to kill me!"

I bend over, hyperventilating.

"Please, try not to worry. I will help you—"

"How? How can you help me?" I pace the small space. "This is insane! What could you possibly teach me to fend off a person so bent on destruction?"

"I'll teach you our history, our—"

"History? Are you kidding me? How will history keep Abby safe? What if this guy shows up and you're not here?"

"I will teach you how to master the original form of martial art. Its meditation is—"

"I'm gonna to fight this guy by meditating? Are you nuts?"

"Mu-tubu-udundi puts human biorhythms in accordance with Earth's energies, allowing control of one's defense. Adepts aim to exhaust opponents with an intricate series of—"

"Tire him out? That's the plan? Oh my God, I'm going to die!"

Bryce reaches out to me, but I swat his hand away. He looks hurt.

"You won't need to fight, Tess. One strikes only after all other options have been exhausted. And it's irrelevant since I'll be with you."

"Show me." I push him into open space.

Bryce steps forward and pulls me into his arms. "Patience," he says. "Explaining eons of ancient history, lost art forms, and how to connect with forgotten ways will take years."

I try to wiggle free but he holds tight until I surrender, clinging to his chest.

"Years?" I can barely breathe. "I won't be able to defend myself, protect my daughter, for years?"

"Pretend you're a toddler learning to read."

"I'm not a child, Bryce. I am fully capable of—"

"I am not comparing you to a child. I'm hoping the analogy

will help you understand that you will need to learn in progression." His breath hollows out to a whistle. "The fact that you are an adult, an intelligent one at that, is not an advantage. In some ways it will make teaching you more difficult. You have pre-existing biases and opinions. You'll want to ask many questions. Some I can answer and some will need to wait until you're ready. You will get frustrated and mad, but you must remember that I am trying to help you. And that I have your best interest in mind at all times. You'll need to trust me."

I've lost all my fire listening to Bryce's voice.

"I do trust you." I do.

"Tess, Thomas and I are Keepers. We've spent an eternity working with lost souls. We know how they work, how they think, and Thomas can't find a trace of this particular man. He's probably left town and won't come back. You will be safe. Abby will be safe. We'll make sure of it. So, please, please try not to worry."

Bryce gently tugs me toward my easel. He lowers my painting apron over my head and ties it at my waist. A second later a paintbrush is in my hand.

"Find your happy place," he says, pointing to the canvas. The lightness in his voice sedates my nerves, and I close my eyes to focus on the feel of his breath on the back my neck.

"I'm sorry." I'm suddenly ashamed of my outburst.

"Your reaction was delayed but expected." He wraps his arms around me. "I thought you'd wake in a fury."

No, I woke under a blanket of tranquility, thanks to my white knight. Reality knocked the wind from me for a moment, but I'm all right now. I'll get through this, I'll find a way to keep everyone I love unharmed. I'll be strong for Abby. Bryce will help.

"I will," mumbles Bryce. "But this is going to be harder than I thought."

"What's going to be harder?"

"Teaching you. Helping you." He watches our tangled hands moving in tandem, delicately exploring of their own free will. "Helping old souls is my purpose, and I am very proud of what I do. But this, this will be different. I've never had feelings for one of my students."

I suppose I should ask him to clarify his feelings but I don't really need enlightenment. Holding his hand is easy and natural, like we're pieces that form to one. We belong together. His breath catches, and I find myself amused that a man capable of such mythical feats can be so affected by a simple touch. My touch.

We stand like this, me in Bryce's embrace, for a long time. The silence is wonderful, soothing, and after a while I forget he's even there, behind me. I lose myself in colors, textures, the dance.

It's euphoric, like the finest of drugs.

At one point I turn and catch Bryce studying a canvas hanging from the ceiling. The glint in his eyes is back and I watch him, enthralled, wondering what he's thinking.

"It's not fair really. You know my intimate thoughts, and I can only guess what—"

"Soulmates," he says, staring at the sliver of light cutting across one of my paintings. "I was thinking how some Keepers search for their soulmate and waste an entire lifetime doing so. With a population so massive and widespread, most cannot hope to find a past love, even if they believe one is truly out there."

I reach to cup his face, a touch to resurrect his smile. It works and he glows.

"I've never really considered the concept of a soulmate. The idea of having a soul was foreign, so it never came to mind."

Oddly enough, neither does Meyer.

# CONFESSION

## Early February

*Some believe ancient Egyptian texts contain the legacy of a lost civilization on a quest for the immortality of the soul, a belief that immortality may not be guaranteed by simply being born. It may have to be worked for, strived for, the result of a lifetime of choices, the focused power of the mind, an advanced connection to our inner spirituality. Immortality may be a gift that is earned.*

*Forgotten History Magazine*: Archeological Finds Baffle Scientists

**If** bad things really do happen in threes, I hope I've met my quota. I'm not sure my tiny family can endure much more. And I can't stand watching them suffer.

Even at five, Abby senses something is different about the house, something off, something beyond the physical. The vibe of our home has been altered in some intrinsic way beyond description. Abby doesn't recognize the break in. I don't think it's even in her vocabulary. And I'm spending every waking moment making sure she never has reason to suspect a thing. While Abby is at school I shop. Well, we shop. Grams and Gramps won't leave me alone. Karen, Bryce, and Thomas hover relentlessly, Bryce and Thomas seldom in the same room at once, and bickering when they are. It's exhausting. I have a long list of broken items to replace, and most days I barely make it home in time to open boxes, put things together, and dispose of packaging before retrieving Abby from school. Scheming is hard work, but I want Abby to feel secure and safe, so her contentment has become my obsession.

Me, on the other hand, I'm not so oblivious. Nothing will ever be the same.

Thinking that maybe this is a sign to move on with my life, I pack the last clinging remnants of Meyer and surrender them to a local shelter. I watch men cart away our bed, Meyer's and mine, then spend an entire day assembling a new one, a bed without memories. It isn't as hard as I thought it would be. The old me is coming back, slowly but surely, the me with thicker skin. I'm no longer a widow but the strong, independent woman I once was, the chick capable of battling whatever or whomever life throws her way.

A survivor.

All this bravado yet I lie about Maxi. I lie big time. It's a choice I'm not totally convinced I won't regret someday, but I don't see an alternative. Life's harsh realities were part of my everyday upbringing, but I'll be damned if it'll be Abby's. Even Grams and Gramps back me when I tell Abby that while we were in Florida, Maxi was reunited with her family, the family that missed her dearly. They took her home, to a happy house, too far for us to visit but filled with children and quality dog food. The news fostered melancholy in Abby, and she sulked for days, but she swallowed the storyline and is now drawing cheery pictures of Maxi with her family in some foreign farmhouse.

If there is such a place as hell, and deception is considered a whopper of an offense, I'll rot there with a smile on my face.

When I have the chance to slip away from my responsibilities as a mother, I spend time with Bryce. This is another thing Grams and Gramps have rallied to support, even going so far as to nudge me out the door, hoping I'll make my way over to Bryce's estate. It's obvious they think they're participating in a budding romance, and if they actually knew what Bryce and I spent these hours doing, they'd be thoroughly disappointed.

I am the student, and Bryce is the teacher. And it's not some kinky sex game.

"I see you brought another list," says Bryce, pointing at the paper in my hand. He's trying to maintain professional etiquette, but I can see his effort to contain a grin.

I've come to enjoy these hours with Bryce. Even though the atmosphere is a bit stuffy and clinical, I can always get him to lighten up and laugh before I leave for the night.

"Why do we meet in your office?" I ask, following him down the hall.

"You don't like my office?" He turns in the doorway.

I come to an abrupt halt, practically underneath him. His eyes flicker silver and the muscles in his cheek twitch. The effect is disturbing, and I wet my lips in a spontaneous response.

"It's a perfectly nice room," I say. It's a typical office with a large oak desk, leather chairs, and various black and white photos hanging on the walls. A well-appointed man-den. "It's just a little formal, I guess."

"Yes, well, that does help."

To the left is an excellent Monet look-alike. It's taken a massive amount of self-restraint to keep from touching it. A bowl of jellybeans sits on the desk. I know from last week that they're hard as rocks.

"How does formal help me?"

"Not you," he says, tapping on the back of a chair, instructing me to sit, "it helps me."

"This is new." I spin the chair. Usually Bryce has plush yoga mats in front of the window and we sit on the floor while we talk.

"You talk," he corrects. "I try to get you to concentrate."

He's right. Lesson one I demanded to be taught Mu-tubu-udundi. The trick to this ancient martial art is to slow your breathing and block outside stimulants. The sessions haven't gone well. Apparently I have the lung capacity of an asthmatic and the only place I focus is in my studio.

"You won't clear your mind until you've gotten answers to your questions." Bryce sinks into his chair. He points to my list. "We might be a while."

I ignore his smirk and skim through my list titled *Man's Big Questions*. I've actually pulled these from the Internet. I'm not this deep. I was shocked to discover how little, as human beings, we really know about ourselves. Worse, I find it baffling that what we do know is speculative at best.

I clear my throat. "Let's start at the beginning. Where did man come from? Were Atlanteans the first people to inhabit Earth?"

"Man existed for millennia before Atlantis." He taps his pen on the desk. "Humanity first appeared on islands in the Pacific about two-hundred and fifty-thousand years ago. Our pack nature fueled the gradual rise of mankind's first civilization, the Lemurians, and we dominated for a—"

"We?"

"Yes, we. The world was—"

"We, as in you and me, our souls? How do you know, were you there?"

"Our souls date back to the dawn of man, but you need to stay—"

"Did you know me, my soul, were we . . . acquainted?"

"Stay focused, Tess." He rolls his eyes. "The world was a different place then. Several moons revolved around various planets seen with the naked eye. Even Earth itself was different. It was lush, green, untamed. Human beings were not separated by water or religion. We lived together in harmony, on one vast area of land called the Motherland, or Mu. But Mu was more than a place, it was a culture spread over a number of territories across thousands of miles. Lemurians knew the sun personified the order of the universe and attached the human soul to recurring patterns in the cycle of life. We believed personal fulfillment lay in cooperating with nature and considered knowledge the highest form of spiritual attunement. We lived in peace, and through our understanding of natural law, we developed science and art to a high level of sophistication, creating majestic cities with temples, palaces, citadels, columns, and colossal pyramids." He pauses, obviously enjoying a memory. "Even with all these so called powers, most of us were seamen and farmers, nurturing bountiful crops under an enduring sun. We enjoyed life."

I gravitate to the window. The sun is asleep, the moon casting a radiant blue glow over the snow. My soul was there, in this world Bryce weaves with words. Somewhere deep inside I remember, I must.

"What happened? Where did we go?"

"Over thousands of years, Earth suffered a series of natural disasters. A passing comet caused killer tsunamis, plate shifts, seismic activity, and major volcanic eruptions. Mu slowly broke into several parts, some buried, most sinking under the sea."

"Just like Atlantis." What an awful fate.

"Unlike Atlanteans, Lemurians had time to prepare, to amass an immense understanding of weather and astronomy. In fact, our comprehension of science and natural law proved to be our greatest asset, allowing some of us to spread to foreign highlands, to safety, before catastrophe obliterated our entire race."

"Why don't people know this? Why isn't this documented?"

Bryce's pen stops mid-air. "It was," he says. "Try to envision the chaos, the upheaval. Everything was burned, buried, or lost at sea. What was left survived only in the tormented minds of the beaten and broken, in nature's refugees."

I look back to the black line of trees outside the window. "Until all that is left is myth and folklore."

Bryce smiles. "Atlantis has been the jewel of the storyteller's trove, but Mu has not been forgotten." Bryce joins me at the window. "Tales of tall, light-skinned survivors of an epic catastrophe are told across the globe, in diverse cultures, entwined in almost every belief system, all with similar notes of our sunken realm. And not all was lost," he says, bowing gracefully. "The Keepers remember."

I watch the spark in his eyes as it reflects off the glass.

"My grandfather was involved in the preservation and transcription of one of Japan's oldest historical documents, the *Fudoki*, or *Record of Ancient Matters*. Evidence of Lemurian culture exists for those willing to look for it."

It dawns on me that Bryce's soul was actually there, watching everything and everyone he loved killed, and he remembers. His soul remembers. I take his hand and squeeze tight. I can't imagine having to dwell on such awful memories.

I hear the sound of tiny feet only seconds before Sofia runs into the room at full throttle, flying into Bryce's open arms. He dips her formally, holding her tight, and winks at me. Now that Thomas thinks Sofia's presence will keep Bryce from making a move on me, from getting physical, she's allowed over a lot more.

I haven't commented. Bryce is thrilled. Sofia begs for a bedtime story. I watch Bryce negotiate with his niece, raising the ante with every offer. Bryce caves and I laugh. He settles for four books at breakfast and Sofia jumps from his arms, running to the door where Nanna awaits.

I wave to Nanna and she smiles. Everyone says goodnight before Bryce and I are alone again, staring out into the woods.

"Sofia is beautiful. She looks just like you." The moment the words are out, I blush. I can't believe I just called Bryce beautiful.

"I wouldn't mention that to Thomas if I were you. That's a sharp bone for him, that Sofia looks more mine than his."

"Does Sofia know you're a Keeper? Does she know what her father is?"

I know Sofia isn't an old soul, Bryce told me a week ago when I asked about Abby. Our children were born with new souls.

Bryce shrugs. "I'm not entirely sure what Thomas tells her, but my family and I don't censor Sofia, we have nothing to be ashamed of. She knows we're different, hears us talking. But she's too young to understand the perplexity of our world. Someday, when she's older, if Thomas will allow it, we'll teach her everything."

I can see it hurts him to keep things from his niece. I know the feeling. Fudging the truth about Maxi's death and the break in has eaten away at my conscience for days. But part of parenting, part of maturity, I think, is knowing when a child is mature enough to hear the truth. And when they're not.

Bryce leans forward, resting his forehead on the window frame. "When children are born with a strong connection to their old soul, they naturally tap into hidden talents from previous lives. But society frowns upon unusual talents and eccentric behavior, quickly putting the kibosh on what is deemed adolescent imagination at best, or mental illness at worst." He sighs. "It's a shame really, because when nurtured these children bloom, gifted at telepathy, precognition, telekinesis, levitation, and much, much more."

"When I was a kid I used to lie in bed and stare at the ceiling until I could touch it. I swear I'd float, hovering inches from the stucco. I remember telling my mother about it once."

"And?"

"She told me to keep it to myself. That I was silly and adorable."

"A few months ago, I was called to assist with a situation. A four-year-old boy had been lowered into a dormant well to cleanse his body of evil spirits. When I arrived at the remote Turkish village, the boy had been at the bottom of the thirty-six foot shaft for three days without food or water. This was the local clergy's cure for clairvoyance."

"The thought makes my skin crawl, but I'm not surprised. Human beings can be brutal in their beliefs."

Bryce nods. "Not only was the boy's soul capable of recalling the art of telepathy, he knew the power of invisibility. And could explain it. He could describe the use of light to transform physical matter into transparent matter and the use of energy from the seven major centers in the chakra system to project energy. He could, by all accounts, remember man's oldest form of self-defense, invisibility."

"What torturous past did this boy's soul experience to recall disappearing from sight?" The thought makes me shiver, and a few of my more recent nightmares come to mind. "What happened to the boy, did he survive?"

"He's living with a friend of Angitias."

"The witch," I say, remembering the woman from Bryce's

Halloween party.

Bryce grins. "Her friend runs a school for the gifted in Russia, a secluded little place called the House of Ved'ma." I must look confused because he says, "The Russian word for witch is ved'ma, literally meaning, one who knows."

It all comes together. Bryce's powers, the mind reading, the superhuman strength, the memory; these are natural capabilities of the human mind, the soul, but are considered witchcraft. A light flickers in my head. To protect my family, I need to learn how to tap into my soul's inner strength, its knowledge of the mystical. I've got to think like a witch.

Bryce's chuckle pulls me from my thoughts. "Change of plans," he says, grabbing my hand and guiding me from the office.

At the front door he tosses me my coat. He looks downright giddy so I follow without question. I've just finished lacing my boots when he pulls me close placing a knitted hat over my head. We laugh as the puff of wool flops over my face. "I know where you can concentrate," he says, grinning. He opens the door and we step out into the night.

Even in the dark the woods call to me. The moon reflects off the bright white snow, illuminating the forest in shades of indigo. I'm overwhelmed by an urge to paint, to capture the beauty on canvas. The dense packing snow crunches under foot. There is no wind but the air has bite, nibbling the tip of my nose. I remove a glove and reach out to touch the branches of an ancient blue spruce. The needles are chilled, but soft. Furry buds await spring. The silence captures me, trancelike, until I feel Bryce watching, his billowing breath the only proof he's breathing.

"Close your eyes, feel the energy that radiates from the trees," he says.

I tilt my head back and concentrate. The warmth starts at my feet and works its way up my body until a buzz rings in my ears. I feel . . .I feel . . .alive.

I open my eyes and the forest snaps back into place, serene but dormant. The feeling is gone, the cold seeping into my boots.

"Tell me," I say, turning to Bryce, "which came first, the chicken or the egg?"

Bryce laughs, his entire body shuddering with amusement.

"Funny girl. I assume you're referring to which came first, the human form or the soul, and the answer is neither. One does not exist without the other. Some Keepers believe their soul experienced life for millions of years before man. But if this is true, if our soul existed within creatures like dinosaurs prior to mankind's rein, we have no memory of it."

I walk along the tree line, kicking at clumps of snow. A fresh blanket drapes over manmade mounds, and I realize these woods are well-traveled. I spot what looks like a fort and a pyramid of snowballs.

"Who created souls?" I chuck a snowball at Bryce. It hits him in the shoulder, smashing into bits. He looks surprised.

"The great unknown question. Good luck finding someone to teach you that one."

I gather snow into my gloves. "I thought you knew everything." I throw another ball but Bryce disappears and it smacks into a tree.

I hear his laugh before he appears a few feet away. "Keepers contain the knowledge and power of our race. But we're limited in regards to history pre-dating our own creation. This is why religion, legends, and sagas are so popular. They give people something to believe, a neatly packaged answer to the unknown. Most don't care if it's the right or wrong answer, they just like to feel that there is one."

I've never believed in a higher power. I've always thought we humans were the power, and that miracles are within us. I never doubted we are capable of so much more than we understand.

Bryce dissolves, and when I turn he's standing right beside me. He's so close I can't lob the packed snow in my fist so I hide it behind my back. Bryce laughs and I pretend the silver sparks in his eyes don't provoke my stomach to do flips. I step back and stumble into a ditch, a long hole dug behind a rudimentary wall of ice and snow. Under me lies a pile of snowballs, and when Bryce reaches to help me I grab one and aim, but he's disappeared again.

"Nice try!" he bellows from afar.

Suddenly the hole reminds me of an open casket. Meyer comes to mind. "Where do we go when we die? I know where our body goes, back into the earth in one form or another, but what about our soul, where does it go? Does it immediately jump to another body, a newborn?"

Bryce leans over the wall, shaking his head. "Most choose to reflect, to think about what they've learned."

"They go to heaven?"

"Where they go is more a time than place. Some souls call it Spirit World, but that's merely a name of convenience. There, a soul feels at peace, one with Earth's energy. There is no negative emotion, only contemplation, an infinite time for basking in the contribution of life."

"Sounds kinda beautiful."

I hope Meyer is there, at peace.

"It is," says Bryce, "and it isn't. There's no color, yet everything is bright. There's nothing to touch or smell, but the aroma of your favorite bread engulfs you and the memory of a fleeting touch is so strong you'd swear it was real. Eventually you realize the experiences that drive you, make you feel, are memories made while joined with a living being."

I suppose I wouldn't enjoy the scent of grass if I couldn't wriggle my toes in it. And what would love be if you couldn't hold the one you're attracted to, or look into their eyes, or hear them breathing?

A series of thumps followed by flying snow catches my attention and I peek over the wall. Bryce is about twenty yards away, partially concealed behind a similar wall of ice. When he sees I've made out what is obviously the stage of an earlier snowball fight, he laughs and throws another one in my direction.

"Finally, a counter attack!"

We take turns hurling well-packed balls at each other, mine hitting nothing but branches. Bryce is either quick to move or he disappears all together. I lean over to scoop more snow and get belted, the force knocking me over.

"Sorry." he yells.

I duck into the trench, gathering snow for an arsenal. I need time, a distraction.

"Is that the best you can do? You're a Lemurian, a Keeper! Come on, man, I want to see this power in action!"

"You've seen my soul as an eagle." He's not even slightly interested in taking my bait. "What more do you need to see?"

"I'd just witnessed the violation of my private property and the murder of my dog. I was under serious duress." I tweak the line. "I wanna see your tricks.

Bryce laughs and a round of shots pound my barricade, the last leaving a gaping hole at one end.

"Let me see you fly," I say, trying not to chuckle, "or lift a bus or something." My knees are frozen numb and I can hardly move my fingers. I count the mini mounds of snow that barely pass as balls, formulating a battle plan.

"Tess, power has a cost. I don't hurl it around like a toy. I could lift a bus, but why would I?"

I pop up, lobbing an armful of mushy bullets, one at a time.

"To show me you can." I watch Bryce shatter each snowball with a simple wave.

"What about the people on the bus? What about the driver? What about the innocent people walking by or the curious child? Do I disregard their safety to prove something to you?"

The last of my snowballs falls to the ground, not even close to the mark. Okay, so I hadn't thought about the potential passengers. And I've officially lost this snowball fight.

I pout.

"We make choices," says Bryce, stepping over his wall and toward me. "We learn from the decisions we make, the good and the bad." He pulls the hat down over my eyes. "Lifting a bus to show off would be a bad call on my part."

Bryce is right and I know it. Still, there are things I want to see him do, things I want to learn. There is so much I don't know. And speaking of choices, why did he let Thomas hit him?

"Is Thomas stronger or faster than you?"

Bryce shakes his head, in on my game. "I would neither run from nor strike my brother. I love him."

"So you just stood there and let him beat you? Why didn't you stop him?"

"We all make choices. Mine was to allow my brother to vent his frustration."

I amble to the front of the house, aware of how cold I am. I'm half soaked and frozen.

"You don't even sound angry about it," I say.

"I'm not. I would do anything for my brother. There are no conditions."

"Does he know this?" The answer is written on Bryce's face,

setting me off. "He knew you wouldn't defend yourself, yet he hit you anyway. What an ass. Why would he do that?"

Bryce takes my hand. "That's a question you'll have to ask him."

"Maybe I will." When I'm not pissed at him. I look to Bryce, wondering if he heard what I was thinking. "How do you do that?"

Bryce looks away. "Do what?"

"Ha, ha. How do you read my mind exactly?"

He drops the charade. "I don't hear your cognitive voice, and I can't visualize your exact words, although sometimes they come through loud and clear. It's more of a feeling. I can feel your thoughts."

"Can you teach me?"

"Someday. If you learn to clear your mind and concentrate." I roll my eyes and he grins. "Like everything, man is made of electro-magnetic energy. Our thoughts create energy that is dispersed into the atmosphere like radio waves. Anyone capable of picking-up on this transmission can essentially read your mind. The trick is distinguishing other thought waves from your own."

I let go of Bryce's hand and consider blasting the heat in my car.

"I guess that's kind of cool."

"Lemurians rarely communicated using language. They shared memories, images, and sensations, not words. Now, however, it's a necessary skill, one that allows me to assist my students." He sighs. "People's true feelings aren't always great to know. Sometimes I prefer to work blind."

"Ah, so you can shut it off." I dig keys from my coat pocket.

"With you I forget. Partly because you fearlessly say almost anything that comes to mind and partly because I'm so comfortable with you."

I step closer. "Speaking of that, being comfortable, I mean. Why is that?" I'm suddenly hot. I know Bryce prefers to keep these rendezvous a great distance from personal, but I can't shake the feeling that there's something he isn't telling me. "You know I feel the same. I want to know why?"

His complexion turns pasty. "This is not a subject we should be discussing right now."

I lean forward, studying his apprehensive features. He doesn't move, but the muscles in his jaw flex and the glint in his eyes turns bright white. I search for what he's concealing, but if it's there, in those explosive eyes, it's hidden beyond my reach.

"I guess this session is over then," I say, turning back to Magic Carpet.

Bryce slams the car door, the force rattling the windows.

"I was your consort in several lives," he says, the words escaping captivity. He rakes a hand over the back of his neck and fumbles for his pockets.

I stop dead in my tracks.

"How is that possible? How could you have been my . . .You were my lover?"

"I was your confidante, your advisor. In this day you would call me your best friend." He pauses. "And yes, I, my soul, shared your bed."

Bryce watches me slowly break into a grin. What can I say? I don't have a clue what to think, never mind putting a thought through my vocal chords. My mind flashes vivid and sensual dreams I've had of Bryce, dreams I wouldn't dare confess. Instantly I remember the first time we met, at the parent-teacher meeting, when Bryce was naked, wrapped in white fur.

We were lovers.

"You know this, Tess. I can feel it when you touch me with

even the simplest of gestures."

I tear my eyes away and his gaze relentlessly searches for another connection.

"Are you going to deny it?" he asks.

Deny it? I couldn't even if I wanted to. Besides, he's the one with the accurate memory. My dry mouth refuses to form words as I rotate in neurotic spurts in search of the door handle.

Bryce sighs. "I think you've had enough for one night. Head home and get some sleep."

Like that's going to happen now. I open the door in a daze.

"Regarding Thomas," says Bryce as I sit. "You really should give him a chance."

We were lovers. I'm shocked but rather impressed. In any lifetime I imagine Bryce would be a pretty good . . .

Bryce clears his throat.

"I'm leaving town for a while. My family has connections and my dad is trying to help me find out more about this lost soul. Thomas will be keeping an eye on things here," he says, still attempting to draw my attention. I drop the keys, hardly able to see through the explicit visions. "That might be easier to do if you were amicable." Bryce shuts the door.

Somehow I start the ignition. I rub my eyes and try to focus.

Bryce steps back, frowning.

I'm overwhelmingly flushed.

We were lovers.

# PERSPECTIVE

## February 10th

**M**y nights are spent tossing and turning within two extremes. One end of the spectrum has me hot and bothered by Bryce's touch, and the other has me suffering deathly encounters with lost souls. Both have me waking with a sudden jerk, an accelerated heartbeat, and a shortness of breath.

Seldom do I reach a state that forces me to succumb to being medicated, but between life-altering truths and very little sleep, today I'd settle for a swift whack to the head. After delivering Abby to school, I loiter in a steamy shower then spend twenty minutes searching for a pain reliever that hasn't expired. It's futile. If I had Tylenol, it was ditched in the wake of the break in. So I surrender, climbing back into bed with a damp cloth over my eyes, concentrating on the soothing vocals of Sarah McLachlan seeping from the stereo.

I'm hovering on the brink of deliverance when my cell rings, shattering my respite. I grunt as I grope for the phone.

"Tess, Sofia misses Abby a lot."

It takes a minute to register the voice minus small talk.

"She sees her at school, Thomas."

"It's not the same. Sofia craves one-on-one time with her best friend. Is that too much to ask?"

I poke around throbbing neurons, trying to come up with a good reason to say, *yes, yes, that is too much to ask*, but when my probe uncovers only issues between us adults, I wave the white flag.

"I guess not," I mumble, pushing my pride aside for the kids.

"Look, tomorrow's forecast is calling for sunshine. There is a ton of snow and we've got a wicked toboggan hill out back. Bring Abby over and let the kids play a while."

"Fine," I say, curtly. "I'll drop her off at ten."

Thomas groans, obviously frustrated. "Please stay and talk to me. I know we see each other, but it's not the same, and we don't talk anymore. Really talk. I care about you, and it's only fair you hear my side. Please, I also miss my best friend."

I'm not a heartless savage, so his forlorn words wallop me. My head recoils from the impact. I'm mad at the way Thomas has handled all of this, the way he's lied to me repeatedly. But he's also stuck his neck out to help me, to find this lost soul so Abby and I can feel safe again. And aside from our daughters' close ties, I want Bryce and Thomas to resume a healthy relationship as brothers. I guess I should try to salvage our friendship, to return things to the way they were. Sort of.

"I'll stay for tea." If Bryce can forgive and forget, so can I.

"We'll start over," he says.

"We'll start over."


**Abby and Sofia** run to the playroom before I even get my shoes and coat shaken off at the door.

Thomas was right. Abby and Sofia have been feeling the strain in our relationship. I'm ashamed to say that in my self-absorption I hadn't noticed, not until I mentioned the arranged play date to Abby during our afternoon walk from school. Her entire demeanor changed. Immensely pleased, she giggled and skipped the whole way home then danced to her room to pick out specific toys to bring, ones she and Sofia enjoy together. She chattered about her best friend all through dinner then again through breakfast this morning, leaving no doubt that a talk with Thomas is an absolute necessity. Thomas and I need to work out our issues so our daughters can be together.

Of course, like most things in life, this is easier said than done.

"Come on in, I have the kettle on," says Thomas, leading the way down the hall.

Bowls and baking utensils clog the sink, but the counters are spotless and the stainless steel fridge almost glows. I pull out a seat at the table, tucking my foot under my butt as I watch Thomas nervously putter around the kitchen. Squinting, I try to distinguish extraordinary movements from the mundane, but nothing stands out. He looks like a normal guy. Other than the shorts.

"Help yourself," says Thomas, placing a silver tray of fresh baked apple fritters in front of me.

"Well, well, you're pulling out the big guns." The wafting aroma attacks my defenses by way of cravings. "I thought food was the way into a man's heart?"

Thomas leans on the island, watching me. "Whatever it takes."

I take two. "You were right, by the way," I mumble between bites. "Abby's been missing Sofia. I can't recall the last time they played together out of school."

"The last pageant rehearsal—they had a sleepover at your place, and you and I made out in my truck."

It was actually the night of the break in, at Bryce's place, but I keep my mouth shut.

Thomas pulls a chair and sits next to me, picking apple chunks out of his fritter. "I guess we shouldn't talk about the pageant or . . ." He changes his mind. "We're starting over, remember?"

"Sure," I say, even though I feel something altogether different. I'm itching to discuss the part of the pageant where he beat his brother. Or the scenes in which he claimed me like an inanimate object. Maybe we should debate the abundance of lies and artificial pretenses. And what about the fact that he put his mouth on me without revealing a single grain of authenticity?

"How's the painting coming along?" He's straining to sound casual.

I swallow the last of my fritter. "It's not. Between hunting down replacements for house stuff that got damaged in the break in, raising a daughter without a husband, and learning about the mythical world of souls, Lemurians, and Keepers, I don't have enough hours in a day to paint."

Thomas drops his fritter onto a napkin. He rolls it and throws it like a basketball into the garbage can. "If it's all so time-consuming and stressful then stop," he says, his stare lingering on the can across the room.

"Stop." What does he mean by stop?

"Let it all go and live a normal life. Forget about lost souls and house raids—that won't happen again. Stop letting my brother fill your head with a world you're better off not knowing. And don't raise your daughter alone. Be with me."

"Thomas . . ."

"I was born a Keeper, just like Bryce. Yet even with all this knowledge and power, I choose to pretend it doesn't exist and live an ordinary existence. Why do you think that is?"

I stare at him, thinking. "I figured you needed time away, to focus on Sofia after the divorce, just like you said. Was that another lie?"

Thomas looks away. "I'm not so sure the knowledge is a good thing. I don't even know why we bother teaching people. I want better for you, more for you, a different life for you and Abby." He leans forward, hands steepled. "Believe me, you don't want to be part of that world. You want to stay far, far away from it."

"I need to know, Thomas. I want to know."

"Did Bryce give you the 'knowledge is power' speech?" He whips his hands down and leans back in his chair. "It's bullshit. Knowledge would have gotten you killed that day in the coffee shop. That lost soul would've taken your life without so much as an afterthought. The fact that you didn't have a clue what you were seeing is undoubtedly the only thing that saved your ass." The chair legs scrape along the floor. "Did Bryce tell you that?"

"No, but—"

"You're better off oblivious, ignorant, blissful."

I give my head a shake, endeavoring to keep Thomas from getting to me.

"I need to understand who I am, Thomas, to learn how to live with what I see. And Bryce doesn't lecture me. He answers my questions, my many questions."

Thomas laughs. It's not a nice laugh. "You should be learning how to ignore what you see. You should be taught to look right through lost souls, as if they don't exist. If you'd known how to do that, maybe the one in the cafe wouldn't have noticed you at all. He surely wouldn't have ransacked your house. Your dog would be alive, and Sonia wouldn't be at the fucking morgue."

I stand abruptly, toppling the chair. It lands with a sharp crash and I flinch like a deer within gunfire. "You can't think that I had any control over—"

"This kind of knowledge will get you killed." Thomas rises.

"Then who'll raise Abby? Huh? You want a kid with two dead parents?"

I gasp, shocked he'd say something so cruel. Abby cannot be parentless. She just can't. My chest is tightening. For the first time in weeks I actually feel the cold hand of fear. Could Thomas be speaking the truth? Had I reacted differently, would the lost soul have stayed away? Could I have saved Maxi? And what about Sonia, could I have done something to save her? Bryce says there was nothing I could've done, but is he wrong? And what if I was killed? Grams and Gramps are in their eighties and won't be with us for long. Abby only has me. She can't lose the only family she has left.

"I've lived in this town for over a year," says Thomas. "Not once have I seen a lost soul anywhere near these parts. In fact, I hadn't seen much beyond the realm of normal until Bryce moved in. He brought danger here, with his fancy parties and social web of outcasts. Had he stayed out of—"

"Bryce would never knowingly—"

"You're defending him? You don't even know him. My brother has already tossed one woman to those damn souls of purgatory. You wanna be next?"

The heat jumps several degrees. "What are you talking about?" I'm tearing my napkin to shreds. My hands shake. I'm not so sure I want to know the answer.

"Come on, you don't think you're the first, do you?" Thomas sneers. "Bryce's last girlfriend was butchered by a lost soul and he couldn't do shit to save her. Even if he could've, he wouldn't. All that crap about choices and consequences did nothing but lead her to slaughter. Bryce didn't help her. A Keeper's knowledge and power didn't save her." His facial muscles tic under the stress of his locked jaw. "And it sure as fuck didn't save my wife."

Holy shit. I stop breathing for a moment.

Thomas launches into a predatory pace between the table and butcher-block island. He's pulled up his sleeves, mindlessly rubbing the scar along his arm.

"You wanna know the truth about this life? We are here to struggle. We're challenged with nothing but heartache and disappointment, pushing us to our limits. We spend our time suffering and wallowing in a life we can't control. My wife was an old soul. She could see what you see. Her husband hired me because she suffered from nightmares, screaming for mercy in languages she didn't know, and their church had written them off. I tried to help her. Instead of teaching her avoidance, I tried to be the Keeper I was born to be. I told her about our world, our history, our truth. She wouldn't believe me, so I tried harder. I pushed and pushed until I finally had her convinced." He chuckles darkly. "She thought I was an abomination. She made sure she couldn't have more children. All I wanted was a son. I should've had a son. She called Sofia a freak of nature and took off. She went back to him, back to that asshole without a clue. She abandoned her own child!" His hands fist in his hair, the blood drained from his knuckles. "She ran like hell from the world you're fucking volunteering for."

I open my mouth but no words come out.

"Why was I powerless, Tess? Why couldn't I stop her? You wanna know what she did with this reputed knowledge?" He slams the counter with a fist and I jump. "She put a fucking bullet in her head!"

I gasp. His wife shot herself?

My mother downed two bottles of pills while I was at the hospital stitching a run-in with an ex. It was the last sunrise she ever saw, and her death nearly destroyed me. This is the past Thomas struggles with. This is his demon.

"This isn't the life I want for you. This isn't the choice I want you to make. You shouldn't be with Bryce. Be with me. You can paint while I tend the farm. Abby and Sofia will be sisters, and we'll have son. We'll live a simple existence, uncomplicated and safe. I've shunned my work a long time with no intention of returning. It's not all glory and power, as Bryce would have you believe. A Keeper's life is hard work with little reward. We spend our entire lives helping others, but when we need help, who is there for us?"

"Maybe that's why there are twelve of you," I mumble.

"Ah, he told you that, huh? Did he tell you I'm the mistake, the one that shouldn't have been born? The fucking family mishap?"

"He told me how much he loves you."

Thomas's shoulders slump and he rubs his eyes. "He doesn't love me enough to stay away from you."

"Shake the jealousy, Thomas. Work on a relationship with your family, your brother. He cares for you, for Sofia, and wants to be close. As for us," my hand flutters between us, "we won't ever be anything more than friends."

"I know how you feel now, but in time you'll think differently."

"Time won't make a difference, Thomas." I plow into the overturned chair by mistake, grunting in pain. "I have feelings for Bryce, a connection I don't see an end to. We have history."

Thomas blocks my way from the kitchen, his entire frame swallowing the doorway.

"I've heard all about my brother's pathetic theories. Did he tell you he was your lover in past lives? Ha! I'm sure he did. Anything to get you in his bed."

"Thomas, this is none of your business, and you've no right to—"

"Let me guess, he left out the part about the two of you never producing a child together. Never ever. Not in a single past life did you bear his son."

My gaze falls to the floor as bells go off in my head.

"Did he forget to mention you were killed before finding your happily ever after? Every time. Every fucking time! You were brutally murdered in each and every life that mingled with his."

I stumble back and grasp the table to keep from sliding to the floor. My head swims in a lifetime of nightmares.

The brunt of a fist.

The fatal twist of a knife.

The theft of my soul.

Suddenly my violent dreams take on new meaning. Shudders run through my body. A cold sweat leaves the smell of fear on my skin.

"You have no future with Bryce."

Oh my God, what if Thomas is right? I hold tight to the counter, my body going into shock. Maybe it's too dangerous to consider a life with Bryce. Is that what I've chosen, a future with Bryce? My baby girl, Abby, my innocent daughter, her safety comes first. Should I take her away, leave Carlisle and find another place to live, a safer place, somewhere far from lost souls and Keepers? Where? How?

I follow the wall down the hall, slowly, unbalanced. My emotions are on overload.

I'm enthralled with Bryce's lessons, the wonders of this world being unraveled like a good book, but is it all too much for me? Am I making the right choices? Maybe a normal life, the life I had with Meyer . . .

"Be with me," says Thomas, stepping close, too close.

I look up, into his eyes. They're a turbulent storm of gray, and I'm struck by one word: longing. What if the kind of life

Thomas offers would keep my family safe?

"Tess, be with me, we'll have our family. With me you'd be—"

"Lying," I say, pushing past him. A rush of clarity has me heated to a boil as I stomp down the hall to the front door. "I don't want to hear anymore." I grab my coat and boots. Thomas reaches for me and I plow past him, opening the door. "I'll be back for Abby at one o'clock. Have her ready."

Thomas grabs the door so I can't pass. "Promise you'll think about what I've said."

He's not going to let me go until I agree.

"Fine," I say, actually hating him.

He opens the door and I step out without looking back.

Think about what he's said . . .

How can I not?

# PRECIPICE

## February 12th

**M**y toes dangle over the edge, curled against cold stone. I flex and a biting wind rises up the monstrous precipice to burn the tender skin between all ten digits. I stare into nothingness, the unfathomable abyss, as the chill smothers my face, stinging extremities. The spread before me is so dark I might as well be blind. Anxiety builds within my core, setting fire to every internal morsel. I can hear fear in the wind. It should affect me. It should rattle me and attack my senses. It tries, desperately, but my soul is numb and too stunned to run.

*Tap, tap.*

I jump inches from the ground before registering the sound of bone on glass. Bryce stands at the glass-paneled door of my studio, my haven. A pensive smile fails to reach his eyes. He slowly raises his hand to wave.

Somewhere in my mind swims the notion to open the door and welcome him in, but my feet are firmly planted, my toes still wrapped around the ledge of frigid rock. To move would mean stepping into the abyss. Or running in the opposite direction. Bryce opens the door a crack and asks for permission to enter, snapping me from this self-induced trance. I nod and smile awkwardly, crimson paint dripping down my sleeve. Bryce gently closes the door behind him.

I pull at my smock, hiding the tea stains on my clothes. Days of sleep deprivation have left me looking a little worse for wear. Okay, I look like shit. I stare at Bryce, unable to speak. At least one of us looks good. My favorite scarf hangs from his neck, and his dark tailored suit and crisp white shirt remind me of an Oreo cookie. I haven't eaten today.

Seconds into pleasantries Bryce asks, "What's wrong? Something has changed. I can't read you. You have walls up," he says, peering into my eyes.

"For real?" I'm surprised to hear this. I didn't even know I could do that, block his intrusion into my head. I glare right back, losing myself in his hypnotic glow. "I had a chat with Thomas," I say, shaking my head clear. Bryce's expression evolves to concern in an instant. "You were right, your brother has an interesting perspective."

I don't need to repeat Thomas's position. I doubt he's ever held back with Bryce.

"Yes," he says, pulling his spine straight and rolling his shoulders back.

He doesn't look shocked in the least, and for the first time I wonder if his sudden departure was legitimate or just a ruse to get me to speak to his brother. I study him, suspicious, but my stance doesn't prompt a confession and I'm out of energy to bicker.

"You knew Thomas would try to talk me out of . . . everything." I'm struggling to find the right words. Having had days to toil over my thoughts and emotions, my lines are well rehearsed. But now, now that he stands before me with the face of a god and the ability to melt my every defense, I can't bring myself to rant.

"Yes," he whispers, the sound barely distinguishable from

the swish of ceiling fans. "I wanted every option presented to you. As much as it pains me to see you torn and confused, you needed to hear my brother's point of view, your choices. That is life's gift, the freedom of choice."

The studio falls silent. Minutes tick by. Even the blowing wind seems to halt while I process.

Bryce steps closer. "You can tell me anything, you know." His expression desperate. He looks past me, taking in my canvas. Then looks to the floor. "Thomas is a good man. He can give you the life you want, a good life, a different life than . . ." The obstruction in his throat clears. "He'd make you happy if you gave him the chance."

"I don't understand. You want me to be with Thomas?"

"No." He inhales a mouthful of air, moving closer. "I want you to be—" He looks away, studying my canvas, obviously troubled. "If you choose to be with Thomas or to live his way of life, now that you've learned the truth, I will respect your wishes and leave."

"Leave for where?" I ask on a whim.

Bryce deflates, obviously assuming I'd prefer he move from Carlisle, leaving me with Thomas. This is not an option. There is no future for Thomas and me. Since our heated discussion, I've thought about all he said—thought of nothing else—and although some of it scares me, frightens me to the core, I'm not about to let fear choose my path in life. Thomas's picture-perfect existence sounds beautiful. Knowing he's great with Abby even makes it tempting. But I'm not in love with Thomas. And although I'm sure he's being forthright with me, at least some grains of truth in his speech, I know his words are tainted with jealousy, fear, and anger.

I cross my arms, the air suddenly thick with determination. I'm not sure what I want from this life, but I'm sure of what I don't want. And right now I want answers.

"You leave town and Thomas watches over me," I say, standing tall. "How long do you think I'll tolerate being babysat? Maybe I shouldn't learn your truths. Maybe I should learn to run and hide? Maybe I should get as far away from Carlisle and Keepers as possible?"

"You are free to pick any course of action you wish," says Bryce. "But I doubt even Thomas would suggest you abandon the life you've made here. Lost souls are everywhere." He sighs and steps toward me. "I can't find a single reason this particular lost soul was here in town. As far as I can tell, he had no connection to Sonia, and no reason to be here, no family, no friends, not even employment. And I'm not sure if his interest in you is coincidental, spurred by curiosity, or planned, in hopes of eliminating a possible threat to his freedom. But I think he was satisfied with what he saw in your home and left town for good." Bryce sighs. "Look, you want and deserve your independence, your freedom. I can give you that. I can help you. There are worse out there, and there is much you don't know. But I am sure if you don't learn, your nightmares will eventually catch up with you."

He knows. Bryce knows I have gruesome nightmares. And that these scenes, these deathly reenactments are real: history, my history, moments my soul's past had to endure as its body was tortured and stripped of its will. Thomas was telling the truth.

Suddenly I'm pissed, fed-up with feeling powerless.

"Thomas is not divorced," I say. "His wife is dead."

Bryce neither confirms nor denies this fact, which in itself says plenty. The thought of death overwhelms me, and a vision of Sonia lying naked and bloody in the snow attacks my conscience. I snap the paintbrush in two and hurl it and the palette I'd spent hours mixing across the studio, splattering several shades of red across the floor.

"Had I . . . had I . . . in the café . . .?"

Bryce reaches out. "Oh, Tess—"

I push him away. "Tell me the truth, would Sonia be alive?"

"No, absolutely not." He groans. "You can't believe you had anything to do with Sonia's death. Tess, there is nothing you could've done. There is nothing anyone could have done."

Lifting my canvas from the easel, I hitch up my chin. "Your last girlfriend, is she dead?"

Bryce tips his head back and closes his eyes. "Yes."

He flinches as I thrust the wooden frame over my knee, breaking it in half. Bits of wood, paint, and staples fly this way and that.

"How did she die? Was she killed by a lost soul? What happened? And don't you dare lie to me."

"Her name was Lilith and I loved her," he says, voice pained. "I loved her for all the wrong reasons. She was wild and sexy and kept me on my feet, but she had no interest in being a Keeper's wife, and I didn't have the heart to try and change her, to make her into something she wasn't. I didn't have the right."

I shrink back, realizing I've forced him to talk about something private, something heartbreaking, something Thomas shouldn't have told me.

"Lilith lived life on the edge, like every day was her last. It was intoxicating, and I was drawn to her, to the way she soaked up every teeny morsel of every minute, hour, day. But Lilith also liked to play with fire, with danger, with lost souls, and her choices ultimately got her killed. I tried to help her, as a person I cared for dearly, not a student. I told her she'd lose, that her life was worth more than the thrill of the game, but she wouldn't listen. She never listened."

My focus on destruction has faded, ire gone. The canvas in my fists drops to the floor in a heap. Red paint is splattered everywhere.

"These previous lives, when you and I were . . ." I can't say the word lovers while he stands within arm's length. "Was I killed before we could have a family?"

Bryce sways before me, the look of horror tensing his face. He inhales a gust of air, holding it captive. Seconds pass before he regains his composure.

"Yes. I'm sure your nightmares have given you more than enough detail."

Oh my God. I've dreamt over a hundred lifetimes, all ending in death. I look to the canvases gently swaying from the ceiling on delicate chains. Creatures of mythical proportion stare back at me, daring me to rip them from their godlike positions. A renegade tear slides down my cheek and in an instant Bryce closes the space between us, holding my face against his warm chest and enclosing me in his jacket.

"Oh Tess."

We stand like this, me in Bryce's embrace, for countless minutes. His scent is calming, drug-like, sending me over the edge of the precipice to weightlessly drift in the abyss.

When Bryce finally loosens his grip I cling to him. I want to crawl under his shirt and fall asleep on his bare skin. At this moment I want to pretend. I want to live in a world where everything is as it seems. I want to forget these new discoveries and go back to thinking my visions are delusions and my nightmares are nothing more than an overactive imagination. I want Bryce to be a man, not a Keeper.

"What happens if I don't want to learn anymore?" I mumble into his chest.

"This is my fault. I let your eagerness and enthusiasm set the pace. I should've known not to go so far, to give you time to think on it all. No more for now."

"But I want to know." My mind is running in chaotic circles.

"We've been moving too fast in your lessons. We'll slow things down. You need time to absorb. You need to think about what Thomas has told you." His words get lost in my hair, his lips warming my scalp. "I'd prefer you come to terms with your choices without a Keeper's influence. And if you still feel the same about me . . ." He takes a step back so he can peer into my eyes, still holding me tight. "Come to dinner with me. Better yet, come to my place for dinner. Valentine's Day. No kids. No talk of Keepers and souls. Just you and me on a real date."

The sparks in his eyes ignite and I hold tight to this energy, this escape from reality. Valentine's Day. My first Valentine's without Meyer. I have feelings for Bryce, no doubt, but a date on such a day is making a statement.

"I understand," Bryce mumbles, looking away.

His lack of confidence when it comes to my affection baffles me. "You can't possibly think that my hesitation has anything to do with Thomas?" I see his reply in his eyes. "For someone so smart you are awfully dense." I fiddle with my wedding ring. "I don't know if I'm ready for the whole dating thing. And Valentine's is such a . . ." My words die off.

What am I saying? Valentine's is a day like any other, a media inflated holiday meant to boost the sales of overpriced roses that die in two days. I can handle a nice, quiet dinner with Bryce. We can discuss normal things like average men and women do on dates. I can wear that new skirt Grams bought me for Christmas along with my kick-ass red heels. I can put my hair up and dig out the audacious scarlet lipstick I haven't worn in ages.

"Maybe another day would be—"

"Valentine's is fine," I say, peeling the canvas stuck to his pant leg. Red paint drips over his shoes.

"My place, six o'clock." He places a finger under my chin. "Just a date. Just you and me, two ordinary people sharing each other's company."

He's trying to sound reassuring but the grin plastered across his face proves how big a deal it really is, and I start to second-guess myself.

Bryce disappears before I can change my mind. The canvas strip sways in my grasp, and the wind stirs branches into a chorus that sounds kind of like a death march.

Apparently my walls are down.

# BE MINE

## Valentine's

Thomas doesn't give up. Even though I've made my feelings painfully clear, he still called and asked me out for Valentine's. It was nice of him, and he made a grand effort to show his sweet side until I mentioned I already had plans. Then he got cranky. He didn't ask whom my plans were with. There was no need to. If I'd be anywhere other than home on the day of romance, I'd be with Bryce.

Still, my nerves are on edge, jumpy. I'm relieved Bryce suggested a hiatus, but our professional relationship has made it easy not to dwell on my feelings for him. This also includes what these feelings mean long-term. Am I ready for a serious relationship, especially one so convoluted? I'm not a teenager anymore. I'm not interested in a fling or a dead end—both figuratively and literally. I'm a mother. A single mother. I need to think about Abby.

Then there's the beaten-and-left-for-dead thing. According to history, odds aren't in my favor. I'm a strong woman, but come on, that would freak anybody out. I truly refuse to allow fear to dictate my life, but I'm not an idiot, I'm not about to gamble with my life either. I try to remember that my nightmares show only flashes of the past, not my future. And I don't believe my future in this life is predestined. Bryce doesn't either. If he did, he would have left Carlisle the minute he met me.

But what if we're wrong?

I miss Meyer and our uncomplicated life.

I'm wavering at Bryce's front door, heart pounding a mile a minute, glancing over my shoulder at Magic Carpet. Part of me wants to bolt. I can't start a relationship with Bryce. I look up, the impressive mansion daunting. My hands are clammy, even after rubbing them on my coat. I turn back to the door and draw a mouthful of February air. This is just a date, nothing more. I can go home if I want, cower from change, swallow the poor widow pill.

But I am not a coward.

The door opens before I even knock.

"Hey," says Bryce.

I don't know if it's anxiety or the almost six and a half feet of in-your-face masculinity, but I can't keep my thoughts straight.

"Maybe this isn't such a good idea."

Bryce takes my hand and leads me inside. "Dinner is ready," he says, helping me with my coat.

I examine my watch, tapping it in confusion. Where did thirty minutes go? I left on time. I think back to the drive over. Maybe I did wander down a few wrong streets while lost in my head.

"You're far away," whispers Bryce, gently dusting snow from the hair that has fallen over my eyes. He hangs my coat and scarf on the elegant wrought iron swirl that makes up the entryway coat rack. His scarf, the scarf, is there, calling out to me, but Bryce gently guides me through the elaborate stained glass arch showcasing the dining room. He doesn't mention my tardiness. No comment regarding my pathetic smile. I think he's even staying out of my head.

I pause in the doorway, the setting so breathtakingly beautiful I'm rapt. The stunning glass table is illuminated with a dozen tapered candles supported by dainty silver candlesticks, crisp white linens, silver plates, and crystal wine glasses that glow bright in the candlelight. A bottle of wine patiently waits on ice and a crackling fire toasts the atmosphere to perfection. I inhale deeply, reveling in the aroma wafting from the kitchen. My fingertips glide over the soft, finely woven linen. I luxuriate in the sensations, soaking in the ambiance, and my worries ebb away. I can't help but wonder what I've done to deserve this.

Bryce dances to my side and bows regally. "Twenty-nine Chateau Latour," he says, filling my wine glass. His jet-black sweater accentuates his palpable virility and combined with his dark hair sets a dramatic stage for chiseled facial features and combustible silver-gray eyes. I sample the wine, watching him. He's trying to act casual, but I can see he's nervous too.

I smile and Bryce smiles back.

Now there's my white knight.

The nervousness is short lived, and as the hours fly by, we enjoy three courses of meticulously prepared plates of edible art and effortless conversation. We chat about Bryce's renovation woes and geothermal heating. We talk about all the foreign places we've traveled, his list endless. I comment on the embroidered chairs and the grand buffet, their antiquity intriguing, and Bryce weaves a fantastical story filled with discovery and nostalgia. We discuss the many schools we've attended, and Bryce tells me about his parents and his childhood, seamlessly maneuvering around anything out of the ordinary. I discover Bryce knows Mrs. Maples, has known her his whole life. Her late husband was an archeologist and close friend of Bryce's father.

We don't talk about Thomas. No one mentions Meyer. We

laugh over the uncanny similarities in our favorite books, and joke about cinematic duds, the movies that drove us crazy for one reason or another, and the few that made us sprint from the theater. We delve into music, songs that make us dance around like fools, lyrics that inspire us, and instruments we wish we'd learned to play.

Bryce pours the last of the wine and we hold our hands to the candlelight, playfully debating the pros and cons of our long slender fingers vis-a-vis musical brilliance. "You win," says Bryce, tenderly stroking the sensitive underbelly of my wrist. "Your hands are beautiful and talented."

My head struggles with conflicting desires. Part of me wants to surrender, to get lost in the feel of Bryce's touch, the liquid quality of his accent. Another part warns of trouble, of the danger lurking in those silver eyes that cavort with the flicker of candlelight, of a past we might not shake.

*You have been killed in every life that mingled with his.*

Bryce rises from his chair. "Let's relocate," he says. "I'm dying to show you something."

His exhilaration is contagious and I laugh in spite of myself, the wine rushing to my head.

With our wine glasses in hand, Bryce pulls me down a long winding hallway into a dark room. For a moment I panic, wondering where he's leading me, until alcohol dampens my sense of self-preservation and I really don't care. With the flick of a switch a row of pot lights and several wall-mounted lamps jump to life.

At first glance it looks like some sort of sitting room. Within seconds my mind registers the sight and my breath catches in my throat. Gliding to the center of the room, I spin in circles, taking in the spectacle. Magnificent oil paintings are professionally displayed and illuminated. The space is largely standing room only with a few scattered antique benches and an elegant oversized settee richly upholstered in striking earth tones, offering visual impact against the ebony floors and creamy-white walls.

"You have your very own art gallery," I mutter in shock.

Bryce watches me, grinning. "I thought you might like this."

Overwhelmed, I shut my eyes and randomly pick a work of genius to admire first. "Hieronymous Bosch, *Garden of Earthly Delights*, circa 1504," I regurgitate from memory. I step closer, absorbing the painting's power. The smell of ancient oils pummels me and I tangle my fingers in the back of my sweater to keep from reaching out. "You have all three panels," I say, peeking at Bryce for a split second. "This can't be the original." Minutes pass without a response so I steal another quick glance. The look on Bryce's face is priceless, and I shamelessly swallow a huge gulp of wine. *This is the original.* "I thought this painting was at the Museo del Prado in Madrid?" I can't tear my eyes from the masterpiece in front of me.

"It was. On loan from my family until last year, when I wanted it back," he says, very matter-of-fact, not a smidgen of gloating.

I would gloat.

"This is insane! You actually own this?"

Bryce nods, and I'm over the moon with delight. Without delay I step to the next miracle on the wall and Bryce walks me through his collection, his knowledge of fine art rousing my libido. I analyze the brush strokes, the pigments, the awe-inspiring details. All the while, Bryce's velvet voice seduces my intellect. "Redon, *The Cyclops*, circa 1914," he says. "William Blake, *Ancient of Days*, 1794."

"I can't believe you can spend time with these wondrous creations whenever you wish. I'd never leave the room!" We make a slow sweep of the gallery and when we're done I yearn to start again, craving the smooth cadence of Bryce's voice.

"There's a painting at the top of the stairs I'd like you to see." Bryce gently guides me toward a stairway leading up. I move reluctantly, questioning Bryce's motives. "A painting," Bryce repeats, "and then we'll have some dessert."

Heat from his mouth warms my ear and tiny shivers run through me from head to toe. I swallow another gulp of wine.

One step to go and I stop short.

"No way." I'm blown away.

At the top of the stairs, on a large landing outside double French doors to the master bedroom, under custom lighting that calls attention to the abundance of texture, is a painting I recognize. I know every single stroke, every color mix, every ounce of heart and soul that went into creating it.

My heart and soul.

"I—I—" I stammer. I don't know what to say. My head whirls in circles.

"The honor is yours." He rests his hands on my waist.

"Tess Morgan, *Crimson Spirit*," I murmur as I lean into him, allowing his arms to hold me tight within his frame.

I'm in shock. Bryce has my painting on his wall, in this exquisite mansion, among world-renowned artists. As a painter there is little more I want for my work than to have it where it's admired and cared for. I feel like a doting mother, proud of her progeny. Even now, after all these years, this piece still takes my breath away.

I'm so happy I could fly.

"I sold this painting at a gallery showing a few years ago."

"To me," Bryce breathes, his embrace tightening. His sweet scent surrounds me, tugging at my heartstrings and teasing my every defense. "You're humming again. I should call you my angel," he whispers in my ear.

"Because of my painting? The wings?" I say.

"No," he says, his eyes leading mine downward. Our feet hover a foot above the hardwood floor, freaking me out. "Relax. Your heart is racing. Just think calming thoughts and breathe."

I release the tension in my muscles starting at the top of my head, working my way down, just like he taught me. A minute or two passes and I open my eyes cautiously. Total relief only comes when I confirm our feet are firmly on the floor.

"You said there was to be no mythical stuff tonight," I say. "That would include hocus-pocus, don't you think?"

"It wasn't me."

I turn and glare. "How? How did I do that?"

"Well," he says, eyes radiant. "You were able to—"

I press two fingers over Bryce's lips, stopping him midsentence. He bites me and I yank my hand back laughing.

"This is a normal date, two ordinary people talking about regular things. Tomorrow, tell me tomorrow."

Bryce grins. "No parlor tricks," he says, turning me to face another set of stairs. As I turn I see Bryce's bedroom, the huge four-poster bed taking center stage. Bryce chuckles. "Your heart is racing again." He takes my hand.

I follow him down the stairs as quick as my feet will take me.

"You were awfully loud for someone with so few tools out to work with," I tease when we step into the kitchen. Bryce's jaunts to the kitchen during dinner were quite noisy, so I expected to see the telltale signs of labor, but other than a few roasting pans in the sink, there is no evidence of our three-course meal.

"Yes, well," says Bryce, his hearty laugh filling the room, "Clause is a very talented man." He heads to a set of paneled doors on one side of the floor-to-ceiling curtain I vividly recall leading to an outdoor patio. He tugs on a steel handle and a gust of cold air bellows from within, unveiling a built-in Sub Zero freezer. "Dessert is on me." There's a small bounce in his step.

He's adorable like this.

He pulls a bunch of items out of the pantry and sets a long glass bowl on the island countertop. "One banana split coming up," he chimes, rubbing his hands with exaggerated enthusiasm. He glows, luminous, happy.

I examine the inventory and realize he's got all the fixings to make a killer banana split: three flavors of ice cream, bananas, strawberries, chocolate sauce, caramel, and whipped cream. I reach over to help and he affectionately taps my hand with the spoon. "No way," he says. "This is something I can make."

Yielding to his show of domesticity, I pull up a stool and watch him create his masterpiece. The sweet smell of ripe bananas fills the air. A clock ticks, faintly, from the next room. An adorable grin of pride twitches the right side of Bryce's upper lip as he makes swirls with the whipped cream, making me laugh.

"You are rotten to the core," I say when he's done. "There's an entire pant size in that bowl."

"Just for us." Bryce grins and we lean over the granite, clutching silver spoons to dive in.

"Hmm, this is really, really yummy."

Within minutes we're clashing spoons, playfully fighting over a bit of banana. With a chuckle Bryce surrenders, scooping the piece onto my spoon and topping it with whipped cream. "All yours," he says.

I shove the entire spoonful into my mouth and hum through cream-covered lips.

"Whipped cream," mumbles Bryce, reaching to skim my upper lip with his thumb. My breath catches and his pupils set fire. A low grumble trembles in his throat as the tip of his thumb slips between my slightly parted lips, grazing bottom teeth, and I lick sweet cream from his finger.

His smile vanishes, the muscles in his jaw locking.

Another pass of his thumb has me quivering, burning to feel his lips on mine. Goosebumps prickle my skin, the sudden temperature in contrast to the chill of ice cream dripping down my wrist from the spoon suspended in midair.

"I could love you," he says.

Bryce's words echo in the darkness, *love you, love you, love you . . .*

The spoon tumbles to the granite, the tinkling on an endless rampage while I plummet through the black abyss on a slow spiral. Flames lick my neck and face. I see flashes of my wedding day, the birth of my daughter, holidays with Meyer. The inferno rips through my insides, devouring everything in its path, leaving bitter heartbreak to bubble to the surface.

"You have no right to say that," I say, pushing away from the island.

Bryce's hand drops to the countertop with a thump. "You should be loved."

"I am loved—I was. I fell in love, married, and we were happy." I hurl the words like they're objects to inflict pain. "We were supposed to grow old together."

Bryce looks away. "I'm sorry," he whispers.

The weight on my chest is so heavy I can hardly stand it. Melted ice cream forms odd shapes across the countertop, playing games with the unbearable pressure in my head.

"I have to go." I turn for the door.

"Please don't." Bryce steps close. There is no trace of a smile left on his face.

For an instant guilt shakes me. I'm not the only one to have loved and lost. The moment passes and I leave, sucking drips of ice cream from my arm as I bound down the hall. When I reach for my coat, Bryce's intense stare follows my every move. I tuck my jacket to my chest, debating how to say goodbye. Vision hazy, I pull my scarf from the coat rack and reach for the door.

"Wait," says Bryce, catching me full stride, his thick arm holding me tight.

As one we fall back against the elaborate wood trim. My body feels weightless, suspended, my red heels barely touching the ground. My coat, clutched in one hand, hangs to the floor. In my head I'm struggling to pull free, to escape, but my body defies me, snubbing instruction for the feel of Bryce's body pressed close. The air around us hums, electrified, intensifying as time ticks on.

"I can't let you go," he whispers. "Not this time. Please don't go."

"Free will," I say, voice cracking.

He loosens his grip. "You're stealing my favorite scarf."

I look down to see autumn spun into thick braids: Bryce's scarf. The sight sends tiny needles to perforate my rage.

"So I am." I wrap the scarf around my neck.

"Stay with me," he whispers.

Bryce gently prods taut muscles, releasing my grip on my coat. It drops to the floor, and he loosens his hold with the caution of someone expecting a jolt. But I can't move. Not while his intoxicating scent combined with sweet cream and wine coddles live nerve endings and his heart pounds through the back of my knit sweater.

I close my eyes as his warm lips touch my neck, every brush pushing heartache further out of reach.

"Stay." His tongue follows the contour of my ear.

A tempestuous shiver runs through me.

"I can't."

Meticulous fingers unbutton my sweater. "You can," he says, purring seduction. He places soft kisses on my neck, behind my ear, filling my head with sexually explicit imagery. My sweater slips to the floor.

"It's my choice." I stretch—an invitation to taste.

"Um, hmm." His mouth explores my skin, and he groans.

The low rumble in his chest feeds the fever that grows within me with every ragged breath. I squirm, clinging to the ends of the scarf.

Sweet mother of . . . this feels . . . oh my.

I surrender.

My bra hits hardwood and subtle fingers dust over skin that prickles in anticipation. He caresses me as if reminiscing over every plane and recess, playing beyond the boundaries of fabric, increasingly brazen with every stroke. His mouth becomes savage, his heavy breathing creating erotic waves that lap between my legs. Somewhere in a distant realm of my consciousness screams a voice, my voice, asking if I've lost my mind.

*Ignore it*, my body screams.

My skirt falls and Bryce shifts to the faint rustle of material, his sweater being pulled over his head. The feel of his bare skin on mine sends me into an uncontrollable tailspin, my entire body arching against his. My blood boils, the lace underwear and scarf too much to wear in this heat.

"Don't," he says, stopping me from removing his scarf.

Entangling his fingers with mine, he pins them to the doorframe, compressing every inch of our naked bodies. Lace is no longer between us. I push into him, starving to get closer. He's hot, hard, and large against my lower back. Bryce moans, primitive, and my knees buckle in response. His fingers run down my front and between my slick thighs, the contact making me desperate, needy.

Ah. Oh. Ohhhhhh.

Something Bryce mentioned weeks ago comes to mind, something about Keepers and their ability to control cell temperature to kill disease. The worry is wiped from my mind as carnal sounds—embarrassing sounds—fly from my throat, and his play gets rough, turning the frenzied burn into a rage that pumps on the borderline of agony. My hands hurt in his, but my protest gets lost in the feel of his tongue, and when his teeth grab my earlobe, I gasp for air.

*Please* is an inch from my lips when Bryce jacks up my leg and pushes into me.

I cry out.

We move together, the wood echoing vehement cries of passion. Teeth nip my skin, the sensation a lightning bolt of pleasure. His body commands and directs, reveling in the power to shatter me from the inside out.

And if he stops, I'll beg.

Don't stop. Don't stop!

He doesn't stop.

I push into him with all my strength. The blaze devours the last of my control, and I explode, a consuming submission that radiates through my core, vibrating my extremities. My insides pump, nails dig into Bryce's hands. And Bryce releases with a groan, a deep, pulsating heat I feel over my own.

The weight of his sculpted body falls heavy onto mine as he rides tremors, chest heaving, his stubble scraping my shoulder.

Our bodies hold tight to each other, rooted, motionless. Nothing but the sound of relentless panting fills the air. Slowly my mind climbs from the depths and my breathing stumbles upon a tenable pace. My legs ache, fatigued from pushing over two hundred pounds of muscle into the doorframe, and my hands throb between his and the solid walnut.

Bryce loosens his grip but he doesn't let go.

"Stay with me," he whispers.

*Stay with me . . . stay with me . . . stay with me . . .*

I close my eyes as the realization of what I've done sinks in. The world around me begins to shatter, and my mind, taking control, bellows angst. Emotions erupt, panic at hand.

Bryce takes my face in his hands and kisses me.

Worry is replaced by desire.

"Choose me, us." He scoops me into his arms.

I kiss him back. Hard.

And I surrender my soul as he carries me to his bed.

Bryce

# GONE

## February 15th

**I** cover my eyes, protecting them from the relentless sun that gleams in from the windows beside my bed. Then drop my arm when I realize the room is piercingly dark. My head clears. I smell Tess all over me. Thankful she can't see my corny smile, I reach for her.

"Tess?"

I'm the only one in my bed.

I call out, hoping she's in the john, but no one answers and the lights are out. Where is she? She wouldn't have left, would she? I'd have felt her slip away. Surely I would have heard her.

"Tess?"

I grunt and roll over. My hands ache, wanting to touch her. I curse the blackness and for a split second fantasize Tess is here, her silken hair across my sheets, mesmerizing green eyes heavy, earth-shattering smile, but in a blink the vision is gone and I'm in bed alone.

A glutton for punishment, I inhale deeply, tasting her on my tongue. Muscles tense and blood pumps heavy through my veins, making me hard and agitated.

Maybe she's downstairs.

I spring from the bed, driving my toes into the plush carpet while I fumble through my tousled hair, attempting to look half decent, like I didn't just have the best night of my life. I give up, I look thoroughly worked over and it's awesome.

I throw on some boxers and call for her from the top of the stairs. "Are you in the gallery?" It's dark, the lights out. I'm totally confused. She wouldn't leave, not without waking me, not without saying goodbye, would she? Why?

I take the stairs, three at a time, flicking lights on as I go. She's not in the gallery. Or the kitchen.

Bloody hell.

Her coat is gone and my scarf is back on the coat rack.

She left.

I don't understand.

I fall against the doorframe, thoughts of her all too clear, thoughts of her naked, in my arms, in my mouth, under my skin. I rub my eyes with the meaty part of my palms, trying to get control of my body. It wants her, bad. I want her. Now that I've found her, I can't imagine my life without her. Why would she leave? Did I do something wrong?

She must have been overwhelmed and needed space.

The sun hasn't risen but I can't go back to sleep. I need a distraction. I'm restless. I've got to move, to burn, to pound something. On my flight to the basement, to the gym, I stop short at my cell on the kitchen buffet. I want to call her, hear her voice, see her again.

After a delusional moment, I joggle my head clear. I can't call her this early. I have to be patient. Cool. The cell practically leaps into my hand. I put it back down.

"Christ, I can at least wait until morning."

A couple of deep breaths help me muster focus, but the smell of Tess, of sweet sweat encouraging the flow of testosterone takes over and my focus survives all of three minutes.

This woman—this amazing woman—has turned me inside out.

**Twenty hours later** I am going stir crazy. I've lost count of the number of messages I've left for Tess, not one returned. I lay in bed, toiling over each and every detail of our night together, plagued with guilt. Her every word, every expression, tortures me. What have I done? I've blown it, that's what I've done. I found her, finally found the woman of my dreams, and I messed up. She wasn't ready. Maybe she didn't hear me say she couldn't get pregnant, that Keepers choose when to reproduce. Maybe I should've been clearer. I shouldn't have . . . What was I thinking?

"I wasn't thinking, and that's the problem." The dark is a silent audience.

What happened to all my control? For months I've managed to keep my paws to myself, and the one time I get her alone, the first time she lets me in, I screw up.

I thought she wanted me, needed me to prove how I feel about her in more than just words. Maybe I was wrong.

"Fuck," I shout, hoping to dissolve the bitter taste of regret. It's a vulgar word, a term I never use. Instead of making me feel better, it pricks like a thorn, making me miserable and conjuring images of her naked body pressed to mine, the feel of her touch. I moan and the smell of her fills my lungs. I roll onto the other side of the bed with a boner from hell.

Next to wanting Tess, the only thing I want is some sleep, a reprieve from visions of our future, our past, and the mind-boggling lust destined to overtake me. I grab the clock and throw it across the room, tired and frustrated.

Some way, somehow, I've got to get Tess to talk to me. I'll

plead for another chance, beg for forgiveness.

She'll give me another chance.

She's got to.

**Eight hours later** I'm swiping at icicles, pacing at her front door. I can't imagine she'd tolerate twenty minutes of ringing, so she's either not home or she's much more upset with me than I thought. I shimmy the flowers through the door handle. My boots leave tracks in the new-fallen snow as I trek to the back of the house to peek in the garage. Her car is not there.

I think my persistence might be making matters worse. I need to back off. It's not going to help if she thinks I'm out of control, stalking her, suffocating her. Maybe she just needs time. I can give her that.

**Ten hours, twenty-four** minutes, and nineteen seconds have passed since my last shot at reaching Tess. My cell is in pieces across the kitchen floor. I'm pacing like a madman. I can't even bring myself to think about Valentine's anymore. The most amazing date of my life is now nothing but an over-analyzed blur. Moments lumped into categories I've literally written on paper, blocked into squares with titles like *freaked her out, worried her, aroused her, made her smile that smile.*

There's a bang at the door.

"Would you like me to get that, sir?"

I abandon my list. "I've got it, Clause, thank you."

I know who it is.

I open the door and a bouquet of white daises is thrust into my chest, the force sending me reeling back.

"What the hell did you do to her?" roars Thomas.

I stare at the flowers strewn across the floor. There aren't words to say what I did to her.

"Speak, Bryce. Tell me before I lose what little control I have over my temper."

"I don't know what happened." I lean against the door jam.

Thomas points at the mess on the floor. "You gave her flowers. What did you do that requires groveling?"

"None of your business. And how did you—"

"None of my business, are you fucking kidding me? None of my business?" He takes a few steps, boots mashing delicate white petals. "She's gone, Bryce. Gone!"

"What do you mean? Gone where?"

Thomas holds the bridge of his nose with his thumb and forefinger like mother does, squeezing his eyes shut with a malevolent grunt.

"She left. She packed Abby's and her stuff and took off."

I try to absorb this.

"She wouldn't just leave."

The umpteen times she's stormed out on me blend together to form an abominable picture. Her need to run from me is innate, a product of her history, our history, a natural defense.

"Shit, I should've known. I—I didn't think she'd . . ."

"She would and she did," seethes Thomas. "I warned you. I told you she wasn't ready. I said this would happen and you didn't listen. You wanted what you always want, to get laid."

"It's not like that. We have something—"

"Bullshit, Bryce. That's how you play. Did you finally get what you wanted? Is that why she left? Did you push her too far?" What he can't see in my eyes he can read in my head. "Fuck," he spits.

This can't be happening. Our night together, it wasn't like that. She wouldn't just leave.

"How do you know she's packed and left town? Maybe she's just out for the day."

"She hasn't returned my calls and her car's been gone since yesterday," says Thomas, pulling a hand through thick curls, one of many physical features that set us apart. "And I wanted to know what the hell was going on."

I stare at him. "Unbelievable. You broke into her house?"

"Don't you dare lecture me on ethics. Her luggage is gone, along with most of their clothes. She doesn't plan on returning anytime soon."

"I need to find her," I mumble in shock.

"You've done enough. Go away. Eventually she'll come home and I'll be here for her. I'll make her happy. I'll keep her safe."

I glare at my brother. As if I could move and leave Tess. As if I could forget.

"I have to find her." A thought prickles. "She could be in danger. If he followed her, if the lost soul—"

"He didn't. Why on earth would he go after her?"

"You know why."

Thomas swipes an invisible irritant, dismissing the comment. "It was random. He had his fun, his fill with the MacKinnen girl. There's no reason for him to pursue Tess. He split."

I think about this for a moment.

"Thomas, why would he ransack her house?"

Thomas shrugs. "She piqued his interest in the café. Maybe he was attracted to her, liked her, and lost it when he got to the house and saw she had a husband and kid. I'm sure that's it. It sucks that Sonia was killed, but it proves the douche got what he wanted and moved on."

Thomas might be right, but still, I need to find Tess, just in case. But where would she go? Would she go back to Florida?

"She must have gone to stay with her in-laws."

"Bryce, not everyone runs to their mommy and daddy. You don't know her, so don't even try to act like you do."

"Where else would she go?" I say as Thomas looks away, stepping toward the open door. I reach for him and sense it immediately. "Tess isn't in Florida. Why Paris, Thomas?"

Thomas jerks forward, easily releasing my grasp. "Her brother is there. And his girlfriend just left him."

I would remember Tess mentioning this. She talked about Stephen less than twenty-four hours ago, at dinner. I study Thomas, prodding the sudden blockade in his mind. "How do you . . .?"

Thomas turns quickly. "It's irrelevant," he says. "Leave her be."

I feel it, but can't believe it. "Tell me you didn't—"

"Shut up. Of course I did. I wanted to know where she went."

This is the kind of behavior that gets Thomas into trouble. He's impulsive, intrusive.

"It's bad enough you broke into her house, but to read her email—"

"Just leave her alone." He kicks the doorframe.

"I need to find her."

"You need to fuck off." His hands ball into fists. "She'll come home when she's ready. And when she does, you'll be long gone."

That is enough.

"I'm in love with her, Thomas."

"Bullshit!"

"It's not. I didn't intend to hurt you, I would never—"

"Stay away from her or I'll—"

"You'll what?" I yell back. "You can't keep me away from her. And you have no right to try."

Thomas kicks the door again. "She is mine," he growls. He

turns and storms out, slamming the door behind him.

I should follow him. I should set him straight right now. I should knock his self-serving block off and finish this argument once and for all. I should, but I don't.

I slam the door.

I need to find Tess. Now.

**Eleven hours ago** Thomas stomped out of here, and I locked myself in my office on a quest. I'm crashing from an adrenaline high mixed with limited shut-eye, yet I can't pry myself from the chair. I've called airlines, hotels, rental car companies, and when hysteria set in I pulled friends and family into the frenzy. All my talents as a Keeper, all my connections, and I can't find Tess or her brother Stephen.

Something is wrong. Seriously wrong. I feel it in my bones.

My new phone rings and I dive for it. "Tess?"

"Son, please sit." My father's tone has me frantic before my ass even hits the floor. "I have yet to locate your lady's brother, but," he pauses, hesitant, "there is a Jane Doe at Pitie-Salpetriere."

I swallow the silence in one lump.

"It could be anyone." My hands are trembling. My father wouldn't call me with this news if he didn't think . . .

"Son, this woman is five-foot-eight, one-hundred-thirty pounds, and has long dark hair and green eyes." He's describing the flesh-and-blood Tess, and it steals my breath like I've been hit by a truck.

"There is more," Dad says. "She, this Jane Doe, is alive but badly beaten: broken bones, burns, bite marks." The line falls quiet, rocking my soul to its core. "This has lost soul written all over it, Son."

Gravity pulls the phone to the floor.
I need to get to Paris.
Now.

# PARIS

"Pitie-Salpetriere Hopital. Rapide!" I say, slamming the door of the Bentley my dad arranged to meet me at the airport. He wanted to be here with me, but I insisted he stay away. This is going to be difficult enough.

The driver steps on the gas. "Etes-vous bien, Monsieur?" he asks, eyeing me in the rearview mirror.

"No, I'm not all right."

I catch a glimpse of myself in the window. I look like shit. My eyes have burrowed into my skull, and my olive skin exudes stress, a shade greener than Oscar the Grouch. I haven't shaved in days, and I've ripped the sleeve of my leather jacket somewhere between my front door and the runway tarmac. No wonder airport security gave me such a hard time. If I hadn't been boarding a charter jet, I doubt they'd have let me through.

Intuition insists the Jane Doe is Tess. The entire flight I fought this feeling, hoping beyond hope that I'm wrong. Maybe our past, the pasts I've shared with Tess's soul, have me jaded, convinced this is our only destiny. I shake this and concentrate on Abby. Lost souls of this kind seldom hurt children, especially kids with new souls. Children have nothing they want. But this particular lost soul has been unpredictable. I close my eyes and make a silent wish, hoping Abby is safe with Tess's brother, Stephen. Wherever he is.

Brother. Thomas. I sigh and reach for my cell. For once, Thomas answers my call. The conversation, if you can call it that, is short. I tell him about Dad's call and he doesn't say a word. When I say I'm in Paris he hangs up.

"Nous voici, Monsieur," says the driver, pulling the car under a sign announcing the hospital's emergency entrance. He leans to open his door.

I tap him on the shoulder and shove my cell in my coat pocket.

"Merci." I leap from the Bentley.

Once a gunpowder factory, the Pitie-Salpetriere was known for its criminally insane prisoners and even crazier rat population. In 1656, Louis XIV appointed architect Liberal Bruant to build the world's largest hospital in place of the factory, located in the heart of Paris. My soul had come here in 1792, trying to help a lost soul who had been tossed into the guts of the hospital along with over three hundred other prostitutes swept from the streets of Paris. But I was too late. Two weeks later the hospital was stormed by a mob, and all three hundred women were dragged, still in chains, into the street and killed. The lost soul had found the peace she'd craved.

I hesitate at the entrance. I've stepped foot in a hospital only once in my lifetime, when Sofia was born. I've had even less experience with doctors. Bypassing the nurse at the desk, I head straight for the elevators, ignoring inquisitive eyes. I search the directory: cardiology, radiology, maternity. Intensive care, fourth floor.

The creaky elevator rises in slow motion, pausing at every floor. Each time the door opens, the odor that meets me turns my stomach. The police are bound to be watching the door. Will they let me see her? Do I qualify as her boyfriend, her lover . . . her anything? The elevator doors open and there aren't any officers in sight, so I search for the nurse's station. A plump woman in her early fifties looks up from her paperwork. She takes in my face. Then the tear in my jacket.

I decide to speak in English, in case she knows Tess isn't French.

"There is an unidentified woman here. She's been," I can hardly say it, "beaten." Without taking her eyes off me, the nurse lifts the phone and presses a red button. This can't be good. "I think the Jane Doe might be Tess Morgan, a friend. Can you tell me what room she's in?"

The nurse lowers the receiver and points to the hallway on the right. "Four-twenty-eight," she says in English. Her mind is full of doubt. She's not sure if she should be afraid of me or feel sorry for me.

I round the corner to three armed men in uniform. A fourth, hospital security, stops me mid-stride. "May I help you?" His English is brutal. One hand rests on the club at his side.

"I'm here to see Tess Morgan." I pray they tell me there is no one here by that name. It takes all my restraint not to bowl these men over.

A police officer steps forward. "Are you a relative?" he says. He's short but wiry. His thoughts tell me what I don't want to hear. He wants to know how I know Mrs. Morgan.

"No," I answer, clutching the bottom of my coat. I swear the earth might open and swallow me whole. How do they know her name? Has she come to? Is she speaking? "I'm her . . . I'm a friend."

I fell asleep on Valentine's Day thinking I was more, that Tess and I were beyond mere friendship. But she left without a word. Would she still call me a friend?

"Relatives only," says the officer.

"I need to see her." I push toward the door. An officer, the youngest of the three, pulls his gun. I search his mind. He wants to know how I know the woman in the room is Tess Morgan when the media is still referring to her as Jane Doe.

My voice is low when I say, "I need to see she's all right."

"You won't be seeing anyone until you answer questions," says another officer, his English rough. "Identification." He leans in, peeking inside my coat as I reach for a pocket. I slap my passport into his palm. "You are not Canadian," he says, flipping pages.

"No."

"How do you—"

"Please," I plead. "Tess has a five year-old daughter named Abby. Do you know where she is?" All three officers glance at each other, suddenly sympathetic. The hospital security guard walks away. "Where's Abby?" I demand, too startled to be diplomatic.

The room door opens, and a young man steps out, his face red, eyes bloodshot. The first thing I notice is his clothes; he's not dressed like a doctor. Then I spot the hair, the exact same shade as Tess's. "Ce qui se passe?" he says. *What's going on?*

"Stephen?" Part of me wants to pull this kid into a hug. He's here, which means Tess isn't alone. Part of me wants to throw a fist into the concrete wall. Stephen's here, which means the woman in that room, the woman almost beaten to death, is really Tess.

The instant Stephen looks at me he knows who I am. "Bryce?"

I pluck my passport from the officer's fingers and pass it to Stephen. The officer starts to protest, but Stephen raises a hand, studying my passport photo. He's thinking that I look exactly like Tess's description. "How did you—"

"Where's Abby?" I say, grabbing his shoulder.

"She's with a neighbor," he says, turning toward the door. "I can't bring her here."

I sigh in relief. Abby is safe. Stephen takes a step back, and I realize I've been gripping his shoulder hard. Even if I couldn't read his thoughts, I could see them churning in his eyes. He wants to know how I learned Tess was hurt. How I got here so fast. Why I screwed his grieving sister.

I look away. Tess has obviously told her brother about us. I make a move for the door, stopping when Stephen asks, "How did you know my sister was here?"

I stare at the police officer, the young one with the gun in his hand. Stephen isn't the only one waiting for my response.

"I didn't," I say, lying. "My niece and Abby are in the same class at school. Their teacher mentioned Tess had taken Abby to Paris. I had business in Paris today and happened to catch the news while grabbing coffee at the airport. The description of the woman beaten at the park sounded an awful lot like Tess. I couldn't leave Paris not knowing for sure." I'd rehearsed these lines on the flight over. I'm not worried about the officers. My dad has my alibi covered. Its Stephen's approval I want.

Stephen feigns a smile, obviously relieved someone is here to help him through this, and I'm struck by how young he looks. "I haven't been here long," he says. He can't be a day over twenty-one. "My parents are on break in Rio. I've been trying to get in touch with them. Meyer's grandparents are catching the next flight from Florida."

I can't stand another minute in this hallway. I nod toward to the door. "May I?" I look to Stephen. He takes a deep breath and pushes the door open.

In my mind I'd envisioned rushing to Tess's side, holding her hand, maybe kissing her forehead. Now, with her before me, I'm paralyzed three feet from the bed. Her bloated face is several shades of black, blue, and purple, her eyes difficult to locate. Separating the bruises are pieces of white gauze, most spotting thick gobs of blood. A thin cloth is wrapped around her scalp, arched rows of staples peeking through the mesh. Her hair falls in a dull, tangled mass.

A monitor beeps.

I step closer, reaching for the bed. Layers of blankets form over strange lumps barely distinguishable as body parts. Tubes and wires run from bandages to machines and bags. Her lips are swollen and stitched.

I want to touch her. I want to hold her. To do either would hurt her.

A tortured whine pulls my stare from Tess. Stephen's entire body trembles as he crumbles into a chair, face buried in his hands. I know I should say something, anything, but I'm at a loss for words. I round the bed and stand beside Stephen, awkwardly patting his back. His despair is so profound I struggle to block his thoughts.

I focus on Tess, trying to read her, to feel her. The silence is chilling.

"The cops think that whoever attacked her had some sort of dog or animal," says Stephen, voice choked. His stare locks on his sister's hand. The red nail polish has been removed, nails torn short. Taped bandages attempt to cover cuts and blood-stained needles that run fluids into her veins. Her skin is dark and distorted. These hands look nothing like the hands I know. Tess's hands are beautiful, delicate, and capable of bringing me to my knees. I mumble something unintelligible, not even trying to be discreet.

"Tess, can you hear me?" I lean over her tender form. Her

cheek twitches and I catch a train of thought. She knows it's me, knows I'm here. Her mind flips scenes and I snap to attention.

*She's in a park, its dark, cold, but she doesn't mind. Sitting on a rock under her favorite tree, a man approaches her. He steps into the moonlight. His eyes glimmer a strange blue hue. She drops her pen and the letter she was writing to me, gaping at the man before her, the lost soul from the café.*

*This is how I die, she thinks. This is how I always die.*

Beeping sounds cut through the connection in my head, and I pull away, glaring at the machine beside the bed. Red lines jump then fade, the tenor quickening. I turn back to Tess, attempting to concentrate on the flashes of memory playing out in her head.

*The predator paces, a feline stealth working a man's body. Tess slides from the rock and stands tall, fists at her sides. She's afraid, but not afraid. And the lost soul knows it. His chin-length hair falls in reckless curls around his face, the light catching intricate tattoos that trace down his neck, into the folds of his white silk shirt. Tess can smell him, an intoxicating blend of honeysuckle and mandarin that wafts from his skin. He grins.*

Out of the corner of my eye, I witness Tess's fingers inch closer to mine. I search her hand, desperate to find an unmarked spot to touch, to grasp, but the entire surface is discolored and taped. I should have been there. I should've protected her. I should have known she'd run from me. I shift my bodyweight, veiling my shame in shadows.

*Tess sees this man, sees his soul. He knows she sees and he's pleased. She steps to the left and he mimics her movement. She glides to the right and he follows her lead. Not a word is spoken. This is the dance of death. Tess halts, bone still, her chest the only body part in flux. It rises and falls, every breath rallying control. Her eyes lock with his. A breeze rustles the tree's bare branches and her hair blows across her cheeks. The lost soul reaches, gently tucking wisps of hair behind her ear. Her lip quivers, and he smiles.*

"The doctor should be here any minute," says Stephen, shattering my connection with Tess. "The nurse said he checks her every hour." He fidgets beside me, avoiding his sister's face.

"I think she needs something for pain," I say, worried. She needs drugs to dilute these traumatic images, something to help her forget so she can heal. I need her to get better. "She needs to rest."

*The lost soul touches Tess's cheek and she flinches, ever so slightly. He's got her mesmerized, stunned, but she's trying to suppress the sensation of concrete drying around her. His fingers follow the contour of her chin, her lips. She suppresses a whimper as something inside her tugs and pulls toward his touch, a magnetic anomaly. A wicked smirk ignites his face, and a hum lingers at the base of his throat. Her body quakes, fighting the urge to give her soul freely.*

"She's cold again," says Stephen, diving for the blankets stacked at the end of the bed.

Tess shakes, the chill of trauma assaulting her a second time. The motion threatens to yank the IV.

"Shh, you're safe." I steady her arm with the lightest touch possible. Stephen drapes a blanket over his sister and I turn away, straining to hide my emotions. It's killing me to watch him touch her, seduce her, control her. Knowing the replay is wracking her body and causing her pain is unbearable.

*The dance continues, now shrouded in a haze of pain. Tess's entire body aches to defy the lost soul's demands. Again, he steps back, motioning for her to follow. She ignores his command and his teeth clack a warning. He steps closer, slow and deliberate, pausing at her side. He runs his palm across her hip and down her thigh. He grins, eyes narrowed. She backs into the rock, defiant. His snarl bellows into the night as he mats a chunk of hair in his fist and jerks her head back. Fire sears her skin as his lips ravage her neck, her screams echoing through the branches.*

"The police haven't seen a beating this brutal in a long time," says Stephen, pulling me from hell. My hands are balled into fists. I want to pound something. I want to holler. I want something I've never wanted before. I want vengeance.

*Teeth slice into flesh, the pain stealing her breath. Her arms flail until she falls to her knees, a stream of vomit coating the ground. Bites rip through her shoulder, her scalp, agony pushing her to the brink of consciousness. She lashes out, collecting layers of his skin under her nails. Blood splatters across his white shirt and he roars, the frenzy out of control.*

Stephen grabs my arm. "What's wrong?" He's panicking.

The monitors are going wild, buzzing and beeping. Bright red blood oozes though layers of gauze covering Tess's head and shoulders. The cast covering her right leg bangs against the bed rail.

I lie. "I don't know."

Stephen looks horror struck. "I'll get the doctor." He sprints for the door.

"Tess, please, you have to stop," I plead, an inch from her ear. "Don't think about last night. Please. Christ, please, Tess, go to sleep."

*Nails dig into muscles in Tess's legs and she wails. Gripping both calves, he flips her, her head hitting stone before she's flung into a tree. She cries out. Branches tear at her skin and bones pop and snap, the sound melting with the sounds of splitting wood. She clambers, searching for purchase.*

"No, Tess, please!" I fumble around her face.

*Her leg throbs, hanging limp at an odd angle. He reaches for her foot, another snarl ripping from his lungs. Torn from the tree, she falls until stone shatters bones and she rolls to the ground, the earth red with blood. Crumpled and broken, Tess gasps for air as the lost soul towers over her, lighting a cigarette.*

*He's not sated. And no longer smiling.*

"Move," says a man, pushing me aside. He's wide and hairy and would better suit a stampede of buffalo.

"Give her something for pain," I beg, moving out of his way. The short, high-pitched sounds coming from the equipment have me reeling.

"What's happening?" Stephen cries from across the room.

A nurse hovers over the machines, tapping lines and pushing buttons. "Four over," she says in English.

"Four?" the doctor repeats.

"At least."

Stephen approaches the nurse. "Will she be all right? Please, tell me she'll be all right!"

"We will see," she says, nudging Stephen out of the way.

The doctor rips tape from gauze squares on Tess's neck. "More ADB pads," he says. He taps the IV feed. "Fentanyl, 50 micrograms IV," he calls out as the nurse runs from the room. The doctor pulls back the covers and Stephen turns, facing the wall.

"Shit," I mutter on impulse. Without bandages I can better see Tess's injuries, the protruding welts and rows of thick stitches leaking fresh blood. The doctor cuts material with a speed close to my own, and I find myself grateful, grateful that someone here knows what they're doing.

The nurse shuffles back into the room, handing the doctor a syringe. He sticks the needle into a capped tube taped to the back of Tess's hand. "This will help," he says.

Within seconds Tess's trembling subsides and she melts into

the mattress. Her mind drifts until all I catch is a drug-induced fog. The reprieve is overwhelming. I stumble to a chair and sit, sweaty palms kneading my eyes.

When I look up, I'm the only one in the room not freaking out. The doctor is pacing, and Stephen looks like he's about to pass out.

The doctor tosses blood-stained gloves into the garbage. "She's comfortable for now," he says.

"For now?" says Stephen.

The nurse leaves the room and the doctor turns to Tess's brother. "I increased her pain medication. It will help keep her calm." He crosses his arms.

"Calm?" Stephen steadies himself with the IV pole. "She'll pull through, right?"

The doctor sighs and opens the door. "Let's see how she is in an hour or two," he says. He points to the bin where he dropped the syringe. "That'll keep the pain under control. She should sleep."

Now, I have no experience with doctors, but it can't be good when they flee. I look at Stephen. He's the color of ash. He's thinking the same thing.

Not good at all.

# COULD'VE SHOULD'VE

The monitor keeps a slow steady pace with Tess's heart. Stephen and I sit, tightlipped, watching the contraption taped to her mouth rise and fall with every breath. The clock on the wall ticks between us. Like little girls, we've long since lost control over our emotions.

Stephen moans. "I keep thinking of all the ways I could've prevented this," he says. "I can't believe I let Tess go to the park alone. My sister is fearless. Did you know that? She does what she wants, when she wants. I love that about her." He moans again. "But I'd have never let Gabriella go the park alone after dark."

The park? I let her leave the country.

I look at Stephen. "Gabriella is . . .?"

"Gabriella is my girlfriend. Was my girlfriend. She moved out a few days ago, from the student house we share with flatmates. Tess came to cheer me up. I wasn't surprised to see my sister, because she's always been there for me. She's always known what to say to make me feel better, even when I'm being the ass." He attempts a smile. "She appeared on my doorstep, and we talked the entire night, girl troubles and guy troubles." Stephen glances at me, lips taut and cheeks puffed.

I'm the guy in "guy troubles." One of them at least.

Picking my way through Stephen's thoughts, I try to distinguish his feelings regarding Gabriella from Tess's sisterly confessions, but they're so tightly woven I can't separate them. One thing is for sure, Stephen has no concept of Keepers or lost souls.

"She was upset with me," I manage to say.

He seems surprised. "She has nothing but good things to say about you. She's worried it's too soon. She's worried about Abby. Meyer's accident was . . . I've never seen Tess take anything so hard, not even mom's suicide."

Too soon. The words sit heavy on my conscience. It was too soon to ask her to love another. Too soon for her share a bed. Too soon to think she could fight a lost soul. Thomas's words add to my burden, *She's not ready for all your shit.*

"If I'd have backed off maybe she wouldn't have come to Paris," I think out loud like a retrospective fool.

Stephen doesn't argue my point. Misery loves company.

"At school yesterday," he says, "I was so exhausted I could hardly take notes in class. By the time I got home I was a walking zombie. Tess and Abby had dinner ready. It was nice. It'd been a while since we'd eaten together as a family. After dinner Tess suggested I crash with Abby. She wanted some time alone." Stephen shakes his head. "How could I let her go to the park alone?"

There is more than enough guilt to go around. I pushed her when she wasn't ready. I spent two days worrying about the wrong thing. I should have known she'd leave Carlisle, that she'd run from me. I should've known the lost soul would follow her.

"I should've known this would happen."

Stephen looks at me. "If you wanna talk could've should've," he says. "I've got you beat. I went to school this morning without even realizing my sister was lying in a hospital bed. I didn't know she'd been beaten." Tears slide down his cheek, coating his lower lip. "What kind of brother leaves his flat without checking his sister is even home? I assumed she was sleeping with Abby, but I didn't look, I didn't make sure."

I am a Keeper. My head is jam-packed with history, years and years of experience to pull from, to learn from. I was so determined to keep Tess in my life, so caught in the sheer joy of having found her, that I forgot the lessons of our past. I pushed aside all the memories I didn't want to remember, ignored all the nightmares Tess had relived a hundred times.

I leap from the chair with a sudden urge to pace.

"People were talking about her at school today," says Stephen. "Someone had the news on at break and I didn't even pay attention. After work I grabbed pizza and went home, happy as a pig in shit, thinking that Tess and Abby would be there. Not only was Tess not there, but my five-year-old niece had spent the entire day by herself."

"Abby is all right." I work to sound positive.

She won't be all right for long. Eventually she'll want to see her mother. I look at Tess. She's swollen and unrecognizable. This isn't something any child should ever have to witness.

"Abby had no idea where she was or how to call anyone. None of my flatmates were home. She watched French cartoons and ate bread with chocolate milk. For ten hours!"

I'm relieved Abby stayed home with Stephen when Tess went to the park. I shudder to think of what would've happened to Abby had she been with Tess when the lost soul attacked. Even if he hadn't touched a hair on her head, the sight of her mother being beaten would've scarred her for life.

"Abby is safe now," I mumble.

"Thank God the police found my sister when they did."

Stephen fiddles with the blankets. "They said an elderly couple taking a midnight stroll heard her screaming." He closes his eyes and shakes his head, trying to dislodge the image of his sister being beaten.

It's a tough scene to let go of.

The nurse waddles into the room making a beeline to the monitors. "How we doing?" she says, pressing buttons. She pulls a wire from a machine and plugs in another cord before turning to us for an answer.

Stephen's brain fires questions by the second. None of them make it to his mouth.

I say, "She's been sleeping since you left."

"Good." She moves with efficiency, replacing empty bags of blood and clear fluids that hang from the IV stand. While removing soaked bandages from Tess's shoulders, she muffles something unintelligible and a sound hovers in her trachea, unsettling me. I ask what's wrong but she focuses on her tasks. She's heard my question. She's just pretending she didn't. I take a deep breath, readying to ask again.

The door swings open and the doctor walks in. He heads straight for the bed. "I see you've got some shut-eye," he says.

The statement wasn't meant for Tess. She's sleeping. Its sole purpose was to pacify Stephen and me. The doctor skims Tess's chart, the chart that's been hanging on a clipboard at the end of Tess's bed. The chart I hadn't thought to read. The regrets just keep coming. The doctor asks the nurse a few questions and she answers curtly. Her name is Martine. This is the first time I notice the name embroidered on her smock and that she speaks learned English without all the subtleties of a born-and-bred.

Stephen slides in close to the doctor, attempting to decipher medical jargon. "Was she . . . ah, did her attacker . . .?" Images of Tess being raped flash through his mind.

"No," I say without thinking.

Stephen throws me a disparaging glance then softens. "Sorry," he mumbles.

The doctor's stare drifts from me to Stephen and back again. I see the connection take place in his head. "Rape kits are standard procedure in these kinds of cases. Whoever beat her either wasn't aiming for sexual assault or didn't get the chance."

I lock my jaw, the words *he tried* almost pushing their way out.

The doctor instructs us to step outside the curtain while he peels back layers of blanketing. Martine tugs at the gathered material, gently shooing us out of the way. The sound of metal rings irks me and within seconds we're separated from Tess, in a room within the room. The disconnect feels oceans wide. Stephen stands beside me, as worried as I am. He's hoping his parents arrive soon. He strains to hear the muffled commands of the doctor as he inspects Tess's wounds. I can hear every word, but he's talking in medical terms, a foreign language I don't speak. The machines make a new sound and seized wheels drag over linoleum. Every few minutes, Martine sighs.

The clock, now in our territory, ticks louder. I shove my hands in my pockets to keep from yanking back the curtain and demanding answers. And to stop myself from tearing the clock from the wall.

Eventually Martine eases herself through a crack in the curtain. She walks past us and out the door without a word. Stephen and I eye each other, but before we have a chance to speak, the doctor steps out, closing the gap in the curtain behind him and hiding Tess from sight. I'm torn between the urge to barge my way through to Tess and needing to hear what the doctor has to say in terms I comprehend.

The doc clears his throat. "I'm told you have family flying in."

"Yeah, they are on their way." The doctor contemplates the timing, and Stephen stares at the floor, seeing where this is headed. "I told them she's been through the worst of it," he says. "Broken bones and cuts will heal. With time she'll be back to normal, right?"

"I'd rather discuss this with your family present," says the doctor, "But by morning . . ."

"What's wrong?" I'm trying to keep my cool.

The doctor folds his arms over his chest, a neurotic tendency I'm quickly becoming accustomed to.

"Tess has developed complications," he says. "The clinical term is disseminated intravascular coagulation. It's a blood clotting disorder we see in patients who have suffered massive trauma. Basically it means that her body can't stop bleeding. We've been trying to staunch the flow, but her blood isn't clotting. I've ordered another four units of blood for transfusion, but she's bleeding faster than I can replenish it." Years of experience tell him we need time to absorb such a harsh diagnosis, so he just stands there, a slight twitch in one eye.

I pace backwards, hitting the wall. "What does this mean?"

I catch a glimpse of Stephen. His skin is bleached.

"I've got the lab mixing a drug called Leudifor. It's somewhat experimental, but there's a chance it might help. If I can't get her blood to clot, her wounds won't heal, and she'll bleed out."

"Bleed out," Stephen repeats. His body tilts as if a wind pushes him to the right.

I lower my face into shaking hands.

Tess is dying. The doctor thinks she's not going to survive her injuries. He can't wait until the rest of the family gets here because she won't live that long.

"But I thought . . ." I mutter. "This can't be."

"I'm sorry," says the doctor. "We'll do our best but you need to be prepared if our best isn't enough."

Stephen stumbles toward the door, almost falling over my knees. He's about to hurl. "I need to check on Abby," he says. The doctor follows Stephen out, promising to return after seeing to another patient.

I lunge for the curtain, suddenly hot. I want to scoop Tess up, carry her out of here, home, as if none of this ever happened. I search her mind for traces of life, her face for recognition. She looks so vulnerable, so weak.

"You can't die," I say, smoothing a patch of her hair, flattening it to the pillow. "I can't lose you." Tess doesn't respond. Her body is shattered, her mind a sedated black cloud. "I love you. Do you hear me? I love you!"

This cannot happen. Tess can't die. I've got to do something. Now!

But what?

Christ, I'm a Keeper. I can recall every natural disaster that ever plagued man. I can read minds and lift objects a hundred times my body weight. I can manipulate cells and move faster than any other creature on this planet. I can control internal organs, telling my heart when to beat, my lungs when to breathe, sending white cells to heal.

"I'll fix this. You'll heal. You'll get better. I'll find a way."

I scour the monitors, the machines, the IV bags, but everything capable of saving Tess is alien to me. All I know is considered folklore and ancient witchcraft.

Gertrude Maples. Inspiration clips through my skull like the silver ball in a pinball machine. Mrs. Maples will know what to do.

"Hold on, Tess. Do you hear me? You've got to hold on!"

Unable to look away, I grope for my cell. If anyone can help, Mrs. Maples can. Not only is she an old soul, she's the daughter of a Keeper, and the most powerful witch I know. She'll know what to do. She must know what to do.

There has got to be a way to keep Tess alive. I can't lose her. Not again.

# BLACK MAGIC

**A**fter checking the last set of stalls, I surrender the search for Stephen and opt instead to put my plan into action. Consoling Tess's brother will have to wait. Time is of the essence.

I take the stairs a half-dozen at a time, oblivious to passersby. The labs are on the bottom floor of the hospital, in the basement. I stop short at the blood bank. I cock my head, shaking out my arms and shoulders. I need to appear normal, calm. I'm just an ordinary guy. A Good Samaritan.

Stepping inside, I scan the barren room. The walls are bare but for a ten-by-ten sepia print framed in metal and screwed to the wall. The smell of plastic permeates the room, from new chairs, I think. What isn't office space with women in scrubs bustling here and there is room for waiting. Almost every one of the three-dozen chairs is occupied, some people reading books, some flipping through magazines, all bored out of their minds.

"Excuse me," I say, my French clear and local. I hit one of the ladies behind the desk with a bogus smile. "I'm here to donate blood."

The woman doesn't even look up from her computer; she just mumbles something about taking a number. The next card is in the double digits. I'll be here forever.

Tick tock goes the clock.

Tess doesn't have that kind of time.

Desperate, I overlook a personal code of ethics and focus my mind's eye on the power of suggestion, insisting this woman move me to the front of the line. My thoughts are muddled, unpersuasive. I can't concentrate when I'm so tense, so worried about Tess. I try really hard and for a moment I think I've done it, that this woman is about to tell me to go on back to give blood, but instead she says, rather huffy, "Take a seat, sir."

Bloody hell.

Raising the collar on my leather jacket, I lean over the counter to whisper to the woman. "You are obviously in charge." She's the only one in a suit. "You must have the power to make this a quicker process."

The lady sighs but doesn't move, and two nurses gawk at me from over their paperwork. One thinks I'm attractive but not that attractive. The other thinks I look like a bad ass. I glance at the clock. This is going to be harder than I thought.

"Look," I say, dangling a ring-free hand over the countertop. "If I'm not back in an hour, I lose my bet with the guys at the firehouse. And after donating blood once a month for a year, it would be a shame to go down in flames at the finish line."

Come on, lying has to work. Firemen are the gods of the twenty-first century.

The woman rolls her chair back and stands, facing me. Her hand, the one twirling the thick gold wedding band, slaps against her hip. Apparently I'm not the first to spin this tale. "Too busy for this tonight," she says, pulling a plastic card from the stand and sliding it across the counter. "Take a seat." As she walks away, I hear someone behind me snickering.

Okay, so it'll have to be game plan number two.

Tick tock.

I swipe the card and turn, sweeping the crowded room. I pick through the thoughts of everyone holding a card. They aren't seated in order of number but the single digits have congregated in the front row. A man in his late sixties looks up at me. The number seven card teeters between his fingers. He's angry. His wife was diagnosed with cancer last month and his daughter has pressured him into donating blood. He doesn't see the point.

Luckily, I sense the number eight a few seats down. "Miss?" I say, and the lady rests her book on her lap. She smiles and a tinge of pink blooms across her sagging cheeks. It's been a long time since a handsome young man has called her Miss. "I'm in desperate need of your assistance." I squat, our knees touching. "I bet you've loved another in your lifetime."

"Gerard," she murmurs. Moments with her late husband dance through her head.

"Gerard."

"I loved him very much," she says.

Stick with the truth. "You see, Miss—"

"Hanna." Her eyes are a lovely shade of blue.

"Hanna," I say. "The love of my life is fighting for survival. She needs blood, lots of blood, and it's killing me that I'm powerless, that I can't help her. I hate to be from her bedside, but donating is the only thing I can do. I've got to help her."

Real tears threaten to spill so I look away.

Hanna slides her card into my coat pocket and pats my three-day stubble. "You'd have saved some time if you hadn't contemplated the old fart." She points at the angry man being led to the back room.

I stare at her in amazement. "You have no idea what this means to me." I rest my hands on hers. A nurse calls the number eight, and I plant a quick kiss on Hanna's forehead before diving for the door.

The room is bright white and smells like rubbing alcohol. I'm seated in what looks like a dentist chair, and before the curtains close I spot identical chairs across the hall, one containing angry man. He spies me through a slit in the material, apparently entertained by my success with Hanna.

"Bad day?" says the nurse, flicking the flap of torn leather on my jacket. She rocks onto the heels of her running shoes, chock full of energy. She reminds me of Ms. Rainer, young and peppy. I should lie and tell her I'm fine, but I'm too distracted, so I only nod in agreement. I watch her take my forefinger and poke it with a pin. A bubble of blood rises to the surface. "Hemoglobin test," she says, noticing my expression. "Iron. We check your iron." She ties an elastic band around my arm and shoves a thermometer in my mouth. "Blood pressure and body temperature too."

"Ah." I'm clueless.

Like a magician she pulls a rubber bag from her pocket and gives it a good shake before attaching it to a machine that rocks back and forth. The bag contains preservatives and anti-coagulants to keep the blood from clotting in transit. 450 ml is stamped on the front. Mrs. Maples said I'd need at least one unit, so I have to fill it and hope it's enough.

The bag's tubing ends with a needle, a needle the nurse stabs into my arm, a vein now surrounded by pumpkin-colored liquid.

I look away. "How long will this take?"

Growing up, my parents made a point of keeping my brother and me away from doctors. Having our blood tested would only lead to questions. Not only have I never had a needle, until today I'd only seen them in memories or on television.

"A big guy like you," says the nurse, smiling, "scared of a tiny needle." She searches the table for something. "Where's your paperwork?"

"What paperwork?"

The nurse frowns and walks away, shaking her head. A minute later she brushes open the curtain, handing me a clipboard and pen. "You've got fifteen minutes to fill this out." She jams a rubber stick into my left palm. "Hopefully you write with your right."

Once alone, I toss the clipboard onto the table and concentrate on my heart. It's easy to quicken the pace, I only have to think about Tess, about her suffering, how she might not survive the night. Fear, regret, yearning, they come racing back to torment me.

My arm throbs. Closing my eyes, I try to relax tense muscles. I force the blood to pump faster, directing it toward the crook in my arm, and sneak a peek at the bag still riding the teeter-totter.

Only half more to go.

"How are you doing?" says the nurse, and I practically fall from the chair. The paranoia is getting to me. The nurse is behind the other curtain talking to angry man. I can spot three quarters of his frown.

Focus.

The bag is bursting at the seams with ten minutes to spare. So far, so good. I yank the needle from my arm and the puncture wound heals immediately.

Showtime.

From the inside pocket of my coat I produce the bag of blood I'd pilfered from the nurse's station down the hall from Tess's room. It's only half full, the other half I flushed down a toilet. Trying hard to slow my movements, make them accurate, deliberate, I peel the sticker off the front and stick it to the bag filled with my blood. Not bad, it matches the bags Martine attaches to Tess's IV, only the blood is a few shades brighter. Tucking it into the hidey-hole in my coat, I pat it gently. This is going to work. This has to work.

Easing the curtain back, I'm ready to bolt. The nurse is gone and angry man is watching me, wondering what I'm doing. He's seen enough to know I'm up to something. Leaning, he looks past me, at the machine beside the chair. I've forgotten to fasten the blood bag, so it flops back and forth with the machine's momentum.

"Ma'am," yells angry man.

Shit.

I move quick, lunging for the door. The last thing I hear before the stairwell door slams is the voice of the nurse. She's never seen such a scaredy-cat.


**Seconds later I'm** stepping onto the fourth floor landing, my stash warm against my chest. My breathing is heavy. Not because bounding up six levels of stairs is exhausting, but because I'm nervous as hell. Thievery, deception, these aren't my usual gig. I round the corner, anxiously spying the officers outside room four-twenty-eight. They're frenzied, Stephen in the mix.

No. No. No. Please tell me Tess hasn't . . .

I pull Stephen aside. "What's going on?" His eyes and nose are covered in ruby blotches.

"The police thought Tess was married," he says. "They wanted to know why her husband hasn't come back." He glances at the officers, wiping his nose with his shirtsleeve. "Apparently someone was here this morning, before me. Some guy named Beck Morgan, with a Canadian passport to prove it. He claimed he was Tess's husband, even told the cops personal stuff about her."

Like me, Stephen assumed the police discovered Tess's identity when he called in search of his missing sister. In the mayhem, he hadn't noticed the cops knew her name before he'd called, that she'd already been claimed. Stephen hadn't been contacted because the police already had Tess's fake husband, Beck Morgan.

The older cop steps forward, the resulting stench of constricting polyester moving with him. "We had no reason to doubt the man," he says. "He spent about forty minutes with his wife and left to make long-term arrangements for their daughter, Abby. We didn't think anything of it until he didn't return."

"When they asked for the whereabouts of my brother-in-law, I thought they meant you," says Stephen, pointing at me.

I've no time to be flattered.

Who the hell is Beck Morgan and why was he here? Could he be the lost soul? Would he try to finish what he'd started? I try to make the pieces fit, but the blood bag sits heavy in my pocket, making it hard to concentrate. Tick tock. I don't have time for this now. I move toward the door and a young nurse, previously hidden behind an officer's burly physique, steps in the way. She's Da Vinci's Mona Lisa without the smile.

"I was on shift when Mrs. Morgan's husband arrived," she says. "This guy was pure Depardieu."

Depardieu is the guy American director's flag when in need of a French actor. His nose is practically a French icon.

"He was hovering over the patient, worried and concerned. Seemed the real deal to me." She describes him as attractive and well dressed. "Thirty-five maybe, 'round your height," she says, waving at me.

This guy doesn't sound like the lost soul that attacked Tess. "Tattoos, did he have tattoos on his neck?"

"Hmm, no. Don't think so."

The older cop turns to me. "Do you know something you're not telling us?"

Do I know something? What I know would rock your world.

"Just taking stabs in the dark," I say. "If I had a clue, I'd be sure to tell you."

Another lie added to today's offences.

Stephen pipes in, "Could this guy, this Beck Morgan, could he be the one who attacked my sister?"

"There wasn't a scratch on him," says the officer. "Even if she didn't fight back, that kind of beating would leave marks."

Stephen leans on the door, obviously overwhelmed. He's sure his sister would have fought hard.

The third officer says, "This bloke had ample time alone with Mrs. Morgan. If he was here to hurt her, he had the chance and didn't take it."

Lost souls don't need fake passports either. They don't pretend and their victims rarely survive to seek justice. Tick tock. If Tess doesn't survive, she'll be no exception. My attention gravitates to the bag of blood in my pocket. According to Mrs. Maples, I only have an hour before the preservatives destroy the white cells in my blood. And Tess's strength is quickly deteriorating. I'll have to deal with this Beck Morgan later.

Opening the door to Tess's room, I pause to look back at Stephen. "You must be starving. Go eat something," I say, urging him to the cafeteria.

I could probably switch the IV bags without anyone noticing my movements, but for the rest I'll need Stephen and Martine out of the room.

"I'm fine," he says, pushing past me. The thought of seeing his sister, knowing she might not live, has his heart racing.

Mine is just as rampant. How am I going to get Tess alone? I close the door behind us, relieved that the majority of Tess is hidden behind the curtain. I can't bear to contemplate the pain I'm about to cause her. And what if it's for nothing, what if it doesn't work—if this wild plan does nothing but end her life at my hand?

"How is she doing?" I ask Martine.

"Still in Neverland," she says. Her mind adds, *But I've had to change her bandages twice in the last hour.* "What's all the hullabaloo about?" She points her chin to the door.

"Paparazzi," I say too quickly. The police haven't verbalized this hypothesis yet.

Stephen doesn't notice my slip up. "Makes sense," he says. He collapses heavily into a chair, his lithe frame cracking and popping under the stress of the situation. "Assholes. French newspapers and magazines pay well for smut, enough to make an investigation and fake ID worth the effort." He studies his watch. "The morning papers hit the stands by five. If the guy was here for pictures, the cops will have him by noon."

Martine clicks her tongue, shaking her head in disapproval. She mumbles something about the state of humanity and hauls back the curtain before leaving the room.

One down, one to go.

Tess looks at peace, even though the white mesh surrounding her head oozes bright red blood and nothing but blackness fills her thoughts. I've got to get her alone. Stephen won't see my quick movements, but he'll hear me, and he'll definitely hear Tess. She's bound to cry out, and the heart monitor will sound. I glance at the machines. I'll have to unplug them. I don't know what I'll do if the police come to her aid. Maybe I should tell Stephen what I'm about to do, tell him it might save Tess's life. No, he trusts me, but not enough to witness me hurting his sister. I cringe at the thought of moving her, even slightly. My blood will dull the pain, but it won't take it all away.

Christ, I'm going to wish it could.

I move to the other side of the bed, a foot from Stephen. "You look exhausted." I frown, regretting my decision already.

"Just worried," he says, slightly agitated.

Staring at Stephen I try to remember the greater good. That Tess's life hangs in the balance. He'll yell for the police, and that's a complication I can't leave for chance. "Sorry," I whisper.

The words *what for* almost make it to his mouth before I apply a lightning strike of pressure to his carotid artery. I gently rest his head on a folded blanket, mumbling heartfelt apologies. I feel less like myself than ever before. Knocking Stephen out is something Thomas would do, not me.

Tick tock.

Moving fast, I jam the spare chair under the door handle and yank the plugs from the wall. The machines hum then fall silent. The blood bag hanging from the IV stand is almost full. I twist the tubing off the bottom, reattaching it to the bag of blood from my coat pocket, just like I've seen Martine do. It's still warm in my hand. My blood flows down the line, into Tess, and I close my eyes for a moment. This has to work.

Tess stirs, and I leap to her side. "It's me, Bryce. Listen to me. For many lifetimes you were the princess of Lemuria. You were an amazing woman. You are an amazing woman. Back then you were powerful, gifted at levitation, telepathy . . ." I shake my head, trying to stay focused. "More importantly, you were capable of controlling your body temperature to fight infection and heal. I know you don't remember, but somewhere deep inside I know you feel it, feel the knowledge of your soul's past lives. I'm going to help you, but you need to search for the connection. Please, please try."

I shove the extra bag into my coat pocket and grab my cell. Mrs. Maples answers on the first ring. "It's done," I say, steadying the phone between my shoulder and ear. I rub my hands together, creating heat, and Gertrude asks if I'm alone. Her tone is gentle, but I detect a slight warning. I lie and tell her everyone has stepped out, even though Stephen is hunched a few feet away, drooling.

Gertrude tells me to remove any pillows and lay Tess flat.

I shimmy my hand under Tess's neck, gently lifting her head from the pillow.

"Tess, can you hear me?"

Her barely-there nod is accompanied by an image of me in my black sweater, sitting across from her at dinner.

"Try to relax. I need to touch you. It's going to hurt, but you have to try really hard not to cry out." I'm not worried about someone catching me. I'm worried they'll attempt to stop me. "Can you do that?"

Another nod.

Even without the monitors buzzing, I can hear her heart beat fast. Pulling the pillow out from under her, I lower her head to the mattress, forcibly averting my eyes from the fresh blood leaking from bandages covering her shoulders and forehead.

I reposition the phone. "Now what?"

The smell of blood and decay fills my nostrils as I peel the covers back and drop them to the floor.

Bloody hell.

Please tell me I'm not too late.

I repeat Gertrude's instructions in my head, over and over, and rest my hands on Tess's chilled arm, just above the needle that directs my blood into her vein. Goose pimples bloom across her skin. Concentrating on the heat flowing to my hands, I run my thumbs along the inside of her arm, applying pressure. Her elbow is wrapped with gauze and I know there is either a cut or bite hiding underneath, but I try not to think about the pain she'll feel as I push my fingers into these spots.

"I'm sorry," I whisper.

Tess's chin quivers and a tear eases its way through the folds of swollen skin surrounding her eyes. Her mind fights to keep control over the pain.

"I'm at her shoulder," I mumble into the phone.

I emulate Mrs. Maples, a low hum vibrating in my chest. Our future lies in the fate of my scorched touch as I direct blood through veins and into bandages that implode, seeping from the pressure. I press hard, both hands flat on Tess's chest, fingers wrapped around her collarbone, and Tess's back arches from the bed, her chin high in the air.

"She's in pain!"

Mrs. Maples stays calm, her hum picking up momentum until I'm on par, the sound lodged in my throat.

"Around her neck?" I repeat. "What if I strangle her?"

The hum omitting from the phone stays steady, so I wrap my hands around Tess's neck, not a speck of white showing. I squeeze and the buzzing from my throat rises to the back of my mouth, the taste of tin coating my tongue. Tess gasps and her fingers fumble over my face. Her mind is a chaotic mess of excruciating pain and confusion.

"Please forgive me!"

Mrs. Maples' humming stops then continues. A silent slap of discipline.

Concentrate! This could save Tess! This could mean the difference between life and death!

Tick Tock.

I steal a glance at my watch. What feels like forever has only been seconds in real time. Still, I've got to hurry. I can't have

Martine trying to get back into the room or Stephen coming around. I tighten my grip and the pressure from under the bandages pushes against my strength. Fresh blood leaks from around the staples in Tess's scalp and her thoughts fade to black, agony sweeping her in and out of consciousness.

My fingertips feel for broken bones in Tess's face, and she finally cries out, the pain too much to bear. Mrs. Maples' voice raises another octave, forcing me to follow suit. Begging for forgiveness, I fumble about Tess's shattered sinus cavity until her arms fall limp at her sides.

What the . . .? No. I've killed her!

Lowering my ear to her chest, I hear the pounding of her heart, faint but there.

Thank you, thank you!

"I think she's passed out!"

Gertrude's hum cracks and alters to a chant, a low rumble in an ancient dialect I'm familiar with but haven't uttered in centuries. I do my best to keep up while probing Tess's head, the metal staples shifting under my fingertips. Tess's body starts to tremble, and I have to grab the blanket so the cast on her leg doesn't make too much noise banging against the bed rail. Gertrude yells into the phone, reminding me not to stop. I've got to guide my blood through Tess's body, from her chest to her feet, paying special attention to internal organs, quickly. Once I reach her ribs, I'll have to increase the pressure.

I can't imagine pushing Tess's torn and broken body any harder than I have been, but I do what I'm told. This has to work. I have to save her.

Tess screams and I smother her mouth with my hand. She breathes heavy, gasping for air.

I'm so sorry.

I thrust a hand into her cracked ribs, the throb of her heart pressing against my palm, and Tess thrashes, her dull nails scraping over my shirt collar, desperate for purchase.

Please forgive me.

I tear my eyes away to inspect the blood bag. It's almost empty. I've got to hurry. A minute has passed since I knocked Stephen out. I'm running out of time.

"I'm at her liver!"

Gertrude's voice softens to a purr and I try to match the tenor, but my voice is breaking down, my throat dry, my tongue sticking to the roof of my mouth. I watch as tears flow from Tess's eyes, soaking her hair and the sheets around her head. Her nostrils flare with every breath. I grasp the cast covering her shattered thigh. I've got to get heat through layers of plaster without crushing the outer shell.

"Almost done, the bag is almost empty," I mutter into the phone.

Tess's left foot has several fissures that crackle from my touch. Tess moans, then the trembling stops, and she lies very still.

Please make this work, please.

I gulp a mouthful of air and inspect the deformed blood bag. "It's empty."

Mrs. Maples says I'm done; we've done all we can do. She sounds exhausted, sad. She reminds me to switch the bags so Tess continues to get the transfusion she needs and the nurse doesn't have reason to suspect. I'll need to be patient, to give it time. The first hour is critical. Tess's body might reject my blood. And we have no way of knowing if her internal organs are too severely damaged to be healed.

Mrs. Maples warns me for the second time that if I don't call my father and tell him what I've done, she'll have to. She doesn't want to be the one to tell the Keepers, and I don't blame her.

"He'll understand," I say, not really convinced this is true. "He knows I love her."

Gertrude sighs on the other end of the phone line. I owe Mrs. Maples my life, and I tell her so before tucking the phone away.

Stephen groans, a hand flitting to his stomach. He's very pale. I watch as Stephen's eyes roll then squeeze shut. He tries to sit up but falls back into the chair with a thump.

The door handle turns.

Quickly, I wash my hands, drape the blankets back over Tess's body, and plug in the machines. In one fluid motion, I pull the chair from under the door and ease myself into what looks like a comfortable sleeping position. A breeze crosses my face with the opening of the door.

"Hmm," says Martine, fiddling with the door handle. She hates calling maintenance: the guys down there are as old and decrepit as the building itself. Snickering, she closes the door and waddles into the room. She stops two feet from Stephen. In a flash, Stephen slumps forward and pukes on her shoes. I hear her sigh. Guilt should have me jumping from the chair to help, but exhaustion takes over, and pretending to sleep becomes easier and easier. Martine drags the garbage pail in front of Stephen before pressing the red button beside Tess's bed. She calls for maintenance.

One last thought of Tess and I drift off, the empty bag folded neatly in my coat pocket. My blood should clot, closing Tess's wounds. She won't bleed to death. If this works, her body should start to heal, broken bones will fuse, organs will repair, and tissue will rejuvenate. Rest is what she needs now.

Ditto for me.

# IN THE NAME OF LOVE

"You were really out," Stephen says, watching me wake from the edge of the hospital bed. He looks to be in better spirits.

I sit up and he hands me a paper cup coated in tacky coffee bean graphics. I take it, even though I don't drink coffee. My hands are unusually cold and the heat feels good.

"She's better," says Stephen, pointing to his sister.

Tess is better! Alive! I rise from my chair for a closer look, but a sudden spin sets me back in the chair. A boundless weight lifts from my shoulders. I am so grateful it worked, that my blood clotted and my touch didn't kill her. Had Tess died, I'm not sure I would've ever forgiven myself.

Tess looks a tad more purple, but alive. She's alive! Pulling the chair forward to see Tess clearer, a blanket I hadn't noticed I was wearing falls off my lap.

"That was me," says Martine, stepping into the room. Her arms are full of supplies so she kicks at the blanket on the floor. "You were shivering in your sleep."

After a quick peek at Tess sleeping peacefully, hand in her brother's, I retrieve the blanket and drape it across the back of the chair. With my back turned from probing eyes I let loose my true emotions, squinting for clarity. Everything seems foggy, almost surreal. Since when do I get cold? I didn't wake when the nurse covered me with a blanket? I didn't hear her in the room? Studying my watch, I count backwards. There is no way I've been asleep for five hours. I turn slightly, the wall clock slowly coming into view. Nineteen minutes after four.

Stephen smiles when he sees me analyzing the time. He's wondering how I slept for so long without moving a muscle, especially in an uncomfortable hospital chair.

I'm wondering the same thing.

A voice booms from the hallway. "Try to stop me!"

The door flies open and Thomas blows in, all three police officers in tow. Thomas halts at the end of the bed, mouth agape. The younger officer moves forward, handcuffs in hand. "You don't want to do that," says Thomas, eyes still locked on Tess. The room falls quiet and the cop stops mid step. In this state, Thomas is quite intimidating. He stands like a superhero without the cape, his expression resolute, dark. His tension is tangible.

I face Stephen. "This is my brother."

"Thomas," mumbles Stephen. Talks with his sister go through his head before he addresses the policemen. "Thomas is my sister's friend." He says it, but isn't quite sure he means it. Tess has told him about Thomas's temper, about his possessive nature.

"I don't care if he's the pope, when I ask for ID, I expect to see it." The cop looks tired, too old to be working the night shift.

Thomas rounds the bed and slides his hand under Tess's. His thoughts are focused, as if no one else is in the room. Tension rolls from him.

"Here," I say, lifting the hem of Thomas's jacket and reaching into the back pocket of his jeans, "we don't want any trouble." I hand the folded passport to the cop and watch as he forces the pages flat, scowling.

Thomas edges his way into my thoughts. *I blame you for this. If you'd stayed away, none of this would've happened. She'd be with me. She'd be happy, unbroken.*

The cop looks at Thomas before his stare pans to me. "Your brother's last name isn't Waters."

"No, it's Tanis, his late wife's name."

Our parents went ballistic when Thomas took his bride's name. Which is, of course, exactly why he did it.

Again, Thomas fumes with his mind. *Where the fuck is this lost soul? I'm going to tear him to shreds.*

I shake my head. I look at Tess and my heart pounds sharp in my chest. I've never wanted to hurt anything as much as I want to hurt the man that did this to her. My entire being aches for revenge. I don't want Tess hurt again, but there is no way we can kill, not even for this.

The cop jots information on a notepad before tossing Thomas's passport onto the table at the foot of the bed. "Next time," he says, pacing toward the door. He's thinking about how he doesn't get paid enough for this shit.

I apologize to the officer, offering palatable excuses. We are all seriously stressed. We're tired, tense.

I look to Tess, battered and torn, her mind a blank slate, and then to Thomas, attentively stroking her hair. He whispers affectionate condolences in her ear, and the slimy tentacles of jealousy creep over me. The fact that my brother loves Tess isn't the problem. How can I blame him for that? It's that he doesn't care if his love is reciprocated.

Thomas throws me a glance, a sinister squint. *Fuck off.*

I stare back. We've got to stop fighting. Tess needs us to work together. We can't just wait to see if this lost soul comes back for her. We need to know he's moved on, that he'll leave her alone.

Thomas investigates the machines. *I'll hunt him like the animal he is.*

"Meyer's grandparents will be here any minute," Stephen says, following the officers as they step back into the hall. He hangs from the doorframe. "The Morgan's." He's worried the cops will give them a hard time.

He has no reason to worry. The police are exhausted and Grams is a pit bull in the coat of a poodle.

I have no idea how to find this lost soul, but we've got to find him, and soon. I doubt he'll come anywhere near Tess with us here, but when Tess gathers enough strength to think straight, she's going to panic. She's going to worry he'll come back for her, or worse, hurt Abby.

Thomas huffs. *He won't have limbs to touch her with when I'm done with him.*

I look away, frustrated. Hurting this man is not an option. How do we stop a lost soul bent on the kill? We don't. Keeper's offer guidance and history to learn from. We teach in hopes of repentance, knowing every soul is here to learn, to experience, to contribute. Like every soul, this lost soul will pay for his crimes, if not in this lifetime then another. I have to believe he'll pay without more violence. How could I ever live with myself if I acted upon my impulses, my anger? What kind of man would that make me?

I'd give a lifetime to protect Tess and Abby, but not by becoming the very thing I exist to save, not by losing my purpose. We've got to find this lost soul and make sure he stays away from Tess. How is the question—how do we do that? We are educators, not bounty hunters.

Stephen closes the door. "Thomas, how did you know my sister was here?"

"I phoned him." I smile an apology.

A strange look comes over Stephen and he turns, hiding his face from me. "Look, my sister's been through enough without the two of you at it."

Ah, so Tess has told her brother about the constant bickering. I stop myself from pulling Stephen into a hug. His need to protect his sister only makes me like him more.

"We'll be on our best behavior," I say, patting Thomas. "Won't we, Brother?"

Thomas shrugs me off. "What has the doctor said?"

Stephen goes through Tess's struggles from start to finish. "She's doing better," he concludes, "she's out of danger now."

I'm relieved to hear this, so unbelievably relieved. My attention gravitates to the clock and I'm reminded of the hours I've slept, apparently through doctor visits. Thomas watches me, prodding the sudden blockade in my mind. He can tell I'm stunned, but nothing else comes through clearly.

"It was a close call," I say. "The doctor didn't think she'd make it." My intention is to hint at the severity of Tess's injuries, but it comes out defensive, fueling Thomas's scrutiny.

"Where's Abby?" says Thomas.

"A neighbor is watching her at my place," says Stephen. "She had trouble going to sleep, so he and his wife brought her back to my apartment, thinking she'd be more comfortable. The Morgan's called from the airport. They'll be here soon, and I'll head home for a while. One of us should be there when Abby wakes."

Good plan.

More I slept through.

Stephen sits opposite Thomas, holding Tess's other hand. The two of them caress her gently and the sight churns my stomach. My touch caused her nothing but pain.

"Let me get that," says a voice from outside the room. She speaks in English, obviously Canadian, and familiar.

The door swings open and the backside of Mrs. Morgan, Grams, eases through the frame, pausing to check that the wheelchair bolts have cleared. "How is she?" she asks, spinning her husband's chair around to the edge of the bed so quickly that none of us have the chance to assist.

Thomas moves to stand behind a chair, and I rise to offer my seat and give them space. I grab hold of the door, slightly dizzy, I think. I've never been dizzy before.

Meyer's grandfather clings to the seat of his wheelchair, precariously propped so he can study his daughter-in-law. His features appear to melt, his heartbreak so profound I have to turn and stare at the wall. Behind me Grams sobs into the crook of her arm, her mind a medley of questions. Stephen has told her what to expect, but hearing it and seeing it are two very different things. "Who would do something like this?" she mutters into her sleeve.

A person who has lost their humanity, their purpose. A lost soul.

*A dead man,* thinks Thomas.

Mr. Morgan struggles to keep his expression passive. He's seen his share of atrocities, once he even saw a guy on fire, but this is something altogether different. This is personal. Anger attempts to rise to the surface, held back by nothing more than sheer will. Still, he doesn't utter a word.

"The doctor," says Stephen, hoping to offer a distraction, "the doctor will be back soon."

Grams nervously fiddles with the blankets. Every few seconds she steals a glance at Tess's wounds. She swallows hard and closes her eyes. Leaning on Stephen, she wraps her arms around his waist, lowering her forehead to his chest. Stephen looks awkward, but he rests his chin on her head, a moment so touching I feel like an intruder just being in the room.

Minutes pass before Mrs. Morgan stands and turns to me. "Bryce," she says in greeting. Her smile takes effort, but its authenticity shows in her eyes.

I nod. "I'm so sorry."

"Thomas," she says, "we appreciate you both being here. Tess will need all the love and support she can muster." Her hands hover over Tess's taut skin, afraid to touch. She covers her nose and mouth, appalled by the foul odor.

I've become desensitized.

For the first time I notice the bandages are mostly white with only small traces of blood dotted here and there. The swelling has gone down and the dark blotches have taken on a yellowish hue.

The doctor steps into the room followed by a new nurse. Martine's shift must be over. He pauses to scan faces. "Full house," he says, reaching for Tess's chart. After skimming notes he looks at Tess's in-laws crowding the top half of the bed and introduces himself. "I trust you had a safe flight from Florida?" In his head he checks points off a list of things he should say to improve his bedside manner. Last week he'd taken a seminar on the topic.

"Yes," says Mrs. Morgan, "safe, but long. We're just pleased to know Tess is doing better."

Mr. Morgan clears his throat. "She is, right? She's doing better?" For the first time since their arrival, he drags his eyes from the bed.

"Much," says the doctor, grinning like a schoolboy. "She's amazing us all."

I can feel Thomas's glare and his persistent nudging at my barrier, but I refuse to look in his direction. He coughs and points at the door. I ignore him.

"In fact," says the doctor, "we've never seen such a response to Leudifor. She's the talk of the doctor's lounge."

Apparently Stephen told the Morgan's about the drug the doctor thought was a long shot because they don't push for further explanation. When a loved one has been pulled from death's door, one is just grateful.

Thomas excuses himself, his eyes piercing me as he stomps out of the room.

"Good," says the doctor, noticing Thomas's departure. "It's awfully busy in here, and our patient needs her rest." He looks to each of us but no one budges.

A few seconds pass before I make out his thoughts. *Immediate family only.*

"I'll step out."

The doctor closes the door behind me, leaving me in the hallway with Thomas.

"What the fuck did you do?" Thomas pins me to the wall.

"Killjoy." I look from one end of the hall to the other. "Where did the cops go?"

His eyes narrow to slits. "Don't you know? Can't you hear them?" He watches me try. "They're around the corner, waiting to pounce, just like I remember."

Thomas recalls a previous run-in with the police. It was at a hospital in Spain, the first time his wife tried to commit suicide. The cops refused Thomas entry to her hospital room because he'd been involved in an altercation with his wife's ex-husband the week before. It got out of hand and the guy was killed. Thomas swore it was an accident, that the guy didn't die by his hands, and the authorities had the evidence to back Thomas's story. But Thomas's wife wouldn't believe them. She went ballistic, blaming Thomas, and slit her wrists in the tub. The next time she attempted to end her life, she was better prepared. She made sure Thomas was out of the country. And she went straight to the morgue.

"What are you hiding?" says Thomas. "Are you gonna tell me or do I find out the hard way?"

I work the wrinkles out of my shirt, trying not to smile. "Hard for whom?"

Thomas studies me, his expression as impassive as stone. "Why do you need to call Dad?" He leans close.

"I don't," I lie, suddenly remembering Gertrude's threat.

"What does Maples have to do with . . .?" He stares at the silver numbers screwed to the door. "You didn't." He turns toward me, face hard. "She told you!"

"I don't know what you're blathering about."

Thomas grabs me by the shoulders. "Shit, Bryce. Tell me you didn't."

I surrender the game. We never could keep secrets from each other.

"I did." I smile, big, showing my teeth. "And it worked."

"Fuck!" Thomas throws his hands up, pacing on the spot. "Dad is gonna to kill you!"

"Won't that make your day."

"You know what this means, don't you? Gertrude must have told you—"

I stand tall. "I don't care."

"You'll never be the same, Bryce. It isn't like bleeding from a cut or injury."

Thomas stops to stare at me, and for the first time in a long time, I feel the love he had for me when we were kids.

"When my wife was in the hospital, when she'd cut her wrists, Gertrude told me how to infuse my blood, how to control it, manipulate the healing process."

This I knew, this is why I thought to call Mrs. Maples. The term is *bon pa*, which means to recite magical formulas, or mantras, that can manipulate sound to influence energy patterns. Father was livid when he found out what Thomas had considered, what he'd almost sacrificed for his wife to survive.

Almost. He hadn't gone through with it.

"I couldn't," says Thomas, obviously privy to the lack of a blockade in my mind. "The consequences were . . . Shit, Bryce, we're Keepers. We can't sacrifice our gifts for others. Not ever. Not for any reason."

"I love her, Thomas."

Thomas groans and looks away. "When the Keepers find out—and you know they will—they are going to rip you a new one. Bro, you're in a ton of shit."

"I know."

Thomas slumps forward. "Are you all right?"

"I'm fine."

Actually, I'm tired and hungry. And I feel like I've got cotton balls stuffed in my ears.

"Shit, Bryce."

"I've lived over three thousand lifetimes, Thomas. Twenty-two of my best were spent with the soul residing in Tess." I can't seem to stifle the grin plastered on my face. "She was dying. Now she's not."

"Now she's not," Thomas repeats, staring at the door. "You've never done this before, saved her soul."

"Maybe that's why I've always lost her."

One of the police officers wanders past, pretending not to notice us. Chocolate jelly is stuck to his chin. Thomas huffs his disapproval, watching the cop as he rounds the corner. "You might get your hearing back. That and the fatigue are probably temporary. We'll have to test your mind later. I doubt you'll be helping anything inhuman for a while."

He means I won't have the power to change into an animal, which means I won't be counseling any lost souls who have chosen to experience life as another one of Earth's creatures.

"Pity," I say, "can't say I'll miss that talent." I've lived a couple of dozen lives as something other than human, and there is a lot to be said for being top of the food chain.

The door inches open, in need of oil, and Stephen steps into the hallway.

"My sister was awake for a few minutes, but she's burning up, so the doctor gave her something to make her sleep. He's never seen a fever so high, but she seems to be handling it. He doesn't seem worried. He thinks this new medication is some sort of wonder drug." He smiles. "Anyway, Tess will be out for a while, so I'm heading home to spend time with Abby, maybe get some sleep."

I nod. The fever is doing exactly what it's supposed to do, kill infection. Tess has figured it out. She's controlling her body heat, manipulating the cells. The smile on my face grows in increments, and Thomas rolls his eyes.

I yell out to Stephen slowly dragging himself down the hall. "Tell Abby her mother is invincible!"

"I will," he bellows over his shoulder.

And amazing and strong and beautiful and alive.

No matter the cost.

# DAWN

**T**homas, suddenly the attentive sibling, insists I get some food into me. So after checking on Tess, we head two floors down to the cafeteria. The thought of eating processed food has my stomach curdling, but I need water and something with a bit of substance. Thomas stands beside me in line, his tray stacked with freeze-dried, gas-flushed, preservative-packed junk. Mother would go nuts. Not a single item looks appealing to me.

"Are you going to eat that?" I deadpan.

Thomas assures me he is, and the lady at the counter tallies his stash. "He's paying," Thomas says to the woman. He gestures to me then lifts his tray over the cash register and heads for the condiments counter.

Nice. He hasn't changed in years.

*I'm better looking.*

I pay for the food and follow Thomas toward a quiet table in the far corner.

Four feet from the table Thomas stops. "Listen," he says.

Instantly the tray is gone from my hands and we're standing on the other side of the cafeteria. A flat screen television mounted to the wall blasts the news, and a small mass has gathered to watch the local anchorwoman.

"Live, from the steps of Palais PD." The wind blows her hair as she tries to grip the microphone and keep the hem of her skirt down at the same time. "I repeat," she says. "The Jane Doe Butcher is dead. Only moments ago, the body of Adrien Rimkin was found here—" The camera pans to steep stone steps leading to a set of glass doors covered with graffiti. "—on the steps of the old Prefecture of Police building, gunshot wound to the head." Yellow tape marks the parameter corralling a dozen officers milling around a white tarp. "It appears that Rimkin climbed the steps, confession in hand, and shot himself, unable to live with what he'd done the night of February sixteenth, to Tess Morgan, no longer our Jane Doe." A picture of Tess materializes in the left corner of the screen. She's wearing the red dress she wore to Karen's New Year's party, but her hair is shorter.

I close my eyes, just for a second, and a nurse nudges me in the side. "She's here, in ICU," she whispers.

Another photo pops onto the screen and Thomas says, "That's him, the guy from the café. That's the guy I saw on the café's security video."

I look around us but no one is listening. They're all riveted to the television.

The reporter clears her throat. "Rimkin, a twenty-six-year-old Spanish born American, has only one prior involving—oddly enough—tax evasion. According to police, Rimkin's hand written note describes how he met Tess Morgan, less than forty-eight hours ago, at the Roissy airport. Smitten, he followed her to an apartment on Rue Nicolas Houel, where she and her daughter were visiting family. While trying to talk to her at the Jardin des Plantes, he—and I quote—lost control. Police say the note is clearly the ramblings of a deranged mind, and they are relieved to see he's off the streets."

Rimkin's photo disappears and the one of Tess dominates

the entire screen.

"Mrs. Morgan is now in a stable condition at Pitie-Salpetriere Hospital, where doctors believe a new drug called Leudifor saved her from what should have been fatal injuries." The reporter comes back into view, now with the Leudifor logo scrolling across the top of the scene. "What else is this miracle drug capable of? Next, we'll talk to the head chemist at Rideau, the makers of Leudifor."

"Holy shit," I say, eyes glazed over. "I didn't see that coming."

Thomas drags his hands slowly down his face. "Me neither. And I'm not handicapped."

I ignore the jab and try to concentrate on the facts. The lost soul is dead. This is good. This is very good. Tess is safe. I should be relieved. Why am I not relieved? After what this guy did to Tess, I wanted him hurt, killed, obliterated. I got my wish, and without dirty hands. But this isn't right. Lost souls don't commit suicide. Few ever feel remorse, never mind put it to paper.

Am I'm missing something?

By the time my focus returns, the news has ended and the crowd has dispersed. I turn to speak to Thomas but beside me is nothing but space.

*Over here*, he says without using his voice.

I look to the table in the far corner. I'm there in a heartbeat.

"You're eating?" I say, stunned.

Thomas shrugs, dipping fries into mayonnaise. "I'm hungry."

I'm starving, but I can't eat. Not now. My thoughts are jumbled as I try to decipher the puzzle. I don't see why this guy would turn himself in, never mind commit suicide. The police had no idea who he was, and we weren't onto him, not yet anyway. Why wouldn't he just flee?

"Does it really matter?" says Thomas, slurring around a

mouthful of food.

"Well, yeah. I'm elated he's no longer capable of hurting Tess, but his death matters. And it means there is someone else, someone higher up the chain, someone capable of controlling a lost soul. Who killed him and why?"

Thomas has shoved too much into his mouth to speak. *So the guy had enemies. I don't really care who popped the fucker. As long as he's gone, that's one mighty big project off my hands.*

I head to the stairs, pausing only to see what channel the news was on.

I need to see Tess. When she wakes, she'll want to know what's going on, and if the lost soul will return for her. She has to know he won't come back, that the lost soul is dead. The news should calm her soul, help her sleep, allow her to heal.

And I won't give her any reason to worry.

Not yet anyway.

Pausing outside her hospital door, the silver numbers blur as exhaustion clouds my vision. The past twenty-four hours have passed in a whirlwind. The thought of Tess's family watching over her on the other side of this door makes me think of my family, my life, my future. I take a deep breath. I love Tess. I think she loves me, the Keeper and the man. She's alive, she'll heal, and I'll give her the time she needs. I'll give her everything. She'll love me someday, I hope. We'll figure it out and be together. Again.

Someone says my name, and startled, I look up to see Mrs. Morgan propping the door with a rubber stopper. She smiles. "Are you coming in?" she says.

I step into the room, and it looks different. Brighter. Tidier. It even smells better.

"How is she?" I say.

Even Tess looks different. Her hair curls around her

shoulders, clean and combed. The tube taped to her mouth is gone, and not a speck of blood shows on the white gauze squares.

"She's good." Mrs. Morgan rests a warm hand on my arm. "She's been asking for you."

I rush to the bed. "I'm here."

Tess's eyes remain closed, but a tiny smile inches up the right ride side of her lip.

A heartfelt sigh catches my attention and I turn to see Grams leaving the room, guiding her husband's wheelchair through the doorway. "We're going to check on Abby," she says. "You take care of our girl now."

Mr. Morgan gives me a simple wave and I return the gesture. I hadn't even noticed he was in the room.

"Oh, wait," I say, diving after them. "There is no television in here, so you wouldn't have seen the news. He's dead. The man who did this, he can't hurt her again."

Mrs. Morgan just sighs. "The police told us before they left." She kicks the stopper from the door. "We'll be back soon." As the door closes I catch a trace of her thoughts. She aims to find Thomas and distract him, giving me time alone with Tess.

"I really like Grams," I murmur, carefully sitting on the side of the bed.

Tess runs air over her vocal cords, obviously happy to see me. I'm surprised to see she's awake. Her mind is still murky, I think. Maybe it's me, maybe I can't see through the stuffing in my head.

"He's gone," I say, "really gone—the lost soul won't return. Now you don't need to worry, just rest."

I don't mention the lack of lost soul suicide statistics or the feeling I have, the sensation I'm missing something, that this was all too easy. I ignore the fact that the lost soul's death seems more like a concluded loose end than a suicide, and how I suspect there is someone worse lurking in the shadows. Instead, I push doubt from my mind and rummage through the blankets for Tess's hand.

I hold tight and a wave of calm falls over me.

Studying Tess's hand, I recall all the times I've wanted to touch her, to hold her. All the times I've had to show restraint and keep my feelings at bay. My fingertips follow the lines in her palm, the many lives she's lived. I refuse to lose her again. She's not ready for me to love her the way I do, but we'll take things slow.

"Your ring."

The gold wedding band she wears is missing. It's the first time I've noticed. I reach for the drawer beside her bed, assuming her personal belongings are tucked inside. There is a bag, the contents obviously Tess's. The glass face of her watch is shattered, a silver key tainted with blood. Her ring slides along the bottom of the bag, beside a pen and folded sheet of paper.

"This belongs here." I slide the gold band onto her finger. It only fits halfway, but Tess attempts to close her hand around mine.

I can see the paper through the plastic, the blue ink in Tess's handwriting.

*Dear Bryce*, it says. *I should have stayed. I wanted to stay. I'm sorry I didn't call before leaving for Paris, but I knew if I heard your voice I'd change my mind. What you said to me, how you feel, I feel the same. But I need time. Abby needs time.*

Blood splatters cover the remaining words within view and I want to tear the paper from the bag and read more, but I won't invade Tess's privacy any more than I already have. These are her private thoughts, things she wanted to say to me herself. And I'll wait. I'll patiently wait until she's ready to tell me how she feels.

Leaning in close, I dust my lips over her forehead.

"We have all the time in the world."

Our connection is still laced with fog and nothing but a general sense of contentment comes through.

I start to panic. She's recovering quickly. Her mind will be crisp and clear soon.

"I love you," I say impetuously. "I'm so in love with you I've lost my mind." I chuckle and sit back, suddenly hot.

A smile slinks across Tess's lips.

*I could love you too.*

# END OF BOOK ONE

# AUTHOR'S NOTE

The function of myth is to describe and encapsulate an event, truth, or memory of significance. Dividing myth from fact is proof. There are inherent problems with proof: technology, experience, perspective, interpretation. Not to mention politics.

While the world created in *A Keeper's Truth* in regards to lost souls and Keepers is truly a figment of my imagination, there is a wealth of historical documentation, both folkloric and archeological, to support claims of the lost civilizations of Atlantis and Lemuria. There is currently tangible proof of man's existence as early as 250,000 BC, and who knows what tomorrow's technology will uncover? If Lemurians were inundated by catastrophe spanning thousands of years, it's possible that proof of their existence remains buried, undiscovered, possibly leagues under Earth's oceans. Someday the story of Atlantis and Lemuria might cross the line from myth to fact. Maybe it already has and we just don't see it.

As for human beings having souls . . . who am I to say?

Dee Willson

# ACKNOWLEDGEMENTS

Writing is a solitary endeavor, a private relationship between a creator and her cast, yet riddled with an abundance of good fortune, research, learning, confidence, and sheer time.

My good fortune was in stumbling across the entrepreneurial spirits behind Driven Press and BK Publications. They not only saw what I saw in *A Keeper's Truth* but invested their time and money so others could share this story. Suz, Sam, I am forever grateful.

Many books were important in researching this novel, and a vast amount of information can be found in *The Lost Civilization of Lemuria* by Frank Joseph, Bear & Company 2006; *Atlantis and 2012* by Frank Joseph, Inner Traditions International 2010; *Forbidden History* by J. Douglas Kenyon, Bear & Company 2005; *Destiny of Souls* by Michael Newton PhD, Llewellyn Publications 2000; and *Encyclopedia of Spirits* by Judika Illes, Harper One 2009. Your work has changed me forever.

Writing is a constant learning process, so there is a special place on my bookshelf for *The Time Traveler's Wife*. Audrey

Niffenegger, we have never met, but I owe you a great deal of thanks. Your book taught me to be a better writer.

To spend years writing (and editing) a novel, one must have a certain balance of confidence, drive, and insane focus. All of these I get from an awesome collection of fellow writers, dear friends who make the journey extra special. Tanis Mallow, Rob Brunet, D.J. McIntosh, Pam Blance, Melodie Campbell, Rita Bailey, and Kent Rees, this road wouldn't be the same without you. Thanks for holding my hand.

Lastly, there is time. Most have no idea how much time goes into writing, editing, publishing, and marketing a novel, but my family does. They've helped and encouraged me through every arduous step. Vera, I can't imagine a better cover. Mom, you are the best cheerleader a girl could ask for. Dad, Georgia, John, Jamie, your faith in me keeps me going. Jeff, after twenty years I am still the luckiest girl in the room. To my daughters, Tess and Hanna, you are my *everything*.

I love you all.

# ABOUT THE AUTHOR

Dee Willson felt the writer's call at fifteen, when she penned her first novel and received her first rejection letter to go with it. Over twenty years later, with two successful businesses under her belt (both with Canada's largest book retailer, Indigo Books), Dee Willson rekindled her passion for novels. She joined a hardcore book club, published short stories and interviews, contributed to blogs, and wrote the novel *A Keeper's Truth*, followed by *GOT* (*Gift of Travel* ). Dee is presently working on the second installment in the *Keeper's* series, and *Meant 2 B*, a crazy ghost story riddled with fate.

Dee and her husband currently reside in Burlington, Ontario. They are building their dream home on the shore of Lake Ontario, where they expect to watch their daughters frolic in the lake, and possibly grow four heads. Visit her online at www.deewillson.com or on Twitter @denisewillson

www.drivenpress.net

info@drivenpress.net

Join the Driven Press readers' club for:

* a 10% club discount on purchases in our shop every time you buy
* new release updates straight to your inbox
* news of any events or giveaways before anyone else
* special club member giveaways and competitions

Details on our website.

CPSIA information can be obtained at www.ICGtesting.com
Printed in the USA
LVOW07s0845100216

474421LV00005B/179/P

9 781925 296181